Wrath of the Broken One

Tale of the Scorpion Book One

SHAWN E. CRAPO

ISBN: 0692457526
ISBN-13: 978-0692457528

DEDICATION

This book is dedicated to all the fans of *The Dragon Chronicles*.
Thank you for your support!

ACKNOWLEDGMENTS

We must always remember those who have inspired us to live in our own little fantasy worlds. Without their contributions, our lives would be mundane and lacking the magic that makes them worth living. I will always do my best to be a part of that group and bring joy to those I can reach.

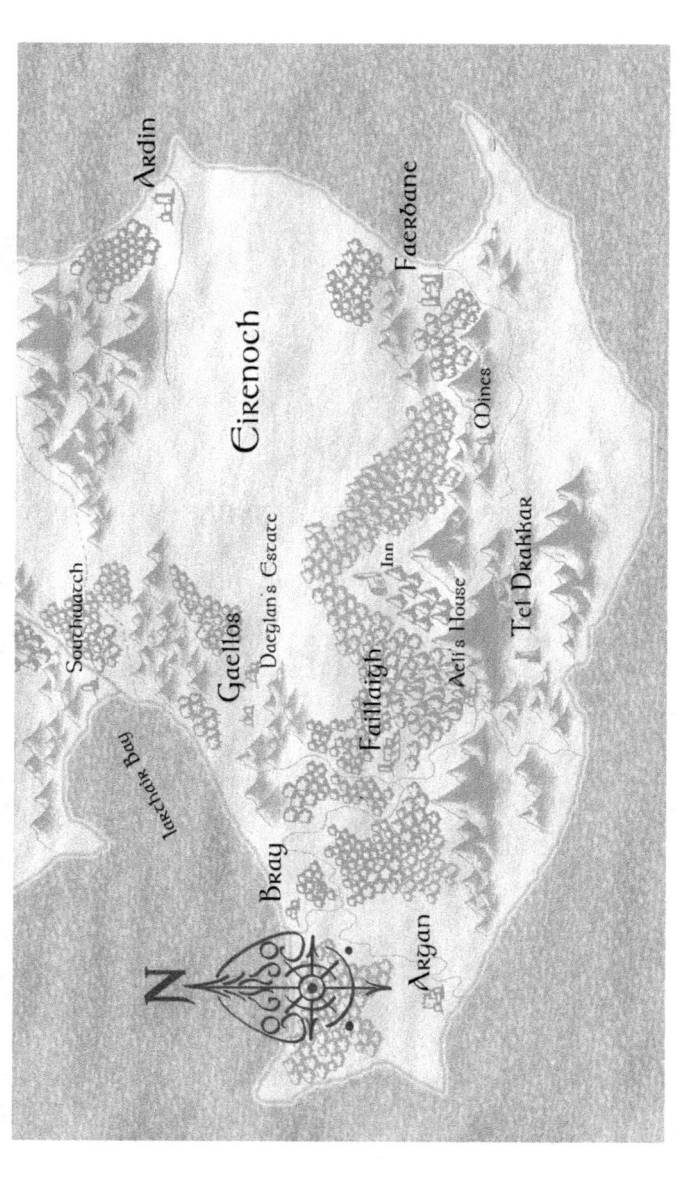

CHAPTER ONE

words were scattered on the floor of the smith's shop. Smoke hung still in the air, broken only by the light breeze that blew through the open windows. The walls were florid with the dim light of the dying forge, giving the entire shop a warm, almost ethereal glow.

The smith lay snoring on a wood and leather couch against the back wall, a flagon of wine lying on its side on the floor beside him. He was a large man, not particularly old, but not that young either. He was balding, somewhat portly, and dressed in the clothes in which he had toiled the entire day.

In the doorway there stood a black figure, still and silent, staring intently at the man that slumbered away before him. He did or said nothing; he merely watched the man as he slept, standing like a statue as the forge crackled in its final sputters of life.

The smith opened his eyes, seeing the stranger in the doorway, and snapped awake. He quickly produced a dagger in his soiled hand, sliding off the couch onto his feet. The stranger calmly held out his gloved hand, palm down, in a gesture of peace. The smith swayed back and forth, still drunk, unsure of whether the man was a threat.

"Calm yourself," the stranger said. His voice was deep, smooth, and commanding.

"Who are you?" the smith slurred. "What are you doing in my forge?"

The stranger reached up to slide back his large cowl, revealing a bald head, a short and sparse beard, and deep-set blue eyes.

"That is not important," the stranger said. "But you need not worry. I am only here to seek your help."

The smith looked him over, lowering his dagger, but

remaining cautious. "I know your kind," he said. "You're an assassin."

The stranger smiled slightly, nodding his head. "That is correct," he said. "But my job is already done. As I said, I am here to seek your help."

The smith scowled, shaking his head in disbelief. "What do you want, then? And what is that accent? You're not from around here?"

The stranger smiled again, clasping his hands behind his back. "Also correct," he said. "I am from Thyre."

"What is an assassin of Thyre doing in Gaellos?" the smith asked.

"Again," the assassin said. "Not important."

The assassin reached into his cloak. The smith stepped back, his eyes focused on the assassin's face. The stranger produced a dagger from a hidden pocket, holding it up by its blade.

"You are Joran, correct?" he asked. "The finest smith in all of Eirenoch?"

The smith cocked his head curiously. "Aye," he said. "You've heard of me?"

The assassin chuckled. "Your reputation precedes you, sir."

He stepped forward, handing the dagger to Joran in a quick, smooth motion.

Joran took it, holding it up in front of him. His eyes widened as he studied its beautiful black blade. It was perfectly formed, forged in such a way to give it a swirled finish that shimmered before his very eyes. It was like looking into a pool of fine, pure oil.

"This is a blade of Khem," Joran said. "An obsidian blade; used by the assassins there. Where did you find this?"

"It was left at a residence," the assassin replied. "One where I was contracted to be."

"You mean you were there to kill someone," Joran said, not asked.

The assassin nodded slightly. "When I arrived," he said. "The contract had already been fulfilled, and this dagger was there, still embedded in the... mark's heart."

"Mark," Joran repeated skeptically. "So what do you want from me?"

"My sources tell me you can identify a blade's origin by its appearance. You have already answered my question. But can you tell me if there is anyone in these lands that bears a blade like this?"

The smith shook his head. "No, sir," he said. "I have never seen one up close. No one here would carry one of these, nor would I ever forge one."

"And why is that?"

Joran scowled again, this time scratching his chin. "It is bad luck to work with this material. It takes your skill with it, they say. Whoever forged this was very skilled, though. It was definitely a man of Khem. But judging by the quality and effort put into it, I would wager the poor fellow has no skill left. A blade like this would have taken much of it."

"The blade appears to be some kind of glass."

"It is," Joran said. "But with the right spells, it can be worked like metal once the basic shape is formed by knapping; like flint."

The assassin nodded. "There are writings on the cross guard," he said. "Can you read them?"

Joran studied the blade carefully, squinting at the writings. "The language of Khem, that is." He shook his head. "I cannot read it. There is only one man I know of who can read this."

"And who is that?"

"Prince Maedoc," Joran said. "He is versed in many strange things; magic, old languages, artifacts."

The assassin chuckled. "A future king interested in magic?"

"Rumor has it he has no interest in the throne," Joran said. "If you need to read this, then show it to him."

The assassin held out his hand, and Joran returned the dagger to him.

"I thank you, Joran," the assassin said, bowing his head graciously. "And I would thank you not to mention our encounter."

"No reason for that," Joran said. "But I would appreciate a little... compensation for my services."

"Of course," the assassin said, reaching into his cloak again.

Joran stepped back slightly, wary of the assassin's movements. But the stranger produced a small ingot and handed it to him. Joran took it happily, biting it with his crooked teeth.

"Adamantium," he said excitedly. "I've been looking for some of this."

"Use it wisely, my friend," the assassin said. "And I apologize for disturbing you at this hour."

Joran smiled, bouncing the ingot in his hand. "No problem,

sir," he said. "It was worth it."

The assassin bowed his head in respect. "Good evening sir."

He left quietly, closing the door behind him. Joran stood for a moment, admiring the quality of the ingot he had just been given. Behind him, the door to his residence opened, and he turned to see the small face of his young son.

"What are you doing up, Angus?" he asked.

The child rubbed his eyes, smiling up at him. "Hungry," he said.

"All right, son," Joran replied. "Let's get you fed and then back to bed. You'll need your rest if you'll be takin' over the forge someday."

Angus giggled.

* * *

Etanos reflected on his encounter with Joran as he strolled down the darkened street. The smith had confirmed what he had already known about the dagger, but there was still the mystery of the writings upon it. As far as he knew, there was no one anywhere outside of Khem who could read Khemite. The fact that the crown prince himself was well-versed in it was surprising.

Despite his dislike for royalty—for obvious reasons—going to Prince Maedoc was likely his best bet. Traveling to Khem was a bit too much just to have someone read a few words on a dagger. But, no matter what the words read, one thing was clear; there was a Khemite assassin here in Eirenoch, and that assassin wanted Etanos himself to know it.

That angered him greatly.

Chapter Two

arret knelt on the kitchen floor of the convent, scrubbing intently at a single spot that had been bothering him for some time now. The cook stared at him strangely, almost lustily, as she admired his corded arms and back. Garret knew she was watching him, and knew what was going on in her head. He rather enjoyed toying with her at times like this.

He had always found it amusing.

"You're going to burn a hole in my back," he said, not bothering to look up.

He heard Helga chuckle and return to her pot to stir the thick soup that boiled inside. He smiled to himself, knowing that she would still take a peek every once in a while as he scrubbed.

"You know," Helga said in her thick northern accent. "That spot has been there since you arrived. I don't think there's any chance of getting it up."

Garret dropped his brush, leaning back on his knees and slumping. "You're probably right," he said. "I've been working on it for an hour now."

"Well, don't let me stop you. Feel free to keep scrubbing if you wish."

Garret grinned. "Later, perhaps," he said. "I think I'll just go back to my room and polish my blade."

Helga chuckled loudly for several seconds before Garret realized why. He covered his face, shaking his head in embarrassment.

"That was *not* a euphemism," he said.

Helga kept chuckling, stirring her pot as she did so. Garret stood and grabbed his shirt, walking away without another word. He passed a few of the younger children who were having snacks at the tables, smiling at them in a friendly manner. They each looked at him like he was an older brother to be admired.

SHAWN E. CRAPO

That was how they perceived him, and that was how he treated them.

"See you later, Garret," a small boy said, smiling.

Garret mussed the boy's hair with his hand and then donned his shirt as he left the kitchen area. Outside, the Headmistress was coming down the hallway, looking him right in the eye. Apparently, she had been looking for him, as she gave him that familiar smile of relief.

"Garret," she said. "I've been looking for you."

"I'm sorry, ma'am," he said. "I was helping out in the kitchen."

The Headmistress smiled, clasping her hands in front of her. "In any case," she continued. "I was wondering if you could go to the market for some ink. All of my couriers are busy, and the other children are far too young to be traveling by themselves."

The *other* children?

"Of course," he said. "It would be my pleasure."

She smiled again. "Thank you, Garret. I know it's difficult for you to always have to do these things, but I do appreciate it."

"It's no trouble," he said. "I don't mind. It's good to have something to do, and I owe it to you for all of the things you and the sisters have given me."

She smiled then, showing Garret that loving expression he had grown to admire. "Speak no more of our help, Garret. Your father was a wonderful man who helped our temple in every way you can imagine. It is the least we can do to repay his kindness."

"His kindness has been repaid," Garret. "I assure you. It is I who should be repaying you."

The Headmistress lowered her gaze, showing what looked like an expression of guilt. "Well," she said. "The time is coming for you to move on. You're a young man now. Even though the children look up to you, it's no good for you to stay here. You are a wonderful young man of many skills. Don't waste them all serving our needs. You owe us nothing. Helping parentless children is why we are here."

Garret pursed his lips, nodding in agreement. "I will stay as long as I am needed," he said, "but no longer. I promise."

"Two vials of ink, please," she replied, walking away.

He watched her as she went, smiling crookedly at the way her hips swayed.

* * *

After retrieving his blade from his room, Garret made his way through the crowded streets of Gaellos on his way to the market. He passed through the various sections of town, admiring the diversity of the classes, and the way they acted toward each other. He had always noticed the lack of animosity between the higher class and the common folk. Unlike other cities that he had heard of, Gaellos seemed more united and friendly — for the most part.

There *were* those in the upper classes who held themselves in higher esteem and treated those below them as cattle. Some of the local lords were this way; and almost all of the nobles. But that was a fairly common thing, no matter where one looked.

He passed a tobacco shop, where several well-dressed gentlemen were sampling the local leaf. The merchant, who had set up a booth outside his shop, graciously allowed them to congregate and converse. It was a good business tactic, Garret knew; one that would draw the finest of customers.

He sniffed the air as he passed, closing his eyes and taking in the aroma. The smell of certain tobacco blends was comforting to him, as his father had been a pipe smoker. He remembered sitting on his father's lap while he read to him, giggling as rings of smoke shot out from his father's bearded lips.

The thought always made him smile, and miss his father as well. He had been taken too soon; before Garret was even five years old. His memories were cloudy, but what always stood out in his mind was the day the local constable came and told him that his father had been killed at the local mill. Though Garret was too young to understand, he knew then that he would never see his father again.

It was a thought that still made him weep to this day.

"Garret!" the tobacco merchant called to him.

Garret turned, seeing Taen wave and smile his toothy smile. He waved back, chuckling to himself as he saw the man's face. If there was one thing he could say about Taen it was that the man had all his teeth — and then some.

"Good afternoon, Taen!" he called back.

"Tell Helga to stop by sometime," Taen said. "I've got something to show her."

I bet you do, Garret thought, grinning. "I sure will, sir," he said.

He continued, reaching the town square in a matter of minutes. The parchment shop was on the opposite side, just around the large fountain that dominated the square. He had always wondered why the town had placed such a pointless structure there. The water was always too warm to drink, and usually stagnant.

What a waste of someone's money.

He circled the fountain to the right, passing the smith's shop. He saw Joran there through the open door, pounding away at something with his big hammer. Little Angus was out front, drawing pictures in the dirt with a stick as a scruffy-looking dog watched and erased everything he drew. Garret laughed as he saw the boy chase the dog away in frustration.

Keeping his eyes on the antics, he didn't see the nobleman whose path he had crossed. He narrowly missed running into the man, lightly brushing his sleeve with barely any contact. Still, he felt his arm being grabbed roughly. He turned his head to see the angry face of the noble's personal guard. His right hand went instinctively to his blade.

"Watch where you're going, boy," the guard scolded him.

Garret pulled his arm away, glaring at the guard. He loosened his grip on his blade but kept his hand there. "My apologies, sir," he said, stepping away.

The guard reached out to grab him again, but Garret sidestepped, leaving him to swipe the empty air. The man reached for his blade, prompting Garret to unsheathe his own. Garret was much quicker.

"It's all right, Baern," the nobleman said, stepping between the two. Garret recognized him as Lord Daeglan. "He apologized. No harm done."

Garret sheathed his blade, relaxing his posture but keeping his guard up. The nobleman pushed his bodyguard away, but the man continued to glare at him, apparently insulted at Garret's superior speed.

"You'll have to forgive him," the nobleman turned and said. "He's overprotective, and a bit zealous."

Garret shook his head, silently turning and walking away. He didn't want any further contact with the two men. He hated nobles and hated their bodyguards even more. Just the look on the nobleman's smug face was enough to send him fuming, and the guard's attitude made it even worse.

It was a beautiful day, and he had been enjoying it up until now. But all he could do was grit his teeth in anger and continue his task. It would do no good to act on his anger, but he knew he could easily take the guard if need be.

He looked back, seeing that Daeglan had engaged in conversation with another man. The guard, however, was still glaring; scowling at him with a murderous look in his eyes. Garret shot him a sarcastic grin, prompting the man's scowl to tighten even more. The guard drew a finger across his throat in a silent threat and then turned back to his master.

Garret ignored the gesture, ducking into the parchment shop and pausing to allow his heart to slow to a more civilized pace. The guard had gotten to him. Though he didn't know the man— had never met or even seen him before—Garret's reaction had been one of hatred. How dare that stranger grab him by the arm? Who did he think he was?

He's nobody, Garret said in his head. *Pay him no heed.*

"What do you need, son?" the shop owner asked from behind the corner.

Garret turned quickly, mildly surprised. He wiped the sweat from his forehead and approached the counter, hoping that the color of his face wouldn't give away his mood.

"I need two vials of black ink, please," he said, "for the sisters."

The man nodded and turned to search his shelves. He was an old man, obviously one who had spent his life as a scribe. His hands were gnarled by years and years of writing, and his palms were stained with ink of various colors. Even his back was bent, probably from countless decades of sitting hunched over a desk.

"Black, did you say?" the man asked.

"Yes, sir," Garret said, putting his hands on the counter.

The shop owner continued to peruse his stock, moving the various bottles to the side and humming off-key to fill the silence. Finally, he found what he was looking for, and set the two vials on the counter with a toothless grin.

"Here you are, young man," he said. "I'll expect payment by the end of the week."

Garret took the ink, stuffing the vials into his pockets. The man paused to study his face, and Garret met his gaze with a questioning look.

"Are you all right, son?" the shop owner asked. "You look a wee bit frustrated."

Garret lowered his eyes, nodding politely. "Yes," he said. "I'm fine. Nothing to worry about."

The man gave him a skeptical look but changed the subject. "Give the sisters my best, then," he said, "and you have a good day."

Garret smiled. "Thank you. You too."

He turned and walked away, but he could feel the man's eyes on him. He seemed like a nice enough fellow, but probably wouldn't understand Garret's anger if he mentioned the reason for it. Nobody would; at least not a shopkeeper.

The street was still crowded when Garret emerged. He took a quick look around to see if the noble and his guards were anywhere near. Not seeing them, he rounded the fountain again, this time sticking to the storefronts. If he spotted the guard, he could more easily duck out of sight that way. Not that he was afraid of the man, but he had no desire to draw any attention to himself or risk doing anything that would make him look bad.

Garret kept his hand on the pommel of his blade just in case. If the guard saw him, he wanted the man to know that he was willing to fight for his honor. He was no coward, by any definition of the word. He would defend himself — and anyone who couldn't help themselves — to the death. He had spent years practicing with his blade for this very purpose. His years at the convent had taught him that there were people who needed protection; *his* protection. There was no one else to defend those children, and he had always considered himself their guardian — from the time he was able to swing a blade.

As the need to blend in became more urgent, Garret decided that taking the alleyways back to the convent was his best bet. Taking one last look at the square, he turned left between two shops and hurried into the sheltered road behind them. Here, he could traverse his way back without being in the open. The rows of buildings would provide some cover.

There were few people here, only a wandering pauper or two. He nodded respectfully as he passed them, keeping his eyes on the areas ahead. It was only when he reached the temple section of town that he began to feel insecure.

Garret turned into another alley heading toward the convent. It was only a few blocks away at this point, and he could make it there without going back onto the main streets. Still, he felt a strange sense of being watched. Maybe Daeglan had dismissed his guard, and now the man himself was wandering town watching him.

He ducked behind a stack of boxes and leaned against the wall. His heart pounded for some reason he could not fathom, and he felt compelled to look in every direction. To his left, there was a man in long robes standing on the opposite side of the street. He had just come from that way and hadn't seen him standing there before.

Garret studied him carefully. He didn't appear to be watching him directly; just standing there casually with his arms folded and his gaze directed at the rooftops. He didn't look like a man of Eirenoch; his skin was slightly darker, and his beard was of a style he had never seen among the people of this land. It was simply a small tuft of hair on his chin, with no mustache or sideburns. His robes were odd, as well. They were multi-layered—like a priest's robes—yet Garret could tell the man wore leather armor beneath them. Only thieves wore leather armor as far as he knew; thieves and rangers, perhaps. This man was no ranger.

Garret suddenly felt a twinge of fear. The stranger looked dangerous, to be sure, and he wanted no part of it. He ducked out of his hiding place, walking close to the wall as he headed back toward the main street. The alley widened somewhat, becoming more of a courtyard where four buildings met. There, out of one of the side alleys, the offending guard appeared.

Garret stopped, gripping his blade as the man strolled toward him. Two others stepped out of the remaining alleys to join him, and the three glaring men came right in his direction. Garret drew his blade, crouching slightly in preparation.

"So you draw against me again?" the guard said, stopping and gripping his sword, showing a smug smile.

The others drew their blades and stepped to the side. Garret looked at each of them in turn, taking note of their positions and what weapons they carried.

"You bring two others to stand against me?" Garret asked. "Are you such a coward that you cannot intimidate me on your own?"

The guard's smile vanished, replaced with a look of rage. Garret had insulted him greatly.

Good.

"I should cut out your tongue, boy," the guard said. "A smart mouth like yours needs to be silenced."

"Have at it, then," Garret taunted him. "Or you can send your friends to do it for you."

That did it. The guard growled in rage, whipping out his blade and charging him. Garret crouched lower, shifting his feet to gain the leverage he needed to dodge. The other two guards charged around either side of him. He was surrounded.

The main guard swiped clumsily, swinging back-handed in a blind rage. Garret easily dodged, spinning to block an attack from the guard on his right. He countered with a spinning kick to the chest, turning again to block a second attack from the first guard. He jumped back and to the side, countering with a slash and side-kicking the other guard in the chest again. He heard the man curse as he was knocked back onto the ground.

The third guard charged, attacking with a thrust of his sword. Garret spun to the side, slashing the man's triceps, drawing a groan of pain along with it. He quickly jump-kicked the man in the back, sending him sprawling into the dirt. Garret backed away, standing in a ready position as the main guard glared.

"It seems I'm quicker than all three of you," Garret said, grinning.

"You insult not only me," the guard said, "but my men as well. Lord Daeglan will have your head."

Garret laughed. "I hope he sends someone better to take it," he said.

"How is *this* for better?" the guard taunted, snapping his fingers.

Other men melted from the alleyways, surrounding Garret and the three guards. They were not dressed in uniforms, but the typical garments of criminals; leather armor and cloaks that concealed them from head to toe. He had seen them before. They were brigands and bandits who robbed peasants on the highways and made life difficult for honest merchants. They were extortionists, thugs, and thieves.

"Nice choice of friends," Garret mocked him.

The guard lunged with his blade, his face twisted in a grimace of rage. Garret spun to the side, backslashing in an upward attack that laid open the man's cheek to the bone. The guard howled in rage, dropping his blade and clutching his open wound.

"*Kill him!*" he shouted.

The thugs charged all at once. Garret sheathed his blade, turning and leaping onto the wall of a nearby building. He grabbed the window sill and pulled himself up, digging his boots into the rough area between stones. Behind him, he could hear the brigands shout and curse. He ignored them, climbing upward as fast as he could, and disappearing over the eave.

He rolled to his feet, crouching as he ran to the roof's peak. He stopped as he crossed over it, looking back to see the heads of a few of his pursuers appearing over the edge. He smiled, turning and leaping across the gap to another building. He ran as fast as he could, varying his route to avoid leading them right to the convent. He could easily lose them, he knew and would have fun doing it.

His only worry was losing the ink before he got home.

* * *

Etanos watched the boy from a nearby rooftop. He had climbed up after the boy had spotted him, and hidden behind a chimney to observe the scuffle. He was highly impressed with the boy's skills; not only at fighting, but climbing and eluding as well.

Through his many years as an assassin, Etanos had trained quite a few promising young fledglings, as he called them, but none of them compared to this mysterious young man. There was something about him that Etanos liked. Perhaps it was his enjoyment of the chase or the way he taunted his foes. Either way, the assassin felt the need to meet this young man. Perhaps he would help him get rid of this obstinate guard and his criminal cronies, maybe offering him training or an apprenticeship.

He smiled at the thought. His order could use more men like this young boy, and he was skilled enough to take to the training well. His only concern was whether such a lifestyle would be suited for the boy. Would it take away his spirit? Would it change the way he looked at the world?

The guild needed heroes, not simple murderers. It needed people who could distinguish between a noble contract and the simple greed of a potential employer. It needed dark knights of justice.

It needed this boy.

CHAPTER THREE

hat have you done, Garret?" the Headmistress asked.

"I didn't do anything," Garret replied, leaning against the door frame of her office. "He attacked me for nothing more than not watching where I was going."

The Headmistress sighed, shaking her head as she sat at her desk. "You know you can't interact in any way with the bodyguards of nobles. Those nobles, especially Lord Daeglan, are nothing more than criminals."

"Then it's about time someone *did* stand up to them," Garret insisted. "They do nothing to help the people. All they do is rob them and threaten prosperity. The king knows this, I know this, and you know this."

"Yes, yes," she agreed. "But it is not our place to do anything about it. Not in this way, at least. That guard could have killed you, and now you have drawn attention to the convent."

"The king has done nothing to change things," Garret insisted. "Maybe it *is* up to us. Who else will stand up for the law?"

The Headmistress folded her hands in front of her. "There is a reason the king's hands are tied," she said. "He cannot engage them directly. Such a tactic would show dissent among the nobles. The king must do things according to law, too."

"Then maybe we should just get rid of the nobles," Garret said.

The Headmistress sighed. "That would be ideal," she said. "But they must be dealt with through the proper channels. You have no idea how much power they hold. Their troops are fiercely loyal, and the king would be hard-pressed to use military tactics against them."

"If their troops are loyal, then they too are criminals, and enemies of the kingdom."

The Headmistress stood, leaning on her desk. She hung her head low. "That may be," she said. "But when the king feels the time is right, he will do something. Until then, we must trust in the Great Mother."

Garret shook his head, sighing in resignation. "I admire your faith, Helena," he said. "I really do. But the Great Mother can't protect everyone. Your order is small, and you have no warriors. What happens in the future if criminals decide to turn their attention to the temples of Gaia?"

"The Dragon will protect us," the Headmistress said. "For to serve one Firstborn, or the Great Mother, is to serve them all."

"There have been no priests at the temples for thousands of years," Garret reminded her. "We must find other ways. But you are right; I may have drawn attention to the convent."

Helena nodded. "Everyone knows you serve us. None of them are willing to lie to Daeglan's guards."

"Don't worry," Garret said, pushing away from the door. "I won't let anything happen to the children *or* the sisters."

The Headmistress smiled warmly. Though Garret could detect skepticism in her smile, he knew she had faith in his resolve. She knew he would protect them to the best of his abilities — whether he owed them or not.

Garret nodded slightly, leaving the Headmistress to her duties.

* * *

"His name is Garret," Joran said to Etanos. "He was raised by the sisters of the Order of Gaia. Why do you ask?"

"I find him interesting," the assassin replied. "His skills are impressive."

"Oh, now," Joran protested. "He's a good boy. He doesn't need to get involved in your business."

Etanos smiled crookedly, raising a brow. "And what business do you think I am in?"

Joran shook his head, stuffing a working blade back into the fire. "Come on," he said. "I knew your business the moment I saw you."

Etanos folded his arms across his chest, turning to look out the window of Joran's shop. "You have it all wrong, friend," he said. "Our guild is not about murder. We are warriors of justice — knights, if you will. Kings hire us to rid them of their rivals, or those that threaten a kingdom's stability. That's how it works, Joran. Kings cannot wage war against their own, even if their own are thieves and criminals."

Joran sighed. "Then your order is different than the others."

"Of course it is," Etanos said. "That's why I came to you about the dagger. There is a Khemite assassin here in Eirenoch, and if he belongs to the order I think he belongs to, then I must rid your land of his menace."

"How noble of you," Joran said. He pulled his working blade out of the fire and set it down on the anvil as Etanos watched. "Now, if you will excuse me, I need to get back to work."

"Thank you for your time, Joran," Etanos said.

"It's all right," Joran said, swinging his hammer down, and throwing off a burst of orange sparks. "But if you're planning on contacting the boy, make sure he takes the righteous path. I would hate to see him become something... undesirable."

Etanos smiled. "You have my word," he said, turning to leave.

"And don't *you* worry," Joran said. "This one's on the house."

Etanos chuckled as he closed the door.

* * *

Garret's mind wandered as he performed his katas in his small cabin on the convent grounds. He had pulled off his boots and his shirt, and stood in a crouched position; his muscles tensed and locked in place as he breathed slowly and deeply. This was how he trained and relaxed at the same time. To an outsider, it wouldn't look relaxing, but to Garret, it was the ultimate way to relieve stress.

He switched positions, turning to face the opposite direction and swapping the positions of his fists. He tensed, tightening his muscles as much as he could, then relaxed and breathed out sharply. During his exercises, he had gone over the previous events in his head. He replayed the fight over and over again, judging his moves and his strikes with scrutiny.

It was the only way to improve one's performance, he had read. The scrolls he had been given had detailed not only the very katas he was currently performing, but the philosophies of the samurai of Kinar as well. Self-scrutiny was self-improvement. To have too much faith in one's abilities could lead to stagnation of skill; not to mention overconfidence. And, as every warrior knew, overconfidence could lead to death.

Without looking, he reached behind him to retrieve his blade. He unsheathed it and swung it into position above his head with a sharp swoosh. He then lifted his right leg, pointing his blade forward. There, he stood still, unmoving for several minutes as he allowed his muscles to tighten in that position. He called it the scorpion stance, as it allowed him to strike swiftly, like a scorpion, and step back to observe its effect without putting himself in danger.

It was detailed in the scrolls, and he had found it pleasing. Not only was it a formidable-looking stance, but its configuration was confusing to those who stood against it. From this position, Garret could strike downward with his blade, kick out with his right foot, or even do a back spin kick with his left. These were all detailed in the pictographs, but Garret had added his own. It was a move he had practiced over and over again until he had perfected its execution with lightning-like quickness.

Letting his right leg drop and swing behind him, he let his left leg bend, and he rolled onto his hip, bringing his left leg around and kicking upward with his right foot; almost straight upward. With this move, he realized, he could easily break an opponent's neck with one quick, upward thrust of his foot, all while maintaining guard with his blade, and pushing himself back onto his feet with his free hand.

Or so he hoped.

It felt effective when he performed it. He would be back on his feet and in the same stance within a split second, ready to strike again. But, he had never tested it; at least not on anything living. In the courtyard, he had practiced it against a dummy he had fashioned. It seemed to work well. The only question was whether he could do it quickly enough against a moving, conscious target — with a sword.

Garret did a few more stretches, holding his blade above his head at either end and squatted down several times. He then laid his blade on the dresser and shook himself off, allowing his muscles to loosen up before plopping down on his bed to daydream.

Tomorrow, he thought, he would practice in the courtyard.

* * *

"Lord Daeglan must be out of his mind," Ergan said. "I can't believe he is allowing this."

Baern grinned, his brow furrowing in anticipation of the night's deeds. "He knows how important it is to assert dominance over these peasants. Give them any leeway, and they will take advantage of our employers, leaving us in the poorhouse, just like them."

"Still," Ergan said as they glared at the convent. "Murdering nuns is bad luck. We could be cursed for life."

Baern glared at him through his fog of rage. "They cling to these ancient and forgotten religions as if they even matter anymore. There is no Great Mother. Nor is there a Dragon, despite what the king believes. He and his line will end, and this archaic trend will die with them."

Ergan sighed, nodding. "All of this over an insult by some worthless man-child of no consequence."

Baern grabbed him by the collar, pulling him within inches of his face. "Do you contest my right to challenge his insult?"

Ergan swallowed hard, his eyes fluttering as he struggled to find the words to alleviate Baern's temper. "N-no," he stammered. "You will have your revenge."

Baern threw him back, drawing his blade and moving to the edge of the forest. Just a few short yards away, the pasture sat unguarded before them, interspersed with the various buildings that made up the convent. There were no city guards in this entire section, as the foolish Sisters of Gaia trusted the townsfolk in an almost sickening way.

Tonight, they would learn better.

Baern turned, signaling to the rest of the men behind them. A dozen of them appeared from the shadows, black-cloaked, and silent as the night itself.

"Kill every nun you find," Baern ordered them. "Set fire to the gardens and buildings and find that boy."

The warriors quickly dispersed into the pasture, spreading out among the buildings, and keeping to the shadows. Baern and Ergan watched, waiting for them to melt into the darkness. When they disappeared completely, Baern turned to his companion, gripping his shoulder tightly.

"Do not hesitate," he warned. "If you show any signs of disobeying me, I will cut off your head and feed it to the pigs."

Ergan gulped, narrowing his gaze at the complex before them. Without a word, the two of them charged.

CHAPTER FOUR

arret's eyes popped open when he heard soft footsteps outside. He lay still for a moment, listening to the rhythmic movements as they circled his small cabin. They were not the footsteps of someone passing by, but the carefully placed steps of someone purposely attempting to move silently.

He slowly sat up, reaching over to his nightstand to grab his blade. Without a sound, he lowered his feet to the floor, eyeing his boots, and laying his blade beside him. The footsteps were near—just to the north—and were fading away. Someone had passed right by his cabin, ignoring it and heading toward the other buildings.

He bent down and grabbed his boots, pulling them on silently, and reached for his blade again. He crept toward his door, pulling it open and peering outside. The moonlight was dim, but he could definitely see the shadows moving.

What the hell is going on, he wondered.

He slipped outside, crouching in the darkness near the door. Ahead, the shadows seemed to be gathering near the chapel and the dorms where the sisters slept. Garret's heart pounded as he watched. Something bad was about to happen, and he was the only one here who could stop it.

As he built up his courage to charge forth, more shuffling sounded behind him and to the north. He turned and crouched behind a bush, seeing two more figures emerge from the tree line. He recognized one of them immediately.

The guard from the alley.

"Bastard," he whispered, gripping his blade in anger.

He started after them just as several flashes of light erupted from the group of shadowy figures. They had drawn their bows, and magical, flaming arrows had flared to life. Before he could react, a dozen fiery missiles raced toward the surrounding buildings, embedding themselves in the rooftops and setting them aflame.

"*No!*" Garret shouted.

The offending guard turned, spotting him as he charged in rage. Garret saw his face, gritted his teeth in rage, and froze. He was torn. He had to choose between facing the guard and saving the sisters and the children. He chose the latter, racing around the two charging guards and heading toward the dorms.

He had to save them.

"*Come back here!*" the guard shouted behind him. "*Face me like a man!*"

Garret was fixated on the spreading flames. Ahead of him, several of the shadowy figures broke off from the main group to block his way. He saw the glint of their blades and the strange garb that helped them blend in with the darkness. He slowed, abruptly changing direction just as he passed one of them. He dodged the man's strike, spinning in the air above the slashing blade, and landing just behind the attacker. He ignored the second attack, desperate to reach the closest dorm.

He leaped onto the wooden porch, bursting through the door. The interior was already burning, with flaming chunks of roof material falling to the floor. In the back corner, he saw several children huddled in terror, clasping each other for safety.

Garret passed them, kicking open the back door that always remained locked.

"*Get out!*" he shouted.

The children remained unmoving, crying out for help as they hid their faces from the horror. Garret reached out to them, dragging them to their feet and pushing them toward the door.

"*Get out!*" he shouted again. "*Get to the front gates! Find the city guards.*"

The children disappeared outside. He watched them flee, waiting for them to reach the safety of the front gates. On a nearby rooftop, a moving shadow caught his attention, and he shifted his eyes to peer into the darkened sky.

Nothing.

He hoped it was his imagination. Surely, these men were not here to kill the children. He took one last look, satisfied that the children were safe, and turned to face the front door. The dark men outside were still spreading themselves out throughout the compound, and he could hear their shouts as they called to each other and issued orders.

He slipped out the back door, making his way toward the other dorms. The children were already gathered outside the next building, and they cried out to him as he approached.

"Get to the front gates!" he directed them.

One of the older boys grabbed the others and led them away. Garret counted them as they fled, seeing that they were all present. He nodded, stopping to glance around. The sisters were housed across the way, and he knew that the bandits would head there next. He started in that direction but froze as he sensed something jumping across the rooftop above him. He looked up, backing away far enough to see onto the roof.

Again, nothing.

Garret shook his head, racing between the buildings to reach the sisters. One of the shadowy figures appeared before him, grinning and hissing in a strange, insane fashion.

"Caught you," the man said, licking his lips.

Garret dropped to the ground in a slide, slashing the man's thigh as he passed underneath. His target groaned, slashing behind him blindly as Garret slid back onto his feet. He kept running, putting as much distance between him and his attacker as he could. But the man groaned in pain once more, and Garret turned to see him fall to the ground. Another shadowy figure disappeared into the darkness.

What the hell, Garret whispered.

With the sisters' dorm in his sights, Garret ignored the chaos around him. The children were safe, but he knew the sisters were still in danger. The bastard guard was nowhere in sight, telling him that the man was probably going to use the innocent women as pawns. Garret would not let that happen.

Another shadowy warrior leaped from the darkness, spinning his blade in front of him menacingly. Garret changed direction, leaping against the side of a building, and delivering a spin kick right to the man's face. He felt the impact against his foot and heard the satisfying crack of the man's jaw breaking. He growled in battle fury, landing on his feet right behind his victim.

He grabbed the man by the cloak, pulling his bloody head up to face him directly. "You made a big mistake coming here," Garret hissed. "Harm the sisters, and I will kill every last one of you."

He threw the man back to the ground and leaped onto the nearby deck. Here, the buildings were larger and contained the dorms of the sisters, and their various offices and classrooms. He had to find them and get them to safety. There was little time before the flames would overtake them.

Before he could enter, he heard the sound of clashing steel. The body of a bandit fell from the roof, flopping lifeless to the ground. Garret glared upward, seeing only the faintest of outlines against the moonlit sky. There was a man there, just a shadow, staring back at him. Garret could swear he saw him nod.

"*Who are you?*" Garret called out.

The man didn't answer; he simply disappeared over the eave in one quick motion. Garret shook his head, not sure as to whether he had actually seen anything. Inside, he heard a piercing scream that brought him back to attention. He burst through the door, desperate to save the sisters. He was immediately choked with thick smoke that billowed throughout the room.

The scream sounded again, and Garret charged forward. He passed by the windows, busting them out with his elbow. The screams were coming from the kitchen, he knew. Helga was in trouble, and he had to save her.

As he burst through the kitchen door, he was greeted by the intense glow of flame at the outer wall. Part of the ceiling had collapsed, and the way was blocked. Helga was there, along with three of the sisters.

"*This way!*" Garret called out.

Helga pushed the sisters toward him, shielding them from the flames with a wet blanket. As the nuns passed by Garret, Helga stopped to gather some pots.

"*Leave them!*" Garret shouted. "*Get out of here!*"

"*I'm not leavin' without me pots!*"

"*Go now!*" he shouted again.

Frustrated and cursing, Helga dropped her armful and dashed toward him. She suddenly lurched forward, stumbling into him with a look of horror in her eyes. Garret caught her, cradling her in his arms as she went limp. As he lowered her to the floor in confusion, he was horrified to see an arrow protruding from her back.

"*Helga!*" he cried out.

He looked up through the flames, seeing the smiling face of a bandit there. The man drew back his bow again, releasing an arrow straight toward him. Garret ducked to the side, slashing at the missile with his blade. The two halves of it clanked against the wall, and Garret leaped up to escape.

…just as the ceiling crashed to the floor.

As he raced to the front door, he heard the agonized screams of the bandit as he was crushed and burned beneath the flaming timbers. Garret smiled at his luck, but his heart was heavy. Helga, the strange but friendly cook he had known his whole life, was dead.

She didn't deserve such a fate.

Garret emerged back onto the outside path, seeing the sisters fleeing toward the front gates. He rounded the building, heading back to the main path to seek out the cloaked bandits. Helena was there, dragging along the remaining children. She eyed him as she led them away to safety, seemingly looking at him with approval, yet worried at the same time.

"Be careful, Garret!" she said as he passed.

The shadowy bandits came from out of the darkness, rushing toward him with mad growls. He poised himself in a defensive stance, standing between them and Helena. Some attempted to circle him, but he leaped back, cutting off their routes and slashing at them with lightning-fast feints.

"Leave the children alone," he hissed. "They have done nothing to you."

Two bandits suddenly fell, cut down by shimmering arrows that streaked from the rooftops. The rest of them scrambled to stand guard, their eyes darting around them in search of the unseen archer. Garret searched as well, seeing the shadow man dash across a nearby roof and leap across to another building, only to disappear again.

Then, from between two of the bandits, the bastard guard and his companion appeared. They strolled casually toward him, their faces smug and confident.

"So," the bastard said, "I found you at last."

Garret said nothing but smoothly transitioned into his scorpion stance. The guard looked at him curiously, nearly laughing.

"What is this?" he mocked. "Some new thing you orphans are doing these days?"

"Come find out," Garret smirked.

The guard drew his blade, his brow furrowing in rage. He suddenly charged, raising his blade over his head in a sloppy attack. Garret kicked up his right leg, swinging it inward and spinning to deliver a backkick at the guard's face. His head was jarred with the impact, and he swung clumsily, knocking himself off balance.

The guard's companion and the rest of the bandits charged as their leader pitched into the ground. Garret rushed a single guard, dodging his blade, and spinning to slash with a backhanded strike. His blade sliced open the bandit's gut, and the howling man crumbled and toppled to the ground with a pitiful groan.

Garret spun into the scorpion stance again, glancing briefly at the fallen bandit. The man was writhing in agony, trying desperately to contain his innards as he moaned. Garret's heart fluttered at the thought of what he had just done. The attack was surely fatal, and he had delivered it. It was his first kill.

He would think about it later.

The bastard guard growled as he charged. Garret knelt, thrusting his blade up with two hands to block the furious downward strike, countering with an uppercut punch to the groin. The guard groaned; grasping his crotch and stumbling away just as his companion came in on Garret's left. Garret rolled out of the way, double slashing as he rose to his feet, catching the smaller man in the back of the thigh.

Garret backed up against the nearby wall, his eyes widening as he saw the other bandits surrounding him. Though his heart was pumping furiously, he did not feel any fear. He felt confident, yet guilty at the same time. He hated the guard and his cronies, but he had no desire to kill any of them.

However, they had destroyed his home; the only home he had ever known. Nothing he did would ever be unjustified at this point; at least not to others. But inside, he knew that revenge would take its toll on his soul.

But that was unimportant at the moment.

Seeking an escape, his eyes darted around the burning buildings. The shadowy stranger streaked into his vision, coming up behind the half circle of bandits that closed in on him. Three of them fell in the blink of an eye, cut down by the shadow's silent blade.

The group, now several men fewer, turned their attention to their new opponent. Garret took advantage of their surprise, charging the bastard guard's companion. He spun in the air, coming down with a thrust of his blade. The companion swatted the attack aside, countering with a backslash. Garret ducked, twirling his blade into an upward slash that caught the man's leg once more.

The companion stumbled away, making room for the raging leader, who came in furiously with his blade striking in an X attack. Garret backed away, blocking each time the furious blade came close. Behind him, he could hear the sounds of his mysterious ally taking down the other bandits.

The bastard's blade caught Garret off guard; barely missing as he spun out of its way, and right into the companion's path. Garret's heart nearly stopped as he saw the impending strike that would surely end his life. But the companion froze as a dagger suddenly embedded itself in his chest. Garret rolled away just in time to avoid another X charge from the bastard. He rose to his feet again, back-swinging and catching the bastard's back plate. He immediately went into his scorpion stance again, glaring at the bastard guard as he turned to face him with a look of rage.

"I will kill you," the guard hissed. "And mount your head on my mantle."

Garret kept his position, waiting for the man to charge. This was the final strike, he knew. This is what would decide the outcome of the battle. He watched the man's face, looking for any sign of his intentions. It was as if the world had slowed down for him; slow enough for him to see every little movement in his opponent's eyes, brow, and mouth.

The man's lips slowly curled into a scowl, and Garret knew the time had come. As the bastard's blade rose, Garret let his left leg go limp, swinging his right leg around to drop his weight on the knee. He gritted his teeth as he swung his left leg behind him, spinning counterclockwise to bring it up with all his might.

The bastard guard struck, swinging wildly in his rage, and bringing his head into just the right position. Garret's heel thrust upward, catching him right in the chin and blasting his head back with all the fury Garret's leg could muster. The guard was jolted upward as his neck cracked like a falling tree.

Garret rolled back onto his feet, spinning around to see the man drop to his knees and pitch forward into the dirt. He stayed in his defensive position for a moment, marveling at how well the move had worked. But that marvel soon gave way to that feeling of guilt. Though the guard had destroyed his home, and the death of an innocent woman, just the thought of killing him sent Garret's mind into a whirl.

A lump began to rise in his throat. He let his guard down, dropping his blade and falling to his knees. Though the convent was burning around him, and the sound of the city guards approaching was growing louder, he could only stare at the man's body in disbelief. He was transfixed.

Suddenly, he felt a rough hand grab the cloth of his shirt from behind.

"Get up," a voice whispered harshly. "It's time to go."

The hand pulled him up, and Garret didn't resist. His world was a blur, and nothing seemed to make sense anymore. All he could do was picture the faces of the two men he had killed. Nothing else mattered.

"Move!" the voice said. Garret blindly stumbled forward, but his mind protested. He shook his head as the man dragged him into the tree line just outside the row of burning buildings.

"I have to—" he stammered. "I have to make sure everyone is safe."

The man pulled him down into a crouching position, turning to face him just as the city guards burst into the courtyard with buckets of water.

"They're fine," the man said. "I promise you. You need to get out of here, and no one can see you leave."

"Why?" Garret asked. "I've done nothing wrong."

"You killed a nobleman's bodyguard," the man reminded him. "That noble will put a price on your head, and it will be an attractive price."

"But my scrolls…"

"Never mind that," the man said. "Whatever they are, you can find new ones. It is time for you to flee."

Garret was silent. He didn't want to leave. Gaellos was his home. The convent was his home, but now it was burning to the ground. What was happening? One moment he was scrubbing the floor, and the next, an entire series of events had turned everything upside down.

He wanted it to end. He wanted to go back to his cabin and relax again.

"I don't want to leave," he said.

"Come," the man said, pulling him back to his feet. "You're with me now. I will make your life a lot more interesting. This place is not for you."

Garret wasn't sure what he meant, but he didn't argue. The confusion and longing were heavy, and he couldn't think clearly. Perhaps it was best that someone else did his thinking for him — at least for the moment.

He sighed, nodding his head and following his new friend through the shadows of the forest. Somehow, he knew, his life was about to change drastically.

CHAPTER FIVE

Who are you?" Garret asked the strange man when they had finally stopped in the forest to rest.

"My name is Etanos," he said. "I am an assassin of the Kingdom of Thyre."

Garret's eyes widened. "An assassin? For the king?"

"Not the king," Etanos answered. "Daelus is not one to employ assassins."

"Then for whom?"

Etanos leaned back, pulling off the glove of his right hand to reveal a tattooed symbol. Garret scooted closer to look, seeing it's finely detailed depiction of a hooked dagger.

"I belong to a guild in Thyre known as the Brotherhood of Perses. This is our symbol."

Garret studied it for a moment, noting how the ink seemed to move beneath Etanos' skin; as if the dagger were alive.

"Who or what is Perses?" he asked, intrigued.

"He is the master assassin of the Firstborn," Etanos explained. "It is he who executes vile and perverse men when the divine demand it. We do the same, but for great and noble men who are unable to do it themselves."

Garret sat back, his mind spinning. "So you are a murderer, then," he said.

Etanos smiled. "Not a murderer, my friend," he said. "An assassin, at least the assassins of my order, help to maintain or restore the balance of power. While we do take contracts to do away with difficult and dangerous men, our guild acts on its own as well, ridding the world of those who would oppress others or cause harm to those beneath them."

"I have never heard of an assassin who did that," Garret said, skeptically. "I have only heard of those who murder people who stand in the way of a powerful man's ambitions."

Etanos nodded. "There are those who do that," he agreed, "which is why I am still here."

"What do you mean?"

"I have come to learn that an assassin of Khem is here in Eirenoch," he explained, pulling a magnificent black dagger from his cloak. "He left this at the residence of a slaver I was hired to eliminate. He got there before I did and fulfilled the contract. He left this behind. I believe he left it for me to see."

"Why would he do that?"

Etanos flipped the dagger over in his hand, studying it carefully. "To tell me something, I think. Perhaps he wanted to make his presence known to me. Why? I do not know. I have no reason to believe he belongs to any guilds in Khem. He may be acting on his own."

"But if he killed this... contract, then he is on the same side."

"Not necessarily," Etanos said. "An independent assassin will take any contract he or she can get their hands on. Sometimes they will have a sense of honor, as I do, and sometimes they may have no honor. They will take contracts for the murder of innocent people, just as the darker guilds do. The fact that this dagger was left behind tells me that this assassin knew I would come, and wanted me to know that I had a rival or an enemy."

Garret was silent. He wasn't sure why this man had come, or why he was telling him this story. It was all too confusing, especially considering the recent events. What did this man want with him?

"I saw you in Gaellos," Garret said, remembering the fight earlier in the day. "You were watching me."

Etanos nodded. "I suppose I was," he admitted. "After I saw you sneaking through the alleys. I was curious, so I followed you and watched the fight."

"I did everything I could to avoid it," Garret said. "But that man just wouldn't let it go."

"You handled yourself well," Etanos said. "I saw the way you climbed up that wall and ran across the rooftops. You are very skilled; not only at that, but at fighting as well. Although watching your techniques, I could see that you could use a little formal training."

Garret sat up again. "Why would you train me?"

Etanos held up the dagger. "Because, my little friend, the world is full of men who must be eliminated. I think you would make a grand assassin, with a little training."

Garret shook his head. "No," he protested. "I couldn't... I could never kill anyone in that way."

Etanos pursed his lips. "You killed two men today," he said. "I saw you. They were evil men who destroyed your home, and you exacted revenge upon them. What is the difference?"

"They hurt my friends," Garret said. "They destroyed the home of the children, and the Temple of Gaia."

Etanos grinned, nodding his head slowly as if to encourage Garret to see the logic in his own words. "And you brought them to justice for their sins."

Garret lowered his eyes, suddenly feeling less sick about the deaths he had caused. Still, the thought of taking their lives troubled him, and Etanos seemed to sense it.

"They were monsters," the man said. "And you slew them. You are a hero. That is what you were meant to be, I think."

"How is an assassin a hero?"

"Because that is exactly what we do; what *I* do. I have rid the world of many evil men, whether by the sword in outright battle, or by a dagger in the back."

"Why choose me?"

Etanos stared at him for a moment. Garret sat nervously as the man studied him.

"When I look at you," Etanos said. "I see myself. I, too, was an orphan. I spent my life wandering the world as soon as I was old enough to do so. I spent all those years as a thief, climbing towers, robbing rich merchants, and smuggling slaves away to freedom. It wasn't until several years later that an assassin found me and gave me a true purpose. He taught me how to use my skills to better the world, and not just to steal."

"Freeing slaves is a noble deed," Garret said.

"Yes, it is," Etanos agreed, "but eliminating those who enslave them is a far more effective solution."

Garret lowered his head, considering the man's words. His perception of an assassin was nothing like the man before him. He did not seem like a murderer. He truly seemed like a man who sided with those in need. He was much like Garret himself.

Perhaps...

"You have piqued my interest, sir," he said. "At least for the moment. I have taught myself how to fight by reading the scrolls the sisters gave me. But I think I could be better trained by an actual warrior."

"Indeed, Garret. I can see that your self-training is based on the techniques of the Eastern warriors; your stances, your attacks, everything. They are a bit sloppy if you ask me, but I can help you with that."

Garret cocked his head, not sure whether or not he should be insulted.

"Where did you get your sword?" Etanos asked him.

Garret pulled out his blade, showing it to Etanos. "The sisters gave it to me," he said. "It is nothing special, but I have never had enough money to buy another."

Etanos tossed the blade to the ground, drawing a curious glance from Garret. "It is the wrong kind of blade," he said. "You need something more conducive to your technique. Tomorrow morning, we shall seek out a new blade for you."

Garret lay back, clasping his hands behind his head as he stared up into the sky. He could see Etanos still gazing at the dagger.

"Why is that dagger of such interest?" Garret asked him.

"The writing," Etanos replied. "It is the language of Khem, which I cannot read. I was told that Prince Maedoc could read Khemite, but I loathe dealing with nobles for the most part."

"I would not seek out Maedoc for such a thing," Garret said. "He will ask too many questions, and see too many things. But I know of another person who could read it for you."

"Oh?" Etanos said. "Who is that?"

"A witch that lives near the southern shore," Garret said. "She knows and sees almost as much as Maedoc, maybe more, but she doesn't ask questions."

Etanos grinned. "And what is this witch's name?" he asked.

"Aeli," Garret replied. "She can help us."

* * *

Now that the sun had come up, Garret was able to get a better look at Etanos. The man was not much taller than Garret himself—perhaps an inch or two. He seemed to be in his early forties, judging by the slight wrinkling around his deep-set eyes, but was quite obviously far more fit than most people of his age.

His head was shaved, and he sported a small tuft of hair on his chin. His ears bore small rings of silver or adamantium, and there was a strange yet intriguing tattoo on his neck, just under his left ear. It appeared to be writing of some kind, but Garret didn't recognize the language.

But what was most impressive was the man's garb. His robes were intricate and layered; shocks of black fabric were draped over what appeared to be finely forged ring mail that was utterly silent when he moved. Over his shoulders were leather guards, styled with the same intricate branding as the gauntlets he wore around his wrists.

Around his waist was a belt that supported his twin blades. They, too, were carved and branded, forged of the finest steel, Garret guessed, with leather-wrapped handles and fine leather scabbards.

The man looked deadly, and from what Garret had seen, he was just as silent. He would make a great teacher.

"The southern shore is rather far from here," Etanos said as he donned his cloak. "We will likely need to travel by horseback."

"True," Garret said. "But we could also follow the river. We might find a ferryman along the way. If not, there are boats in Faillaigh from what I hear. We could hire one there if need be."

"Good enough," Etanos replied. "But I'm not overly fond of water travel."

"How did you get here, then?" Garret asked with a smile.

Etanos grinned. "A ship is quite different from a riverboat, my friend."

"I suppose so," Garret replied. "I've never been on a ship."

"Lead on," Etanos said, gesturing for Garret to take the lead.

Garret retrieved his blade, just in case, and headed to the west. There, near the foot of the small clump of mountains, they would find the Laer River and follow it south to Faillaigh. It was a scenic route, to be sure, and Garret looked forward to seeing the city again. He had been there once with Helena a few years back and was impressed with the city's architecture and the size of its market. Maybe he could find a good blade there.

"What kind of blade do you think is more suited to me," he asked, stuffing his own in its scabbard.

"Your technique suggests a blade similar to those of the East," Etanos replied.

"A katana?" Garret asked.

"Not necessarily. I noticed that you have added a few attacks of your own; the thrusts and parries. I would suggest a saber.

They are slightly curved, like a katana, but also have a point and can be used for blocking if need be."

Garret nodded curiously. He had never seen nor heard of a saber but trusted Etanos' opinion. The man obviously knew his weapons. "We could find a smith in Faillaigh," Garret said. "But I don't have any money."

"Don't worry," Etanos said. "Everything will work out the way it was meant to be. You will have your blade."

* * *

Questions were building in Garret's mind as they trudged through the forest toward the river. He wasn't sure how to ask them but was also too curious to keep them to himself. He kept thinking back to his first kill, wondering if what he was feeling was normal. Maybe Etanos had felt the same way when he had first taken a life.

"What was your first kill like?" Garret asked, still picturing the bandit writhing on the ground.

"Likely the same as yours," Etanos said. "I was young and inexperienced; acting on impulse. But it was justified, I think."

"Who was it?"

"A noble of Thyre," Etanos replied. "He had been harassing a local merchant's daughter, using his rank to try to get his way with her. As much as the merchant protested, the noble took her anyway. His guards beat the man to death in his own home and took her. I followed them back to the noble's house and killed him."

"Was it a big fight?" Garret asked.

"Not quite. I simply slipped into his house after his cronies left, and put a dirk in his back."

Garret nodded. "And how did you feel afterward?"

Etanos pursed his lips in thought. "Not good," he said. "But good at the same time. I knew I had done the right thing, despite how cold it seemed. I was not as skilled then and probably would have died trying to rescue the girl if I had faced him in open combat. I suppose I brooded for a while. But, I got over it, just as you will get over your first kill."

"I can't stop picturing it," Garret said, staring off into the forest ahead of them. "I could hear his moans as he died. It was disturbing. I almost felt sorry for him."

Etanos grunted. "That happens," he said. "But when dealing with the vile, you must learn to recognize that they do not deserve pity. If it helps, think of the suffering that they have caused other people. When you do that, it's easier to turn off your empathy. And remember, those are the people that have no empathy to begin with. Once you realize that, you can administer justice without a second thought." He clapped Garret on the back. "But that may take some time."

Garret hoped that he was right. There was no telling how such negative thoughts could affect him if he held on to them. They could very well lead to hesitation in future combat, possibly leading to his death. But was killing someone without a second thought any better? How would *that* affect someone's soul? But, then again, why should anyone feel guilty about taking the life of someone who didn't deserve to have one; someone who took life from others?

It was a difficult argument to make sense of, Garret thought, but perhaps Etanos was right; in time he would grow to realize that there was no reason for guilt. Killing an evil person was a good thing. It would prevent that person from harming others. But how could one tell who is evil and who is not? How did assassins distinguish between good and evil, especially if they had never met their victims before?

"What about your first contract?" Garret asked. "How did you know... how does *any* assassin know if his contract is justified."

"Well," Etanos said, stopping in a small clearing within a clump of fallen trees. "You have to trust your Grandmaster. You have to trust that he will accept contracts he believes are truly justified. If he receives a request and does not believe the target is genuinely deserving of death, it is refused." He sat down on a fallen tree, urging Garret to rest as well. "But even if a contract is accepted, it is up to the recipient to judge for him or herself firsthand."

"By observing the target?" Garret asked.

Etanos nodded. "Yes. The assassin will observe the target until he or she has decided whether to take the contract or not. If the target is deserving of death, he is eliminated. If not, the assassin may return and report his doubts to the Grandmaster."

"Have you ever refused a contract?"

"A few times," Etanos said, pursing his lips. "There have been contracts where I have simply not felt right about it. Even those who seemed to be exactly as described are not always so easily killed. You have to trust your gut. Always trust your gut. It will never lie to you."

Garret nodded. That made sense. Helena had said that on several occasions. "So who was your first contract, then?"

Etanos thought for a moment, making gestures as if he were recounting a *long* list of contracts. "That would have been a sea captain named Valeran," he said finally. "Rumor had it that he traded slaves off of the coast of Pashir. The contract never specified with whom he traded, but that, of course, didn't matter. I went to him, observed him for three days, and decided the contract was justified; but not for the reasons that had been detailed to me."

He paused for a moment, scratching his chin. There was an odd, uncomfortable look on his face.

"For what reasons, then?" Garret asked.

Etanos scowled. "Well," he said. "He was not exactly the person he was portrayed to be for one. He was not a he, for one, and *she* wasn't a slave trader."

Garret leaned in closer. "What was she?"

"She was a meat trader."

Garret sat back, underwhelmed. "What?"

Etanos glared at him, raising an eyebrow as if trying to convey his meaning that way. He sat unmoving for a moment as the phrase began to sink in. Garret gasped when he realized that he meant *human* meat.

"I can't believe it," Garret said. "Who would eat another person?"

Etanos grunted, standing again and stepping out of the clearing. "There are those who do, my friend," he said as Garret followed. "There are those who do."

"So how did you kill her?" Garret asked, eager to hear the story.

"I snuck onto her ship late at night," Etanos began. "Her crew was drunk and half dead, laying naked and stinking on the deck. I walked right past them, as if they weren't even there, and found her in the galley. She was also naked, rubbing herself with the blood of her victims. The dead were hanging on hooks all around her, and she had slaughtered them like pigs; naked and drunk with lust."

Garret couldn't believe his ears. His heart was racing with horror as he pictured the scene. He couldn't imagine Etanos' reaction at walking into that situation. It must have been sickening. From the look on Etanos' face, his guess was correct.

"Then what did you do?"

"I ran her through with my blade," Etanos said. "Making sure she knew she was about to die beforehand. While her life slipped away, I forced her to watch as I set her crew on fire. The ship burnt down to the keel with her and all twenty-five of her disgusting crew aboard it."

Garret was silent. What an incredible story, and a disturbing one at that. Just the thought of the woman's actions made his stomach turn, but then he noticed something else. He felt anger toward her as if he had known the people she had murdered. He pictured their faces alive and happy; enjoying and struggling through life only to be slaughtered by an insane monster and her crew of heathens. They all had families and friends; people who loved them and cared about them. What right did she have to take that all away?

She deserved to die.

As Garret's anger surged through him, he felt Etanos' firm hand on is shoulder. "You see," the man said, "it's a lot easier than you thought."

* * *

They reached the river by late afternoon. The trail had led them right to its bank, where several hundred yards of it were landscaped and well-kept in either direction, with carefully placed sandstone slabs and river rock flattened into the dirt to serve as a brush-free path. The river itself was a mere ten yards wide here, and the trees on either side rose to an incredible height, curving over the water to meet in the middle like a high, vaulted hall.

Here, the air was cool and moist, and the pleasant sound of slowly moving water gave it an aura of peace and tranquility. Etanos stopped and crouched near the bank, closing his eyes and smiling pleasantly as he took it all in. Garret joined him, feeling the calm rush over him like a comforting blanket.

"We should stop here for the moment," Etanos said. "If you would gather some wood, I will find us something to eat."

As Garret stood to go off in search of fallen branches, Etanos produced a small bundle from his cloak. It appeared as three curved pieces of flattened wood, tied together with a black cord.

Etanos unwrapped the cord as Garret watched, and then held out the bundle before him. With a flick of his wrist, the bundle sprang open, popping together and forming an elaborately designed bow.

Garret's eyes widened and he felt a rush of excitement and envy.

"That's amazing," he said. "I've never seen anything like it."

Etanos grinned. "Then I bet you've never seen anything like this, either."

He grabbed the bowstring, raising the bow out before him, and pulled. An arrow shimmered into life, knocked and ready to fire. It shone silver, with greenish tendrils of energy swirling along the shaft.

Garret shook his head in disbelief. "Where did you get that?" he asked.

Etanos relaxed the bow, and the arrow faded from existence, just as magically as it had appeared. "It was a gift from a wizard I met in Kinar," he said. "I saved his life from brigands, and he was *most* appreciative."

"He must have been," Garret said, grinning.

"I'll find us a rabbit," Etanos said. "Find some wood."

Garret leaped up with excitement, heading off into the brush. He heard Etanos creep back into the tree line on the opposite side of the path. Though he wanted to see for himself how the bow worked, he trusted that Etanos would be better off hunting alone. He was silent and skilled, a seasoned hunter, and Garret was still clumsy and about as silent as a starving dog.

So, he wandered the area in search of wood, practicing being silent and creeping through the brush. He imagined himself as a skilled ranger or an expert assassin in search of signs of his target's passing. As he gathered various-sized branches, he studied the dirt and the positions of the weeds. He noted their broken stalks and the way they were bent over, judging by their shape and the degree of damage how long ago his target had passed.

He had no idea what he was doing.

Laughing to himself, he juggled his armful of branches, pressing it close to his chest, and returned to the bank. Etanos had already returned and was crouched over and preparing a carcass for the fire.

That was quick, Garret thought. It had only seemed like a few minutes.

He piled the sticks near the bank, reaching out around him to gather some tinder. Etanos expertly cleaned the rabbit, laying out its pelt and tossing the innards in the river for the fish to consume.

"Did you sense them?" Etanos asked.

"Sense whom?" Garret asked, producing his tinder box to light the fire.

"There are men in this forest," Etanos replied. "They are all around."

Garret knew who he was referring to. "The rangers," he said. "They are always around and watching. They protect the forest."

"They are very skilled," Etanos said. "But not skilled enough to be invisible to me."

Etanos grinned, bringing over the finished coney. Garret had the tinder smoking by then and bent down to breathe it into life. Etanos gathered the sticks and placed them over the tiny embers as Garret blew gently into the smoking pile. Soon a small fire was going, and the two sat back to relax while their meal cooked.

"They won't bother us," Garret said. "As long as we don't cause any harm to the forest, they will leave us alone."

"I admire their cause," Etanos said. "But I also admire their skill. There are quite a few professions that require stealth, and as far as being noble or... rotten, so to speak, they could go either way."

Garret shrugged. "I've heard that the rangers have no concept of good or evil; only balance. They care only for the forest and those that dwell within it. Anything that upsets the balance of life is their enemy, whether it is good or bad."

"Much like the druids," Etanos said. "They have the same cause, though on a much grander scale."

Garret nodded. "When you meet Aeli you may have the same impression of her. She is also much like a druid but is more focused on the spirits of the Earth as a whole. She can heal, commune with the Great Mother, and create life. But she isn't bound by any rules, as she doesn't belong to any particular faith."

Etanos chuckled. "And *that* is why people call her a witch."

"True," Garret agreed. "Just don't call her that to her face. That is unless you *want* to live out your life as a frog or something."

CHAPTER SIX

After a good meal, and a moment of rest, the two set off again, just in time for the evening cool to set in. Etanos had dried the remaining rabbit meat over the fire for later use, ensuring they wouldn't have to stop again for a while. They followed the river to the south, staying close to the bank to keep an eye out for ferrymen.

The riverside was pleasant, and the sounds of trickling water, birdsong, and frogs filled the air with an almost tangible sense of peace. The road was easy going; covered in a fine layer of pine needles from the nearby forest, creating a comfortable path for them to walk upon.

They spoke frequently, commenting on the wildlife, and exchanging questions and stories about each other. Etanos freely gave any information that Garret desired, which was quite a new thing for the young man. Most of the questions he had asked the sisters at the convent had went unanswered; not that they were unwilling to answer, but that Garret's questions were out of their scope of knowledge. He wanted answers to the grittier questions in life, and Etanos seemed to be a valuable and limitless source of knowledge.

Not to mention, one of the very few men he had ever had the opportunity to speak to.

He was a seasoned traveler, Garret knew, and would likely be a storehouse of information; one that Garret was grateful to have met. The man's demeanor was unlike what Garret would have pictured for someone of his particular profession. He had always pictured an assassin as being morose, quiet, and reserved. Though he did possess these qualities to a certain degree, Garret surmised that it was not due to his personality, but the fact that he was always staying aware of his surroundings. It was not introverted behavior, but absolute awareness.

There was nothing that could ever escape this man's notice.

Garret wanted that, too.

"Where did you learn to climb?" Etanos asked.

Garret shrugged. "I'm not sure," he said. "I just climbed trees like any boy, but added some of my own moves to make the process quicker."

"The jumping and grabbing?"

"Yes," Garret said. "Exactly. But I watched how animals did it. Squirrels and things. Of course, they're a lot smaller and lighter, and miss less often."

Etanos chuckled. "Yes, they do. I fell a few times in my youth. But it's the falling that makes you better."

Garret smiled. "Yes, it does."

"So," Etanos said. "Tell me of your childhood."

Garret shrugged. "There's not much to tell," he paused to think for a moment. "I was raised by my father before he died. When that happened, I was taken to the convent where the sisters took care of me along with the other children. They educated me about useful things; the world and its countries, people, cultures. They taught me about nature, the Great Mother, the Firstborn, everything."

"So, you weren't beaten or scarred by trauma, then," Etanos mused, not asking a question.

"No," Garret said. "It was a good life. A bit boring, but good."

"So when did the interest in combat come into play?"

"Helena noticed me watching the military parades," Garret said. "I insisted on going whenever the King's Guard was around during the celebrations. I also took an interest in some travelers from Kinar when they came to Gaellos during a circus. I was fascinated by their fighting techniques, but also those of the warriors of Eirenoch. She even took me to the forest once, to meet some of the rangers. I was *very* intrigued with them. Helena bought me the blade to practice with, hoping maybe I would grow up to join them in honor of the Great Mother."

"And these scrolls you spoke of?"

"Katas," Garret said. "Illustrations of the eastern fighting techniques. But it was more than that. There were meditation positions that I learned to help clear my mind and focus my attention and awareness. I'm not sure they ever worked, though. They were just pictures, after all. I couldn't read the writing that would have told me what I was supposed to do."

Etanos nodded. "Those are very good things to learn," he said. "A warrior is nothing without focus, regardless of other skills. What good is a sharp blade and a quick hand without the discipline to control them?"

Garret studied him for a moment. "Did you learn from the eastern teachers?"

Etanos nodded. "Some things," he said. "I met a samurai once who was traveling the world on some kind of spiritual journey. I traveled with him for a year or so, learning everything I could."

"Did you learn fighting techniques from him?"

Etanos shook his head. "No. He was impressed with my skills and thought my techniques were best suited for my agility. But he taught me the principles of meditation and balance. This is what led to my decision to become an assassin. I felt I could make a difference by ridding the world of the wicked, one silent assassination at a time."

Garret was beginning to understand now. Despite the dark nature of the trade, assassination was sometimes the best method of fighting the wicked, as opposed to outright battle. Anyone could fight in open battle, but the problem was that sometimes, the valiant could lose. No matter how good a warrior was, there was always someone better.

"Sometimes," Garret said. "The Great Mother works behind the scenes, as well. So, I would suppose that an assassin could be Her hand, in a manner of speaking."

Etanos smiled, gripping Garret's shoulder. "You are beginning to understand now," he said. "I'm glad to hear it. I would hate for you to get the wrong impression of our trade. Sure, there are those out there who do it for the money or fame, but there are those of us who do it for the greater good."

"I think I could do that," Garret said. "I want to work for the greater good."

"Very well," Etanos said. "Then you shall be my apprentice. We start training immediately."

"Immediately?"

"Immediately," Etanos repeated. "And this is your first lesson."

"I don't understand," Garret said, confused.

"You have learned the basic principle," Etanos said. "That our trade is not that of the common opinion. We are not murderers or cowards. We do our business behind the scenes to avoid drawing the attention of the public. The less the public knows the better. They are safer that way. If a rebel forms a militia to get rid of a sour nobleman, everyone knows, and everyone is in danger of treason. A single assassin on a mission to destroy the same noble puts only himself in danger. That is our noble cause, my friend. We keep the people safe in more ways than one."

"And the downside," Garret added, "would be the lack of recognition. But that is what we must sacrifice, for..."

"The greater good," Etanos finished his thought. "Excellent, Garret. Lesson learned."

Garret smiled. "All right then, when is the next lesson?"

* * *

The river became wider when the two reached the north edge of Faillaigh. The shipping companies were the first buildings they could see, and the docks came into view soon after. At this hour, there was not much activity, but the sight of the setting sun reflecting off of the calm waters was awe-inspiring.

Here, the path gave way to a paved road lined with cobblestones and decorated with wooden lamp posts and well-trimmed foliage. A small sign that read, "*Faillaigh*" was posted near the left side of the path, partially obscured by the lush, low-hanging branches of a large oak.

There were no people in sight, but a few stray cats were seen scurrying across the road. Etanos and Garret watched them as they stepped onto the cobblestones, chuckling at their apparent terror at being spotted.

"I've always liked cats," Etanos said. "They're quiet and keep to themselves. Plus, they keep one's house pest-free."

Garret grinned. "Anything that keeps the mice out of the pantry is all right with me."

Etanos gazed up at the sky, glancing briefly at the height of the sun over the horizon. "It's getting late," he said. "We will find an inn and rest for the night. I see no reason to bother any ferrymen at this hour. We can get a fresh start in the morning."

Etanos removed his cloak, turning it inside out and unfastening a flap of fabric. He shook it out, turning it over and refastening the flap in a different position. When he donned it again, it looked completely different. It was now hunter green, with edges of brown, and the new flap covered his leather breastplate like a tunic. He reached into the small of his back, bringing out two ends of a canvas belt, and tying them together at his waist.

When he was finished, he looked at Garret, grinning. "That's better," he said.

Garret chuckled. "Interesting," he said. "I can still see your boots, though."

Etanos looked down, frowning. "Hmm. Think of how often you look at a man's boots. Probably not often."

Garret shrugged. That was true enough.

The road gave way to a wide landing that stretched into the water on one side and opened up into an outdoor lobby on the other. There were a few shops surrounding the lobby, all open for business, and several commoners were wandering around or speaking with the merchants. Nestled in the trees was a larger building, two levels, with a deck that surrounded the second floor. The front door was open, and the sounds of laughter and chatter wafted out from within.

"That looks like a tavern," Etanos said. "We'll see if they have rooms for rent."

Garret followed him inside, nodding politely to all of the patrons who stood just outside the door. The tavern itself was fairly empty, with only a few tables being occupied; albeit, with very loud patrons. Etanos headed straight for the bar, where the barman stood polishing mugs and silverware. He looked up when the two approached, giving them a crooked, nearly toothless smile.

"Evenin', sirs," he greeted them. "What can I get for ya?"

"We need a room for the night," Etanos said. "If you have any."

The barman set down his mug. "Aye," he said. "For you and your... young boy?"

Etanos glanced at Garret. "Yes," he said, "for me and my nephew. We are traveling to the south shore to find his father."

The barman grinned. "All right then. There are a few rooms on the second floor. Two copper crowns a night for ya."

Etanos fished in his cloak, producing a handful of coins. He held it out to the barman, who looked it over carefully. "I only have coin of Thyre," Etanos said. "I haven't been here long."

The barman nodded, reaching out to pluck two copper coins

from Etanos' palm. "These'll do," he said. "Is there anything else you need?"

Etanos sat down on a stool, urging Garret to do the same. "I'll have a pint of your finest ale," he said. "And a half pint for my nephew here."

The barman chuckled, turning to fetch two mugs; one large, one small. "Will this be the boy's first ale?" he asked, filling the mugs from a keg on the back counter.

Etanos looked at Garret, who grinned excitedly, nodding. "It appears so," Etanos said.

The barman set the two mugs in front of them, fishing a few more coins from Etanos' palm as he held it out. "So how old are ya, boy?" he asked.

Garret picked up his mug, sniffing the ale. "Fifteen," he said.

The barman grumbled, but shrugged and returned to his mug washing.

"Is there a smith in town?" Etanos asked him. "Maybe one that specializes in foreign weapons?"

The barman furrowed his brow. "Not that I know of," he said. "But there's a merchant who *sells* weapons from other lands. He's in the town square, on this side. You'll know his shop when you see it. It's the biggest one on the square."

"Thank you," Etanos said.

Garret took a sip of ale, swishing it around in his mouth before swallowing it. It was warm going down, and the bite was just enough to fill his senses with a pleasant, refreshing boost.

"That's good," he said.

Etanos grinned. "It's good in small quantities," he said. "But it will dull your senses and slow your reaction time. Never drink ale before a mission. When you're done, drink all you want."

Garret grinned, taking another sip. Etanos turned in his stool to look around the tavern, glancing at every person seated at the nearby tables. They ignored the two of them for the most part, Garret noticed as he looked, and they seemed pleasant and content.

"Working class," Etanos said. "Just plain, ordinary people enjoying some ale at the end of a long work day. Quite different from the noble class. These are the people who are best served by our trade."

"I wonder what they all do," Garret said.

"These are probably fishermen," Etanos said, "judging by the location of the tavern... and the smell of fish, of course."

SHAWN E. CRAPO

Garret sniffed. "I don't smell it," he said. "But all I can smell is the ale."

Etanos grinned. "See?" he said. "I told you; it dulls your senses."

Garret laughed but was unsure as to whether the ale was the cause. Maybe Etanos' senses were just better than his; more acute somehow. Either way, he couldn't smell anything other than the ale, and the faint scent of smoked meat.

"Is there a tower here in town?" Garret heard Etanos ask.

"A tower?" the barman repeated. "Why?"

"Any tower at all."

"Well," the barman said. "There's the old bell tower a few blocks away. Why d'ya ask?"

"I was just wondering," Etanos replied. "Do you think anyone would mind if my nephew and I climbed it?"

Garret turned around, looking at his mentor. The barman leaned his hands against the bar, eyeing Etanos curiously.

"Now why would ya want to climb the bell tower?" he asked.

Etanos shrugged, smiling. "He could use the practice," he said, nodding toward Garret.

The barman glanced at Garret, turning back suspiciously. "Ya wouldn't be planning to rob anyone in town, eh?" he asked.

"No, sir," Etanos said. "We are acrobats, not thieves."

"Oh," the barman exclaimed, skeptically. "Yer acrobats, eh? And where's yer circus?"

Etanos grinned. "That is why we're meeting this boy's father at the coast. But he needs a bit of practice, and a bell tower sounds perfect."

The barman sighed, going back to polishing his mugs. "Just beyond the stables, inside the wooden arches."

"Thank you, sir," Etanos said, then turned to Garret. "Finish up. We'll rest for a few hours and then climb the tower."

* * *

Though Garret enjoyed the slight numbness in his body and the pleasant sensations of euphoria, the ale made waking a bit too abrupt. The room had been comfortable, with a small fireplace that kept it cozy and warm, and the beds were soft yet firm. He had fallen asleep quickly, slipping into a deep slumber with a smile on his face.

But now, Etanos stood over him, shaking him and insisting he awaken. "Time for lesson two," the man said.

Garret rubbed his eyes, not wanting to open them. His body was still asleep, and his mind, though conscious, was not quite there yet, either.

"Come on, Garret," Etanos insisted. "This is part of the lesson."

"Waking up drunk is part of the lesson?" Garret mumbled.

Etanos chuckled. "No," he said. "Doing your work while not at your best. The ale will simulate fatigue; both mental and physical. This test will help you overcome the strain of working with very little sleep, which may happen often. Now, come on. Let's have at it. The tower waits."

Garret sighed, sitting up as Etanos slid him his boots. He slipped them on quietly while Etanos looked out the window, and then stood on slightly wobbly legs. Etanos led him out the door and down the dark hallway of the inn.

There were still a few late-night patrons in the pub; mostly evening shift guards who had just been relieved, and a few night owls who enjoyed their ale in the wee hours of the morning. There was a different barman at this hour, but he had been made aware of their presence. He nodded quietly as they passed, grumbling something under his breath.

"How do you feel?" Etanos asked Garret.

Garret assessed his physical condition, coming to one simple conclusion. "Like I could sleep for a week."

"Good," Etanos replied. "You'll have that feeling quite often."

They stepped out into the night air, and Garret immediately felt the chill of early morning. He bundled his cloak around him tightly, locking out the cold, but still, he shivered. Etanos point off to the east, just past the wooden arch that separated the shipping area from the rest of the town. The tower stood black against the dark blue sky; tall and thin like a blade thrusting upward into the night.

"Oh, that looks like it's going to be cold," Garret said.

"It will be," Etanos said. "But you'll forget all about your discomfort as you climb."

Somehow, Garret doubted that, but he followed his mentor anyway. They kept to the shadows, not wanting to alarm anyone of their presence, and weaved in and out of the buildings. When they heard people approaching, they hid; not for the purpose of concealing their passage, but for practice.

"Always practice your techniques when you can," Etanos said. "And be wary of your presence. If you can hear yourself, chances are others can, too."

Just a few minutes later, the two stood at the base of the tower. It didn't seem quite as tall up close as it had seemed from a distance, but it was still taller than anything Garret had ever climbed. It was intimidating, to be sure.

"Once you see your path," Etanos said, gazing up. "The rest of the world fades away."

Garret knew exactly what he meant. Every time he saw a building, he wondered if he could climb it, and how he would do so. Once he discovered the route he would take, the handholds along the way almost seemed brightened and highlighted in his vision, as if they were the only things in existence. As he gazed at the tower before him, the familiar visions came. He saw his route, and it became his only focus.

"Ready," he said.

Etanos charged forth, and Garret followed. The two silently leaped onto the side of the tower, grabbing on and pulling themselves up without so much as a sound, gripping each handhold as it came within reach. Garret stared upward, his eyes focusing on every brick that offered even the smallest purchase.

From the corner of his eye, he saw that Etanos was much quicker, and used his legs less often than Garret did. He saw the man leaping upward to grab his next handhold, pulling himself up with very little effort. His movements were almost primate-like in their fluidity, and Garret struggled to keep up.

"Don't worry about your speed too much," Etanos said. "This is practice, for building strength. When you're on a mission, your primary focus is getting there as silently as possible."

Garret kept climbing, hand over hand, foot over foot. His only thoughts were reaching the top and not looking down. Every foot he rose above the street was just another step in a long flight of stairs, so to speak. There was no ground beneath, only the path ahead. As his focus became stronger, he gained ground, coming up even with Etanos. His mentor grinned, picking up his speed and pulling ahead again.

Near the upper third portion of the tower, they came upon a window. Both of them climbed around it, slowing their pace and leaning inward to peer inside. There was nothing but an empty room, with a single beam of moonlight illuminating the dusty floor.

"Watch the windows as you pass them," Etanos said. "You never know when someone might need to piss. I learned that one the hard way."

Garret chuckled to himself as he pictured it, but kept his focus. The climb seemed to get easier, despite his growing fatigue. He had never experienced much fatigue while climbing. It must be the ale, he reasoned.

Finally, the top openings of the bell tower came into view, and Garret grabbed the ledge just behind Etanos. They pulled themselves up and over, landing silently inside the roofed enclosure where a huge bell hung silent and alone.

"Good work," Etanos said. "How do you feel?"

Garret grinned, feeling the rush of excitement that always accompanied a good climb. Though his hands ached, and his breath was labored from the ale, the feeling was good.

"A bit tired," he said. "But good."

"Excellent," Etanos said. "Now here is your reward for the climb."

He turned to the city below, sweeping his hand out before him. Garret leaned against the stone railing, gazing out over the rooftops. Throughout the city, lamps illuminated the streets, and the windows of everyone's homes dotted the gloom like motionless fireflies.

"It's beautiful," Garret said.

Etanos folded his arms, smiling as he too enjoyed the view. "Yes, it is," he said. "Sometimes, when I come to a town, I climb the highest tower to get a good view of the bustle of life. You can tell a lot about a town this way; its layout, what sections of town are the most active, and if you look closely enough, what areas to avoid."

"And if one were a thief," Garret added. "Which houses would be the best to rob."

Etanos laughed, pointing to a large, well-lit property to the north. "I would say that one."

Garret nodded as he studied the mansion that sat in the block's center. It was likely the home of the local lord, whoever that was. He pictured Lord Daeglan in his mind and the smug look on the man's face when he had encountered him in Gaellos. How he hated him. He was beginning to understand Etanos' aversion to nobles.

"Bell towers are also a good place to rest during a mission," Etanos said. "The belfries are usually empty. If you know anything about the city you're in, you will know when the bell is rung and can time your rest appropriately. But, always be gone by the time the bell rings."

"I have no idea when this bell rings," Garret said.

Etanos pointed upward, toward the top of the bell. There were no ropes attached to the pulleys; only those that supported the bell from its thick, wooden beams. "I would say this one never rings anymore," he said.

"I wonder why," Garret said.

"It doesn't matter. Shall we descend?"

Garret nodded, standing to look over the side. Etanos produced a thin, black rope from his pack, attaching a small hook to the end and tossing it over the wooden beam that held the bell. It wrapped around, securing itself with a tiny *clank*. Etanos then dropped the rope over the side.

"We'll take the easy way down," he said. "You've earned a reprieve for the night."

Etanos swung over the side, planting his feet against the stone and walking his way down with a firm grip on the rope. Garret followed, finding it difficult, but much faster than climbing down. His hands were already cramped, however, which made holding the rope even more painful than it would have been otherwise. By the time they reached the bottom, Garret was spent.

Etanos clapped him on the back, grinning. "Very good," he said. "Next time, be sure to wear gloves."

Garret looked at his hands. His palms were chafed and scratched, and his fingertips were rubbed nearly raw. He gritted his teeth, squeezing his hands in pain. "Good idea," he said.

Etanos chuckled. "And *that* would be lesson three."

CHAPTER SEVEN

arret awoke the next morning sore but motivated to start the day. Etanos was already awake, waiting for him to rise while rubbing a tan-colored compound into his elaborate leather boots. He smiled as Garret sat up; nodding toward a bowl of stew he had brought and placed on the nightstand. Garret ate it eagerly, watching his mentor tediously working.

"What is that you're rubbing into your boots?" Garret asked.

"Goose fat," Etanos said. "It keeps the leather supple and prevents cracking and rotting. It looks like your boots could use some too. But, we'll worry about that later. Today, we shall find you a good blade and a pair of gloves. We can also get some other equipment you might need."

"Other equipment?" Garret asked.

"You'll need some climbing gear specially made for people like us," Etanos said. "Buying it will be tricky, though. We may have to find a fence, as opposed to a public merchant."

"What is a fence?" Garret asked.

"Someone who sells black market goods," Etanos said. "Usually a thief or a criminal."

Garret finished his stew and placed the empty bowl on the nightstand. "I would think someone like that would know a thing or two about that dagger you found."

"Possibly," Etanos agreed. "But if word got out that I was looking for its owner, I may lose the element of surprise."

That was logical, Garret supposed. If there was anyone who could read the language of Khem other than Maedoc or Aeli, it would be a worldly criminal experienced in smuggling and pawning. He decided to drop the matter.

He reached over to grab his boots, pulling them on just as Etanos finished wiping the excess goose fat off of his boots. The assassin inspected the leather, twisting it and bending it, seemingly satisfied. He pulled them on and laced them up, returning a set of small daggers to their tiny sheathes along the boot shaft.

"Are you ready?" he asked, standing.

Garret stood, gathering his cloak and the empty bowl. "Ready."

* * *

After returning the empty bowl to the barman on duty, the two stepped out into the early afternoon air. The city was a bustle of activity, with the merchants already at their booths and stands calling out to passersby. It was a clear, beautiful day, and Garret was immediately awakened fully by the bright sun and pleasant breeze—and the smell of scones and shepherd's pie blew through the air like bait.

They made their way to the center of town, keeping to the main streets. Etanos still had his cloak inside out, making him appear somewhat normal, and he whistled and smiled while they walked.

"Remember," he said. "You're my nephew, and we are on our way to meet your father at the shore."

"I remember," Garret said, grinning. "But I doubt anyone will care."

They passed an old man standing near the entrance to the town square. He was dressed in colorful rags, and juggling several bottles in the air to the amusement of the townsfolk who gathered near him. They watched him as he passed through, smiling and laughing when he stopped to do tricks.

"That man is a thief," Etanos said. "An experienced one at that."

"How can you tell?"

"Look at his movements," Etanos replied.

Garret looked, noticing nothing at first. But as the man moved through the crowd, Garret noticed that he tended to keep close to those of higher station. He seemed to be following a particular pair of men whose clothing was that of city officials; possibly magistrates or court officers.

"If he is a thief," Garret asked, "then why is he performing for coin on the street?"

Etanos prompted him to keep walking. "It is a front," Etanos said. "He is scouting out the area, or possibly gathering information from those men. People tend to be loose-lipped when they think no one important is listening."

"So he's a scout, then," Garret said. "But for whom?"

Etanos shook his head. "Probably a guild in town," he said. "Or a small troop. Either way, it's not our concern."

They continued on to the square, leaving the thief behind to do his business. Garret was interested in what the man may have been doing but was more interested in the upcoming visit to the merchant that the barman had spoken of. There, he hoped, he would find a weapon that best suited him.

The square was busy. Most of the storefronts that lined the four sides were obscured by the crowds, and neither Etanos nor Garret could read any of the signs. However, the barman had said the foreign trader's shop would be the largest building.

…and there it was.

A three-story shop dominated one side of the square. It was of an odd architecture that stood out among the other buildings. The corners of its roof were turned up, and the support beams and columns that tied each of the walls and floor together were painted bright red. It was similar in appearance to the buildings of the eastern lands; quite a contrast to the dark wood and plaster structures that surrounded it.

"That must be it," Etanos said. "The barman was right."

Garret grinned. "It sticks out like a sore thumb," he said.

"Or maybe a strong thumb on a broken hand."

Garret understood Etanos' metaphor for the most part—but not completely. Nevertheless, he grinned, and the two of them wove their way through the crowd toward the impressive structure. As they neared, the unmistakable scent of jasmine filled the air, telling them that the merchant was burning a large quantity of incense.

The building itself sported a large pagoda, where various tables of small items were set up and manned by young men of both Kinar and Eirenoch. They chattered skillfully with the locals, providing an almost entertaining sales pitch at each of their stations. Garret glanced at the tables where each one worked, seeing stacks of silk, small trinkets and idols, and various perfumes, waxes, candles, and scented oils.

It was truly a diverse marketplace, and Garret looked forward to going inside.

"Do you see anything interesting?" Etanos asked.

"Everything looks interesting," Garret said. "But nothing looks useful."

Etanos pointed to a table where a young man of Kinar sat stoically; overseeing the sampling of the incense he was selling. "Find something that smells pleasant," he said. "That will be for a later lesson. Meet me inside."

He handed Garret a handful of coins to purchase anything he liked and disappeared into the shop. Garret approached the table, drawing the attention of the young man, who smiled and bowed his head respectfully.

"Good afternoon, sir," the young man said. "What pleases you?"

Garret pursed his lips, looking at the tableful of powders, cones, and sticks. There were many colors to choose from; presumably of different scents. He wasn't sure exactly what he was looking for and simply shrugged at the young man's question.

"For what purpose do you seek your scent?" the young man asked.

"I'm not sure," Garret replied. "My teacher told me to select something pleasant."

"Is your teacher a warrior?"

Garret shrugged. "I suppose so," he said, thinking that the answer was better than saying that he was an assassin.

The young man reached forward to pick up a light brown powder that was piled upon a plate. He held it up to Garret's nose, allowing him to sniff it. It was sweet and musky smelling; rather pleasant and not too strong.

"This is Nyaga-alu," the young man said. "It is derived from the lotus flower and is very soothing. Warriors use it for meditation. I would assume that is why your master suggested you find something pleasant."

Garret nodded. "All right," he said. "How much is it?"

"Ten copper crowns for a king's ounce."

Garret counted out the coins, dropping them into the young man's hand. He was given a small pouch in return, and a polite bow to close the deal. "I thank you, sir," the young man said.

Garret turned and stuffed the pouch in his cloak, seeking out the door to the shop. As he neared it, a voice to his left side caught his attention.

"Boy," the voice said.

Garret turned to look for the voice, wondering if someone

was trying to get his attention. There was an older man there, waving him over. He was a man of Kinar, like the others, and was as old as the hills from the looks of him. Garret walked over reluctantly.

"Yes?" he said.

The old man held out a dagger, offering it to him as if it were a gift. "This is for you," he said.

Garret studied the dagger carefully, skeptical as to the man's intentions. "I don't have enough money for that," Garret said. "I'm sure of it."

The old man laughed, showing his toothless smile. "No, no, no, my friend," he said. "It is already yours. Take it."

Garret studied the man, seeing no ill will in his eyes. Still, the situation was strange and rather out of the blue. Why would a stranger give him a dagger for no reason whatsoever? Garret looked at it carefully. It was beautiful, he noticed; much too ornate and skillfully crafted to be given to a stranger. Its blade was as long as his hand, highly polished, and imprinted with runes of unknown origin. Its pommel was gold, and the handle was wrapped in the finest of black leather.

"Why would you give this to me?" Garret asked. "I — "

"It is yours," the man said. "It has *always* been yours."

Garret scowled but reached out to take the dagger anyway. As his hand touched it, he felt the strangest of sensations. A cold rush went through his body. He suddenly felt a sharp pain in his chest, coupled with a strange feeling of love that he could not explain. Then, he realized that the cold rush was a sensation of falling into a body of water. He could even picture it.

"Where did this blade come from?" he asked, breathless.

The old man smiled. "Someday, you will see."

Garret looked down at the blade again, studying its surface. The carvings seemed to spell out his name but in some other language. That was not possible, he knew, but he was sure. He looked up to question the man, but he was gone. There was only another table, with a strange man with an eye patch staring at him suspiciously.

"What are you looking at, boy?" the man asked.

Garret shook his head, turning away. He shoved the dagger in his belt, wearily walking toward the shop's door. He felt strange, as if the dagger had imparted some dark magic into him, or perhaps some odd vision. He wasn't sure which. The pain in his chest had subsided, but there was still the strange feeling of love that was slowly fading as well.

What was happening?

"Garret," the voice of Etanos called to him.

Garret looked up, shaking his head to clear his thoughts. Etanos stood there in the doorway, beckoning him to come inside.

"The merchant has some good blades," he said. "Come and see."

* * *

The shop was an eclectic mix of many different items; from spices to weapons, and candles to hunting gear. The merchant had just about everything. The shelves were fully stocked, almost to the point of overflowing, and many of the larger items were stacked or stuffed into corners. Garret felt overwhelmed at the thought of how the man kept track of all of his stock.

Etanos led him to a smaller section, where a separate room had been set up for swords and daggers. Hundreds of beautiful weapons were hung from the wall; weapons from every corner of the world, and all blended together in a pleasing sequence from straight to curved to the exotic.

"Hitaro here has collected blades from all over the world," Etanos said. "I think he has the perfect blade for your style."

Hitaro, a middle-aged man of Kinar with a samurai's garb and hair to match, looked Garret over, scratching his chin as he judged his build. "Something lightweight," he said. "Definitely curved, but not too curved."

He turned and retrieved a blade that he and Etanos had apparently discussed. He held it out to Garret, presenting it to him hilt first. Garret grasped its tightly corded handle and held it up. It was lightweight, but not too light; just about right. Its handle was adorned with a golden cap as its pommel, with a golden crossguard that spiraled at either end, and its blade was long, narrow, and curved ever so slightly to its pointed tip.

"This is a saber," the merchant said. "It is used primarily by the warriors of Thyre and sometimes Anwar. It is very versatile in its uses, as it is both strong and supple at the same time. Try it out."

Garret stepped away, giving the blade a few slow swings to test its balance. It was perfectly weighted; not too blade-heavy, and not so handle-heavy that it would take away the blade's momentum. He swiped it from side to side quickly, barely hearing the *swoosh* as it cut through the air. That meant his swing was nearly perfect, and the blade had complimented his style to make it so.

He put himself into his scorpion stance, raising his right leg and holding the blade, pointing forward, over his head. His right hand was stretched out before him, held open with the palm facing outward. Hitaro approached, studying Garret's position as Garret held still. The merchant grunted, turning to retrieve another weapon from the wall.

"Your right hand is in a defensive position," he said. "But it has no defensive weapon. Try this."

He handed the long, thin, dagger-like weapon to Garret. "Hold it with the blade pointing outward as if you are stabbing with it. It will guard your wrist, and be in the perfect position for swiping if need be."

Garret did as he was told, going back into position. As he held the blade, he realized its potential as both a defensive and secondary offensive weapon. It felt good.

"How does the saber feel?" Etanos asked.

"I like it," Garret said. "It's much more balanced than my old blade."

"Then we'll take it," Etanos said, nodding to the merchant. "And the dirk, too."

"Very good," the merchant replied. "It includes a belt and scabbard, and a whetstone that tucks nicely into this side pocket." He showed the belt to them, demonstrating how the small, square stone slid easily into the small pocket. "I'll give it to you for ten gold crowns."

Garret's eyes widened. He had never seen ten gold crowns. However, Etanos produced the coins from his purse as if it were nothing, handing them to the merchant, who bowed politely with a smile.

"I hope the blade serves you well," he said. "Good travels to you, my friend."

Garret strapped on the belt with Etanos' assistance. As the man was adjusting the straps, he stopped and pulled the dagger from Garret's old belt, looking at it with a raised brow.

"Where did this come from?" he asked.

"An old man gave it to me outside," Garret said.

Etanos furrowed his brow. "He just *gave* it to you?"

Garret nodded, noting the strange look in Etanos' eyes. "Yes, why?"

Etanos was silent for a moment, and then shook his head, stuffing the dagger back into Garret's belt. "It's a nice blade," he said. "It just seems odd, that's all."

Garret decided not to reveal the strange sensation he got when he touched the dagger. It was probably his imagination, anyway, or at least something completely unrelated to the dagger itself. It would just raise more questions.

"There we are," Etanos said, pulling the belt into its final, comfortable position. "How does that feel."

"Good," Garret said, testing the position with a reach from his sword hand. "Did the merchant know I was left-handed?"

Etanos grinned. "Yes, I told him. That's why he chose this belt. There were others of better quality, but this one was better suited for you. I hadn't thought of adding a dirk to your arsenal. I suppose it would work better than the dagger."

Garret was silent. His thoughts kept going back to the dagger. He wasn't sure why; it was just a blade like any other blade. But he felt there was something about it that wasn't quite right.

"Are you all right?" Etanos asked.

Garret nodded. "Yes," he said. "It was just strange that that man gave me something out of the blue."

"Well," Etanos said. "Perhaps he knew you would need it someday. Pay no attention, it's probably nothing."

"I suppose so," Garret replied, halfheartedly.

"All right then, let's find you some better clothes. You can't go sneaking around in peasant garb."

Garret grinned. "True," he said. "But it feels strange having things bought for me. No one has ever really bought things for me."

"Don't worry, my friend," Etanos assured him. "You will earn them. Trust me."

CHAPTER EIGHT

here was a hunting shop on the opposite side of the square. Etanos had decided that buying dark clothing from the same shop where they had just purchased weapons would likely rouse suspicion. Garret agreed, somewhat; not that he thought the merchant himself would care, but others in the shop might see a connection.

And that would be bad.

They made their way into the shop, quietly browsing the racks of clothing that were interspersed throughout by function. Fishing clothes were near the fishing nets, earth-toned hunting clothes were near the bows, and the leather armor was near the spears and other missile type weapons.

Garret stopped to admire a fine set of throwing knives. They were of black, dull metal; wrapped in leather straps, and ground to a fine point. They were of the highest quality, and Garret could do nothing but stare.

"Are you any good at using throwing knives?" Etanos asked.

Garret shrugged. "I've never tried," he said. "But it seems like a good thing to learn."

Etanos grinned. "We shall try them, then."

He grabbed the set off the shelf and handed them to Garret. "Carry them," he said.

An old man in hunting clothes approached with a smile, holding his hands up as if he was relieved to see the two of them. "Welcome," he said. "How can I help you gentlemen this fine day?"

"My nephew and I are hunting on the southern shore in a few days, and his clothing is inappropriate, as you can see."

The old man's smile widened as he looked at Garret. "Ah, yes," he said. "I have the finest selection of ranger gear in Eirenoch. The king's own rangers have shopped here, you know."

Somehow, Garret doubted that. And by the wry smile that appeared on Etanos' face, Garret guessed that he did, too. The merchant quite obviously dealt in stolen goods, as his demeanor was somewhat shifty and nervous.

"Something more suited for night hunting in the ruins, perhaps," Etanos said. "No browns or greens. Grays and blacks would be better."

The old man shrugged. "Very well," he said. "But I'm not sure where there are any ruins other than the temple. No matter."

He led them to another rack, where various types of uniforms were arranged by color. There were matched sets of black and gray tunics, black boiled leather harnesses and armor, and cloaks of black silk and wool. There was even a shirt of banded leather mail, with black iron studs and buckles that held the whole thing together.

Garret's eyes were immediately drawn to it.

"Ah," the old man said. "I see your... nephew is enamored with this cuirass."

He took the leather shirt off the rack, holding it out for Garret to see. "This is fine leather; supple yet firm. It would likely not protect you from a deer's antlers, but should help absorb some of the impact should you come too close." He winked; quite obviously skeptical of their stated intentions.

"It's a bit large," Garret said.

"It's adjustable," the old man assured him.

"How about this and a tunic to go over it?" Etanos said. "And a cloak and some good boots."

"Do you plan on hunting without pants?" the old man asked with a grin.

Etanos chuckled. "Fine," he said. "And some pants."

Over the course of the next half hour, Garret was fitted with all of the garb necessary. The merchant offered to dispose of his old clothes, which likely meant he would wash them and resell them. Etanos urged Garret to walk around, bend and stretch, and make exaggerated movements; all in an effort to ensure the clothing was not restrictive in any way.

The clothes fit perfectly, and Garret felt a little more like a rogue than a homeless orphan. It was a good feeling.

"Ah!" he heard a voice behind him.

He turned, seeing the merchant roll his eyes as a young man

in silks approached. He was around Garret's age, clean-cut, and with a gait that didn't quite convey the noble station he seemed to possess.

"Gil," he said. "I thought I asked you to save that leather cuirass for me."

The old man shook his head, ignoring him. "Pay no attention to him, lad," he said, drawing a grin from the young man. "If he wanted it, he would have bought it weeks ago."

The young man chuckled, clapping the old man on the back. "I jest, Gil," he said. "Who is this... fellow and his benefactor?"

Etanos folded his arms across his chest, obviously annoyed with the young man's presence. The old man sighed. "I don't ask questions, Ferrin," he said. "You know that."

Ferrin held out his hand, and Garret reluctantly shook it.

"This is *Lord* Ferrin," the old man said, exaggerating the word *lord* with mock enthusiasm. "He's not a *lord* of anything, other than being an annoying little piss ant who works as an errand boy for Lord Darragh."

From the corner of his eye, Garret could see Etanos size up the young man, relaxing his posture somewhat. Ferrin leaned in closer and whispered loudly in Garret's ear so Gil could hear.

"I think he's getting senile," he said. "He forgets that those of us who do the dirty work are the true nobles."

Garret raised an eyebrow, glancing at Etanos, who flashed a crooked smile.

"What is your name, friend?" Ferrin asked.

"Garret."

"Well then, Garret, it was a pleasure to meet you. But it seems that I have arrived too late to purchase the items I had my eye on. Enjoy them."

He winked knowingly, patting Gil's shoulder as he turned and walked away. Gil shook his head in frustration. "He's a pain in my arse, that one. Always asking for credit."

"Does he pay?" Etanos asked.

Gil grumbled. "Most of the time."

"Fear not. We have funds. How much do I owe you?"

Gil scratched his chin, motioning for Etanos to follow him to the counter. Garret remained near the racks, watching Ferrin as he interacted with the other customers on his way out. He laughed and jested with them, shaking their hands when he could, full of smiles and laughter that drew strange looks from everyone.

He seemed friendly enough, Garret thought; definitely not the noble type. Though his clothing was that of the upper class, he seemed more like the merchants of Gaellos as opposed to a noble. And that clothing, he noticed, was more like a farce of some kind. It was as if Ferrin was masquerading as a nobleman, but was something else. Even his boots didn't fit his station. They were functional and rough; not fancy or ceremonial.

There was something different about Ferrin, but Garret couldn't quite figure out what that something was.

"Are you ready?" Etanos asked as he returned.

"Yes," Garret said, strapping on his baldric. "But I have a question. What was your impression of Ferrin? You looked skeptical of him."

Etanos grinned as they made their way to the exit. "He's in no way a noble," Etanos said. "And has no interest in serving any noble."

"What do you mean?"

"That boy is a thief, and has always been a thief."

Garret scowled. "How can you tell?"

"Did you notice his boots?"

So, Garret was right. They were not the boots of a noble. "I did."

"For one, nobles don't wear boots. They consider them the garments of the working class. That boy was not only wearing boots, but they were the boots of a thief. If you hadn't noticed, they made no sound as he walked. They were meant for sneaking and scaling walls."

Garret grunted as he realized Etanos was right. Ferrin had made little noise.

"And his hands were rough, as well," Etanos continued. "They were definitely not the hands of a silk-spoiled messenger or errand boy."

"Interesting," Garret said. "I wonder how he got into such a high position in a noble house."

Etanos shrugged. "Thieves are tricky," he said. "I'm sure he *stole* the position somehow."

Garret chuckled.

"Forget about him for now," Etanos said. "We have a witch to meet. It is time to find a ferryman to take us downriver."

* * *

Having returned to the docks, Garret and Etanos scoured the hectic crowd of mariners, shippers, and dockworkers to find passage down the river. There were very few ferries for hire; most of them booked by freelance couriers taking bartered goods down to the plantations south of town. Garret found them amusing when he saw how stacked the flimsy rafts were with boxed items and supplies. They all looked like they'd tip over any second.

There was only one unoccupied ferry that they could see. It was near the south end of town, parked at a dock that sported an outdoor tavern built right into the water. It was a rickety booth, supported on stilts and manned by a single barman who leaned on his tiny counter staring out at the water. A single patron sat across from him, lazily sipping a large mug of frothy ale.

"This looks promising," Etanos said, somewhat sarcastically.

As they walked down the dock, the barman's eyes lit up. He raised his arms in the air in a welcoming gesture, flashing a mostly toothless smile. That seemed to be a common thing here.

"Well met, strangers!" he shouted, a bit too loudly. "You look thirsty!"

Etanos shrugged, but Garret knew he would buy a mug of ale to be polite.

"I *am* thirsty," he said, "and in need of transportation."

The barman gave an encouraging nod, nudging the half-asleep patron. "Janos!" he said. "You have customers."

The lazy man shot up in his chair as Garret and Etanos sat down. Etanos ordered an ale and turned to the now excited patron.

"We need a ride downriver to the coast," he said. "As far as you can get us."

The barman brought a mug of ale, glancing at Garret to ask is he wanted anything. Garret shook his head.

"I can take you all the way down if you wish," the patron said in a thick accent.

"Where are you from?" Etanos asked.

"Northern Thyre," the man said, recognizing Etanos' accent. "It sounds like we're kin."

Etanos shook his hand. "It's always good to meet fellow Thyreans," he said. "Perhaps a discount, then?"

Janos chuckled out loud; probably a little longer than was necessary. "Probably not," he said humorously. "But I'll treat you right anyway."

The barman guffawed, smacking his hand on the bar and leaning in to laugh in Garret's face. Garret leaned back, smiling uncomfortably. What an incredibly odd pair of men.

"We need some discretion," Etanos added.

Janos pursed his lips, nodding with understanding. "Of course, friend," he said. "No questions asked. Twenty silver crowns for the entire distance. I have to come back upstream after all. Money up front."

"Of course," Etanos said, sealing the deal with a handshake. "Though I won't ask how you get back upstream."

"Well," Janos said. "That would be a question, now, wouldn't it?"

CHAPTER Nine

hey were on the river within the hour, squatting near the edge of Janos' raft as it drifted slowly down stream. Janos pushed it along with a long pole, tirelessly digging it into the riverbed, pulling it out, and pushing it in again. The man's thin and tightly corded build told Garret that he had been doing this for quite a while. In fact, he seemed to be a little lopsided.

Though the going was slow, this way was safer for them. The road south of Faillaigh was dangerous, as was said, and there were twists and turns that could potentially get them lost. It was in the south where the forests were so thick that one could lose their way and end up hopelessly stranded in the middle of nowhere.

"How far south does this Aeli live?" Etanos asked.

Garret shrugged. "Rumor has it she lives close enough to the shore to go there every day, but far enough north that those of Faillaigh have met her."

Etanos stared at him for a moment, then sighed. "So you don't know, then."

"Sister Helena says we will know we are far enough south when we see the old dragon tower between two peaks."

"Are you looking for Tel Drakkar?" Janos asked.

"Not exactly," Garret said. "Just looking to see it in the distance."

"I thought you said no questions asked," Etanos said.

Janos grinned, shrugging. "Just trying to help, my friends."

Etanos winked at Garret, turning to Janos. "Do you know anything of a witch in the south?"

"A witch..." Janos repeated. "Maybe not a witch, but a priestess."

Priestess, Garret repeated in his mind. If this Janos referred to her as a priestess, then he must know her, or at least he must have heard of her.

"Her name is Aeli," Garret said. "Do you know her?"

Janos pursed his lips. "I've met her," he said. "What do you want with her?"

"Just her help," Etanos said. "Nothing more."

Janos grunted, looking them over for a moment. "If what you say is true, then I will tell you how to find her. But be wary; if you have any intentions of harming her, you will not succeed. There is a reason people call her a witch."

Garret gulped. "We assure you, Janos," he said. "We have no intention of harming her."

"I'm not the most respectable man in the kingdom," Janos said. "But I am an honest businessman, trying to succeed in a corrupted town. The two of you, however, seem dangerous to me. You must understand my concern."

"We are *very* dangerous," Etanos said, "but we are only dangerous to those who harm others."

Garret grinned. He liked that statement. Feeling dangerous was exciting; feeling dangerous to the rotten was even more exciting.

"Very well, then," Janos said. "When we arrive at your stop, I will let you off and point out the path you must take. You need to keep watchful on the road, though. There are things in those woods that even the Black Witch of the North would not cross."

"What is the Black Witch of the North?" Etanos asked.

Janos flashed his toothless grin. "You've not heard of the banshee?" he asked.

Garret knew the stories but had never heard of the creature being referred to as a witch. The banshee was a dark entity; the shade of something once divine and pure, but defiled and ripped from grace, trapped to wander the earth in pain and anguish for all eternity.

Etanos said nothing, evidently knowing what a banshee was.

"Of what things do you speak?" Garret asked.

Janos grumbled. "I don't know what you'd call them," he said. "But some call them revenants. Wraiths, sometimes."

Garret's eyes widened. He suddenly regretted suggesting they go to Aeli. Perhaps traveling to Morduin to see Maedoc would have been the better choice. Etanos glanced at him with a crooked grin, seeing his apprehensiveness.

"Are you afraid of ghosts, Garret?" he laughed.

Garret gulped again as his mentor stared. The man's grin widened until he began chuckling. Janos soon joined him. Garret laughed half-heartedly as Etanos clapped him on the shoulder.

"He's just jesting, Garret," Etanos said. "Thyreans do that."

Garret glanced at Janos, who winked — halfheartedly.

* * *

The forest eventually became thicker, so much so that the branches of the trees on the shore hung out over the water. Some of them even protruded from the water itself, precariously balanced until such time as their roots lost hold and they would go toppling into the river.

The river itself narrowed to only twenty or so yards in width, causing the water to flow slightly faster than it had before. Still, the ride was slow and smooth, and Janos expertly guided them through without incident.

Etanos seemed to be enjoying the scenery. His gaze went from east to west as he admired the trees and the distant mountains that poked up among them. Garret knew that soon they would see the tower of Tel Drakkar, and Janos would shore the raft to let them off. But, for now, he would enjoy the ride, as well.

"There's a mine far to the west," Janos said. "It's about a day's ride. A little closer, along the road through the forest, is a trading post and an inn, if you're interested."

"An Inn?" Garret asked. "Out here?"

Janos chuckled. "Aye. Many people enjoy the solitude here; hunters, trappers, and furriers. *Jax's Pub* is where they all go to meet. It's been there for generations, along with the name Jax."

"What do you mean?" Garret asked.

"Four generations of men named Jax have run that place," Janos said. "I think they're just too lazy to paint a new sign."

He laughed out loud again. Etanos grinned and glanced at Garret.

"That's funny," Garret said. "Have you met any of them?"

Janos nodded. "Sure," he said, scowling. "But I couldn't tell you who's who. There's a very strong family resemblance that makes me thankful there are no daughters." He grinned widely. "They would probably not be very pleasing to look at."

Etanos pointed off to the southeast. "Is that the dragon tower?" he asked.

"Aye," Janos said. "That would be it. I would stay away from there if I were you. It's a bit out of the way, anyway. We still have a few more miles before we reach the road. Then I'll point you in the right direction."

"Where we will need to be watchful, right?" Garret said.

"That's right," Janos replied.

"What is in the dragon tower?" Etanos asked. "Or Tel Drakkar as you called it."

Janos shook his head. "Nothing, as far as I know. It's been abandoned for as long as I can remember."

"It was the old temple of the Dragon," Garret said. "Where the Priests of Drakkar and the Knights of the Dragon would meet and lead the people in worship of the Dragon."

Etanos grunted. "Such things are not suited for me," Etanos said. "I respect the Firstborn, but my heart lies with the Great Mother."

"Mine, too," Garret said, "for obvious reasons."

He thought about Helena then, and poor Helga. He remembered holding Helga in his arms as she died, and how Helena had given him that one last look before leading the children away in desperation. His heart felt heavy as he pictured her beautiful face; a face he would likely never see again.

He wished things had gone differently.

"Do you see the docks ahead?" Janos asked.

Garret and Etanos looked downriver. There was a large pavilion near the shore, with a long dock that protruded halfway into the river's width. It was well kept, from what they could see, and there was a single small boat tied up there. Though no one was visible, Garret guessed that the boat belonged to someone who was nearby.

"That's where I'll drop you," Janos said. "From there, you'll take the road east. When it splits, you'll want to take the path south. The road itself goes in two directions; to the post, and the pub. Just follow the path south. You'll eventually find Aeli. Or, rather, she'll find you."

"The path isn't a road?" Etanos asked.

"No, the path is a path, which is why it's called a path, and not a road. It's a rough one at that. There was no reason to build a road in that direction since no one really goes that way other than a few hunters." He paused and smiled. "Not very often, though."

Garret winced slightly. He had no desire to go traipsing

around in a dangerous forest. But he had promised Etanos that Aeli was the best choice in deciphering the writings. Besides, she would be able to provide other things, as well, such as some spells they might need later on. For what purpose, he wasn't sure, but it was always good to have resources just in case.

Janos steered the raft toward the docks, and all three of them kept their eyes open for the boat's owner. There was no one in sight, but Garret guessed someone was near, hunting or fishing. Or maybe someone from the opposite side of the river was visiting the pub or the trading post.

A small flock of loons uttered their strange howls before flying off, giving Garret the shivers. It was an incredibly odd sound that resembled the cackles of a lunatic playing a flute. That was what he imagined anyway; a cross-eyed and stinking lunatic, sitting on a stump, playing an obscene tune on a flute carved from bone — probably his mother's leg bone.

"I see no one," Etanos said. "I'm not sure whether that's a good thing or a bad thing."

"Hmm," Janos grunted. "That could go either way."

He slowed the raft once they neared the docks, and Etanos and Garret stood to disembark. Janos grabbed onto the peer, steadying the raft. "Off you go," he said. "When you are ready to return, just call my name."

"Are you staying here?" Garret asked as they stepped off.

"No," Janos grinned. "I just like to think that someone somewhere is calling my name."

He chuckled as he pushed the raft away, waving to them with a strange and disturbing smile. They stared at him, not quite sure what to think of him.

"He was an odd fellow," Etanos said. "Nuttier than squirrel droppings."

Garret turned to look at the road. It was sheltered in the trees; shadowy and twisting as it disappeared into the forest. Though wide and smooth, it gave Garret a sense of confinement, as the trees curved over it and met at the top, giving it the appearance of a dark, green, and frightening tunnel.

"Well," he said. "I guess this is it. Shall we begin?"

"Stay close," Etanos said, nodding. "Keep your eyes and ears open. And don't let your awareness overpower your unconscious feelings. Sometimes, your instincts may tell you things that your brain won't."

"What about the boat?" Garret asked.

"Ignore it," Etanos said. "I have a feeling its owner is around somewhere. Keep your ears open for him too."

* * *

The road was much darker than the open air. The canopy above blocked most of the sunlight, casting long, twisting shadows on the ground. There was a thick mist that rolled across the path, obscuring their view ahead, and the moisture it brought made Garret somewhat uncomfortable. Etanos, however, didn't seem to mind. He did, however, notice the uncomfortable expressions Garret was making.

"In your life as an assassin," he began, "you may experience long periods of discomfort. You will get used to them, and they will make you stronger."

"It's just the moisture," Garret assured him.

"That is exactly what I mean," Etanos said. "I've been on missions where I've had to endure being wet, cold, muddy... you name it. But, if you're dedicated to your craft, you must learn to ignore your discomfort. That pretty much sums up any path you may take."

Garret nodded silently. He supposed that was correct. Making a living—no matter what it was—was a matter of dealing with displeasure. He supposed even a barman had unpleasant moments doing his job; dealing with hostile patrons, remembering what everybody drank, and keeping his tavern secure and safe. Then there was the frequent vomiting...

"I remember on one mission I took, the mark was so difficult to figure out, that I watched him for three days. I spent two of those nights watching him in the rain. I was chilled to the bone, but it was worth it. I finally discovered that the contract was not justified. He was not a criminal or anything of the sort. He was simply sneaking around to meet his love." He turned to Garret with a smile. "She was a peasant, and he was a noble."

"Ah," Garret said. "I suppose that *would* look suspicious to an outsider."

It was true. If a noble had a relationship with a peasant, it would have to be one that didn't draw attention. If he were found out, he could lose face to other nobles, and possibly be ousted. That was just the way it was. Despite the king's indifference to a noble's personal life, the nobles themselves had a strict code of conduct that was common among their kind. Any deviation from that code was frowned upon.

"He snuck around for good reason," Garret said. "*And* for a noble cause."

"What cause is that?" Etanos said.

"Well," Garret said, pausing. "Because he loved her, despite her class."

Etanos smiled. "I suppose that's a noble cause," he said. "But not one that I have ever risked my reputation for. But if I had simply carried out the assassination, then I would have killed an innocent man, so his cause was definitely something to consider. That is why you must observe and judge for yourself before fulfilling a contract."

"I see," Garret said. "Observe for as long as it takes, no matter how uncomfortable you must be."

Etanos grinned, nodding and scruffing up Garret's hair. "Very good," he said. "You're catching on. There are a lot of lessons you must learn, and we will cover them as they present themselves. You learn fast, and you have a good heart."

"That would seem to me to be counterproductive," Garret said.

"Not at all. That's why I chose you. A heartless assassin gives the rest of us a bad name and doesn't stay in business long. In fact, an assassin who kills indiscriminately may find *himself* a target."

That made sense, Garret thought.

"I have killed two assassins during my career," Etanos continued. "They were indiscriminate, taking contracts for the sole purpose of collecting the rewards. I have the feeling that my Khemite friend may be another."

"We will find him," Garret said. "And if he is what you say he may be, then he should be eliminated."

Even as the words left his mouth, Garret felt strange saying them. Though he had always been in favor of punishing those who harm others, he had never considered simply removing them in such a permanent way, arrest, imprisonment, and even public humiliation, yes, but never this way. It *did* seem like the better, more effective, solution. Criminals could buy their way out of prison if they had the right connections. And nobles could even avoid punishment for their deeds altogether.

Why *not* just take them out of the picture? It was better for everyone. Dead men can no longer perform evil deeds.

"This looks like our path," Etanos said, stopping.

The road continued to the east, as was described, and also split off to the north. A rickety sign had been placed at the corner, pointing north and east, reading *Trading Post* and *Jax's Pub*, respectively. Among the trees on the south side of the road, there was also a small break that opened up to a narrow, rocky path that led downward and into the shadows.

"It looks dangerous," Garret said. "But I suppose it's the only way."

Etanos grumbled. "Keep behind me," he said. "And watch your back. I'll keep on the lookout for any traps. Make sure no one follows us."

Garret gulped nervously and fell in step behind him as he entered; looking back at the road one last time before the path fully swallowed them.

CHAPTER TEN

errin reached Gaellos by sundown, having ridden hard and fast after being relieved by Lord Darragh. He rather enjoyed his days off, and usually spent them doing no good. Tonight, however, was official business, and there was no time for playing tricks or burglarizing the local nobles.

Tonight, the guild would be reborn.

He studied Joran's shop for several moments from the concealment of a nearby alley. The smith was in the process of closing his forge, waiting for the last customer to vacate before closing the large shutters that surrounded his outdoor displays. The last customer, however, was obviously chatty, and seemed unwilling to shut his mouth long enough for Joran to close up shop.

Ferrin sighed impatiently. He had planned on meeting Joran at this hour to retrieve a set of daggers that he had commissioned a few weeks ago; ceremonial daggers that would be used to identify fellow members of his newly-born brotherhood. They would all wear them proudly, displaying them discreetly to identify themselves to the others. It was a brilliant plan, Ferrin thought, but now this gum-flapper was delaying things to an uncomfortable degree.

Ferrin could see Joran's frustration as he nodded and shrugged along with the customer's incessant chatting. He could tell that the stranger was a city guard out of uniform, as his blade was held in a scabbard of brown leather with golden vines wrapped around its length—standard issue in Gaellos. He seemed to be asking questions, which Joran was trying to avoid as much as possible, answering only briefly to hurry the man along.

Finally, as Joran pretended to yawn, the guard nodded in defeat, walking away and disappearing into the darkening alleys. Ferrin stood and rushed across the square, reaching Joran's shop just as the man was pulling the last of the shutters into position. The smith looked at him, rolling his eyes and sighing.

"What do *you* want?" he asked.

Ferrin slowed, holding his hands out and smiling. "What do you think?" he said. "We had a transaction to complete, remember?"

"Yes, yes," Joran said, standing aside so Ferrin could enter. "Come in. But let's make it quick. Do you have the money?"

Ferrin ducked inside after taking one last look at the street to ensure no one had seen him.

"You look even more suspicious when you're trying to be discreet," Joran said.

"Sorry," Ferrin grinned. "Habit."

Joran pulled the shutters closed, leading Ferrin into the forge. There, he went to a cabinet behind the stacks of ingots he had stored and retrieved a rolled-up length of canvas.

"That's all of them?" Ferrin asked, excitedly.

"One dozen fine daggers with the sigils you gave me pounded right into the blades."

He set the bundle on the counter, carefully unrolling the cloth and revealing the stack of daggers. Ferrin's heart pounded when he saw them, and a wide smile spread across his face. He reached down to grab one, holding it up to the dim firelight and admiring its craftsmanship. The blades were finely forged and polished, the handles wrapped in the finest leather stolen from Lord Darragh's stock, and the tiny symbols of a cat's paw were pounded into the steel right at the base of the blades near the cross guards.

"Excellent work, friend," he said. "These will serve us nicely."

"I'm not usually in the business of dealing with gangs," Joran said. "But money's been tight lately."

"Gangs?" Ferrin said defensively. "We are a guild, my friend, not a gang."

Joran snorted. "What's the difference? You steal, gangs steal. Everybody steals."

"Well," Ferrin said. "We steal for the benefit of the people. You know as well as I do that the nobles in the south are rotten to the core. It's our job to make sure they don't pilfer the peasants into such a hole that they can't even feed their families."

"That's the king's job," Joran reminded him. "Not yours."

Ferrin grinned, stuffing a dagger into his belt. "The king is too old," he said. "And he has other things to worry about. Therefore, we work for him behind the scenes."

"You speak as if this little guild of yours is already a thing."

"We are," Ferrin said. "We've all been in business for quite a while. Now is the time for us to organize and become official."

"And what are you going to call yourselves?" Joran asked. "The Cat's Paw?"

Ferrin chuckled. "No sir," he said. "We will have no name, only the bond of brotherhood, and justice for the common man."

Joran stared at him skeptically. "So you say," he mocked.

Ferrin shook his head, grinning. "You'll see," he said. "We'll be well-known. But not so well-known that everyone knows our names. That's the way it has to be. And when your son takes over your forge, he will also inherit our respect and our business."

"Leave my son out of this," Joran said. "And you mind yourself. You belong to Darragh's house. I find it hard to believe that you will ever have the time to conduct this guild of yours while serving him."

Ferrin nodded in agreement. "That is true," he said. "But someday I will take over Darragh's house and I will lead the guild in secret. I will keep the nobles in line and make sure they do the job they are supposed to do, no matter who takes over the throne."

"Well, that's a noble cause, I suppose. Good luck with that."

"Luck is not what I need, Joran," Ferrin said. "What I need is for everyone to work together; my guild, the merchants, and those nobles who remain loyal to the people, and the throne."

"Then you should oust Lord Daeglan," Joran said. "He is not loyal to anyone but himself, not even to the Great Mother."

"What do you mean?"

Joran turned to close his cabinet, sighing. Ferrin could tell that he was upset.

"In case, you hadn't noticed," he began. "The convent has been destroyed."

Ferrin shook his head. "I came from the opposite side of town. Explain."

"There was a fire, and several of the sisters were killed. Though the children made it out safely, the guards found the bodies of assassins, all wearing the same robes, and the body of Lord Daeglan's bodyguard."

Ferrin was shocked. Though he knew Daeglan was scum, he never guessed that the man would resort to murder or the destruction of a beloved temple. "When did this happen?" he asked.

"A few nights ago," Joran said. "After a strange visit from an even stranger man."

"What man?"

"It was an assassin," Joran said. "But not affiliated with Lord Daeglan or anyone local. He was from Thyre, I believe."

Ferrin thought back to his encounter with the young hunter and his older companion. There was something about the older man that struck him as odd. Perhaps this was the same visitor.

"Was the man bald with a small beard, deep-set eyes, and a black cloak that was quite obviously reversible?"

Joran nodded. "Sounds like him," he said. "But I don't know what a reversible cloak is."

"What did he want?" Ferrin asked.

"He wanted me to identify a blade," Joran said. "It was an obsidian dagger; one from Khem."

Ferrin nodded. "I believe I met him in Faillaigh," he said. "He was with a young man about my age; one with blond hair tied back and strangely cold blue eyes. The other man called him Garret, I believe."

Joran's eyes lit up at the mention of the boy's name. Ferrin noticed, cocking his head in question. "You know him?" he asked.

Joran nodded, seeming relieved. "Yes. He was the groundskeeper at the convent and acted somewhat as a mentor to the children. I'm glad to hear that he got out safely."

Ferrin nodded. "He did, apparently. But where are the sisters and the other children now?"

"Lord Daeglan had them transported to his estate outside of town."

"Of course he did," Ferrin said, shaking his head. "What a way to cover his tracks. He likely ordered the destruction of the convent himself."

Joran nodded. "He always had his eye on Sister Helena, the Headmistress."

"This is not good, Joran," Ferrin said. "She is in great danger at his hands. I must get her out."

"You and who else?" Joran said. "Your guild?"

Ferrin smiled. "Precisely," he said. "And we will bear these fine blades as we do so."

Joran chuckled. "Flattery is nice, Ferrin," he said jokingly, "but the price remains the same regardless."

"Of course," Ferrin said, throwing a bag of coins on the counter. "Double the price, in fact. Thank you for the information. This… Garret interests me. I must find him and this assassin. I want to know what they're up to."

He rolled up the bundle of daggers, tying it off with his belt and slinging it over his shoulder. "Thank you for your help, Joran," he said. "If I need any more weapons or information, I will surely come to you. If anyone else comes asking questions and bears these daggers, I would appreciate it if you would help them, too. The guild will pay you handsomely for your troubles."

Joran nodded knowingly. "Done," he said. "Now get the hell out of my forge."

* * *

Ferrin snuck through the alleyways of Gaellos with his package full of daggers. He had a specific destination in mind; one that was unknown to the nobles, and most of the townsfolk. Deep below the surface was an old compound, once used by the ancient Order of Baleron, dedicated to the worship of the Sidhe. Thousands of years ago, this divine race, also known as the Alvar, had lived on Eirenoch, acting as kings and protectors of the primitive peoples.

Now the compound was abandoned, and the crypts and chapels emptied, re-equipped, and repurposed for another order; the Thieves' Guild. Ferrin and many of the local youth had found the tunnels years ago, and throughout their growing brotherhood, rumors persisted that one day the Thieves' Guild would be reformed and would reside here for all time.

That dream was coming to fruition.

Outside of town, near a rocky mine entrance, were the crumbled gates of the ancient catacombs. Throughout the years, the vegetation had obscured them to the point of near invisibility. They had gone forgotten for ages, yet maintained and guarded by the rangers, who themselves had learned their craft from the Alvar in ages past. Other than them, only the learned sons of local historians knew the truth, and they happened to be very good friends of Ferrin's and had similar ambitions.

It was Ferrin who decided to organize them into a group of peasant heroes; thieves and burglars united for the specific purpose of thwarting the greedy and evil schemes of the local nobles and their merchant cronies. So far, things had gone well. Money that was stolen from the people through insane taxes was returned to them. Regulations and bureaucratic attacks against small-time farmers and peddlers were thwarted through clever means, resulting in the success of the local shops over the rich merchants who filtered their money elsewhere—or into the pockets of the nobles.

It was an effective organization thus far, but they were missing one very important thing; a base of operations. Here, underneath the city of Gaellos, the new Thieves' Guild could meet, make their plans, and offer shelter to their traveling fellows. Though there were many other places for the thieves to meet in just about every town, *this* would be the location of the actual guild.

And where Ferrin would lead them.

Fortunately, though the catacombs were held sacred by the rangers, Ferrin had convinced them that the new guild would treat the ruins with the utmost respect, and use them for the most noble of causes. Besides, Ferrin had told them, the rangers had a compound of their own; in the north *and* the south. If these catacombs were left abandoned, then they would simply crumble away to nothing, and be forgotten for all time.

It had been, apparently, a convincing enough argument.

And now, as Ferrin ducked into the rocky entrance, that argument came to mind as he beheld the dark form of his friend, Kuros.

"Ho there, thief," Kuros jested as he pulled back his bow. "You stand on hallowed ground."

Ferrin grinned. "Move it, ranger scum, or I'll have your head."

The creaking of a dozen bows suddenly surrounded Ferrin. He knew Kuros had brought his company.

"All right," Ferrin said. "You got me."

Kuros chuckled, signaling his men to relax. He studied the bundle Ferrin carried, raising his eyebrow in curiosity. "What have you got there?"

Ferrin dropped the bundle, unwrapping it to show his friend the stash of daggers. The ranger's eyes widened; almost as wide as his smile.

"I know Joran's work when I see it," Kuros said, picking up one of the daggers and spinning it in his hand. "Yes. Definitely Joran's work. What are these for?"

"These, my friend," Ferrin replied, "will be for the top thieves in the new guild. They will be symbols of rank and prestige, and only the finest, most scrupulous among us will have them."

"Including you, no doubt," Kuros said, grinning.

Ferrin shrugged as if offended. "Of course."

"Well," Kuros began, "you'll be happy to know that my captain has rendered this area protected, and you will have free passage. You won't have to worry about the city guards trespassing. This is ranger territory now."

"Excellent," Ferrin said. "Everything is falling into place. This is a dream come true."

"Don't be hasty, now," Kuros warned. "There is a price. As you know, you will be responsible for maintaining the catacombs underneath, but there is something else."

"Yes?"

"Baelion requests that you act as protectors as well," Kuros said.

"Of course," Ferrin said. "But to whom, specifically."

"To the orphans," Kuros said. "We take some of them, mostly the boys, but there are many here in Gaellos who are far more suited for your purposes. You will take them, train them, and if they choose to, they can join us when they are older. Both of our orders are needed, and the rangers are dwindling in number. We need more members, but we do not have the resources to keep and train orphans. You do. You keep them, train them in your ways, and we will pick our new members from them."

"Are you speaking of the orphans that lived in the convent?"

"As of now, yes," Kuros said. "But also in the future. The convents are disappearing, and children are wandering the streets, starving, and turning to crime. While we can round up those who wander into the forests, and set them straight with a purpose and a life that suits them, not all of them are suited for the life of a ranger. Some would be better suited for city life. Those, you will keep."

"So, we give them a home and training, and then you come and steal them away?"

Kuros grinned. "That's the deal," he said. "It is of mutual benefit. Keep to the plan, and we watch your back. The nobles and their ilk will never invade your territory."

Ferrin nodded. It seemed like a good plan. He and his friends had the resources to care for street urchins, and what better way to educate them in the ways of the world than to expose them to it in the most truthful and revealing way possible?

"What a character builder," Ferrin said out loud.

"What?" Kuros said, cocking his head.

"Nothing. But it's a deal. I will tell my friends, and we will let you know when we are ready."

"Good," Kuros said. "We will keep watch on Lord Daeglan's house. If there are any signs that the children are in danger, we will rescue them, but we will be counting on you to take the ones we can't use. And... vise-versa, of course."

"I'm sorry?"

"If there are children you don't believe are suited for thievery, then the rangers will take them. We do have similar skill sets, after all, just different venues."

"Venues," Ferrin repeated, chuckling. "Good analogy. All right then. Good night, Kuros. I have to drop these off and return to Faillaigh before the morning."

"Right," Kuros said. "Or master will have your hide."

He turned and disappeared into the shadows, leaving Ferrin to squat in the hollow alone.

"Rangers," he whispered, shaking his head.

CHAPTER ELEVEN

he forest was surprisingly well-lit for being as thick as it was. Etanos and Garret had little trouble traversing the path, as the moonlight that filtered down through the canopy was bright and consistent; almost as if the forest was inviting them to explore it. They were surrounded by the sounds of insects, frogs, and the occasional tramping of deer and other animals, and the air was pleasant for the most part; only slightly chilled and damp.

Though neither of them had spoken much since they left the main road, Garret sensed that Etanos was feeling the same thing that he was. There was a strange, foreboding feeling that hung in the air like a cold blanket, and it gave Garret chills that he had never felt before. Etanos' silence told him that he wasn't just imagining it.

Perhaps it was the prospect of meeting with a witch. Though Garret knew that's not really what she was, he suspected she maintained that image in order to keep people away. Doing so would, of course, require the casting of certain spells; perhaps a spell that could cause those who sought her out to have these very same feelings.

Or perhaps it was just the forest itself.

"Maybe we should stop for the night," Garret said, finally, unsure as to whether he would even be able to sleep.

Etanos slowed, dropping down to one knee and peering ahead into the gloom. "That might be a good idea," he said, "but not here. We'll find a better spot where the branches are not so low-hanging."

A rustling to their left caught their attention, causing Garret to shudder and reach for his blade. Etanos calmly held out his hand, scanning the shadows. Garret's spine tingled in anticipation, and his breath quickened.

"Calm yourself," Etanos whispered. "It's likely just a deer."

Garret gulped, loosening his grip on his sword slightly. After a few seconds, the sound moved to the area in front of them. Etanos shifted his gaze and pivoted on his foot. A pair of eyes appeared from the darkened underbrush, and Garret's heart skipped a beat.

"What is that?" he whispered harshly.

The eyes suddenly bolted across the path, glaring at them as their owner's gray hide disappeared into the weeds on the other side of the path. Garret sighed in relief.

"Just a coyote," Etanos said. "Nothing dangerous."

He stood, moving forward again as silently as a cat. Garret followed, keeping behind him with a death grip on the hilt of his saber. They continued through the darkness, keeping their eyes and ears open to all the sights and sounds that engulfed them. Garret's only thoughts were the dangers that Janos had mentioned; revenants, wraiths, and the like. He pictured their ghoulish eyes peering at them through the darkness and felt their foul breath on the back of his neck.

Try as he might, Garret was only making things worse.

Etanos stopped again, turning to him with a curious look. Garret realized that his teeth were chattering, and had caught his mentor's attention.

"You're going to scare yourself into a frenzy," he said. "There are no undead in the forest; only animals and two handsome men with swords."

"And a witch..." Garret added.

Etanos grinned. "You said not to call her that."

Garret shrugged. "From what I've seen and felt so far," he said, "it doesn't seem too far-fetched."

"Next lesson," Etanos said. "There is nothing to fear. Ever. You *are* the darkness. You *are* the creature that stalks the night."

Garret nodded skeptically, pursing his lips in an attempt to keep them from quivering. "I *am* the darkness," he repeated.

Somehow, he didn't believe it. Etanos didn't seem to, either.

But a new sound caught their attention, shifting it away from Garret's chattering teeth. A melodic voice echoed through the forest ahead, and a dim glow slowly spread through the trees. Etanos motioned for Garret to follow him into the brush, and the two squatted near the path as the strange sound neared.

Someone was singing. It was a man, mumbling a flat-toned

ditty to himself as he walked along the path. He carried a torch, and as he became more visible, it was clear that he was a hermit of some sort—or at least he *looked* like a hermit. He stopped singing for a moment as he rounded the bend, and when he came into full view, he began again.

There's a hole in me britches,
where I scratch me itches.
My tunic is ragged and wet.
There's a hat on me head,
that's dirty and red.
And I lost me brown boots in a bet.

Garret grinned, staring at the man curiously. Though the two were as silent as could be, the stranger stopped, seeming to sense their presence. He turned his face left and right, scratching his thick, raggedy beard with a dirty hand.

"Who are ye?" he asked. "Where ye be?"

Etanos slowly stood, and the man turned to him, backing away only slightly.

"There ye be," the man said, cackling in amusement. "Now why ye be hidin' in the dumps? Are ye tryin' to scare an old man?"

"Forgive us, sir," Etanos said, dragging Garret to his feet. "We weren't sure whether or not you were dangerous."

The man cackled again, slapping his knee. "Good one, aye," he said, smiling to reveal a mouthful of nothing. "So yer not plannin' to rob me, then?"

Etanos held up his hands. "No, sir," he said. "We are simply travelers on our way to the coast."

"Ohh," the man said, his mouth gaping open as he looked the two of them over. "The coast, eh? Well, there are easier ways to get there than trapesing through the woods."

"We are from farther north," Etanos said. "This area is new to us."

"Uh-huh," the man grunted. "I don't believe that yer from farther north, young man. This one, maybe, but not you. Where ye from, really?"

"Thyre," Etanos replied. "My name is Etanos, and this is Garret."

The old man looked at Garret, smiling and nodding as he sized him up. "All right, then," he said. "Whatever yer up to, it's none of me business. I suppose ye don't look like bandits, otherwise ye woulda robbed me, eh?" He cackled again. "Ye wouldn't o' got much, though."

"We are not bandits," Etanos said, "I assure you."

The man narrowed his gaze, stepping closer. "Then why ye be in me forest?"

Etanos cocked his head. Garret sensed something then as if the old man wasn't what he appeared to be.

"I asked you a question, son," the old man said, his strange accent disappearing suddenly.

"We are travelers," Etanos said again. "Nothing more."

"We seek Aeli," Garret blurted out.

The old man turned to him, shoving the torch in his face and studying him closely. "And why do you seek her?" he asked.

Etanos gently pushed the torch away, and the old man turned back to him, glaring suspiciously.

"We need her wisdom," Etanos said. "Nothing more."

The old man nodded slowly, looking at Garret one more time, and then stepped back. The torch flared into life, as bright as the sun, obscuring their view. Garret and Etanos both shielded their eyes from the glare. When it died down, the old man was gone. In his place stood a beautiful woman with eyes of the brightest blue, and hair as black as pitch. She was dressed in a hunting cloak with patterns of green and brown, and her tunic was of green silk that shimmered in the torchlight.

Garret's heart thumped as he beheld her, and he could clearly feel the energy that emanated from her body. It was an Earthy energy; as if a dryad had suddenly appeared before them in all its divine glory. Slowly, the energy faded, and her appearance became somewhat normal. Still, Garret couldn't take his eyes off her, and his heart still pounded with excitement.

"I am Aeli," the woman said. "What is it you want from me?"

Etanos bowed his head in respect. Garret still stood frozen.

"I have something that I would like you to see," Etanos said. "But my friend here is cold and tired. We weren't expecting to see you so soon."

Aeli approached Garret, staring into his eyes with a soft, kind expression. Garret could feel a gentle calm settle over him as she neared. Her gaze was comforting and warm, and it filled him with a pleasant sensation that soothed his cold fingers and slowed his heart to a more normal pace.

"He is afraid as well," Aeli said, reaching out to stroke his cheek.

The feeling of her finger on his skin made him quiver, and he gulped loudly; embarrassingly so. She grinned, dropping her hand and turning back to Etanos.

"Follow me," she said. "I don't have visitors often, but it would be nice to have someone to talk to for a time."

* * *

Aeli's cottage was small and quaint. It was nestled in a semi-circle of pine trees, all adorned with hanging lamps driven by some sort of magic that illuminated the whole clearing with a pleasant greenish-blue glow. The roof was high and pointed, and a short, limestone chimney billowed smoke in a steady stream that rose into the trees and glowed with the lights below.

A stone walkway led up to the wooden door, which was decorated with a wreath of dried vines and a large, brass bell. Garret felt a twinge of sadness as he saw it, as Helena had always decorated the convent in a similar way during the winter solstice. But that feeling was overcome by the feeling of warmth and peace that surrounded the whole area. It was quite a contrast to the forest behind them, which was dark and somewhat foreboding.

Aeli's home was an oasis of comfort in a sea of darkness.

The woman led them to her door, stepping in first and waving her hand to light the lamps inside. As Garret and Etanos stepped in behind her, they were both immediately wrapped in a comforting cloud of cinnamon and ginger scent. Garret took a deep breath to take it in, closing his eyes to picture Helga's kitchen. She often used the same spices in her pies, and just the smell of them brought back memories of her cooking.

"Welcome to my home," Aeli said. "Please make yourselves comfortable. I will put on some tea."

"Thank you," Etanos said, sitting down at the crooked wooden table.

Garret took a seat next to him, letting his eyes wander around the eclectically-furnished great room. The kitchen and den were one, with only a small countertop separating them. Pots and pans hung on the kitchen walls and ceiling, and a large, wood-burning stove dominated one corner. In the living area, there was a fireplace with a pot hanging inside, and the shelves were all stacked with clay jars and hung with herbs of all types.

Aeli put on a pot of water, lighting the stove with a wave of her staff. She gathered a handful of herbs from two different jars and sprinkled them inside, stirring them with a wooden spoon. She then joined them at the table, smiling warmly.

"It is customary for guests to introduce themselves," she said.

Etanos smiled. "Forgive me, my lady," he said. "I am Etanos of Thyre, and this is my friend, Garret of Gaellos."

Aeli nodded in greeting, her smile still lighting up the room. "It is a pleasure to meet you both," she said. "What is it I can assist you with?"

Etanos reached into his cloak, producing the dagger and staring at it for a moment before speaking. "It is rumored that you can read Khemite," he said. "I was hoping you could decipher this writing for me."

Aeli cocked her head. "You came all this way just for me to read some writing for you?"

Etanos shrugged. "As far as either of us knows," he explained. "You are the only person who can read it."

Aeli reached for the dagger, taking it in her hands and studying it carefully. She mouthed something unintelligible, raising her eyebrows as she deciphered the writing. Garret waited in anticipation as she sounded out the syllables, translating them in her head.

"I believe it says *The Broken One*," she said, "if I remember the words correctly."

"The Broken One?" Etanos repeated. "I'm not sure what that means."

"This is an obsidian blade," Aeli said. "It's not something the average person would carry. Where did you find it?"

Etanos cleared his throat, apparently reluctant to explain. "It was found in the heart of a man I was contracted to eliminate."

Aeli raised her brow again. "You are an assassin?" she asked.

Etanos nodded. "I belong to a guild in Thyre; one of the oldest. But we are not murderers, only those who work to maintain the balance of power."

"I understand," Aeli said. "I, too, work to maintain the balance, but the balance of nature."

"Are you a druid?" Garret asked, intrigued.

Aeli shook her head. "No. My mother passed my abilities down to me. I am not quite sure what a druid is... or does. But now I must ask, young Garret, are you too an assassin?"

"Garret is my pupil," Etanos said. "I saw great strength in

him, and a great heart. I feel that he has the potential to become a great assassin someday."

Aeli stared at him for a moment, sighing. "Perhaps. Though I don't agree with your methods, they can be effective when no other option is available. The rangers can act in much the same way, though they act on their own."

"Is there anything else you can tell me about this writing?" Etanos asked.

Aeli studied the dagger again, running her fingers along the blade. Though she did not seem to enjoy touching it, her expression showed them that she did, indeed, feel its power.

"All I can tell you," Aeli said, "is that keeping this blade will only draw unwanted attention to you. Its owner has a bond with it, and would be able to sense its presence."

"That would explain why he left it behind," Garret offered.

Etanos nodded. "True. But that still doesn't explain who this assassin is, or why he wants me to know that he is here."

"That I cannot answer," Aeli said. "But I hope I have helped you somewhat."

The teapot began to whistle, and Aeli went to retrieve it. Etanos seemed blank as he stared off into space, not even noticing when Aeli returned to pour three cups of sweet-smelling tea.

"Etanos," Garret said. "Is there anyone in your past that may have a vendetta against you? A rival assassin, maybe?"

Aeli looked at Etanos as he thought. "Not that I know of," he said. "The only rivalries that exist are between guilds; not between individual assassins."

"You said you have killed some who have acted on their own... those who gave the guilds a bad name."

Etanos folded his hands on the table before him. "True," he said. "But dead men cannot seek vengeance, or hold grudges."

Aeli slid his cup in front of him, urging him to drink. "Think on it tonight as you sleep, my friend," she said. "You may both rest here for the night." She turned and pointed toward a ladder in the far corner near the fireplace. "My loft is empty and warm. There are blankets there if you need them."

"Thank you," Etanos said. "And I thank you for your help."

Aeli smiled, placing a gentle hand on his shoulder. "I wish I could have been more help," she said. "I feel that your journey has been a waste of time."

"Not at all," Etanos said. "I am now curious as to who this

Broken One may be."

As he stared at his mentor, Garret began to feel that same curiosity. Someone was searching for Etanos for some reason, and not just to kill him. If that were the case, then the dagger would never have been left behind; the assassin would have just waited for him to arrive and fought him then and there. Why the game?

"There is more to this mystery than we can figure out at the moment," Garret said. "I, for one, could use some sleep."

"Very well," Etanos said.

"Finish your tea, my friends," Aeli said. "It will help you rest, and will relieve your pains."

* * *

Aeli's loft was warm and inviting, as she had said. Garret felt comfortable wrapped up in the furs that were piled on one side. He had slipped off his boots and his leather armor, and positioned himself near the chimney. The heat from the fireplace below radiated from its stones, and gave him comfort as he curled up near it.

Etanos lay on his back, staring up at the peaked ceiling with a blank expression. Garret knew that he was still thinking back at his past, trying to remember anyone or anything that may bring to light whoever or whatever had left the dagger.

"A Khemite assassin," Garret said. "Why would a Khemite assassin be looking for you?"

Etanos shook his head. "Khemite assassins are no different," he said. "There are guilds there that follow the same code of honor, and there are those who do not. It is the same wherever you go."

"Perhaps an independent one, then?" Garret offered. "One of those you spoke of before."

"I do not believe that any of them were of Khem," Etanos replied. "It is possible, I suppose. But the name *The Broken One* perplexes me."

Garret had to agree. The moniker made no sense to him. Why was this assassin broken, so to speak? Was it a metaphor, or a literal characteristic? Surely Garret himself was broken in the emotional sense. He had lost his home and possibly some of the sisters who had raised him. He *did* hold a grudge against Lord Daeglan, whom he knew was responsible for the destruction of the convent. Though the noble was not personally involved in the attack, Garret knew that his guard would never act on his own.

Garret grunted to himself, drawing Etanos' attention.

"What is it?" Etanos asked.

"I believe I have a personal vendetta, as well."

"Against whom?" Etanos asked. "Lord Daeglan?"

Garret nodded. "Exactly."

Etanos rolled onto his side to look Garret in the eye. "And what kind of thoughts do you have about him?"

Garret thought for a moment, remembering his encounter with Daeglan at the market. Though the noble had stopped his bodyguard from skewering him right there in public, Garret did not doubt that he had allowed his guard to not only corner him in the alley but to lead the attack on the convent as well. Why? He did not know.

"I think I need to know why he wanted the convent burned to the ground," Garret said. "Surely it couldn't be just because of me—unless, of course, his bodyguard pleaded with him to allow it."

"The guard felt affronted by your humiliation of him in the alley," Etanos said.

Garret nodded. "I would imagine so."

Etanos rolled onto his back again. "But that would not explain the order to burn down the convent," he said. "You are right. There must have been another reason. A noble would never risk his title for a simple act of revenge; especially for one of his guards. Any other noble would have simply warranted a personal attack against you, not against an entire convent."

There was only one explanation, Garret thought. Helena.

"He wants the Headmistress," he said. "He wants her for himself."

"Then burning down her home would not be the best way to go about that, would it?"

Garret shook his head. "I suppose not," he said. "Unless he offered some kind of aid to her and the children... and the other sisters, of course. It would be a way to cover up the fact that he had ordered it burned down and look like he was offering them his help."

"So, what do you have in mind, Garret?"

The answer was simple. Lord Daeglan had destroyed the convent, killed Helga and some of the sisters, and left dozens of children homeless; all for the affections of a woman who would despise him if she knew the truth. There would be no justice, at least not in the conventional sense. Nobles were rarely held accountable for their actions. No matter who knew what had happened, nothing could ever be done about it. Daeglan would get away with it. Garret could not let that happen.

"Lord Daeglan must die," he said.

Through the shadows, Garret saw Etanos grin.

CHAPTER TWELVE

The pleasant aroma of cinnamon awoke Garret in the morning. He opened his eyes, seeing the empty loft, and hearing the faint sound of voices in the kitchen below. He stretched; pulling on his boots and gathering his cloak and pack, and then descended. Etanos was there at the kitchen table, studying the dagger as Aeli wrapped several small cakes for them to take on the road. She smiled at Garret when he sat at the table.

"Good morning, young Garret," she said. "Help yourself to a muffin or two."

Garret took a muffin from the plate that sat in the middle of the table. It was moist and flaky, flavored with cinnamon, and drizzled with white, sticky syrup.

"Aeli is quite the baker," Etanos said, smiling. "She was kind enough to bake more of these for us to take with us."

"It's nothing," Aeli said. "As I said before, I don't get a lot of visitors."

"So where are we going, then?" Garret asked.

Etanos put the dagger into his cloak, shrugging. "I suppose until we figure that out, we will simply continue with your training. We shall travel back to the north, I think. We may find something along the way that interests us."

"If you are looking for sights to see," Aeli said, "or business to tend to, I would suggest following the road to Faerbane. You may find what you're looking for there. Perhaps even the answers you seek."

Garret had never been to Faerbane but heard it was beautiful. It was the major port city of Eirenoch, the gateway to the mainland. There, a giant estate stood right at the river, overlooking the falls that emptied into the sea. Rumors persisted that one day, Prince Maedoc would rule from there when he became king — *if* he became king.

"Faerbane sounds good," Garret said. "What do you think, Etanos?"

Etanos smiled crookedly, eyeing Garret as a father would, nodding slowly. "It sounds good to me," he said.

Aeli came and sat the bundled cakes on the table before them. "Here you are," she said. "These will help you along the way. They are infused with herbs that will keep your strength up and will help you stay alert."

"Thank you, Aeli," Etanos said. "And thank you for your help last night."

Aeli shook her head humbly. "I only wish I could have been more help to you."

Etanos reached into his cloak and produced his bag of coin. "I will gladly compensate you for your help," he said.

Aeli held out her hand in protest. "No. My help was offered to maintain the balance. The Great Mother will repay me in her own way."

Etanos nodded, stuffing the bag back into his cloak. He placed his right hand over his heart and bowed low. "Then I thank you again," he said. "And we shall be on our way."

"Good luck to both of you," Aeli said. "And mind yourselves. Keep watchful wherever you go. I know that out there, somewhere, someone seeks your attention."

"Then we shall be invisible," Etanos said. "Take care, Aeli."

* * *

"She seemed lonely," Garret said as they set off on the path back to the main road.

"I imagine the life of someone like her would be fairly lonely," Etanos agreed, "especially considering the rumors that would persist."

"She didn't seem like a witch; at least, nothing that would resemble the tales of witches that I've heard."

"Agreed," Etanos said. "I have the feeling she is much more than a simple trickster. You asked if she was a druid. Though she says she is not, she has more in common with the druids than she realizes."

"Have you met a druid before?"

"Not directly," Etanos said. "But I've seen them wandering the wilderness of Thyre. Their kind are few and far between, and most of them are simply followers. Their leaders, the actual druids, are seemingly nowhere to be found."

Garret nodded, knowing that on Eirenoch the Great Druid Jodocus was rather elusive himself. Few people other than the rangers had ever seen him, and fewer still had encountered him for at least a thousand years. But everyone knew he was there, working on his own to ensure that the balance was maintained.

"I have the feeling that the life of an assassin is a lonely one, as well," Garret said. "But that is fine with me."

"It can be," Etanos said. "But an assassin must always make time to mingle. Being social is the best way to gather information about your mark. But one must learn to be inconspicuous when doing so. Too many questions and someone will eventually figure out what you're doing. Taverns and markets are the best places. And, if you can find them, thieves are also a good source. They usually demand a bit more gold, but their information is typically more detailed."

Garret thought of Ferrin, who was a member of a noble house. Surely Ferrin, being the thief he was, knew *everything* about his employer, and would probably use that to his advantage one day: maybe even to usurp Darragh's title.

"Do you think Ferrin would ever kill his lord?" Garret asked.

Etanos shook his head. "Not likely," he said. "He doesn't seem like that type. Ferrin is smart, I can tell. He would use other means of destroying Darragh, I imagine. Blackmail, perhaps. Why do you ask?"

Garret wasn't sure why he had asked. There was just something about Ferrin that intrigued him, as if the young man was important somehow, or was at least planning something important. He decided, however, to let the matter go for the moment.

"No reason," he said.

From the corner of his eye, he knew that Etanos was looking at him skeptically. But Garret simply grinned, leaving his mentor to guess.

* * *

In the early evening, Garret and Etanos reached a large sign that indicated *Jax's Pub* was to the north. The road continued to the east, where another sign indicated that the mines were in that direction.

"So," Etanos said. "How do we get to Faerbane from here?"

"The river originates just west of the mines," Garret said. "I remember it from my maps. We can follow the river from there, and we will end up on the cliffs behind the castle."

Etanos held out his hand suddenly, training his ear to the road ahead. Garret stopped and listened, staring at Etanos for clarification. Soon, the sound of galloping horses echoed down the road, followed by the angry shouts of several men.

"Hide," Etanos said, pulling Garret to the side of the road.

They crouched in the brush, ducking down as far as they could as the galloping became louder. Soon, a horse-drawn wagon thundered into view, its driver wide-eyed and fearful. Behind him, several men on horses pursued him at a distance, firing arrows in an attempt to take him down. As he approached, Etanos drew his bow, flipping it open and drawing it back.

"What's happening?" Garret asked, gripping his blade.

"I'm not sure," Etanos said. "But we're going to stop it."

The wagon passed, and the horsemen came into full view. They were all dressed in banded leather mail, with painted faces and the same angry scowl. Apparently, the wagon was of great interest to them, and they were desperate to catch it.

"Bandits," Garret mumbled.

Etanos let loose. The arrow streaked like lightning through the air, striking the ground just ahead of the lead horse. The beast howled like a banshee, skidding on its legs as the arrow burst into a ball of blue flame. Its rider was pitched forward into the ground, landing with a thud and tumbling violently right past them.

Etanos dropped his bow and drew his blades, leaping from the brush. Garret followed, seeing the wagon slow behind them. The riders, seeing their leader taken down, bore down on them, their blades and their bows poised to strike.

Garret dodged an arrow that streaked toward him, rolling out of the way just as it whizzed past his head. Etanos took down a rider with a slash of his blades, spinning around to take down the next. Garret rolled back onto his feet, rising to face a bandit that charged him. He blocked the man's attack, immediately countering with a back slash that knocked the man's blade right from his hand.

The remaining riders dismounted, racing to circle the two of them. Etanos spun and sidestepped to keep them in his view, feinting and striking out to keep them at bay. Garret faced two of them, his saber held above his head, and his dirk out before him in a defensive position.

One of the bandits charged, feinting left and leaping to the right. But Garret was too quick. He struck to his left just as the bandit landed, catching the man off guard with a slash to the thigh, and instantly back slashing the other leg. The bandit howled as he collapsed, gripping his leg. The other bandit charged as well, delivering a quick strike that Garret dodged and parried with his dirk. He spun around, back slashing with his saber, connecting with the man's blade as he struck again.

The bandit sidestepped, striking diagonally just as Garret spun again and blocked with his dirk, thrusting his saber. The bandit leaped back just in time, throwing a punch with his free hand, and catching Garret in the face. The impact knocked Garret back, and he was sent into a daze, his vision blurring and his head spinning.

Through his haze, he heard a double slash of steel, and a groan of pain, followed by the sound of a body hitting the ground. Garret fell onto his backside, dizzy and blind; dropping his blades as he felt his consciousness slipping away.

Soon, the world was black.

* * *

"Garret," a voice said. "Garret, are you all right?"

He opened his eyes, seeing nothing but a blurry form above him. Was it a face?

"Garret," the voice said again. "Wake up."

He felt a hand on his face gripping his jaw and shaking his head from side to side.

"Are you there?"

Etanos' face came into view. Garret blinked as it materialized. His mentor was staring down at him, his face uncomfortably close.

"There you are," Etanos said, smiling.

Garret groaned, closing his eyes as the pain in his head peaked and then subsided. He opened his eyes again, seeing the grin on his mentor's face.

"First time, I imagine," another voice said, its accent thick.

Etanos chuckled. "That must have been quite a punch," he said. "Are you all right?"

"I think so," Garret mumbled. "I'm still alive, right?"

"Somewhat," Etanos said, helping him up to a sitting position.

"What happened?" Garret asked.

He looked over to the man who squatted next to Etanos. It was the wagon driver. He was scraggly but dressed in the clothes of a merchant — an independent merchant.

"Ye took a fine one to th' face, ye did," the man said. "Knocked ye clean out."

Garret rubbed his eyes. "That was a fist?" he asked in disbelief. "It felt like a hammer."

Etanos and the merchant chuckled as they helped Garret to his feet.

"It was a fist," Etanos said. "A well placed punch."

"Aye," the merchant added. "If it 'hadn't o' been fer yer friend here, ye'd be skewered fer sure. Good effort on yer part, tho'."

Garret looked around for his blades, seeing them lying nearby. He reached down to fetch them and felt the dizziness return. Etanos steadied him, holding him up with both hands.

"Thank ye both fer helpin' me," the merchant said. "Those brigands were after me goods."

Garret looked at the bodies that were scattered on the road. There were six in all, now dead and out of business. Three horses remained, wandering aimlessly on the side of the road.

"Who were they?" Garret asked. "And what were they after?"

"Local gang lads," the merchant said. "*The Red Hand,* I believe."

"The Red Hand?" Etanos said. "From what city?"

The merchant went to his wagon, opened up a bag, and reached inside. "No city, really," he said, producing a small pouch. "They have a base outside o' Faerbane, but nothing inside. Last I heard, they were holed up at the mines."

The merchant brought Garret the pouch, opening it and producing a pinch of dried roots. "Here," he said. "This'll help the swirlin' in yer head."

Garret took the root and ate it. It was bitter and chewy, but almost immediately calmed his dizziness.

"Their armor looks familiar," Etanos said. "Do you recognize it, Garret?"

Garret walked over to a fallen bandit, crouching down to move aside the man's cloak. He studied the armor for a moment before he realized that it was nearly identical to the armor worn by the bandits at the convent.

"These are from the same group that was with Daeglan's guards," he said.

Etanos nodded. "It seems this group is connected with the nobles," he said. "At least Daeglan."

The merchant grunted. "That can't be good. But that does explain why they were after me wagon."

"Why is that?" Etanos asked.

"I deal in herbs," the merchant explained. "Healing herbs like the one I just gave th' boy. I was on me way to Argan to deliver a shipment to th' healers there."

Garret stood, curious.

"The nobles of Faillaigh and Gaellos don't like Lucas or his kin," the merchant continued. "Don't like 'em at all."

"Who is Lucas?" Garret asked.

"He be the young healer there in Argan. Doesn't get along with the nobles at all. That's why they try to shut him down, and that's why they hired the gang here to stop me deliveries."

Garret looked at Etanos, who studied him carefully as if expecting Garret to say something. Garret grinned.

"Then I think it's time we put a stop to it," he said. "Shut them down for good."

Etanos grinned. "Where do we find this base of theirs?" he asked.

"Don't know fer sure," the merchant said. "Like I said, they hole up at the mines sometimes. But if you're planning on shutting them down, it'd be a good idea to speak to the magistrate in Faerbane. He don't like vigilantes. Get yerself a warrant, and they're all yours."

"I believe it is already warranted," Etanos said. "This gang is responsible for burning down the convent in Gaellos; presumably at the behest of Lord Daeglan."

The merchant scowled. "Well, if that bastard is next on yer list, I'd be getting' a warrant for that, at least."

Etanos nodded, turning to Garret. "What say you, Garret?" he said. "Are you ready for this?"

"Of course," Garret said, grinning.

"Let me repay yer kindness," the merchant said, going to his wagon. "I've got all sorts of good herbs in me wagon."

"No worries, friend," Etanos said. "We'll just take two of these horses. You can have the other, I suppose."

"All right then," the merchant said. "If yer ever in Argan, look me up. Name's Geir."

"Thank you, Geir," Garret said.

The merchant went back to his wagon as Etanos and Garret selected two horses. Though they were thin and somewhat broken down, they were fine mounts and would serve the two of them well on their journey.

They checked the horses' packs for any supplies that might be useful. Both were filled with dried meats, a skin of water, and wrapped bread. Garret strapped his pack onto his horse, patting the beast on the flank. There was a large scar there, just above the hip, telling him that this horse had seen many a battle; or at least many a whipping.

"Poor thing," Garret said. "I hope its life is better from now on."

"Don't get too attached," Etanos said. "We may have to abandon them if things don't go well at the mines."

Garret nodded. "Right," he said. "But at least they'll be free of those scum."

"True," Etanos said. "Come. We should get to the mines before nightfall. We'll need to scope out the area before we make our entrance. And if we face open battle again, just remember not to block with your face."

Chapter Thirteen

o," Garret said as they traveled the road east. "Where did I go wrong during the battle?"

"Well, my friend," Etanos said, thinking for a moment. "It seems to me like you were focusing only on your opponent's blade. Keep in mind that when your opponent fights one-handed, his other hand is always free as a secondary weapon."

"I see," Garret said. "It never occurred to me that he would use his fist."

"It's a common mistake," Etanos assured him. "It's one that many a beginner makes. Fortunately, it *was* just a fist and not another blade, or a shield, even."

"A shield?"

"Of course. A shield can also be used as a secondary weapon."

Garret thought about it for a moment. He supposed a shield could be used to bash an opponent after an initial attack. He pictured it in his head, swinging a blade and then following through by spinning around in the same direction and bashing the opponent with a back-handed strike with the shield. It seemed effective.

"All right," Garret said. "I can see how that would work."

"Good," Etanos said. "But with a fist, the strike could come as a jab, haymaker, or even a backhand. Any way you look at it that secondary weapon, be it a fist, a blade, or what have you, can be just as dangerous as the primary weapon. Sometimes it can even be more dangerous, especially if your opponent tricks you with a feint and then strikes with that second weapon."

Garret understood. It was starting to make sense. Again, he pictured the scenario in his mind, faking an attack with a sword just to set up a major strike with a dagger. He nodded, grinning. Another good strategy.

"In other words," he said, offering his example, "sometimes, the secondary weapon is used as the primary."

"It's called trickery," Etanos said, grinning. "Assassins do it all the time. It may seem deceitful, but you must remember that it is either kill or be killed. You must do whatever it takes to win the battle, or at least escape with your life. There is no shame in surviving."

"Hmm," Garret grunted.

"When it comes to trickery," Etanos continued, "you have a distinct advantage."

"What is that?"

"You are left-handed," Etanos explained. "That is a rare occurrence and one that few people expect. You can use that to your advantage in many ways. You could learn to take a right-handed stance at the beginning of a battle, even learn to fight that way for a time, and then, when your opponent least expects it, you can switch back to your natural stance and strike with a left-handed blow. *Nobody* would ever expect that."

Garret grinned as he thought about the tactic. It was brilliant. Why hadn't he thought of it before? What better way to surprise an opponent than by switching hands? He had always thought that being left-handed was a surprising thing to face anyway. But making your opponent think he's facing another right-handed warrior, and then suddenly switching...

Brilliant!

"I will have to try that," Garret said.

"Good," Etanos said. "Practice your right-handed stance, and then we will see how you do. Perhaps when we rest for the night, we will try it out."

Garret continued picturing different strategies in his head as they rode. Only occasionally did he pay any attention to the landscape around them. There wasn't much to look at anyway, just trees, the path, and the distant mountains. The tower of Tel Drakkar was far behind them, and only the familiar, jagged rim of the mines could be seen in the distance. There, nestled in the crater of an ancient meteor strike, Garret would carry out his first real mission.

His anticipation grew with every passing moment. Though he knew the two of them were about to put themselves in grave danger, he had faith that Etanos would not have suggested they do it if Garret was not ready, or skilled enough. There was, after all, no guarantee that they would face open battle. They were merely planning on investigating the mines, and the gang, to gather information and possibly hinder them somehow.

But the one thing that stuck in Garret's mind was the gang's connection to the nobles. Both Darragh and Daeglan had some affiliation with them. That much was clear. But what that affiliation was, or why it existed, remained to be seen. Daeglan had hired them to destroy the convent to cover his tracks. That meant they were mercenaries for hire, not just a band of thieves. Darragh used them to hinder the lives of those he didn't like, Lucas the healer, for example.

But what was their true allegiance? Who was their leader, and where was he or she based? That was exactly what Garret wanted to know.

"The Red Hand," he said out loud.

"That's what Geir called them," Etanos replied.

"Who do you think they are?" Garret asked. "Some kind of guild?"

Etanos shook his head. "Doubtful," he said. "They are most likely mercenaries, swords for hire. They're just a group of would-be soldiers, assassins, thieves, all banding together for mutual profit."

"I wonder if they work on their own or if they're simply bandits for hire."

"Likely both," Etanos said. "I've seen many a similar group. They are usually unorganized for the most part, but some of them have been around long enough and have enough members and funds to become somewhat of a guild."

"There are militias in Eirenoch," Garret said. "Sword Sisterhoods and Brothers-in-arms types."

"Those are everywhere," Etanos said. "And they usually work as reserve troops for their king or a local temple. These lower-level gangs will work for anyone who offers them enough money; much like the less scrupulous assassins I told you about before."

"Then they definitely *should* be put out of business."

"Agreed," Etanos said. "But first, we investigate and find out everything we need to know to take them down. Then, if the situation warrants it, we will eliminate their presence at the mines — provided there aren't a thousand of them gathered there, of course."

"I think we could handle a few dozen," Garret said, grinning.

Etanos chuckled. "Your confidence may very well be your downfall," he said. "Confidence is no substitute for a good sense of caution. But, I agree. A few dozen... no problem."

* * *

By the time the sun had set, Garret and Etanos had reached the rim of the mines. They found themselves on rocky terrain that was sparsely wooded, with a massive wall of stone that rose high above them on a steep and treacherous slope. There, on the other side, was the crater where thousands of years of mining had taken place. Generations of men and women had lived there, tirelessly mining the unique and magical metal that an ancient meteor had deposited when it crashed into the Earth.

Though having been depleted throughout the centuries, there remained veins of the material over which countless rival prospectors had fought. Now, after having been abandoned for the most part, the entire complex was under the control of the criminal mercenary band known as the Red Hand. Why they had chosen such a desolate and isolated location was anyone's guess, but Garret suspected those two aspects were that very reason.

There was only one road into the crater, and that would quite obviously be guarded. The bandits would have either blocked it off or posted guards at various places to keep out not only potential miners but the king's soldiers as well. Such a highly defensible route would be nearly impossible to assault, and it was no surprise that the location remained secure against any type of invasion or attempts at reclaiming it.

Garret explained the mine's history to Etanos as best he could. The sisters had given him a fairly detailed history of Eirenoch itself, and had given him a great deal of education about its old structures; including the mines. It was, however, not complete. The finer details of the mine's operational past, and its long list of occupants, were mostly conjecture. But, the sisters had been as thorough as they could be; relating every nugget of information they knew themselves.

Now, as the two sat crouched on the edge of a nearby cliff, they stared in wonder. Over the edge of the rocky wall, they could see the stone and wooden structures that had sat there for centuries. Brick and stone buildings were built against the inside of the rim, connected by various wooden walkways. A few towers jutted high into the sky near the opening to the outside, and those were likely lookout points occupied by sharp-eyed guards. It seemed that the only way in would be up the side of the rim; traversing the dangerous, rocky slope and going over the top.

Etanos sighed as he scanned the scene. Garret sensed his frustration, knowing that his mentor was thinking the same thing that was going through his mind.

"It would be best if we viewed the complex in the daytime," Etanos said. "There is not much to see at the moment."

Garret nodded in agreement. Though there were fires and torches lit all over the inside of the crater, little could be seen on the outside. They would need daylight to plan their ascent up the slope, lest they run into any blockades that would cause them to retrace their steps and plan the whole thing out again.

"Observing is a good idea," Garret said. "It would give us time to prepare as well."

Etanos stood, looking back at the tree line and up at the tops of the pines that lined the cliff.

"Let's climb up and observe what we can in the moonlight," he said. "The inside should be fairly visible. We can plan that out, at least."

Without another word, the two backtracked and chose a tall pine to climb. It would offer them a good viewpoint into the crater and looked fairly easy to ascend.

"Be careful," Etanos said. "And remember not to look down."

Garret grinned just as Etanos jumped up to grab a branch. He followed, leaping onto the trunk and pushing off to grab a smaller branch. With a slight groan, he pulled himself up and began the arduous task of climbing in the darkness. Though he could barely see Etanos, he could hear the man's huffs and puffs as he climbed hand over hand. It was difficult to keep up, as Etanos was surprisingly agile for a man his age.

"Hurry," Etanos said. "You're almost thirty years younger than me."

Garret grinned as he climbed, knowing that Etanos would probably beat him to the top. Though he was quite skilled at climbing, Garret had never done it for any reason other than the thrill. Now, he was doing it for a purpose, and the task seemed more difficult than it had been before. But he pressed on; using every ounce of strength he had to keep up. Finally, Etanos paused near a clear space in the trunk and balanced himself on a thick branch that led out to an opening in the foliage. Garret followed, holding onto a smaller branch above.

He looked out over the crater, marveling at the bustle of activity that was observable in the light of the many torches that burned within. Countless dots of light were spread about, and many buildings could be seen. Many figures moved among them; some of them alone, some in groups.

"Well," Etanos said. "There are definitely more than a few dozen."

Garret sighed. "So, how do we proceed?"

Etanos reached into his cloak, producing a small hand-length cylinder. He held it out and flicked his wrist, and the object extended to four times its length. He grinned, placing the tapered end against his eye.

"What is that?" Garret asked.

Etanos moved the object from side to side, pausing in various places and grunting here and there. He then handed the object to Garret.

"It's a spyglass," he said. "Look through it."

Garret placed it against his eye. Through it, he could see everything he could before, but now it was all closer and more detailed. He grinned. What a fascinating object! He scanned the area below, noting the layout of the complex. It was like a small town, with several concentric rings of buildings and a square in the center dominated by the mine entrance. It was a huge mound of rock, surrounded and supported by wooden beams and stone retaining walls.

"I can see the entrance," Garret said. "I wonder if that's where the leader resides."

"Someone in that position would likely occupy one of the larger buildings," Etanos said, "unless he liked the darkness of a mine."

"That wouldn't surprise me," Garret said. "But you're right."

He moved the spyglass to the buildings in the inner ring. One of them stood out somewhat. It sported a tower taller than many of the surrounding observation platforms. Though it was dwarfed by the towers near the entrance, it seemed like a good place to keep an eye on things.

"I bet he's in there," Garret said, handing the spyglass back. "Look at the building close to the center, with the tower."

Etanos looked through the glass, studying the building for a moment, and then slowly nodded his head.

"That looks good," he said. "But it will be difficult to reach it."

"We will have all day tomorrow to plan," Garret said.

Etanos nodded, pressing the spyglass back into its former state and stuffing it in his cloak.

"Let's get some rest," he said, "and we'll watch some more in the morning. Unfortunately, there will be no fire tonight."

CHAPTER FOURTEEN

ord Daeglan's chambers were dark and silent. The light of a few candles cast dancing shadows on the wooden walls, and the slight wind that wafted in from the open windows gently blew the silk curtains about in a ghostly fashion.

He sat in his large chair, facing the double doors that opened to the balcony. In his right hand, he held his pipe, staring out at the darkness of night as he puffed his favorite herbs and waited.

Soon, he knew, the mysterious assassin would arrive in all her dark glory, appearing as instantly and frighteningly as always. He looked forward to their meetings, as she impressed him in many ways, despite the utter terror she inspired within him by her appearance. He lived for these moments; those moments that set his heart into a fearful rhythm. It gave him a sense of his own mortality, and it was a sense that inspired him to be great.

Fear was a great motivator, he felt; one that could drive any man to do either his best or fail miserably. He liked to think that he always did his best. Failure, in his eyes, was not an option.

He was suddenly overcome with that feeling all at once, and he knew that his contact had arrived. There was no sound, movement, or any other sign of her appearance; only that feeling of dread that she always brought with her. Soon, though, she would make her presence known with that familiar clacking of her boots, and strange, metallic whirring that always accompanied her — when she wished it.

Daeglan smiled as he heard her boots approaching from outside the doors. They only made noise when she wanted them to; that was her thing. Those who knew her, or knew *of* her, knew how she used that sound to carve fear into her victims' hearts. It was the sound of impending doom. It was the sound of imminent death.

It was a sound he loved.

Through the white curtains, a silhouette appeared. It was merely a shadow; one of dark and horrible origin. The assassin herself was evil incarnate; a veritable demon that walked the Earth in material form. Though he knew that she had once been human, her present nature was one of pure darkness and sorcery. Even her shadow exuded a plague of fear and death.

She was pure, dark perfection.

"Well met, Ammarah," Daeglan whispered.

The shadow stepped into the room with a slow and foreboding pace, her boots gently clanking as she walked. The candlelight revealed the glint of metal underneath her black hood where her face would be. Now, it was a mask of iron, forged to display a permanent, menacing scowl. Her black armor shined dimly, and her long cloak billowed almost purposely in an aggressive, witch-like fashion. Her eyes, burning red cinders of demonic energy, glowed brightly beneath the shadow of her cowl, and her raspy breath droned like a rattlesnake's tail in Daeglan's ears.

"I come at my own behest," she replied, her voice a chorus of tormented whispers. "Do not presume to call me familiar."

"My apologies," Daeglan said. "Please, make yourself comfortable."

Ammarah stepped forward, her breathing becoming louder as her frustration grew apparent.

"I will make myself comfortable as I wish it," she said. "You will reveal to me now your reason for summoning me."

"Very well," Daeglan said. "I have received some new information. It seems our... arrangement requires some alteration."

The red in Ammarah's eyes grew brighter, and she stepped forward, raising her right foot and placing it on Daeglan's chair, right between his knees. She leaned in closer, her eyes burning with wrath. Daeglan's heart raced, and his breathing quickened as a wave of lust came over him.

"There are no alterations," she hissed. "I will decide how our partnership proceeds. Is that understood?"

"Of course," Daeglan said. "But my alteration comes with a benefit to you."

Ammarah paused for a moment as the fire dimmed in her eyes. She removed her foot from Daeglan's chair and stepped back, turning away and cocking her head to the side. "I'm listening."

Daeglan puffed on his pipe, blowing the smoke up into the air and staring at it as the candlelight illuminated its billowy mass.

"I believe I have located your man," he said. "This assassin you seek."

"I seek him not," Ammarah said. "His location is always known to me."

"Yes," Daeglan said. "But he has a prodigy, it seems, and I happen to know that they have recently been in Faillaigh."

"I am aware," Ammarah said. "But who is this... prodigy?"

"He is a young man named Garret," Daeglan replied. "He was an orphan under the care of the sisters at the Temple of Gaia."

Ammarah turned back to him. "The temple which you allowed to be destroyed," she said, not asked.

"Yes."

She cocked her head again, her eyes returning to their fierce glow. "What a man you are," she said, "to kill nuns and children."

Daeglan shrugged. "I have killed no one," he said. "It was my bodyguard who decided to burn it down, with my permission, of course. But, if he murdered nuns and children, then that is on *his* soul, not mine. Besides, the Headmistress is under my protection now; she, *and* the children."

"Your protection? I doubt that was your motivation for bringing her here."

"Of course it was," Daeglan protested. "I offered her my protection as a man of honor."

Ammarah hissed. "And who will protect you?"

Daeglan was silent but felt the pleasant stirring in his loins.

"Why do you bring this up?" Ammarah asked. "What is in it for me?"

"Your reason for being here," Daeglan reminded her. "To torment and ruin this assassin before sending him to Hell. That is your wish, correct?"

"You presume to know my wishes?" she accused. "How is that your concern?"

"It is your motivation to serve me," Daeglan said. "You can kill the boy, thus tormenting your target, and ridding me of a pest."

"And how is this boy of any threat to you?"

Daeglan leaned forward angrily. "He killed my bodyguard," he hissed. "And he knows now that it was *I* who destroyed the convent. If such knowledge were to reach the wrong ears, I could be ruined; my title stripped away, and my lands forfeited."

Ammarah chuckled. "And why should I care?"

Daeglan shook his head, grinning. "You shouldn't," he said. "But by killing this boy and his mentor, you will serve us both. Consider it of mutual benefit, and part of your payment for our arrangement."

Ammarah clasped her hands behind her back and paced slowly. "I still have not decided whether to accept your original contract."

Daeglan shrugged again. "No matter," he said. "This is simply a side proposal. Do it, and I will reward you, and you will have what you want and then some. Killing the king is a separate contract."

Ammarah approached him slowly, her hand moving to her blade. "I remind you again," she said. "You tread on dangerous waters. Conspiring against the Firstborn and their servants will incur their wrath. You run the risk of damning your soul to an eternity of torment."

Daeglan smiled, not the least bit daunted by her words. In fact, they excited him. "Well then," he said. "We will finally have something else in common."

Ammarah's eyes glowed brightly. Whether in anger or pleasure, Daeglan couldn't tell.

And he didn't care.

* * *

Helena's heart fluttered when she felt the dark presence in the main building of Daeglan's estate. She awoke suddenly, with a feeling of terror that she could not explain. Even from her small cottage near the edge of Daeglan's estate, the sense of doom was strong. So strong that it had lured her back into consciousness.

Such was the nature of the Great Mother's power.

She stood at her window, looking out toward the largest of the buildings where Daeglan himself lived. There was a single window lit from inside; only by candlelight, but bright enough in the night to be visible. She knew that in that room, something mysterious and dreadful was present. Whether it was Daeglan himself, she could not be sure, but no man could possess so much hate, so much darkness, that it could be felt this strongly.

Not even by a member of the Sisterhood.

Helena felt the tug of duty on her heart. This very presence was why she and her sisters existed. It was their duty to protect the lands from such things. Only they possessed the power to dispel this evil, this utter hatred that stalked the night. But, in the aftermath of the burning of the convent, Helena realized that they were powerless. The fire had prevented them from retrieving their arms and armor from the vault. They were without weapons.

There was nothing they could do.

Only by returning to the ruins of the convent could they hope to arm themselves. But, that was impossible. There was no getting there; Daeglan would never let them leave.

"Damn you, Daeglan," Helena cursed him under her breath.

Under the guise of offering his help, Daeglan had imprisoned them here; all of them, the sisters and the remaining children. They were trapped without any hope of escape, and no means of raising any kind of insurrection. Even if they could arm themselves, attempting to revolt against Daeglan would put the children in danger.

There had to be another way.

Perhaps if she offered him what he truly wanted…

"Helena," a voice said softly behind her.

She turned, seeing Ailin, the youngest of the sisters, standing there. Her eyes were wide, and her brow was furrowed lightly.

She knew.

"Do you feel it?" Helena asked.

Ailin nodded her head, curling her lips back in fear. Helena went to her, embracing her tightly. She knew the young woman was terrified; this darkness was beyond her experience. If there was a revolt, Ailin would not be able to fight at their side; she was too new to the Sisterhood. She had never held a blade in her life, and would likely never do so.

"Do not fear, Ailin," Helena said. "When the time is right, we will escape, and we will destroy whatever it is that Daeglan has brought."

"I cannot take the fear, Helena," Ailin sobbed. "It is too much to bear."

Helena stroked Ailin's hair, trying desperately to find the words to comfort her. The young woman trembled in her arms, and Helena could feel the wetness of Ailin's tears against her blouse.

"I need you to be strong," Helena said. "I know it is difficult, but you must remember that the Great Mother watches over us."

She leaned back, pulling Ailin away so she could lift up her face. "The children need you to be strong as well. We must get them out, and lead them to safety. Only by being strong can we do this."

Ailin swallowed, her tears coming faster, but her lips pressing together in determination. "I will give my life for them," she said.

Helena smiled. "I know you would," she replied. "But there is something else you must do."

Ailin's brow furrowed again.

"Lord Daeglan seems to trust you," Helena said. "Like me, you have caught his attention. He trusts you enough to have free run of this estate. He does not believe that you are capable of standing against him. Use that to your advantage. When you can, flee."

"Flee?" Ailin repeated. "Flee to where?"

"To wherever you can find help," Helena said. "Go back to Gaellos and find someone who can help us retrieve our weapons."

Ailin was silent but nodded her head. She understood, at least. Now, the question was, could she find a way to escape without alerting Daeglan? As far as Helena knew, Daeglan thought the Sisterhood was simply a gathering of docile nuns. If Ailin was able to escape, she did not believe he would have any reason to think it was of any consequence to him; just one nun who slipped through his fingers.

On the other hand, if anyone were to find out that the Sisterhood had been held captive, or that Daeglan had anything to do with the convent's destruction...

"Go back to sleep," Helena said. "All will be well."

She embraced Ailin again in hopes of calming her enough for her to sleep. There was much planning to do, and all of the sisters would have to remain vigilant if they were to escape. If only there was a way to ensure that the children would be safe.

She thought briefly of Garret. He would protect them, she knew; he always had. But he was gone. She had seen him fighting the bandits alongside another man; a stranger she had never seen before. Though she did not know his fate, she had faith that he had made it out alive, and was out there, somewhere, safe and moving on with his life.

Perhaps Ailin could find him, and tell him of their fate. Or, perhaps he already knew that Daeglan had perpetrated the burning of the convent, and was plotting to help them escape.

Helena sighed, not sure whether her hopes were even realistic. Garret was still just a boy, after all, not a military leader. But what of this other man, this dark stranger that had appeared from nowhere? Who was he? Why had he come?

The questions plagued Helena's mind as she held Ailin. Gradually, the young girl began to relax, and Helena dropped her arms and sent her on her way. Soon, Ailin would be able to do her duty and find a way to get the word out to those who could help.

She only hoped that Ailin would find the right person.

* * *

Ferrin lay quietly atop the roof of Darragh's private balcony, casually sprawled out and waiting for his lord and his guest to step outside below. Sometime earlier, past midnight, an unknown guest had arrived, and Ferrin knew that Darragh preferred to talk business outside. The guest's identity was unknown, but the carriage in which they had arrived was oddly non-descript; too non-descript to belong to someone of no importance. It was almost as if its occupant was trying to hide their identity.

And that meant that, whoever it was, their presence was one of the utmost secrecy.

Though the night air was colder than he preferred, Ferrin had taken his hiding spot to eavesdrop regardless. Such an important guest would bring information that may be valuable to Ferrin's plans, or detrimental to them. Either way, he couldn't resist the temptation to listen.

Now, as the sound of locks being opened below caught his attention, his excitement and anticipation grew. He scooted closer to the edge, quietly positioning himself to view the balcony below. Darragh stepped out, placing his hands on the railing and looking out over the lamp-lit lawn that surrounded his estate.

"Now," Darragh said to his unknown guest, "we can speak in private."

"I would prefer the indoors," a female voice said.

Darragh turned, smiling. "I don't trust my servants," he said, "any more than I trust Daeglan or any of the other nobles."

"Very well," the woman said. Her voice was commanding and even-toned. "But if we are all going to work together, you could at least pretend to get along with each other."

Darragh chuckled. "I will do my best."

There was a moment of silence as Darragh's guest, still hidden from view, gathered her thoughts. Ferrin could hear her pacing, but still could not see her.

"There has been a change of plans," she said. "We may have to delay things until the near future; perhaps a year or two."

"What change?" Darragh asked, folding his arms across his chest.

"I am with child," the woman said. "And this has changed things drastically."

Darragh nodded his head, as if in realization. A smile spread across his face; a rotten smile that Ferrin knew all too well.

"This could be a good thing," Darragh said. "Definitely for you, at least."

"The spirits tell me I will have twins. Girls. Do you know what this means?"

"Yes," Darragh said. "Someone to carry out your dark legacy; one of them, at least."

The woman laughed quietly. "Correct," she said. "And when they have been confirmed in court, then we will proceed. But, not until then."

"What of your son?"

"He is of no consequence," the woman said. "Despite his skills, he is not much more than a normal man. He does not have any divine blood at all, it seems; neither mine nor his father's. He merely has the gift of sight."

Darragh turned back around. "So then these twins will carry on your blood?"

"They will," she said. "Or I will end their lives myself."

Ferrin furrowed his brow in disgust. What kind of woman would kill her own children?

Darragh sighed. "I suppose we will have to let Daeglan know as soon as possible. He still plots with this assassin."

Assassin, Ferrin thought. *What assassin?* He thought back to his encounter with the assassin at Gil's shop. He seemed shady, even shadier than Ferrin himself. But he was with Garret, and Joran had said that Garret was living at the convent at the time of its destruction. Surely this assassin was not the one Daeglan just mentioned.

"This assassin is aware of more things than Daeglan," the woman said. "He plays a dangerous game with this woman, or whatever she is. She is much more than just an ordinary murderer. I sense a great amount of hatred in her; hatred that could spoil things if it were to interfere with her mission."

Darragh nodded. "She delays anyway," he said. "Daeglan has had a hard time keeping her interest. She seems focused on something else; *someone* else. Another assassin, he says."

Ah, Ferrin thought. *The plot thickens.*

"That *is* disturbing," the woman said. "She must not be allowed to depart. You know as well as I do that the king is the son of the Dragon. He cannot be killed by any ordinary man. His nature will require someone of her... abilities."

Darragh chuckled. "What?" he said skeptically. "She is just a woman, like any other woman. Don't let his words fool you. There is nothing magical about her. She speaks as if she stepped out of Hell itself, but there is no reason to believe she is any different than her kin."

Ferrin's interest was growing by the minute. What was this talk about divinity? Who was this mysterious assassin, and why was there reason to believe she was something other than just a woman? The questions were stacking up in Ferrin's mind, almost to the point of making him forget that there was a plot to kill the king.

The woman stepped into view. She was clothed in a red cloak, her face concealed. Ferrin pursed his lips in disappointment. He wanted to see her face.

"Be careful, Darragh," she said. "Things are not always as they seem. Get word to Daeglan that we are delaying our plans, and I will take care of the rest. When we are ready, we will strike, and the throne will be mine. Then, you shall be rewarded."

Ferrin scowled. What was this woman saying? Why would she have the throne?

"Very well," Darragh said, bowing. "Your will be done, my Queen."

114

Ferrin's heart skipped a beat.

CHAPTER FIFTEEN

After scoping out the mines for most of the night, Garret and Etanos had found a small cave in the bedrock within the forest. It was warm and dry, and hidden from the outside by trees and brush. They would sleep away the day and awake in the early evening to prepare for their incursion. Etanos had promised to give Garret a few more pointers on his stance, and his defensive moves once they had awakened.

"I can feel them again," Etanos said as he pulled his cloak around him.

"Who?" Garret asked. "The rangers?"

Etanos nodded. "They're all around. It seems they've been following us."

"There are several companies of them," Garret said. "Three or four, at least. But I've never heard of them coming this far south. The nobles here don't like them, at least the ones of Faillaigh and Gaellos."

"Well, I'm sure they'll leave us alone. We're not doing anything to disturb the forest."

"They've likely been watching the mines," Garret said.

"If they were in this area, then I wonder why they didn't protect Geir on the road."

Garret shrugged. "None of their concern, I suppose. They protect the forest, not the road."

"I saw another city in the distance to the west," Etanos said. "Is that Argan, the town Geir spoke of?"

"Yes," Garret replied. "There was a temple there once, deep underground. I don't know whether anyone still goes there, but I hear some of the past knights are buried there."

"Who is the governor there?"

Garret thought for a moment. "I'm not sure. The last I heard it was Lord Halek. He is one of the few nobles of the south who still have loyalty to the throne."

Etanos smirked. "No doubt he is constantly at odds with the others."

"I hear he is a great man," Garret said. "He opens his estate to those who are in need. He is constantly building things and hiring the townsfolk to do the work. He pays well and takes care of them. I would assume he also finances this Lucas and the other healers."

Etanos lay back, closing his eyes. "I hope he has good security, then. He's a man among monsters."

Garret sighed. Etanos was right. Daeglan was a monster, to be sure, and from what Garret heard of Darragh, *he* was no better. Halek may be the one noble in the entire South that deserved to be called *noble*. However, Garret had never met the governor of Faerbane, nor of Ardin or Bray. Perhaps Halek was not alone, but there was no way of knowing.

"Get some sleep, Garret," Etanos said. "Tonight, you become an assassin."

* * *

The setting sun awoke them both as it shined directly into the small cave. Curiously, the golden orange rays illuminated the walls in a strange, shimmering fashion, drawing their attention as they opened their eyes. It was like a flame dancing on the stone.

"What the hell is causing that?" Garret wondered out loud.

Etanos pulled out his dagger, tapping the stone with its tip. A small chunk of it came loose, and Etanos held it up to the sunlight. He grunted and handed it to Garret, who did the same. It was some kind of amber-colored crystal that shimmered in the sunlight as if it had a life of its own. The sunlight almost seemed to bounce around inside, trying to escape. The effect was mesmerizing.

"It's beautiful," Garret said. "I wonder what it is."

He cupped the stone in his hands, leaving only a small space between his thumbs. Inside, the stone still gave off light, as if it had absorbed some of the sunlight and kept it as its own.

"It's still glowing," he said. "It must be some kind of magic crystal."

Etanos chipped off a few more chunks, stuffing them in his cloak. "We may find someone who knows what it is," he said. "Take some for yourself."

Garret drew his dirk, chipping off more small chunks of the crystal. He felt a wave of excitement rush over him, thinking perhaps he had stumbled on some magical stone that he could use to enchant his weapons somehow. Anything that could keep the light of the sun within its depths was surely capable of transferring it to its bearer.

If he ever saw Aeli again, he would ask her.

"All right," Etanos said. "Before we go, let's do a little sparring."

Garret grinned, stuffing his crystals into his pack and scrambling out of the cave. He met Etanos outside, already prepared with his blades drawn and his feet set for battle.

"Take it easy," Etanos said, grinning. "We're not there yet. First, we will meditate."

He cleared the leaves and scrub from the ground around him, forming a space large enough for the two of them. Then, he sat cross-legged, beckoning Garret to take the space across from him. Garret grumbled, putting away his blades and reluctantly plopping down.

"Meditation may seem like a waste of time to those who have never done it," Etanos explained. "But, its effects are very beneficial, especially for those like us. The incense will help you in the future, and you must always remember to use it if you have trouble getting into the proper state of mind."

He closed his eyes, placed his hands on his knees, and allowed his posture to relax. "Find a good balance," he said. "And allow your body to go limp. Let your muscles and tendons relax. Take as long as you need."

Garret closed his eyes, slouching. He focused on relaxing each of his muscles one by one. It was more difficult than he expected, and he found himself jerking upright when he felt himself lean. Gradually, he found a good balance, and the muscles in his back relaxed, followed by his legs, his arms, and finally his face. It was much different than what he had done in the past; only having the drawings to go by.

"Your breathing is important," Etanos continued. "Breath in deep through your nose. Feel the air go into your lungs and through your body. When you feel its energy wane, let it out slowly through your mouth."

Garret breathed deeply, taking in as much air as he could. He held it for a moment, and then let it out without forcing it. He repeated several times, concentrating on each and every breath. He suddenly realized that focusing was the point. By concentrating on his breaths, he became unaware of everything else.

It was quite relaxing.

"Now, with your mind clear, listen to everything around you, every rustling of the leaves, the swaying of the branches, the footsteps of every tiny insect. Open your mind and your awareness."

Garret pictured the outside world in his mind, basing his vision on everything he heard. The forest came to life within his consciousness and eventually took full form. Every tiny sound created a little piece of that reality and imprinted itself in Garret's mind. Even Etanos' breathing painted a picture of the assassin sitting there across from him.

"Now," Etanos continued, "without opening your eyes or changing your posture, rise to your feet and keep crouched."

Garret pushed up with the sides of his feet, rising up and uncrossing them to a crouching position.

"Put yourself in your scorpion stance," Etanos said, "Clenching your fists. Keep your eyes closed."

Garret lifted his right leg, turning his body to the side and putting his arms into position to strike. He held his stance, barely moving a muscle as he waited for the next command. Suddenly he sensed movement and reacted subconsciously. He dropped his right leg, stepping to the side and spinning, swiping back with his left hand to block the fist that he sensed.

His fist impacted with his mentor's.

"Good," he heard Etanos say. "Keep your eyes closed."

Garret felt a rush of pride. He had blocked an attack he hadn't seen. How he did it was unknown, but he suddenly realized that he was being taught how to fight in the dark. Etanos was an excellent teacher.

Another attack came at him, and he skillfully blocked, sidestepping and countering with a punch of his own. He felt Etanos block and immediately counter with a double attack. Garret blocked both attacks, spinning around and taking the scorpion stance again. Etanos came at him quickly, and Garret dropped into the upward kick as he did with the bastard guard in Gaellos. His foot missed, and he felt Etanos' hands wrapped tightly around his ankle.

A foot to the back of his knee flipped him over, and Etanos rolled him into a tight hold. He struggled to breathe, but it was no use; he was helpless.

"You can open your eyes now," Etanos said, releasing him and chuckling.

Garret rolled onto his back, breathless, staring up at his smiling teacher. "That hurt," he said.

"Good," Etanos replied, holding out his hand. "You got lucky with that kick in Gaellos. Work on it more when you have the time. One of the biggest mistakes one can make is to be too eager to use a new move as soon as possible."

Garret got to his feet, wiping the dirt from his cloak. "But it's a good move, right?"

"With a little practice and good timing, it *will* be. But don't expect to break someone's neck every time. Rely on your other moves when possible, and use that as a last resort."

Garret nodded. "I will have to meditate more often," he said. "I could almost see your every move, or... sense it."

Etanos grinned. "Sometimes, you may find yourself in the dark and will need to be able to sense your opponent's moves. Now you know how."

Garret felt a boost of confidence. Etanos' training had given him the means to expand his awareness. Perhaps, in the future, he would be more aware of that secondary weapon every warrior carried, whether it was a blade, a fist, or a shield. He would be ready for anything — he hoped.

"We still have a few hours of daylight left," Etanos said, drawing his blade. "Let's work on that right hand of yours."

Garret grinned, drawing his blades again.

They spent the next three hours sparring. Garret tested out his new blade, finding it well-suited for him and easy to wield. His attacks were much quicker and more accurate than they were before.

Etanos seemed impressed with Garret's skills, but offered his advice on occasion, suggesting ways that Garret could improve each attack. The assassin was familiar with Eastern techniques and helped Garret to perfect them as well as he could. Garret listened intently, eager to learn everything he possibly could in such a short time. He even learned some new moves; both offensive and defensive. But he also remembered Etanos' advice; *don't be too eager to use a new move.*

It would be a hard thing to avoid, Garret felt, as everything he learned was sure to end the fight quickly. However, the most important thing to remember, Etanos taught, was how to avoid direct confrontation in the first place. An assassin must eliminate his target as quickly as possible, preferably without resorting to outright battle.

Get in, retire the target, and get out, he had said.

Tonight, though, there would be no specific target. It was merely an observation mission to gather more information about the gang itself. But, if the opportunity presented itself, their forces would be dwindled in secret.

It would be a long night.

* * *

As the sun began to set in the west, the two observed their side of the crater's wall. There were a few clear paths up the side, with slopes that were traversable with some effort, but they were also guarded. At least four men stood along each path, heavily armed, and seemingly more observant than the guards in the towers.

However, Etanos did not seem worried. As they had agreed, a few dozen were no problem. Four guards should be easy.

"We'll take the path on the left," Etanos said. "Those guards are farther apart, and the path over the rim is much lower."

"I should have practiced with my throwing knives," Garret said, having forgotten all about them.

"There will be plenty of time for that," Etanos said. "One weapon at a time. Eventually, I'll teach you how to use a bow."

That sounded good. Garret had always wanted to learn archery.

"Are you ready?" Etanos asked.

"Ready," Garret replied, not sure whether he was or not.

Etanos was off, and Garret followed right behind him. They crept down the slope toward the left path, keeping behind the rocks that lay scattered about. Ahead, the guards walked slowly along their routes, their eyes moving from side to side as they scanned the landscape. Approaching them would be difficult, but when they did, they would face them one at a time.

"I will take out the first guard," Etanos whispered. "Watch and learn."

Garret nodded, feeling his heart beating with an

apprehensive droning. He wasn't sure he was ready to kill just yet but would know for sure when it was his turn.

"Stop here," Etanos said, pointing to a large rock that sat beside the path.

The assassin moved to the other side, crouching behind a smaller rock. He pressed a finger against his lips, looking at Garret as the two waited for the guard to pass. Garret could hear the man humming and mumbling to himself as his boots kicked up rocks. His heart pounded furiously as the target came closer and closer. Etanos glared, poising his dagger to make the killing blow.

When the man passed by, the assassin went into action.

He leaped up silently, grabbing the man around the neck with his left arm, and plunging his dagger into the guard's back. Garret stared wide-eyed as the guard struggled. Etanos put his weight on the man, dragging him down to the ground until his struggling stopped. He then pulled the man behind the rock, wiping his dagger on the dead man's cloak, and nodded to Garret.

"That's how it's done," he said. "I will take the next one if you're not ready."

Garret shook his head. "No," he said. "I will do it."

Etanos clapped him on the shoulder and the two of them proceeded up the slope. Though the sun was almost completely set, the path was illuminated enough for them to see the next guard. He too plodded along, keeping his attention focused around him. This time, Etanos lagged behind, staying near Garret as he ducked under an outcropping.

"Remember," Etanos said. "Do it as quickly and quietly as possible. It won't always be this easy."

Garret nodded, drawing his dirk and gripping it tightly. His heart was still pounding; not only with fear, but with a sense of regret for something he had not yet even done.

"They're criminals and murderers," Etanos reminded him. "You are the knight. You maintain the balance."

The guard stepped into view and passed by. Garret crept behind him, quickly catching up. He grasped the man's shoulder, spinning him around, and mindlessly plunged his dagger up through the man's chin. There was a gurgle of blood as the guard dropped his spear and clasped Garret's hand. Garret drew the blade out and stepped back, watching as the man crumbled to his knees and pitched forward into the rocks.

Garret stared at him in shock.

"Hide the body," Etanos whispered.

Garret shook his head, bending down to wipe off his blade on the guard's cloak. He grabbed the man's shoulders, dragging him behind the outcropping and rolling his body underneath the underbrush.

"Good work," Etanos said. "A bit risky, though."

"I wanted him to see me before..." he paused, not knowing what he was saying.

"It's all right," Etanos said. "If it helps with the guilt, then by all means do whatever it takes."

Garret nodded, staring back at the body as the two continued up the slope. Though he felt a twinge of guilt, Garret's mind was not as scrambled as it was the night of his first kill. It was simply a shocking moment; one that he would eventually get used to, he supposed.

"I'll take the next one," Etanos said.

They crept forward another twenty yards before the third guard came into view. Curiously, the man was standing still, staring out over the path, but oblivious to their approach. They hid behind another large boulder, waiting for the man to descend. But, he seemed to be reluctant to do so, merely standing there as if sensing that something was wrong.

"Dern," the guard called out. "Are you pissing again?"

Garret glanced at Etanos, who raised his eyebrows, shrugging.

"Dern," the guard said again. He sighed loudly, and began descending, cursing under his breath. "I swear you piss more than an old man."

The crunching of rocks came nearer. Garret moved behind Etanos as the assassin drew one of his swords.

"Watch this," he whispered.

Just as the guard appeared, Etanos dashed across the path. Garret heard the swipe of steel as he quickly passed behind the guard, and saw the man topple without even a groan. Etanos grabbed the man and dragged him into the shadows, emerging again with a grin.

"What was that?" Garret asked.

"A quick slash to the spine," Etanos said. "Painless and instant."

Garret was impressed. The attack had been lightning-fast, and the guard had died instantly. He didn't even have time to drop his spear before he fell to the ground.

"Now, last one. Ready?"

Garret nodded.

They continued, traversing the rocky slope until Etanos motioned for Garret to stop. He stared up for a moment, waiting for the next guard to come into view. Though Garret couldn't see him, it was clear that Etanos could, and he seemed reluctant to continue forward.

"What is it?" Garret asked.

Etanos shook his head. "He's not moving," he said. "He's facing the other direction, up the slope. I don't think he's coming down."

"What do we do?"

Etanos reached into his cloak, pulling out his bow. He flicked it open and drew it back, raising it up as the glow of the magical arrow faded—presumably at his command. Etanos aimed and loosed. There was a thunk, and a slight groan as the guard was hit. Then, the sound of the man's body tumbling down the slope followed.

Garret watched him tumble by and then glanced up at Etanos.

"All right," Etanos said, putting away his bow. "Now it begins. Follow me close."

Garret fell in step behind him, glancing back at the guard as he continued to tumble down the rocky path. He wondered how long it would take before he reached the bottom.

CHAPTER SIXTEEN

he entire mine complex was lit with lamps and torches, making it visible from one side of the crater to the other. There were men everywhere; from heavily armed guards in leather armor, to lighter infantry with ranger-like garb, much like the bandits that had attacked the convent. Stone roads with deep grooves led away from the center shaft, upon which large iron carts were pushed around by what appeared to be slaves.

Garret and his mentor lay prone in a small depression in the crater's rim, passing the spyglass back and forth as they planned their strategy. Etanos glared at the guards that surrounded the enslaved, his teeth visibly gritting with anger. While Garret himself was shocked and angry at the sight of his countrymen in chains, Etanos seemed enraged.

It was quite obvious that freeing the slaves would be their objective.

"I never would have thought that this could happen in Eirenoch," Garret said. "If the king knew about this, he would kill every last member of this band of thieves."

"And they would deserve it," Etanos growled. "But since the king is not here, it is up to us."

Garret looked back down, noting the large number of guards and other warriors that were present. There were dozens, if not hundreds, of them everywhere. They were vastly outnumbered.

"How are we going to do that?" Garret asked. "We are only two. They are... who knows how many?"

"This is where our skills will come into play," Etanos said. "We will find a way to set things in motion before we are discovered. We may even find and kill the leader before anyone knows we're here."

Garret nodded, still skeptical, but eager to help his countrymen escape.

Etanos pointed to a larger building below that sat near the inner slope. There, the walls of the crater had been eroded to the point where there was a nearly vertical surface, and the building itself was a mere five or so yards from it. It was quite a drop, however, nearly fifty feet, and the only way down from this point was over the edge.

Etanos produced his rope, rising to his knees to wedge its hook into a secure spot between two layers of rock. Then, he tossed the rope over the side, watching as it fell to its full length.

"When we get to the bottom," he said, "we will have to swing over to the roof."

"That sounds fun," Garret said, grinning.

Etanos returned the gesture, grabbing the rope and swinging over the side. "Follow about ten feet above me," he said. "If you lose your grip, I want to make sure I have enough time to get out of the way."

Garret chuckled. "Funny."

Etanos dropped into the darkness as Garret pulled on his gloves and grabbed the rope. Garret swung his legs over the side and slid down slowly, keeping the shadowy form of Etanos in his sight. He adjusted his grip to alter his speed, gritting with the strain of holding the thin rope. It was painful, but he knew every second of discomfort would build his strength and make future rappelling that much easier.

"Slow down," Etanos said. "There's a guard below, behind the building."

Garret stopped, looking down. "What is he doing?"

"What do you think?"

Garret grinned, but suddenly had an idea. He reached into his cloak to retrieve a throwing knife. Though he had never thrown one before, he could probably drop it and take out the guard. They were blade-heavy, after all, and should fall straight down.

Conceivably.

He twisted his right leg around the rope, clasping it with his left, and leaned back to hang upside down. His face was right above Etanos' head, and the man glanced up at him with a curious look.

"What are you doing?" he asked.

Garret showed him the throwing knife, dangling it down as

he aimed. Etanos rotated toward the wall, giving him room.

"If you miss, we'll have to climb back up."

"Don't worry," Garret replied. "I can't possibly miss if I just drop it."

"Overconfidence," Etanos reminded him.

Garret ignored him, closing one eye and lining up the dagger with the man's head. It was quite a distance, and the man's head made a small target, but he was confident he could hit it. When he was sure he was lined up, he let go of the knife. It sailed straight down, glinting slightly in the light as it descended. After a few seconds, a groan sounded, and the guard fell straight back.

Garret grinned.

"Good job," Etanos said. "Now you have to climb all the way down to get it."

Garret hadn't thought of that. "Damn it," he said.

Etanos rotated back around, continuing his slide down. Garret reached up and pulled himself upright again, following right behind him. They reached the bottom without incident, dropping onto the ground behind the building. Garret retrieved his knife, and Etanos flicked the rope several times until the hook came loose above. He stepped to the side as it fell to the ground, making only the slightest of sounds as it hit.

"This building looks unused," he said, rolling up his rope. "Check that door over there."

Garret went to the rear of the building. It was stone and brick, with glass windows at about shoulder height. The door that opened up to the back was wooden, with a large keyhole and lever-type handle. It was locked. He looked into the nearest window, seeing nothing but darkness inside.

"It's empty," he said. "But the door is locked."

Etanos joined him, crouching at the door and producing a set of lock picks. Garret watched him as he fiddled with the lock, poking and probing with the picks until he heard a click. Etanos then reached up and pulled down the lever, opening the door slowly and listening inside.

"Clear," he said.

Garret was intrigued. He now had two things he wanted to learn: archery and lock picking.

"Pull the guard inside," Etanos said.

Garret returned to the fallen guard and dragged him by the shoulders, pulling him inside the door. They rolled his body under a stairway and scanned the room they were in. It was sparsely furnished, with dusty chairs and a large table. There were two doors, rows of small windows along the front and back walls, and a number of old, useless sconces that probably once lit the room.

"Nothing of interest here," Etanos said. "This outer circle of buildings must be abandoned. We'll go to the next circle and take to the rooftops."

Garret nodded, following him back outside. They crept to the front corner of the building, scanning the street in either direction before dashing across the road to the next building. There, the lamps lit the street, and the buildings here seemed occupied. The grooved roads connected them all in a network of drop-off points where various materials were separated from the carts. Slaves pushed the carts from building to building, while armed guards directed other slaves to pick minerals from them and carry them inside to be processed. Smoke billowed from some of the buildings, telling them that those were the smelting areas.

"There aren't many guards here," Etanos said. "But I can see more of them on the rooftops. We should take them out first."

Garret looked up, seeing several guards with bows stationed at various points on the rooftops of each building. The roofs were multi-tiered, with plenty of places to hide, and the two circles of buildings were connected with high catwalks made of wood and iron. Guards walked along them, overseeing the activity below. Thankfully, the upper levels were not as well-lit as the ground level.

Garret followed Etanos to the rear of the building, and the two mounted the wall. They climbed to the roof and pulled themselves up over the eave, crouching there and planning their route.

"We'll take out the guards one by one," he said. "Then, we'll worry about the ones on the ground."

Garret nodded, following him to the peak, where they would leap to the next roof. There was a chimney there across the gap, where a guard stood, half asleep. Etanos stared at the man for a moment, looking at the ground behind the building. He then pulled out his bow, summoning an arrow and taking aim. He loosed, hitting the man in the small of the back. There was barely a groan as the guard arched his back in pain, tumbling down the peak and over the edge to the ground below.

Impressive, Garret thought.

Etanos shouldered his bow and leaped across the short gap, landing cat-like on the other roof. Garret followed, landing not so cat-like next to him. They stayed still for a moment, waiting to see if anyone heard them.

"Try to be a bit more flexible when you land," Etanos said. "You'll make less noise."

Garret shrugged.

They crept forward, resting at the peak and peering into the gloom at the other rooftops. A catwalk stretched across the road from the next building, and two guards patrolled it, walking in opposite directions. They each observed their side of the ground level below, passing each other periodically as they walked back and forth.

"We'll ignore them for now," Etanos said. "If we kill them, they may fall to the street below."

Etanos led Garret to the edge of the roof, judging the distance. It was farther than the last gap, and the roof was slightly higher. Etanos backed up a way, still keeping low, and leaped across. He caught the edge, hanging there for a moment before pulling himself up. He then turned and motioned for Garret to jump across.

Garret watched the guard as he reached the end of the catwalk. The man stood there for a moment, gazing into the shadows, and then turned to cross again. Garret jumped across, barely catching the edge, and losing his grip. Etanos caught his right hand, pulling him up to safety before he even had time to panic.

"That was close," Garret said, his heart suddenly pounding. He looked over the edge at the ground below, imagining himself splatting on the stones below.

"You hesitated a bit before you jumped," Etanos said. "Remember when I told you overconfidence would kill you?" Garret nodded. "The opposite will kill you, too."

"I misjudged, I think," Garret said.

Etanos shook his head. "You hesitated. Don't do that."

Garret pursed his lips. He felt shameful to a certain degree, but more embarrassed than anything. Then again, he had almost fallen to his death. Perhaps Etanos was right. He hesitated somewhat; just a little reluctance, he guessed. It *was* quite far.

Etanos continued, staying low behind the roof's peak until they reached the opposite edge. The next building was too far to jump to. However, one floor down, there was a balcony whose edge was just close enough to jump across. Garret searched the wall, looking for something to grab onto. There was only a decorative ledge, barely a foot wide—and even that was sloped and featureless.

"This will be more difficult," Etanos said, lowering himself over the edge. "Follow me down, and we'll get a closer look."

He dropped down to the balcony, immediately pressing himself against the wall and peering into the balcony door. He signaled to Garret to drop down, but to stay on the opposite side. Garret swung his legs over the edge and lowered himself as far as his arms would reach, and then dropped. He now stood across from Etanos, who pointed to the room inside.

There was, apparently, someone in there.

Garret leaned in close enough to get a one-eyed view of the interior. Though the room was dark—lit only by a single lamp— he could see the shadows of two men on the wall. They were speaking in low voices—too low for Garret to hear their conversation. He glanced at Etanos, whose hand was poised around the grip of his dagger. Garret drew his dirk and reached out to tap the glass. Etanos nodded his approval.

Garret rapped a single knuckle against the glass, and the two leaned back, hugging the walls on either side of the door. The men inside stopped talking, and their footsteps were heard approaching the door.

Slowly, the door opened, and the two men stepped outside. Garret and Etanos both stepped forward, grasping their targets around the mouth and plunging their daggers home. The men slumped down after a brief struggle and were dragged into the room and dropped on the floor.

"Good work," Etanos said. "Taking the initiative; I like that."

Garret grinned. "I wonder what they were talking about."

Etanos shook his head, going to the table where the two men were having their conversation. There was a map there, marked with red lines of unknown purpose. They appeared to follow the minor roads, and even the rivers, as if marking trade routes or something similar. Garret studied them, trying to make some sense of their purpose. When Etanos looked at him for an answer, he simply shook his head.

"They don't make any sense to me," he said. "Obviously, they are routes of some sort. But, for what?"

"Distribution of the metals mined here?" Etanos offered.

Again, Garret shook his head. "Most of the blacksmiths along these routes are well-known and honorable," he said. "I doubt they would buy metal mined by slaves."

"Unless they were unaware of what was going on here."

Garret shrugged. "True," he said. "I don't suppose the Red Hand advertises the fact that they use slaves... or that they even run the mines now."

Footsteps sounded outside the door, causing the two to reach for their blades and separate, going to the shadows as someone approached the room. The door opened quickly, and a guard stepped in.

"You two need to finish the map," the man said as he entered. "Lord Daeg—"

He froze as he looked up, seeing the bodies of his comrades lying on the floor. His eyes immediately went to Garret's position, shot wide open, and he turned to bolt back out the door. Without thinking, Garret reached for a throwing knife, drawing it out and flinging it at the man's back. The knife caught him in the base of the skull with a wet *thock!* He pitched forward, slamming into the wall, and crumpled to the floor.

Garret exhaled quickly, surprised that he had gotten such a good shot. Etanos stared with a grin.

"Excellent hit," he said, going to the man's body.

Etanos dragged him behind the table, dropping him near the others. Garret stood frozen with disbelief.

"I can't believe I hit him," he said. "I didn't even realize I was throwing the knife until it was already flying through the air."

Etanos pulled the knife from the man's skull, wiped it off, and tossed it back to Garret.

"That's instinct, my friend," he said. "I knew you had it in you. It was bound to come out eventually."

Garret slid the throwing knife back into its belt and gathered up the map on the table. He rolled it up, stuffing it in his boot. He opened the door again, and he and Etanos stood on either side of it to listen. Apparently, something was happening in this building, and Garret knew they would have to investigate.

"So," Etanos said. "What do *you* think?"

Garret shook his head. "Something here is being smuggled," he said. "And I doubt it's just materials."

"What are you thinking?"

"People maybe?"

Etanos Shrugged, giving him an agreeable glance. "It's as good an idea as any," he said. "Let's find out."

Etanos crept out the door first, moving to the opposite wall after glancing left and right. Garret followed, staying behind him and crouching as he decided which way to go. He listened closely, hearing no sounds from either direction. The only difference between left and right was the dim light that came from around the left corner.

"There may be something that way," Garret suggested.

Etanos nodded, hugging the wall as he approached the corner. As they neared, the sound of voices echoed down the hallway. Etanos peered around the corner for a second and then turned back to Garret.

"Two guards about ten yards down the hall," he said. "Facing the opposite direction."

Garret drew his dirk, giving his mentor a nod. Etanos turned back and crept around the corner, his own dagger in his hand. Garret followed close, padding along as silently as they could. The two guards stood still, not making any indications that they were on patrol, or even interested in having a conversation.

They passed two open doors, one on each side, leading to small bed chambers with multiple bunks. They stopped to peer inside each one, making sure no one was slumbering away in either room. Then, as they turned back to the hallway, Garret's foot scraped against the door. They both dashed into their respective rooms, crouching near the doorways as the guards came to attention. Garret's heart pounded. He looked across the hallway, seeing Etanos shake his head.

"Did you hear that?" a guard asked.

"I didn't hear anything," the other said. "Have you been hitting that pipe again?"

There was a moment of silence, then, "What is *that* supposed to mean?"

"Nothing," the other said. "Let's go look."

Garret pressed closer to the door, seeing Etanos do the same. His mentor nodded, holding up his blade. Garret guessed he meant they were going to kill the guards as opposed to letting them pass by.

"Where the hell is Velkin?" a guard said. "He was supposed to grab the map."

"Who knows? He's an idiot. He probably got lost."

Just as the two guards came into view, Etanos leaped up. Garret grabbed the guard nearest him from behind, wrapping his arm around the man's neck and jabbing his dirk into his back. Both guards struggled for a moment as they suffocated and bled until finally, they went limp. Garret and Etanos dragged their prey into their respective rooms, dropping them onto the lower bunks.

"Another close one," Etanos said as they met outside again.

"Sorry," Garret said. "I need to watch where I'm going."

"New boots," Etanos said with a grin. "You're just not used to them yet. Come."

They continued down the hallway to the guards' post. There, the hallway ended with an alcove on either side and a stairway leading down. Each alcove was decorated with a strange statue depicting a hammer-wielding miner. The statues were old, cracked, and covered in dust; obviously uncared for.

The stairway was dark, the same width as the hallway, and led down to a dimly-lit open area. They crept downward, listening for any signs of life. As they reached the bottom, they saw that the room was small, empty, and open to the outside. The front door was closed, and the windows on either side were sealed shut. Outside, the bustle of activity was barely audible.

"The office must have been the only area of interest," Etanos said. "That means the map was what was being guarded."

"If the man I killed with the throwing knife was sent to fetch it, then someone is expecting him."

Outside, the cracking of a whip caught their attention. Through the window, they could see a guard walking among the moving carts, directing the enslaved men to their appropriate destinations. He whipped them savagely for no apparent reason as they passed; already struggling to push the heavy carts.

"He's coming this way," Garret said. "Maybe we could lure him inside and convince him to help us out."

Etanos nodded, watching as the man neared. Then, he reached out and pushed down the door's lever, pulling it open and staying behind it. The guard's attention focused on the door, and he watched it closely, evidently expecting someone to emerge. He continued tormenting the workers, glancing at the door occasionally; each time, his expression became more stern and curious.

Finally, he coiled up his whip and hung it on his belt, drew his blade, and headed for the door.

"He's coming," Garret whispered.

Etanos readied himself, moving to the edge of the door and wiggling his fingers in anticipation. The guard stopped a short distance away, gripping his blade, and peering inside.

"Velkin?" he called. "Are you in there?"

When there was no answer, the guard shrugged and shook his head. "Idiot," he cursed. "Can't close a damn door."

He went right for the opening, carelessly coming into the room. *"Velkin!"* he shouted, just as Etanos leaped up and grabbed him from behind. Garret kicked the door closed, keeping watch at the window as Etanos dragged him deeper into the room.

The man struggled to break free, but Etanos threw him to the floor, smashing his face with his fist, and knocking him limp.

"Quiet," Etanos said calmly as the man grasped his nose.

Etanos held him down with a knee, drawing his dagger and holding it to the man's throat.

"I need some answers," Etanos said. "And you're going to give them to me or I will jab this dagger into your brain. Understand?"

The guard nodded, wide-eyed.

"The map," Etanos continued. "What is it for? What are the red lines?"

"T-tunnels," the guard said.

"Tunnels for what?"

The guard shook his head, seeming unwilling to answer. Etanos punched him again, knocking his head against the stone floor. The man groaned with the impact, and blood ran from his shattered nose.

"The network," he groaned.

Etanos pressed the tip of his dagger against the guard's throat. "You're going to have to be more helpful," he hissed, leaning in closer. "What network?"

"To connect our bases," the guard said. "The slaves will build them once we clear out the mines."

"Where is your leader?"

The guard turned his head, ignoring the question. Etanos pressed the dagger harder, drawing a pained growl from him.

"Where is your leader?"

"There *is* no leader," the guard answered. "Only bosses. They are all equal."

"Fine," Etanos said, glancing at Garret. He looked back down, leaning in closer. "Then where is the boss of this mine?"

"In the armory," the guard said. "The stone building on the north side of the center ring."

Etanos nodded, grinning at Garret. "Perfect," he said. "Right where all the weapons are. We'll give the slaves a good supply of them once we kill him."

Garret grinned. Etanos gave the guard one last punch in the jaw, knocking him senseless. "Thank you, sir," he said, rolling the man over and searching his pockets.

Garret looked back out the window, seeing a patrol of men going by. They ignored the building but looked around curiously. They were probably looking for the guard who was now unconscious on the floor.

"We might have company," Garret said. "Guards outside."

Etanos grunted as he tied the man's hands with his own belt. Another swatch of cloth was bound tightly around his face between his teeth. Etanos stood, grabbing the guard's collars.

"Help me drag him back upstairs," he said. "We'll hide him and get to the armory. This operation is about to be shut down."

Garret grinned, feeling the pride of accomplishment. The mission—as it were—was going well. Not only would they shut down a major hub of a criminal network, but they would be freeing several slaves, as well. With the map, the locations of the other bases would be easy to discover, and the entire network could be brought to its knees.

And the common folk of Eirenoch would be none the wiser.

CHAPTER SEVENTEEN

uros and his company emerged from the thick forest just north of the mines. Having seen the strange foreigner and his young companion following the path east, Baelion had ordered the young lieutenant to follow them and observe their behavior. The old ranger was suspicious of everyone, as most experienced rangers were, but this oddly dressed man seemed much too out of place to be any ordinary traveler.

Baelion trusted Kuros to lead the company quite often as of late. The young man showed promising leadership abilities, and the men trusted him and followed his orders as if he were their captain.

It was a good feeling for the young ranger, and it only encouraged him to perform his duties to an even greater degree of proficiency.

The rim of the crater rose high above them, and the rangers stood at its base, scanning the darkness for any sign of the pair's passing. Scouts that had been dispatched earlier reported that several bodies were lying near the base along one of the paths. Strangely, they said, there were no signs of battle—the victims had not even drawn their weapons.

"We may be dealing with a rivalry here," Kuros mused. "Two men, one of them my age, enter a known criminal compound for unknown reasons. If the bodies had not been found, I would assume the two are members of this organization. But that is, apparently, not the case."

"They're criminals," Turgon said. "The two strangers may be hired assassins and would have no qualms about killing lesser guards. I've seen this before, back in Taryn. That's the way these gangs work. Very chaotic."

"Still," Kuros protested. "They've done nothing that would indicate any wrongdoing. They killed an entire group of these scum on the road."

"Sure," Turgon said. "But why would they just walk into a nest like this? That would be suicide. They *must* be connected with them somehow."

"Or," Kuros said, clapping his friend on the back. "They are more skilled than we thought."

Turgon smiled, shaking his head. "Always the optimist," he said. "Shall we assist them, then?"

Kuros grinned. "I think it's time to put this organization to rest," he said. "Orders or not. The people need these mines back."

"No doubt Ferrin would love to get his hands on some of that metal," Turgon joked.

"Right," Kuros replied with a laugh. "He'll be the first one to visit."

Kuros drew his bow, signaling to the rest of the men to follow as he started up the slope. Tonight, he would lead the company in his first military action. He only hoped he would keep them in one piece.

* * *

Etanos climbed onto the balcony's railing, judging the distance to the ledge across the gap. Garret watched him in anticipation, unsure as to whether he could make the distance himself. He was, however, confident that Etanos could make it.

And he was right.

The assassin leaped like a panther, grabbing onto the ledge and pulling himself up to a small window that was higher up. He used the sill as a ladder, stepping up onto it and reaching up to grab the eave. When he had rolled up onto the roof, he turned to look at Garret.

"It's not that far down," Etanos said. "So, if you miss, it won't hurt too bad."

"I won't miss," Garret grumbled, climbing onto the railing. "Not this time."

He balanced himself, focusing on the ledge as he steadied his heartbeat. He closed his eyes, taking a few deep breaths and picturing himself leaping across. When he was confident enough, he opened his eyes, took a deep breath, and leaped.

His knees slammed against the hard stone wall, jarring his bones, but his fingers caught on to the ledge. He growled lightly as he pulled himself up, swinging his left leg onto the ledge to get leverage. Etanos reached down to offer his assistance, but Garret shook his head. He pushed up with his leg and grabbed the windowsill, pulling up just as Etanos had done.

He reached the eave with a triumphant smile, prompting a chuckle from his mentor. Etanos clapped him on the back.

"Good," he said. "You're catching on. Let's take out all the guards we can on the way to the armory. We'll start with guards on the catwalk."

"What about the patrol below?"

"As long as they don't fall," Etanos said, "the guards below will never know."

Garret nodded and followed Etanos up the peak. Across the gap, the closest guard was approaching the end of the catwalk, where he would stand for a moment before turning around. Both guards would have to be taken out at the end of their paths, or else they could very well fall to the street below.

From their viewpoint, Garret and Etanos were higher up and had a better view of the street. The patrol that had passed by was long gone, leaving only a few scattered guards here and there among the slaves. Garret glared at them with hatred, his heart pounding as the image of a Red Hand burned in his mind. He would remember that symbol forever and would hunt down any man that bore it.

His hatred was obvious.

"Ease your anger, my friend," Etanos said. "Anger only leads to poor judgment."

Garret sighed. Though Etanos was right, he couldn't help the feeling. He was seeing his countrymen enslaved and tortured — by his countrymen. It didn't make any sense to him. Slavery was evil in any case, but to enslave your own people...

That was unheard of.

"I know what you're feeling, Garret," Etanos assured him. "I feel it, too. It's probably not as strong in my case, since these are not my people. But I do feel it. To see another man enslaved is infuriating, no matter what the circumstances."

"I will never allow a man to remain a slave," Garret said. "If I see a slave, I will free him, no matter what the cost."

He felt Etanos' firm grip on the back of his neck, and he knew his mentor was proud to hear his words.

"That," Etanos said, "is the heart that drew me to you. Never forget that vow. And never forget that justice must sometimes come in the form of a deadly shadow; a silent hand that watches over the people and keeps them safe without their knowledge."

Garret gritted his teeth but breathed deeply and slowly to calm himself. Though the symbol still lingered in his mind, his blood cooled, and his heart began to slow. He would not allow his anger to cloud his vision or his judgment. To do so would only result in failure; now and forever.

"Ready," he said.

Etanos reached out and pried a shingle from the roof, waiting for the guard to reach the end of the catwalk before tossing it across the gap and onto the far side of the roof. The guard was alerted to the sound, and drew his blade, ascending to the roof's peak. He stood at the peak for a moment, peering downward and pointing his sword around as if warning the empty air.

Etanos drew back his bow, letting loose an arrow that plunked right into the side of the guard's head, just behind his right ear. The lifeless man pitched forward without a sound, tumbling and sliding to the eave before coming to rest right at the edge. His sword fell into the gutter, clanking slightly with the impact.

The two then turned to watch the other guard as he reached the end of his path and started back to cross to their side. Etanos readied his bow again, and Garret watched the street below. There was a guard on the opposite side of the street, just below the higher guard's current position. Closer to their side was a slave perusing a cart brought to him by another man, picking out several choice samples of materials.

Garret shifted his attention back to the guard on the catwalk. The man mindlessly walked across, keeping his attention focused on the street below him. When he reached the end of the catwalk, he stopped, looking around as usual. But, as he began to turn back, he suddenly paused, turning around again as if realizing he had not passed his companion. He drew his blade, frantically searching the rooftops.

Etanos fired just as the man opened his mouth to shout. He fell in place, toppling forward onto the roof and dropping his blade. Garret winced as the sword clanked on the gutter and tumbled to the street below.

Etanos cursed in his own language; a word Garret didn't

understand, but whose meaning he could guess.

Garret pulled himself up to the peak, peering down to the street. The man he had seen earlier was looking around suspiciously as if taking note of the positions of the guards. The slave who brought the cart looked up in confusion, and the two glanced at each other, shrugging. The foreman bent down to pick up the blade, stuffing it in his coat and nodding at the other man.

Etanos sighed. "Well," he said. "That's one-armed slave. Only a few hundred to go."

* * *

"What the hell is going on here?" Kuros wondered out loud as he and his company observed the mine from the rim.

He was surprised and angered to see the scene below. The mines were active, and there were men among them who were working against their will. He shook his head in disbelief as he watched uniformed men whipping and shouting at them in anger.

"Slavery?" he hissed.

He looked at Turgon, whose jaw was clenched tighter than Kuros had ever seen it. Even his face was red with rage, and a thick vein pounded quickly at his temple.

"This is an outrage," Turgon said. "The king would slaughter every last one of these devils."

"The king is not here," Kuros growled. "It's up to us."

Turgon nodded aggressively, his grin widening. "We will send them to hell at your order, brother," he said.

"Sir," a voice said behind them.

Kuros turned to see a younger ranger creep up, his attention focused on the southwest.

"You should see this," the ranger said.

Kuros and Turgon followed him to another gap a few yards away. The young ranger pointed to a group of several buildings in the second inner ring. Kuros peered into the darkness, seeing two shadows running quickly along the rooftops, leaping across them with great skill and stealth. He smiled as he realized that these were the two strangers they had been watching.

"It's them," he said. "I knew they were up to something."

Turgon chuckled beside him. "Something good, I see," he said. "I was wrong."

Kuros shot him a humorous glance. "You're always wrong," he said. "That's why I'm in charge."

Turgon laughed, shaking his head as he drew his bow. "Well," he said, knocking. "We'll just see which one of us is the better archer."

* * *

"We'll cross here," Etanos said, pointing to an abandoned catwalk.

They crept across quickly, avoiding the gazes of the guards that were around. They were becoming more frequent on this side of the compound, and there was little chance the two of them could reach their destination without alerting them. They would have to kill them all.

As they reached the inner ring of buildings, two guards appeared on the peak of the roof before them. Etanos motioned for Garret to take the guard on the left, and the two drew their daggers. They crept up behind them, staying in the shadows of the oddly placed chimneys, and silently took them out, dragging their bodies into the darkness.

Garret could see the armory on the opposite side of the circle. It loomed above the other buildings, with fortifications at each corner. Guards were posted atop the short towers, visible under the burning light of some magical spell.

Below, at the center of the circle, the mine entrance was bustling with activity. Slaves worked the winches that brought carts full of material to the surface, placing them on tracks that would distribute them to the appropriate processing buildings. Guards were all around the structures, and it was clear they were heavily armed, especially for thieves. From the looks of it, it was quite a large operation.

"This isn't a simple group of thugs," Garret said.

Etanos shook his head. "No," he agreed. "This organization is much larger than that. It's hard to believe they could operate under the king's eye,"

"They've been paying off the nobles," Garret guessed. "It's the only explanation. The nobles have always been greedy. They would kill their own mothers for a chunk of whatever is coming out of that mine."

"And silence those who would get word to the king," Etanos added. "They've got the revenue, and the arms, to do so."

"Not for long," Garret said.

Etanos flashed a crooked smile. "I like your spirit," he said. "Let's get to that armory."

They crept to the edge of the rooftop, crouching behind the peak and scanning the path before them. There were at least half a dozen guards posted atop the buildings between their position and the armory, scattered randomly on each rooftop. Etanos drew his bow, pulling back and taking aim at the nearest one.

But the guard fell before he loosed, dropping in place and sliding down the slope a short way before coming to rest near the edge.

"What the hell?" Etanos said.

Garret scanned the area, looking for any sign of the archer. He could see nothing, only the torches and lamps that lit the streets, and the men who pushed the heavy carts.

"It came from the north," Etanos said. "But it's too dark to see anything."

He stood, putting away his bow and leaping across the gap to the next roof. Garret followed, landing squarely and silently behind him. They approached the guard's body, and Etanos plucked the arrow from his back, showing it to Garret.

"Do you recognize it?" he asked.

The arrow was simple, unstained wood with crow feather fletching and an iron point. He nodded knowingly.

"Rangers," he said. "That's what they use."

Etanos dropped the arrow, shrugging. "This is getting more interesting by the moment."

* * *

"Excellent shot," Kuros said. "My turn."

He drew back his bow, aiming at the next guard. The two strangers leaped across to his target's roof, sneaking along the edge near the gutter. Kuros loosed, watching his target until his missile struck. The guard collapsed straight down, sliding only briefly. The strangers stopped again, looking around in confusion.

"Take down the rest," Kuros said. "We'll spread out around the rim and keep a close eye on what's going on. Keep them covered until we figure out what they're doing."

Turgon nodded and turned to order the men to take position. Kuros watched the strangers, admiring their persistence, and noting the fact that the older one seemed to constantly glance at their exact position. His awareness was more acute than the younger man's; much more acute than the average thief.

He was something different altogether; someone to be feared.

Kuros looked forward to meeting him.

* * *

Etanos paused as the third guard fell. The two crouched at the peak and watched as each guard toppled in turn until the rooftops were cleared. They now had an unhindered path directly to the armory, with only the guards at each corner tower keeping watch over the streets below.

Garret followed Etanos closely, noticing how he continually glanced at the north side of the dark rim. He guessed that the rangers were up there, somewhere, but there was no way of telling. He trusted in his mentor's instincts, however. They had consistently been correct in the past.

"Can you see them yet?" he asked as they leaped to the next roof.

"Not yet," Etanos replied. "But I know they're up there. I can tell by the direction the guards fell, and the angle of the arrows in their flesh. That's one thing you must learn."

Garret focused on his running as he listened. The leaps across the gaps were getting easier, and he felt a strange sense of calm settling over him. It felt like he was watching himself run, jump, and creep from someone else's body. It was a strange feeling, but one that gave him confidence in his abilities.

The last rooftop was taller than the rest, but he and Etanos leaped across effortlessly, catching onto the eave and pulling themselves up without a second thought. There, under the shadow of the two closest towers, they paused.

"The angle is too high for a bow," Etanos said as he assessed the guards' positions. "We'll climb up, keeping to the outsides — but out of the lights. Take your guard out with your dirk, and I'll hit the other two towers with my bow."

Garret nodded, seeing his path up the tower begin to flicker with life in his mind. On Etanos' signal, they burst from the shadows and latched onto the towers; Etanos on the left, and Garret on the right. Garret glided up silently, following the golden path with very little effort. He glanced across at the other tower, seeing Etanos disappear around its side.

When Garret neared the top, he slowed. He could hear the guard walking back and forth above him, mumbling curses to himself. Garret pressed against the stone, listening for the guard to walk back across to the far side. When he heard the guard sigh and walk in the other direction, he pulled himself up over the edge and dropped into the tower's enclosure.

Without a sound, he drew his dirk and crept up behind the guard, grabbing him around the neck and jabbing the dirk deep into his back. There was very little struggle as he dragged the man to the floor; only a slight moan and a jerk.

He had killed him almost instantly.

He wiped his dirk clean and peered over the battlement to the next tower. Etanos was already poised to fire his bow across the roof to the next two towers. An arrow streaked across, then another; both hitting their targets. Etanos nodded to him, pointing down.

There was a trapdoor on the floor. Garret straddled it and pulled it open carefully. A ladder led down into the torch-lit room below. He mounted it, gripping its sides and sliding down quickly, drawing his dirk at the bottom. He was in a small room the same width as the tower. It was all but empty, with only a few crates piled in one corner near the door. Mice scurried away as he moved to the door to look out.

The room opened up into a square hallway that connected all four towers. From his room, Garret could see two doors opening into a center area, probably the central stairway. Etanos whispered to him from down the hall, and he met him in the center.

"There are probably doors on all four sides," he said. "And the room in the center is likely guarded."

"Where do you think the leader is?"

Etanos shook his head. "One floor down, I would imagine," he said. "From what I saw, it's the only floor with windows that opened to the center. That would be a good place to oversee things."

There was a sudden squeak of metal to their right as the door handle turned. Etanos grabbed Garret and pulled him behind the door just as it opened. Two guards stepped into the hallway, closing the door behind them. They barely had time to part ways before the assassins were upon them.

With quick and silent blades, Garret and Etanos dispatched them, dragging their bodies to the corner room on Garret's side. After piling them behind the crates, Etanos grinned.

"Well, I suppose the room isn't guarded anymore," he said.

He was right.

The room was perfectly square, with a vaulted ceiling and a large stairway that dominated the center toward the south wall. The rails that surrounded it were old and rickety, and the room's floor was pitted and rotted somewhat from water dripping through the roof throughout the years.

The stairway led down to another room, where the two men could see the feet of a pair of guards facing their direction. They were posted just outside a set of double doors where the leader was most likely stationed. After assessing the view, Etanos pulled Garret behind the railing.

"We need to get the guards' attention and draw them up here," he said. "There's no way of knowing whether there are more guards down there or not, but it's the only way to proceed."

Garret had an idea. He reached into his cloak and retrieved a handful of the fiery crystals they had found in the cave. They sparkled brilliantly in the dark as he opened his hand, casting flame-like light on the walls around them. Etanos grinned. He reached out and grabbed a few of them, tossing them against the wall at the top of the stairs. They bounced off, flickering as they impacted the stones, and came to rest just at the edge of the top step.

They heard the muffled whispers of the guards below, and the shuffling of their boots as they reluctantly stepped forward. Garret could make out the words, "What is that?"

Etanos drew his bow, and Garret pulled out a throwing knife. They waited in silence as the guards debated with each other. Finally, their boots hit the stairway, and the two assassins readied themselves. The guards ascended, keeping their spears at the ready as they climbed. When they reached the top, they stopped, staring down at the crystals.

"Where did those come from?" one of them asked.

Etanos took him out with an arrow, and Garret flung his knife at the other, catching him in the shoulder. The guard turned with a groan just as his partner collapsed, and Etanos finished him off with another arrow. Garret immediately rushed to their bodies, pulling one guard out of view. Etanos grabbed the other, pulling him behind the railing. Then, they fetched the spears, tossing them aside.

Garret retrieved his crystals, stuffing them back into his cloak as they descended the stairway. The hallway below was empty, lit only by torches on either side of the double doors. Smaller stairways opposite the door led downward on either side, disappearing into the shadows below. Etanos approached the doors, pressing his ear against the wood to listen while Garret kept watch on the stairways.

"A group of men," he whispered. "Four, at least; maybe five, or more."

The sound of footsteps echoed up from one of the stairways. Garret moved to the other, and Etanos followed him. A few seconds later, two men in rags appeared, escorted by a single guard armed with a long spear pointed at their backs. The men stopped at the double doors, standing to the side as the guard set his weapon against the wall.

"The boss will decide what to do with you," the guard said. "I hope for your sake he will be merciful."

As the guard reached for the door, one of the men looked up. Garret grinned back at him, and the man's face brightened. Without thinking, Garret drew his dirk, pouncing on the guard and drawing him back. He silenced the struggling man for good, dragging him to the larger stairway. Etanos gestured for the men to stay silent until Garret returned, having pulled the dead guard up the stairs with the rest of them.

"Where is the armory?" Etanos said.

"The ground floor," one of the men replied. "It's unguarded from this side, but there are men stationed just inside the main doors."

Etanos nodded. "Go up these stairs and hide," he said. "When we return for you, you will lead us to the armory, and we will clear the way for the slaves to arm themselves. Take the weapons you see up there."

The men reluctantly agreed, staring at each other in fear as they wandered up the stairs. Etanos waited for them to disappear, then reached out for the door handle, drawing one of his blades and glancing at Garret.

"Are you ready?" he asked.

Garret put away his dirk, drawing his saber and taking a few deep breaths. "Ready," he said.

Etanos turned the handle.

The door creaked as it opened, and six men slowly turned to see Garret and Etanos standing there with weapons drawn. A richly dressed man in a fine tunic stepped away with a look of horror on his face. The others drew their weapons.

"Who the hell are you?" a man in chainmail asked.

Etanos strode confidently into the room, drawing his other blade. Garret followed behind, eyeing the tunic-wearing man, obviously a merchant.

"We are knights of the kingdom of shadow," Etanos said. "And we have come to put an end to your enslavement of the people of Eirenoch."

The man in chainmail laughed. "The two of you?" he mocked. "We have over one hundred men at this mine. Guards, get these rats out of my sight."

The remaining four men charged. Garret rolled to the side as a spearhead was jabbed in his direction, and he rose and spun to slash at his attacker's legs. The man screamed as his tendons were severed, and Garret finished him off with a thrust to the back. He immediately charged the second opponent, striking in a diagonal attack while leaping from side to side. The guard was caught off balance as he tried to strike, and Garret back-swung, slashing a deep gash into the man's flank.

Etanos had finished his opponents and charged the leader. The tunic-wearing man was sidling around the perimeter in an attempt to escape. But Garret cornered him, pointing his blade at the scowling man's face.

"Who are you?" Garret demanded.

The merchant suddenly charged forward, and Garret heard the ring of steel as a dagger was drawn. The blade shot toward him as the merchant thrust, almost in slow motion. Garret's senses seemed to slow everything down, and he effortlessly stepped to the side, spinning around and ending up back-to-back with the merchant. He turned his blade and thrust backward, feeling the resistance of flesh as it poked through the man's back.

The merchant dropped his blade, and Garret withdrew his own, turning to watch the man crumble to the floor. Though he was mortally wounded, he was still alive and attempting to crawl away. Garret grabbed the cloth at the back of his neck, rolling him over to look down at his face.

"I asked you a question," he said. "Who are you? Why are you working with these thugs?"

Through the sounds of Etanos and the leader battling the man's whispers were barely audible. But Garret knew better than to lean closer. There was no telling how many daggers the merchant had stashed in his cloak. Instead, he pulled the man up to him, letting his arms hang limply behind him.

"Who are you?" he demanded again.

"Lord Daeglan... will have your head for this," he choked. "You and your precious Helena."

"What?" Garret hissed. "How do you know me?"

The merchant began chuckling weakly. Garret's heart raced in fury as he stared at the man's mocking expression. The hatred within him built as he pictured Helena's face, begging for mercy at the feet of Lord Daeglan. But a noble wouldn't harm a sister. He wouldn't dare.

"Where is Daeglan keeping her?" Garret hissed.

The merchant fell limp and lifeless, dangling in Garret's grasp. Frustrated, he slammed the man back onto the floor, standing up to glare at the leader who now battled his mentor. Fearlessly, Garret came up behind the man and waited for Etanos to see him. When he caught his mentor's attention, Etanos round-kicked the leader in Garret's direction. The man spun and stumbled toward him, and Garret met him with a thrust to the gut.

The leader dropped his blade and fell to his knees. Garret kept his grip on the man's cloak, glaring into his face as blood trickled from his crooked lips.

"Where is Lord Daeglan's house?" Garret asked.

The leader choked and spit, nearly losing consciousness. Garret slapped him in the face. *"Where?"*

"East of Gaellos," the leader mumbled. "But you'll never get inside. Not with Daeglan's assassin around."

Garret shot Etanos a curious glance. "What assassin?" Garret demanded. "Who?"

"I don't know... her... name."

The leader's eyes glazed over and his head fell back. Garret dropped him, looking at Etanos for answers. The assassin seemed troubled, yet still unsure of who the man was referring to. A female assassin? Who could it be?

"He said *her*," Garret said. "What is he talking about? Could this be the assassin who left the blade?"

Etanos shook his head. "I'm not sure," he said. "I've known a few women in the guilds, but they were all friends; good assassins with honor and integrity."

"Then it must be someone you don't know," Garret offered. "Or someone from another guild."

"The only other woman I know of who killed for the darker guilds is dead," Etanos said. "It can't be her. But surely there are others."

"Are you sure she's dead?"

"Of course," Etanos said, putting away his blades. "I killed her."

CHAPTER EIGHTEEN

pread out," Kuros commanded his rangers as they descended into the mine complex. "Take out the guards on the rooftops first."

Turgon followed him closely as he approached the outer ring of buildings. They crouched in the shadows, peering through the gaps and watching for any movement. The rooftops were well guarded, with guards posted at every other building. On the street, various patrols and solitary overseers were visible; all keeping a watchful eye out for any misbehavior among the slaves.

Kuros sidled near the edge of a smaller building, watching down the street as a patrol of four men approached. They were armed with spears and escorted someone of apparent importance. Their charge was dressed in shining armor and red silks, quite a contrast to their own drab, brown leather.

The armored man walked in front; his attention turned toward the buildings of the outer ring. This was their route, Kuros assumed, keeping watch on the perimeter. He wondered if the two strangers had even noticed them, or if they had even been present at the time. Perhaps the patrol had been alerted to the breach and was sent to investigate.

No matter.

Kuros knocked an arrow and waited for the patrol to enter the shadow of a larger building. When they faded into the darkness, he loosed. Around him, several other arrows swooshed to their targets, and the entire patrol fell to the ground with barely a sound. In seconds, the dark silhouettes of cloaked rangers swarmed in and gathered the bodies, dragging them behind the outer ring.

Kuros and Turgon moved on.

"If my guess is correct," Kuros said, "the larger building where the strangers were headed is where the weapons would be stored."

"And likely where the leader is," Turgon added.

The two rangers entered the middle ring of buildings, where the activity was more prevalent. Carts were being moved throughout, pushed by men in filthy rags. They would occasionally stop at checkpoints while other men gathered materials from them, and then proceed to the next building.

"Each of these buildings must process a different material," Kuros guessed. "But they don't seem large enough."

"Likely they're just for storage," Turgon said. "They may be processed somewhere else. But I'm not sure how they would be transported."

"Watch out," Kuros said, stopping him with an outstretched hand.

A guard appeared on the rooftop just across the road. He stepped over the peak, descending the slope until he reached the gutter, looking down at the street below. A passing guard looked up and yelled something to him, and then went on his way. The guard on the roof turned and began his ascent back up the slope.

Kuros put an arrow in his back, and the man toppled forward, sliding on his stomach for a few feet. Turgon waited for the patrolling guard to cross into the shadows, and then shot him as well. Again, a swarm of rangers gathered up his body and carried him away. This time, the men pushing the carts were wary of their presence, but went about their business, wisely not drawing attention to the shadowy figures that were among them.

"Baelion would not approve of this," Kuros said, knowing the captain would likely be furious that they were operating out of their element.

Turgon chuckled. "You're right," he said. "But Baelion is not here."

"And neither are the king's soldiers," Kuros said. "That's why we are here."

He motioned for Turgon to follow him onto the street. They crouched behind a cart pushed by two older, but well-muscled men. They walked with it, drawing strange stares from the two. Kuros went to the rear of the cart to speak to them.

"Don't look at me," Kuros said to the man on his side. "Just answer me as well as you can. Do you understand?"

"Yes," the man mumbled, keeping his gaze on the road ahead.

"How many soldiers are here?" Kuros asked.

"At least two hundred," the man replied. "Sometimes more."

"Where is the leader?"

"In the armory. The large building on the north side."

"How many slaves are here?" Kuros asked.

The man shook his head. "I'm not sure. There are some above and some below. Most of those below never see the light of day. They sleep down there, eat down there... they never leave."

Kuros gritted his teeth furiously.

"Guard ahead," the man warned them.

Kuros eyed the road ahead. A guard appeared among the slaves, brandishing a whip and a brightly colored Red Hand sigil on his leather breastplate. Kuros narrowed his eyes at the man, slowing to fall behind the slave who pushed the cart. Turgon fell in behind him, drawing his blade. The guard crossed in front of them, and as they passed, Turgon grabbed him and dragged him into the alley.

Kuros kept pace with the cart, scanning the rooftops ahead. There was another guard near the peak of a roof some ways up. Kuros drew his bow, waiting until the cart passed in front of the building, and shot upward along the slope. The guard fell back, disappearing into the darkness as Turgon returned.

"Done," he said.

Kuros stood slightly, putting his hand on the slave's shoulder. "Keep going," he said. "Don't draw any attention to yourself. We'll take care of the rest of the guards."

The man nodded silently, a grin spreading across his face. Kuros and Turgon ducked into a nearby alley, regrouping with several other rangers who followed them from behind.

"The larger building is the armory," he told the others. "Our strange friends are in there. I can only guess that they plan to arm the slaves. It will be a mad rush once they begin, and the area will swarm with guards. We will make our way there and cover the entrance, protecting the slaves, and keeping the guards at bay."

The rangers nodded, and the group set off across the road. Kuros was anxious to meet the strangers, and get a sense of why they were here, whether they told him or not. It was obvious they were here to liberate the mines. But why? Why risk entering a hornet's nest with only two strong? What was their motivation?

Who were these strangers?

* * *

"Footsteps," Etanos whispered.

Garret pressed himself against the wall near the edge of a large archway. Etanos crouched across from him, listening closely as a pair of guards approached. They waited in silence until the pair crossed the threshold, springing into action and dragging their targets down to the floor, finishing them off quickly.

"No reason to hide the bodies," Etanos said.

Through the archway was a large room lined with tables and chairs; all arranged perpendicular to the entrance. There were three tables to a side, with six chairs at each, and topped with empty goblets and half-eaten dinners. Garret's stomach growled as he saw them, drawing a mirthful glance from Etanos.

"Don't worry," he said. "We'll eat when this is over."

They crossed the room to the heavy wooden door on the other side. Etanos listened briefly and then reached out to open it. There was another hallway on the other side that ended to the left and stretched about twenty yards to the right. On the opposite side was another archway that opened to a well-lit room. The sounds of clanking steel echoed from it, telling them that they were heading in the right direction.

Etanos crossed the hallway, keeping to the wall as he crept toward the arch. Garret followed close, keeping his back pressed against the stone. His heart beat quickly, and that strange feeling of focus came over him again as the clanking became louder.

Etanos stopped at the edge of the arch, peering around to view the room inside. After a few seconds, he turned back.

"Armory," he said. "One man inside, sorting through the weapons."

"Slave or bandit?"

"I can't tell," Etanos said. "He's wearing neither rags nor armor. Maybe we'll talk with him."

Garret nodded. There was no reason to kill the man, especially without knowing whose side he was on. He followed

Etanos into the room, slowing as his mentor held out his hand behind him. The man was hunched over a rack of weapons, apparently taking inventory of some kind, oblivious to their presence. Etanos crept around him toward the opposite side of the room, his blades out. He gave Garret a nod, signaling he was ready.

Etanos cleared his throat.

The man turned quickly, startled. He gasped when he saw Etanos standing there and spun to run in Garret's direction, freezing in place when he saw *him*. Garret grinned. The man's face twisted into a mask of terror.

"Stay calm," Etanos said. "We only want to talk."

"Who are you?" the man asked, backing away.

Etanos lowered his weapons. "The question is, who are you?"

The man shook his head. "No one of importance," he said. "I just keep track of the weapons."

"Are you with these bandits?" Garret asked.

Again, the man shook his head. "Not rightly," he said. "I am just a bookkeeper from Faerbane."

"Why are you here?" Etanos asked. "Were you taken from your home?"

"No," the man replied. "I came here several years ago to keep track of the iron that was mined here when the mines were freely operated by the common folk. I was here when the Red Hand took over, and they took me out of the office and put me here."

"To keep track of the weapons?" Garret asked, skeptically. "Why such a change?"

The man shrugged. "Because I can count, I suppose," he said. "But I guess I do it too well. They didn't want me to know how much material they were taking. I'm not sure why."

"Well," Etanos said. "You have a new job now. You will help us liberate these mines. We need to get these weapons into the hands of the slaves. Do you understand?"

The man nodded fearfully. "All right," he whispered. "But I don't know how we will do that."

"What is on the other side of this door?" Etanos asked, pointing at the far end of the room.

"The main hall," the man said. "That's where the entrance is. It opens up to the street. There are guards posted inside and out."

"How many?"

The man shook his head. "At least four in the hall," he said. "And maybe two outside."

"You can walk freely throughout?" Etanos asked.

The man seemed nervous but nodded.

"Then you will go outside and let the slaves know what is happening. But you will not say anything to the guards, other than to ask those just outside to come into this room. Do you understand?"

"Yes," the man replied.

Etanos stepped to the side, motioning for the man to exit. He and Garret followed him to the door, taking position on either side. The man opened the door and stepped through, leaving the door open behind him. They heard him speaking to the guards outside.

"I need to move a rack," he said. "But it's too heavy. Two of you should do it."

"Move it yourself," one of the guards replied. "That's your job."

"I'm sure the boss would disagree. Help me move them or I'll tell him about your secret stash."

Garret heard the guard sigh. "Fine," he said. "Come on."

The bookkeeper returned, followed by the two guards. He fell in behind them and closed the door as they passed through. Garret and Etanos dispatched the guards quickly, pulling them into the corners.

"Go now," Etanos said. "And leave the door open."

The man grumbled, exiting the room again. Garret and Etanos returned to their positions, peering into the main hall as he went toward the front door. The two guards paid little attention to him, simply staring into space when he neared. But they turned in his direction when he spoke, facing the outside as they engaged in conversation with him.

Etanos motioned for Garret to follow him, and they quickly crossed the main hall without a sound. The bookkeeper kept his composure as they closed in, not giving any indication that he saw anything. Then, the guards were silenced quickly and painlessly. The bookkeeper lowered his head, whispering under his breath as the bodies were dragged away.

"Guards outside," he said. "Near the buildings on the other side of the street.

"Pay them no attention," Etanos said. "Walk among the men and tell them to charge all at once. I will take out the guards across the street. That's when you will lead the charge."

"All right," the bookkeeper said, his breath coming in gasps as the moment neared.

"Relax," Garret said. "Freedom is near."

The bookkeeper glanced at him meekly for a moment before turning around and entering the bustling crowd. They watched him pass by various carts, whispering to the men who pushed them, and casually talking to the foremen. No one looked in their direction or even made any noticeable gestures to indicate they had been made aware of what was going on.

Once the bookkeeper had made his rounds, he returned. He walked casually to the door, stopping and turning toward the street. Etanos crouched behind him, drawing his bow, and aiming for the pair of guards that seemed to be looking in their direction.

"Ready?" Etanos said.

The bookkeeper took a deep breath; Garret did as well.

"Ready."

Etanos loosed his arrow. It streaked brightly across the street, flying level to the ground, plunging into the heart of one of the guards. The man stumbled back in horror, and his companion cried out in shock.

"Sound the alarm!" he shouted.

Etanos took him out with another arrow, and the swarming began. Garret ducked to the side as the crowd charged toward the door. Etanos waved them in, stepping aside as they burst through with the fury of a herd of cattle.

"Grab everything you can!" Etanos called to them.

As the last of the men passed them, Garret returned to his position at the doors. Several smaller groups of men were still running in their direction and following close behind were dozens of guards.

"They're coming," Garret said. "Lots of them."

Etanos put away his bow, drawing his blades and twirling them into position. Garret's heart pounded with excitement. This would be a rough battle, he knew, but he felt that familiar focus settle over him. He drew his saber, stepping out into the night to face the enemy head-on.

He was ready.

* * *

"It has begun," Kuros said.

The roar of activity echoed through the streets as if the slaves had suddenly begun shouting all at once. Several of them nearby dropped what they were doing, rushing the guards that were interspersed among them. The rangers joined the rush, following the men through the alleys, picking off every guard they could see. Everyone seemed to be rushing toward the center circle, guards included, where the sounds of clashing steel could be heard over the battle cries of insurgent slaves.

"*Protect them as best you can!*" Kuros shouted to his men.

They followed the mob into the center area, where the mine entrance was spewing guards and slaves alike. The guards were taken down with vengeance, and the sound of alarms echoed up from the depths and the buildings all around them. The rangers pounced on the guards or took them down with arrows. The slaves took their weapons and joined in the fight, some of them going back into the mines to rescue the others.

All around, guards began to flood into the center, rushing toward the armory. A mob of armed men burst from the doors, led by the two strangers. They clashed with the rushing guards in a chaotic explosion, releasing their fury on their captors. Kuros and his men climbed to the rooftops, taking a position to fire at the mass of guards that poured in from the outside.

"There they are," Kuros said to Turgon, pointing out the strangers below.

Turgon glanced down after firing an arrow at the squad of guards that passed by below. "They've started a revolt," he said. "I hope they were ready for it."

Kuros grinned as he watched them. Their fluid movements were impressive, almost ranger-like in the way they used their surroundings to their advantage. The older man was obviously a seasoned warrior, though not one who typically fought face-to-face. He was possibly a ranger himself, from another land, perhaps. Who or what the younger man was, Kuros could not guess.

But his curiosity was cut short as another shadow appeared on top of the armory. There, at the edge of the roof, standing atop a buttress, was a dark-cloaked figure. It stood menacingly, staring down with two blades held out to its sides. The black cloak it wore billowed around it like dark flame, and there was a strange glow to its eyes. Kuros glared at it, noticing the subtle hint of curvature at the figure's hips.

It was a woman.

Kuros pulled back his bow, knocking an arrow and waiting for the figure to make a move. He wanted to be sure it was not a third member of the strangers' party. Though the answer was not obvious, a strange feeling of dread settled over the ranger as he watched her. She was not as she appeared to be.

* * *

Ammarah glared down at her target with the fury of vengeance. Her eyes narrowed at the sight of the assassin below; her heart pounding furiously as she pictured his face in her mind. Through her iron mask, she hissed, gnashing her teeth in a manner befitting of a beast about to take down its prey.

She would have his head... and his soul.

But she remembered Daeglan's words about the boy; this stranger that the assassin had taken under his wing. Etanos would not be killed just yet. No, she wanted him to suffer first. She wanted him to know the pain of loss; the agony of losing someone he loved.

She would take this boy from him. She would slaughter him before Etanos' very eyes. She would fall upon him like darkness itself and bask in the glory of the assassin's tears.

She would have her revenge.

* * *

Garret rushed toward his enemy, leaping from side to side as he drew back his saber to thrust the killing blow. Just at the last minute, he withdrew his strike, spun around the guard's back, and jabbed with his dirk, catching the man between the shoulder blades. His target fell, and Garret switched his stance to charge the next.

He was in full battle mode now; moving like a shadow and striking like a serpent without thought or hesitation. His focus was pure and unhindered as if he was an automaton brought to life by some mad wizard. But, despite his near tunnel vision, he was completely aware of his surroundings.

He felt unstoppable.

A guard came at him with his sword raised. Garret spun to the side, slashing at the man's flank as he passed, and delivering a spinning kick at his back. The guard was pitched forward onto the ground, and Garret landed squarely in the path of another guard. The man's blade came down in a diagonal slash, and Garret blocked it with his dirk, flipping his saber in his hand and back thrusting into the man's gut.

He growled in fury as he pulled out his blade and sought out his next target.

Through the chaos, he could see many attacking guards falling to the ground, struck by the arrows of unseen archers. He knew that the rangers were up there in the shadows, assisting the battle from the rooftops as they would in the forest. He could even see their silhouettes on occasion.

But it was another silhouette that caught his attention. He saw its shadow on the ground below him and looked up at the armory's roof as the dark shape came down against the moonlight. He dodged its descent, rolling out of the way as the shape slammed into the ground like a small meteorite.

The entire battle seemed to stop then as the dust cleared. Even Etanos, who was surrounded by guards and slaves alike, paused for just a moment to turn to the new spectacle.

There, on the street, a dark figure was crouched. It was a black shape, cloaked in what seemed like darkness itself, and emanating a fury that Garret had never felt in his life. He backed away, as did all the men who surrounded him, as the figure's shining metallic face turned toward him.

His heart sank, it seemed. There was a strange sense of dread that came over him as he saw the glowing red eyes that burned from behind that iron mask. He was staring at the face of death itself.

And it had come for him.

"*Garret!*" he heard Etanos shout through his haze. "*Run!*"

Garret was frozen in place. He tried to move his legs, but they would not budge. All he could do was stare at those hellish eyes as the shape leaped toward him. He felt his legs buckle in terror, and he sank slowly to his knees, raising his blade in a desperate attempt to shield himself from his attacker's fury.

But his effort came too late.

A dark blade appeared in the attacker's hand, bearing down on him faster than he could react. As he stared at the figure's burning eyes and the iron mask that bore a permanent scowl, he felt the blade penetrate his cuirass just above his left collarbone.

It burned like nothing he had ever felt. The blade seemed to puncture his very soul, tearing into his essence like the fang of some unearthly creature of darkness. He cried out in agony, falling back as the weight of his attacker fell upon him and drove him to the ground.

His vision swam as he impacted the street, but through the swirls of reality, he could still see those eyes that burned right into him. They narrowed as he gritted his teeth with the pain. All around him, the world was becoming black and featureless. Everything faded from existence until all he could see were the darkening crescents of red that glared at him from what seemed like Hell itself.

Then, there was nothing.

CHAPTER Nineteen

tanos gasped as he saw Garret fall. The shadowy attacker had taken him down quickly; much quicker than any normal human could. Etanos could only watch helplessly as the figure withdrew its blade and stood over Garret's seemingly lifeless form. He cursed himself for not being there to protect the boy, and for his hesitation when the dark attacker appeared. Whatever the nature of this new enemy, it was obvious that it was not of this world.

Despite his fears, Etanos would not let his young friend die. He shouted at the top of his lungs as he charged, ignoring the chaotic battle around him, desperately trying to get the stranger's attention. There was nothing else in the world; only the black silhouette of his protégé's possible killer.

He reared back his blades to deliver a furious attack as he neared, seeing the glowing red eyes of the stranger as *she* turned. Her face was obscured by a scowling mask of gleaming iron, with those burning eyes showing through black holes in the metal.

She sidestepped and countered as Etanos attacked. The two began a deadly dance of clashing blades, spinning and flipping, twirling and growling, as their swords clanked together in an endless song of steel.

Etanos felt his rage course through him. It burned in his veins like fire, driving him forward toward the deadly she-devil. Though he knew it would cloud his judgment and his skill, he could not quell the anger. He could only direct it at his enemy, hoping that his senses would not be dulled by it.

As he let loose a barrage of spinning attacks, his opponent blocked and parried with perfect timing. She was a master with her blades, striking back with equally quick attacks, matching Etanos' strength, speed, and skill. She drove him back with furious spinning moves, appearing as a mere dark blur among the sparkling glints of her blades.

Etanos could not connect a single blow. Every strike he thought would finish her swiped only empty air, or was blocked by her blades. For every attack he had, she had a parry and a counter. She was, in effect, infallible--and she was as quick as lightning. Much quicker than anyone he had ever faced.

He backed away then, spinning his blades into a guarded position. As he did so, the woman turned and charged the gathering crowd of victorious slaves. She spun into them, cutting down at least a dozen in the blink of an eye before calmly striding back to face the assassin once again. The remaining slaves fled to the alleys, and the cloaked men stood in front of them, ready for another surprise attack.

Etanos glanced over at Garret's body, seeing the boy trembling. The movements gave him hope, and he turned his eyes back to the dark stranger. She stared at him strangely; her head cocked as if she were amused. Then, he heard her chuckle. It was a cackling sound, full of hate and malevolent desire.

"Who are you?" Etanos whispered.

She did not speak, but lifted up her right blade, pointing it straight at him and cocking her head to the other side. The gesture seemed familiar to him; her entire existence seemed familiar. Though he couldn't place her fighting technique, it was one that he had seen before.

But when... and where?

"You will beg for death," she said finally, her voice throaty and alien. *"And I will give it to you."*

Etanos growled, twirling his blades in defiance. He charged again, this time more focused and determined. He feinted to the left as he struck, changing direction at the last second, and spinning to double-slash at her face. Though his first blade was blocked, he felt the second catch the dark warrior's mask, and he heard her shouts of rage.

As he spun around her to attack from behind, an arrow streaked in, catching her as she turned. She howled again, grasping the shaft that protruded from beneath her left breast. Etanos reared back for the killing blow, but she ducked away, racing toward the outer wall of the armory. Etanos dropped his blades, drawing his bow, and fired repeatedly as she ran straight up the stone face and disappeared over the eave. His arrows struck the stone, fading away as their magic dissipated. Not a single one had hit its mark.

Etanos turned and ran to Garret. The boy was squirming on the ground, seemingly unguarded and vulnerable. But as he neared, he saw the shadowy figure of another man standing nearby. He was dressed in an earth-toned tunic and cloak, bore a katana at his side, and held a bow in his hand.

Etanos ignored him, crouching next to Garret and pulling him up to look into his eyes.

"Garret," he said, shaking the boy's head. "Wake up."

Garret's eyes were turned back, and the whites were exposed and bloodshot. He was groaning with the pain, and his face was a mask of torment. There was a large puncture wound just below his right collarbone that pulsed and quivered with some dark magic. Garret moaned in agony as the blackened wound grew, and his skin was deathly pale. He was near death, Etanos knew, and if he didn't do something soon, Garret would die.

He looked up at the slaves who had returned. They all looked on with pity, lowering their eyes as Etanos scanned their faces. He closed his own eyes, hanging his head in defeat. There was nothing he could do. He had failed his student; this boy that was so eager to learn.

"There is only one person who can help him," the nearby stranger said.

Etanos looked up at him as he gulped back his tears. The man was young, probably not much older than Garret, but there was an uncharacteristic wisdom in his eyes; something Etanos had never seen in someone of his age.

"Aeli," Etanos said her name.

The stranger nodded. "The slaves are safe now," he said. "My men and I can get you to her quickly."

"*Kuros!*" another man shouted from nearby.

The stranger turned, directing his gaze up to where another man was pointing. Etanos turned his eyes there as well. There, on the peak, stood the strange woman. She was like a ghostly shadow against the sky, holding a torch in one hand, and another object in the other. As the crowd watched, she brought the torch over to her other hand, and the sparkling flare of a fuse came to life. Laughing, she casually tossed the object down toward the entrance to the mine.

The crowd of slaves began shouting and roiling chaotically as they attempted to flee. The stranger grabbed Etanos' arm, shouting right into his ear.

"*Run!*" the young man said.

Etanos snatched Garret up and laid him over his shoulders. He ran as best he could, following the young man toward the west entrance that they had avoided earlier. The mob was running in the same direction, everyone helping those who fell in the chaotic exodus to safety.

"There are horses near the entrance," he heard the younger man say. "*Turgon, get the people to safety and return to the compound!*"

Just then, a huge explosion rocked the entire complex. The ground shook and cracked with the impact, and the buildings around them began to crumble. Etanos stumbled but regained his balance just in time to avoid a falling beam. Behind him, he heard the ground fall away as the mines underneath collapsed and caved in. The buildings were torn apart, and the destruction was catching up to them as they raced toward the entrance.

The stranger grabbed his arm, pushing him toward a low-lying wooden building where horses were panicking and bucking.

"Take one and follow me," he said.

Etanos threw Garret over a horse's back, leaping up right behind him. He spurred the horse forward, leaping over the fence just as the ground crumbled around them. The horse protested but charged on right beside the horse that the stranger had taken.

The entrance came into view ahead. The free men were pushing through it, and the cloaked strangers were guiding them while others guarded their escape. There were still random guards following close behind, and the strange men were picking them off one by one.

They weren't about to let them escape.

Finally, as the crumbling died down, Etanos rode into the gap right behind his escort. He followed the young man closely as he charged down the slope and into the dark forest ahead. He knew exactly where they were going, but trusted the young man to know a quicker way. He was, after all, a ranger. That much was obvious.

"Who was that woman?" the young man asked.

Etanos shook his head in confusion. He had no answer. He only wanted to get Garret to Aeli. As he gazed down at the boy's face, he saw the darkness creeping into his young features. Something was happening. Something had to be done soon.

"My name is Kuros, by the way," the ranger said. "And I will get you to Aeli as quickly as possible."

* * *

Ammarah watched the mine complex collapse from the crater's rim. She chuckled as the buildings crumbled and fell into rubble, shaking the very ground with their weight. Such power; such destruction.

Such amusement.

Though entertaining to her, the crumbling death of the mines was nothing compared to the satisfaction of watching her nemesis suffer the pain of losing his beloved student. The look on his face as he saw the boy wounded on the street was more than she could ever imagine. It was a look that she had longed to see on the bastard's face.

Pain and suffering, she thought. *Just like you caused me.*

Ammarah threw her head back and laughed into the sky. The sight of the full moon was a welcome addition, increasing her elation even more. Tonight, she had gained a small bit of vengeance for what Etanos had done to her, and it was only the beginning. She would make him suffer more before the end. She would take everything from him — everything he loved — before she finally put her dagger in his heart.

Her revenge would be sweet.

But where was Etanos off to now, she wondered. Who were these green-clad men who led the pitiful slaves to safety and helped him escape? Where were they going?

She glared down at the gap where the men were lined up in a mass exodus. Though some of them had been injured in the destruction, most of them were now out of harm's way and taking the road west to who knows where. She wondered how amusing it would be to attack them at this very moment when they were celebrating their newfound freedom.

It would be amusing, indeed. But, she thought, they were of no consequence to her. She would let them live.

Her target was heading west to a separate destination; somewhere to get help, Ammarah imagined. Perhaps she would follow them and toy with them. She could make the suffering all the more enjoyable.

Ah, yes, she thought. *The game continues.*

Perhaps she would kill a few of the slaves on her way there, after all. That would be amusing.

***

"Keep moving, men," Turgon said to the weary slaves as they finally emptied onto the road. "You're free now. No need to stay here any longer."

As he looked at the faces of everyone who had escaped, Turgon felt a deep sense of relief for them. They were beaten down, he knew, broken and lacking of will, but now they were free. Their expressions were those of disbelief as if this entire ordeal was just a dream from which they would awaken any second now.

Turgon went to the nearest man he could find; an older native with scars on his face and hands that were gnarled from years of forced labor. The man looked up at him with tired eyes, staring at him almost blankly, yet with a slight glimmer of hope. He put his hand on the man's shoulder, gripping it slightly to give him some comfort.

"You can go home now, sir," he said. "Or wherever you wish."

The man shook his head. "I have no idea where home is anymore," the man mumbled. "It's been so long."

Turgon pursed his lips. "I'm sorry," he said. "If you have nowhere to go, then we will see to it that you find a nice place to rest."

"Aye!" another voice from the crowd said. "Jax's pub still be open, yah?"

A dark shape suddenly passed by overhead, moving across the rocks like the shadow of an eagle in flight against the moon. Turgon saw it out of the corner of his eye and turned to track it as it spanned the gaps in the rim as if they were nothing. Three slaves groaned in turn, gripping their guts as they fell to the ground. The men around them went into a panic, either running away or staying frozen in place.

"*Get down!*" Turgon shouted.

A cackling sound echoed from the darkness, fading away as the dark shape disappeared. Turgon scrambled over to the fallen men, rolling them over onto their backs to see if they were still alive. They were all pierced with black arrows, fletched with crow's feathers.

"By the Dragon," Turgon exclaimed. "Who could fire so quickly?"

He stared down the road to the west, where Kuros had led the stranger on horseback. The dark warrior was after them, Turgon guessed, and his friend would be a target. His sense of duty prevented him from abandoning the newly freed men, but his friendship with Kuros would protest—no matter how hard he tried to ignore it.

But ignore it he must. Duty called, and he would not leave these poor men to die.

"Come," he said to the other rangers. "Let's get these men to safety."

* * *

Garret's breathing was becoming ragged as the men bounded through the brush. The trail was rough, and the horses were not used to forest paths; especially those that were as black as pitch. It was only through the dim light of the moon that they were able to make out even the slightest difference between trail and tree.

"We must hurry," Etanos said, the sense of urgency becoming overwhelming.

He could almost feel Garret's pain as they rode on. The boy's moans were getting to him, and the guilt that was building threatened to burst forth in a howling scream of rage. This was all his fault, he knew. If he hadn't ripped the boy away from his life, he would not be lying face down on a horse with his life slipping away.

No, he thought. *Maybe worse.*

"We're almost there," Kuros assured him, spurring his horse on.

Etanos hoped that Aeli could help him. Though she had not revealed her power at their last meeting, Etanos had the sense that she was as powerful as any druid or magician he had ever heard of; perhaps even more. If anyone could heal Garret, it was her. She was his only hope.

Ahead, the glow of Aeli's magic lanterns began to illuminate the forest; bathing it in a pleasant green glow. Kuros led them straight toward it, slowing his horse as they came upon two mighty oaks that grew together like an archway overhead. Etanos hadn't noticed it during their first visit.

"Aeli," Kuros called out. "Aeli, we need your help."

Etanos dismounted, pulling Garret off of the horse, moving through the oak archway, and cradling him as he crouched in wait. There was a shuffling sound nearby, and several small things moved rapidly around them in the brush. Then, as Kuros was about to call out again, the magic lanterns flared brighter, lighting up the clearing where Aeli's familiar cottage stood.

"Etanos," Aeli's voice came from the darkness. "You have returned."

Aeli stepped from the shadows, allowing her staff to come to life, lighting the clearing with its magic. She looked down at the assassin, seeing Garret's limp body lying in his arms. Her eyes widened with horror, and she knelt beside them, placing her hand on Etanos' shoulder.

"What has happened?" she asked softly.

"He was wounded in battle," Etanos replied. "By someone not of this world. Can you help him?"

Aeli gazed down at Garrett's face. Her expression became pained as she did, almost mimicking Garrett's pain. Her eyes became saddened and weary, but somehow still full of life—and hope. Etanos felt her sympathy, and it was strong.

"Bring him inside," she said. "Kuros, I will need your help. Fetch some water from my well."

Kuros nodded, dismounting and going to the well near the opposite side of the house. Aeli rose with Etanos, leading him inside.

"This is grave indeed," Aeli said. "The Broken One has found you."

CHAPTER TWENTY

eli knelt in front of her hearth, with Garret's head in her lap, and her hands held out at shoulder height. Etanos knelt at Garret's feet, watching Aeli as she chanted strange words in a language that he had never heard. He glanced over at Kuros, who sat mesmerized by the woman's spell.

Though intrigued by what was happening, Etanos could only feel the guilt of allowing his student to fall in battle. He was not prepared for the appearance of the mysterious warrior, nor was he prepared for the horror that she brought. Never in his life had he felt such a great sense of hatred coming from one single person. Nor had he ever felt fear. But this woman, who apparently knew him, had brought those feelings to him with little more than her presence.

The Broken One, he repeated in his mind. *The Broken One.* This was the assassin who had left the obsidian blade. This was the assassin who sought him out.

But why?

Was it mere competition, or had the two of them met in the past and parted on less than amicable terms? Had Etanos done something to harm her? The questions were daunting, and there seemed to be no logical answer. All he could do was wonder and wait to see what the future would bring.

"Etanos," Aeli spoke softly. "There is a small shard of this attacker's blade in Garret's flesh."

Etanos gazed into her eyes as she spoke. Her face was saddened and worried.

"But the pain of its removal will be too great for him to bear," she continued. "I will bear it for him."

Etanos glanced at Kuros again. The ranger shrugged.

"Kuros," Aeli said. "When Etanos cuts open the wound, you will ensure that it is clean."

Kuros nodded.

"Cut it open?" Etanos said with disbelief.

"It will have to be cut open to reach the shard," Aeli explained. "I will ensure that Garret's soul is safe from harm. Do not worry."

Etanos wasn't sure what she meant, but he trusted her, and so too did Kuros, it seemed. The ranger nodded to Etanos encouragingly. Etanos sighed.

"All right," he said.

Aeli closed her eyes again, sweeping her hands around in slow circles as she gathered the energy for her spell. Glowing wisps appeared around her, and Etanos could feel the tingling of magic on his skin. As he watched in wonder, Aeli's eyes fluttered open revealing hollow white sclera that seemed to shimmer like silver.

She then lowered her hands, grasping Garret's face gently. She knelt farther, bending her head down until her face was directly over his. She moved her lips just above his, opening his mouth with her thumbs. Then, she gathered breath, inhaling deeply as the glow around her began to brighten. Suddenly, she rose slightly, drawing her breath inward with a sharp gasp. A bright vortex of light appeared from Garret's mouth, swirling its way upward into Aeli's.

Etanos' heart pounded with the sight. It was as if Aeli were inhaling Garret's soul. He watched as Garret's body became still, and the last swirls of energy left him. Then, Alei's breath slowed, and she slowly sat back up, her eyes now wide and glowing.

"Now," she said.

Etanos drew his blade and held it above Garret's wound. He cut away the fabric of his tunic, then the hard leather of his cuirass until the wound was laid bare. Swallowing nervously, he cut into the boy's flesh, gently slicing the wound until he widened it enough to see the pulsing shard of dark metal. Aeli groaned in pain, clenching her teeth in response every time Etanos moved bits of flesh out of the way.

He looked up at her again, reluctant to cause her any more pain.

"Do it," she hissed. "Take it out."

Slowly, he lowered the tip of his blade into the wound, prying up the shard carefully. It resisted, pulling small chunks of muscle with it, and drawing tiny squirts of blood. Aeli's groans became more urgent the deeper he cut, and the harder he pried.

Finally, he was able to reach in with his other hand and grasp the point. The metal seemed hot and stinging between his fingers. But he held on, gritting his teeth as Aeli's groans became low screams. Kuros' eyes were fixated on the gash, but he was ready with a clean cloth in his hand, dripping with the water he had fetched from the well.

Etanos closed his eyes, grasping the shard as tightly as he could. He pulled with all his might, hearing the tearing of Garret's flesh as it finally came free. Aeli's moans subsided, and her breath came in heavy gasps.

"Now..." she stammered. "Clean the wound."

Etanos held up the shard as Kuros reached in to wash away the blood and tiny chunks of flesh. The shard was black, like the obsidian blade, and almost seemed to have a life of its own, a dark life. It was horrifying.

"Throw the shard in the fire," Aeli said.

Without a word, Etanos tossed the shard over Aeli's shoulder. It bounced off of the back wall of the fireplace, flaring into a ball of dark magic that flashed with the light of some hellish sun. Etanos and Kuros both shuddered with the unearthly sound, shielding their eyes from the devilish light.

"Kuros," Aeli whispered. "Hold the cloth over the wound tightly to stop the bleeding."

Kuros did as he was told, pressing the cloth down with a firm grip. Aeli bent back over Garret's face, opening her mouth over his once again. With a few quick breaths, she released his energy, and it streaked back into his body. He convulsed as it entered him, and his moaning returned.

Aeli's eyes returned to their usual green color. She smiled gently, reaching down to cover the wound with her hand. A soft, green glow began to show beneath her fingers, and Etanos could feel its warmth, and see the effect it had on his young friend Garret's pained look softened, and the color slowly returned to his skin.

When Aeli removed her hand, the wound was completely healed over, and Garret's skin was as smooth and pink as it once was. She leaned back again, holding her hands up at her sides as the spell faded. The wisps of magic slowly dissipated, and the strange tingling in Etanos' skin subsided.

It was over.

"You both did very well," she said with a smile.

"Will he be all right?" Etanos asked.

"He will be fine," she assured him. "He will need to rest for the night at least. I will watch over him."

"What do we do now?" Kuros asked.

Aeli looked at him, smiling. "Help Etanos carry Garret up to the loft so he may rest. You may also rest here if you need to."

"I think I need some air," Kuros said.

* * *

After carrying Garret's sleeping form up the ladder and tucking him safely into bed, Etanos and Kuros sat outside in the lush garden. The crickets and other night creatures sang their beautiful songs, and the cool night breeze calmed their senses. It was a nice break from the night's chaos, and the peace was a much-needed reprieve for both of them.

Etanos was lost in thought, however. The mysterious woman had gotten to him greatly, and her identity was an enigma that tugged at his very soul. Not only that, but her nature was that of something other than human, it seemed. Never had he encountered anyone or anything that came close to causing him as much revulsion as this woman had.

Still, there was a strange familiarity with her that he could not place, and that, he guessed, was the reason for her repulsiveness.

"We were watching the two of you," Kuros said, staring up at the moon.

Etanos nodded. "I know," he said. "For quite a while. What was it that made you follow us to the mines?"

"Baelion ordered it," Kuros said. "But I was curious. We hadn't planned on entering the mines, just seeing what the two of you were up to."

"We hadn't planned on it, either. But when we saw the men being held as slaves, we both knew what we had to do."

Kuros pursed his lips, shaking his head. "I never would have dreamed that such a large operation could work under our noses. But then, we stick to the forest and the roads that go through it."

"This is a much larger operation than just the mines," Etanos said. "Garret has a map that shows the locations of other bases."

"Oh?" Kuros said, leaning forward.

Etanos nodded. "There are many of them located all over the south of Eirenoch," he said. "Some of them oddly close to the estates of the nobles."

Kuros grunted. "Why doesn't that surprise me?"

Etanos glanced at him, noticing that he was lost in thought. "You've had dealings with the nobles?"

"Lords Daeglan and Darragh are under our watch," he said. "Daeglan has taken in the children and the nuns of the Temple of Gaia in Gaellos. We are watching him to ensure they are all safe. And as far as Darragh goes, my friend Ferrin is a member of his house."

"And what sorts of things is Darragh doing to draw your attention?"

Kuros shook his head. "He has been suspected of smuggling things in the past," Kuros said. "Various things; nothing specific. Never slaves. Not that we knew of anyway."

"Tell me of this Ferrin," Etanos said. "Garret and I met him in Faillaigh."

Kuros nodded. "That is where Lord Darragh's estate is located. I can't tell you much about Ferrin, other than that he is a shady one. He has plans to take over Darragh's estate; that I know. Other than that, he keeps to himself."

"He is a thief," Etanos said.

Kuros glanced at him briefly and then lowered his eyes. He knew.

"What is he up to?"

Kuros pursed his lips again. "I cannot tell you much," he said. "But I can tell you that the things he is involved in are for the good of the kingdom. Make no mistake."

Etanos thought about it for a moment. He supposed that was good enough. There was probably a reason Kuros was not going into detail. He wouldn't press the matter. After all, *he* worked in secret—behind the scenes—and was training Garret to do the same.

"I am no one to judge," he said, smiling.

Kuros chuckled. "I gathered that. So, tell me, where are you from?"

"Thyre. I grew up there but learned my trade in various places. I've been just about everywhere in the world."

"So what brought you to our little island?"

"A contract," Etanos said. "But that's when things changed. That's when I discovered the existence of this... woman. She is a rival of sorts, I suppose, but I have no idea who or what she is."

He brought out the obsidian blade, looking at it for a moment before showing it to Kuros. The ranger's eyes widened as he beheld it, and he reached out to touch it but hesitated.

"Is that..." he stopped.

"An obsidian blade," Etanos finished him. "Left at the mark's house for me to find. It belongs to her."

"Very strange indeed," Kuros said. "I don't know much about your trade, but that sounds like a challenge to me."

Etanos nodded. "Definitely," he agreed. "And one whose reasoning escapes me."

"So you have no idea who this woman is, or why she taunts you?"

Etanos shook his head. "None," he said. "I have made no enemies that I am aware of. At least, none that are still alive."

Kuros grinned. "You sound like King Magnus," he said. "But little does he know the enemies he truly has here in his own kingdom."

Etanos thought for a moment, realizing why Kuros had said this. Sometimes, a man doesn't even know who his enemies are. Overconfidence.

"You are right," he said. "I should think harder."

"It is clear that Daeglan has new enemies now," Kuros said.

Etanos nodded. "Garret loves the sisters and the children," he said. "He will want to rescue them if he thinks they are in danger."

"I doubt they are in any immediate danger," Kuros said. "Daeglan is more of a whore monger than a criminal. But in light of what has happened with the convent, he is stepping into that area now. This new information about the network is disturbing. We will keep a closer eye on him, and the children."

"Regardless of their immediate danger, Garret will no doubt do whatever it takes to get the sisters and the children out. But I'm not sure where he plans to take them."

Kuros grinned. "That is not a problem," he said.

Etanos glanced at him, seeing the roguish expression on his young face. Again, he didn't press the matter.

Kuros turned his head suddenly, shooting Etanos a hunted look. Something was out there. Etanos felt it too. The two of them jumped up quickly, drawing their blades and moving out into the center of the clearing. Behind them, the door to Aeli's cottage opened, and she stepped out, staff in hand and an angry stare on her face.

"I am sorry, Aeli," Etanos said. "I fear I have brought this evil to your doorstep."

Aeli stepped out into the clearing to stand beside them. "Do not worry, my friend," she said. "I do not fear her."

Etanos tightened his grip on his blades as the sounds of the night creatures subsided. Kuros held his bow ready with an arrow knocked and his eyes narrowed as he peered into the darkness. Aeli stood stoically, her face undaunted and still.

A low cackle echoed through the shadows, and a strange whirring sound followed, interspersed by the gentle clanking of steel on the ground.

"What is that?" Kuros whispered.

Etanos shook his head. He squinted in the darkness, barely making out the shadowy form that emerged from the tree line. Only the fiery glow of red eyes betrayed their enemy's position.

"Begone from this place," Aeli called out. "This is a sanctuary of Gaia. You are not welcome here."

Somehow, Etanos thought, the woman did not care. Her red eyes blinked, and she stepped forward into the green glow. The faint light reflected off her iron mask, accentuating the black, empty holes where her demonic eyes burned. Etanos could see the scowling expression carved into the metal and the odd way her head was cocked to the side—that same familiar gesture.

"Am I not a child of Gaia?" she spoke, her low whisper echoing across the clearing.

"You are no longer of this Earth," Aeli replied. "Return to the darkness."

The woman stopped, raising her blades in yet another familiar stance. Etanos narrowed his gaze, feeling that strange sense again. He knew this woman, he was sure. But who she was remained a mystery; a mystery that drove his mind into chaotic flashes of his past. There was only one woman in his past whom he had faced in battle; one woman that had always carried with her the veil of darkness.

One assassin whom he had killed...

"Ammarah," he whispered.

The woman chuckled in the distance, her blades quivering in anticipation. He knew that gesture, too. He took a defensive stance just as she shot forward. He spun to the side as she struck, swiping his right blade in a wide arc. She rolled underneath it, coming to her feet and immediately countering with a spinning charge. Kuros fired at her, but she cut the arrow out of the air and continued her charge.

Etanos stepped from side to side as her blades came at him, dodging and parrying after every sharp swipe. His blades glanced off of hers, sparking in the moonlight as they connected. From the corner of his eye, he saw Aeli step away, gathering magic for a spell. Kuros drew his blade and circled to Ammarah's flank.

She immediately broke away, flashing toward the ranger quickly with a double, diagonal attack. He blocked both blades, ducking out of the way just as a neck-level back slash cut the air above him. Etanos charged her, but she went back into the defensive, dodging his initial attack and countering with a leaping spin attack. His blades came up just in time, halting her in midair, and he kicked out with his right foot, connecting with her gut and sending her sprawling to the ground.

Aeli let loose a burst of green fire that engulfed Ammarah and sent her reeling in anger. Kuros quickly rolled over to his bow, firing another arrow that struck the assassin square in the hip. She howled in rage, plucking the arrow out and charging him. Aeli blasted her again, knocking her away.

Aeli slammed the end of her staff into the ground and swept up with her open right hand, bringing thick saplings up through the ground that knocked the assassin away. With a growl of rage, Ammarah chopped at them, cutting down a few as she attempted to charge again, but Aeli kept them coming, blocking her approach and driving her into a frenzy.

Kuros fired his bow again and again, but the arrows bounced off of the assassin's limbs with metallic clanks. Then, with a call to the spirits of the Earth, Aeli released a more powerful spell. Brilliant white-hot fire shot from her staff, engulfing the dark assassin in its hellish grasp. She thrashed and screamed with the fury of a thousand demons, chopping down the saplings around her.

Aeli kept the blast going, driving her back farther and farther as Etanos and Kuros both fired arrows into her thrashing form. Her screams echoed in Etanos' mind, bringing back the memory of her previous death—or what he thought was her death. The horror of that memory pulled at his soul; the memory of watching her plunge to a fiery end.

He had defeated her on the rooftops of the temple of Imbra. He had watched her burn alive, and fall to the stone far below. He had looked down upon her lifeless body from above as it burned. She was dead — she had to be. Yet here she was, burning again in front of his very eyes.

He froze then, unable to comprehend this reality. Time seemed to slow down as he watched her thrash and burn, cutting down the saplings around her to escape. Bewildered, he fell to his knees, his eyes locked on Ammarah's form. She turned and fled, streaking across the clearing like a flaming comet.

The flames around her died out as she reached the tree line, and Etanos could hear her howls of rage through the chaotic pounding in his ears. They were the tormented cries of a young assassin in the throes of death; the horrified sounds of a person experiencing a gruesome and traumatic end.

Etanos closed his eyes, feeling the pangs of guilt course through him. He dropped his blades, covering his face and lowering his head as his breath became labored. Everything around him disappeared, all but the sounds of Aeli calling his name and the firm grip of Kuros' hand on his shoulder.

"Etanos," Aeli's soft voice said.

He dropped his hands, still struggling to breathe. He felt her hand on his head, pulling him to her, wrapping him in her warmth. She was comforting, and he could feel his horror melting away as he listened to her heartbeat. But still, the vision of the young woman glaring at him as she fell to her death was burned into his mind's eye. It was a vision he would never escape.

Not until she was dead once more.

"Kuros," Aeli spoke again. "Help me take him inside."

Ammarah sped away, enraged. Though the witch's magic had not physically harmed her, its effect was agonizing. The familiar pain of immolation came flooding back to her, breaking her focus, and causing her to flee. In her eyes, that was a show of weakness.

She had survived a similar fate so long ago; having been defeated by the bastard assassin and left to burn in torment. The pain of her flesh being consumed by flames remained etched in her mind, and it was what had fueled her for all of these years.

She had used it to further her aggression and build her reputation as a creature to be feared. But the witch's fire, along with the sight of her enemy's face, had proved to be a daunting combination.

One that had almost led to her defeat.

Never again would she allow her memories to cloud her focus. Her intent was clear, and she could not allow anything to stand in the way. Etanos *must* be tormented to the point of giving up. He must be made to feel the same pain that she had felt; not only the physical pain, but of solitude as well.

Then, and only then, could she end his suffering.

As she slipped through the trees like a shadow, she cried out in rage. Her ghostly screams echoed through the darkness, causing the wildlife to flee, and the spirits of the forest to shudder in terror. To them, she was a demonic presence that did not belong here, yet one that was far too fearsome to confront.

This she knew.

Even Etanos feared her. She could feel his fear and that of the ranger who accompanied him. They would not forget their encounter. It would be forever etched in their minds and in the mind of the witch that had protected them. She would not soon be forgotten.

Not again.

She laughed then, picturing the look of recognition on the assassin's face; that look of horror that told her he remembered her. He remembered their last battle, she knew, that battle on the rooftops of an ancient temple, where he had mistakenly believed that he had defeated her. But she had not been defeated that night. Not at all. It was that night when she was taken away by the strange, sub-human shaman, that she had truly been born. It was the night she became a dark specter of vengeance.

The night she became something more than human.

CHAPTER TWENTY-ONE

errin arrived in Gaellos in the early morning; equipped, and funded for the errands he was asked to run by Lord Darragh. Despite having overheard the disturbing conversation between his lord and the queen herself, he humbly agreed to do Darragh's bidding without question. There was no reason, yet, to bring suspicion upon himself by revealing his knowledge — or acting strangely for that matter.

It was his "willingness" to do Darragh's bidding that had elevated him above the nobleman's other servants. In the past five years, he had never questioned what his lord asked of him, and had put himself in awkward situations just to prove his loyalty — as it were.

But, behind the ruse, Ferrin was about as loyal as a hungry dog presented a nice, fat sausage by an intruder. He would gladly step over his master's body to gain the advantage, should the opportunity present itself.

Such were his ways.

The previous night's events, he realized, had presented him with that very opportunity. He could very well achieve his goals if he played his cards right. However, considering the situation, proceeding with caution was his best bet. A plot against the king would surely give him the leverage he needed to oust his lord but knowing that Ferrin had revealed such a plot would send Darragh into a vengeful fit.

But still, though he had no love for the king, a plot against him was unreasonable and dangerous. Magnus was a fair and just king, he knew, and his death would only allow Queen Igraina to take his throne and bring the kingdom to its knees. She was not, by far, the noble character Magnus was. Her origins were unknown. It was likely she was not even a native of Eirenoch.

But what could a simple servant boy do?

Should he warn the king somehow, he wondered. Or was there another option? Who would listen to him and take him seriously? Who would do so without revealing that it was he who had informed them? How would he even go about doing so?

Frustrated, Ferrin shook his head, sighing into the morning air. He entered the town square with his charge; a pack of items ready for shipment to Taryn. Trinkets for various merchant friends, Darragh had said.

Trinkets...

He entered the town square with a spring in his step—no reason to appear any other way than his usual lively self. He waved at the merchants who were setting up their outdoor displays, and the bar wenches who winked as they cleaned the pub tables. He gave them crooked smiles as he passed.

No time for chatting.

The trading company was just now opening as he walked up. Tam Caill, the local shipper, was out front, sweeping away the night's clutter with a straw broom. He grumbled when he saw Ferrin, the same way everyone did.

"What is it, now?" Tam asked, scowling.

Ferrin mocked a hurtful look. "Well," he said. "That's no way to greet a customer."

"What have ye got?"

Ferrin followed the man inside, unpacking the items and setting them on the counter.

"Just some items Darragh would like shipped to Taryn," he said. "I don't know what they are, but their destinations are clearly marked."

Tam flashed his toothless grin, marking the items into his log book as he read the recipients' names.

"Master tells ye not, eh?" he joked.

Ferrin smirked, drumming his fingertips on the counter. "I don't ask," he said. "And I don't care."

Tam chuckled as he figured out the shipping rates in his head. "Eleven gold crowns," he said.

Ferrin counted the coins and set them on the counter. Tam swept them into a box, writing out a receipt.

"Should arrive th' day after t'morrow," he said. "Got a wagon goin' there today."

"Thank you, Tam," Ferrin said, stuffing the receipt in his pocket. "Have a fine day, sir."

Tam waved him away without looking up. Ferrin went back outside, wondering what to do next. The plot still weighed on his mind, but he was unsure as to how he could make any difference. Perhaps sending a letter to Prince Maedoc would suffice. But then, revealing a plot right in a letter could be dangerous; not only for him, but perhaps Prince Maedoc as well.

"Bah," he said to himself.

He would worry about it later, once he had more information. Still, all the talk about assassins was intriguing. He had met the older assassin and his young apprentice—so he seemed—just the other day. But who was this woman of whom the conspirators spoke? And why was it implied that she wasn't human?

Who was she? Perhaps Kuros would know—wherever he was.

As Ferrin was about to turn into the alley, the sight of a cloaked woman caught his attention. She emerged from the alley on the opposite side of the square, dressed in a blue cloak with golden trim around the hood. She was young—perhaps a few years younger than he—lithe, and absolutely the most beautiful woman he had ever seen in his life.

He felt himself staring after her as she walked meekly through the growing crowds. She seemed aimless as if wandering with no real destination. She was lost, perhaps. Ferrin felt sympathy for her, realizing that despite her dress, she may be a beggar. She might need money, or food, or even shelter.

She might need… him.

Slicking back his hair, he rounded the fountain and fell in step behind her, quickening his pace to pass by her casually. He ducked between two approaching commoners, coming around in front of her and then crossing her path. He purposely slowed, causing her to sidestep and slow her pace to go around him.

"Oh," Ferrin said, turning in her direction. "Pardon me."

She slowed, turning in his direction. He saw that her eyes were weary as if she hadn't slept, and her gaze was absent and bleak. She said nothing but glanced at him briefly before turning away and continuing her purposeless gait. Ferrin followed her, thinking of some way to strike up a conversation.

"Miss," he called out to her. "Are you all right?"

That was brilliant, he thought.

She stopped suddenly, just as two leather-armored men emerged from a pub. They wore the familiar symbol of the Red Hand on their breastplates, and their cloaks were frayed and black. He caught up to her, pulling her aside as the two men approached.

"There you are, darling," he said, putting his arm around her and leading her away from their path.

She didn't protest but kept her head turned toward the men as they passed.

"Just look ahead," Ferrin whispered. "They won't bother you if they see you with me."

He led her closer to the fountain, where a large pergola stood. They ducked underneath, and Ferrin watched the two men as they disappeared into the crowd. Then, he turned to his companion. She stared at him wide-eyed and nervous—not particularly frightened, but guarded and cautious.

"Why did you flee from those men?" he asked her.

"No reason," she answered. "They just looked dangerous."

Her voice was enough to knock him off his feet. Not only was she beautiful, but she had the voice of the divine.

"Indeed, they are," he said. "It's a good thing I found you when I did." He bowed low. "I am Ferrin, a servant of the House of Darragh."

She backed away. "You're a noble, then?"

"Well, no," he stammered. "Just a servant. But don't let that fool you. I'm not like them."

He smiled, trying his best to get her to return the gesture. She did not.

"What is your name?" he asked.

She hesitated but swallowed sharply and answered. "Ailin," she said.

Ferrin nodded, smiling. "That is a beautiful name," he said, truly meaning it. "You seem troubled. Is there anything I can help you with?"

She shook her head, nervously glancing around. "I—I don't think I should discuss anything with a stranger."

Ferrin nodded, disappointed. "Very well," he said. "But if you change your mind, I am always here to help. I have connections. Maybe connections that would be useful to you."

Ailin lowered her eyes, looking around quickly before moving her cloak slightly to the side. Underneath, she wore a medallion emblazoned with the symbol of the Temple of Gaia; a triangle-shaped arrangement of swirls joined at the center. Ferrin immediately recognized it.

"You're a Sister of Gaia," he said.

Ailin closed her cloak, grasping it tightly around her. "Yes," she said. "I'm an initiate, but a protégé of Helena, the headmistress and captain of our order."

"How did you escape Daeglan's estate?"

Ailin shook her head. "Daeglan pays me no attention," she explained. "I can come and go as I please."

Ferrin nodded. "But you seem troubled," he said. "Do you need help?"

"I do," she replied. "But I cannot talk to you here. Is there a safe place we can go?"

Ferrin thought for a moment. The first place that crossed his mind was Joran's forge. He took Ailin's hand. "Come with me," he said.

They made their way around the square, walking casually so as not to attract attention. The two Red Hand men were nowhere to be seen, but Ferrin wasn't taking any chances. Despite his station, he wasn't well known among those who worked covertly for the rotten nobles, and he wore no sigils to indicate his affiliation.

"Where are we going?" Ailin asked.

"To a friend's," Ferrin said. "We will be able to talk there."

They rounded the last corner, heading straight for Joran's shop. The man was just opening, unlocking the doors, and rolling back his shutters as they approached.

"Joran," Ferrin greeted him. "May my friend and I have a moment in your forge to speak privately?"

Joran glared, annoyed. "I got up this morning hoping I wouldn't see you today," Joran said. "But, fine, have at it. I've just now lit the fire."

Ferrin led Ailin inside, where the smoke of the newly lit forge was beginning to billow around the exhaust port in the ceiling. She looked around curiously, wide-eyed like a child as she beheld the formidable-looking blades that lined the walls.

"Joran is a fine craftsman," she said.

"He is," Ferrin agreed. "The best. Now, tell me what troubles you."

Ailin paused for a moment to gather her thoughts, then, "Daeglan has less-than-noble motives for taking in the sisters and the children."

"I gathered that," Ferrin said, nodding.

"He, like the other nobles in his circle, is against the faiths and would see them gone."

Again, Ferrin nodded.

"What he doesn't know is that our order is more than just a convent," she continued. "We... *they*, rather, are warriors of Gaia."

"Warriors?" Ferrin echoed. "Knights?"

"Somewhat," she said. "Though I have not yet been anointed as a sword sister, the others have."

"So what do you need?"

"When the convent was burned, we had no time to arm or equip ourselves. It was our duty to see to the safety of the children before all else. Once they were safe, we would have armed ourselves and fought against the Red Hand and Daeglan's men, but the city guards came and put an end to the attack."

"And the convent was burned to the ground," Ferrin added.

"Yes," Ailin said. "But our vaults are underground. That's where the armory and the inner sanctum are located."

"Underground, you say?"

"In a secret vault, located deep within the old tunnels."

Ferrin smiled. The Thieves' Guild was in those same tunnels. He had no idea there were other parts of it his friends had not yet explored.

"How did the sisters get to this sanctum and its armory?" Ferrin asked. "Through the entrance outside of town?"

"No," Ailin replied. "There is an entrance within the convent's grounds. How do you know about the entrance outside of town?"

"Well," Ferrin said. "Let's just say that I frequent the tunnels on occasion. My friends and I."

"Why?"

Ferrin sighed. "We have an order of our own," he said. "One that secretly serves the people and stands against the nobles. We have been doing so behind the scenes for several years now but have just recently begun organizing into something more… official."

Ailin smiled. "A den of thieves?"

"You could say that," Ferrin replied. "We work together with the rangers when we can. We have even agreed to take in orphans when needed and train them to put their skills to good use; either for the king's rangers or in… other ways," he gave her a wolfish grin, drawing another beautiful smile.

"Then I have definitely found the right man to help me," she said.

Man, he thought. She had referred to him as a man. That was a welcome change. Everyone else called him *boy*.

"I am, indeed, the best man for the job," he said. "Whatever that is."

He had no idea why he was telling her his secrets. Perhaps he trusted her because she trusted him. Or perhaps it was her smile or the fact that the sight of her made his heart pound like it never had before.

"I need to get the order's weapons inside Daeglan's compound," she said. "But I cannot do it myself."

"Ah," Ferrin said. That was possible, he thought. At the moment, he had no idea how he could pull it off, but it was still possible. For her, he would make it possible.

"I want in on this," Joran said, coming from around the forge. "I've been wanting to see Daeglan swing from a tree since I first met him."

"How can you help?" Ailin asked.

"Well," Joran said. "I *am* the town smith. I'm sure there's something he needs that only I can supply."

"We would need a reason to get in," Ferrin said. "His estate is well guarded. The only way in that I know of is right through the front gate."

Joran cleared his throat. "Keep in mind those bandits, whatever they're called, go there frequently. They're up to something, I say. All of them are."

"Who are they?" Ailin asked. "They had a hand in burning down the convent."

"Just criminals," Ferrin said, guessing.

Joran chuckled. "They're more than just criminals," he corrected. "They're a whole network, I tell you. But some of the nobles have been using them as mercenaries. They'll do anything for the right price."

"Smuggling, hired muscle, I wonder what else," Ferrin mused. "In any case, we'll have to interrupt one of their shipments and take over its delivery. We can set up a roadblock somewhere along the road."

"You will have to figure out their routes first," Joran said.

Ferrin nodded. "True," he said. "Maybe Kuros can help. The rangers have been scouting Daeglan's estate for quite a while. They would know their routes."

"Then," Joran added, "you'll have to remember that Daeglan will want to inspect anything that comes through the front gates."

"No problem," Ferrin said. "The weapons and armor can be hidden in a false bottom. I know just the place to get such a wagon."

He turned to Ailin, smiling when he saw the hopeful look on her face.

"It is settled," he said. "As our first act of defiance, the Thieves' Guild will help you liberate your sisters. You have my word."

Ailin sighed, seeming relieved that she had found someone to help her.

"Joran," Ferrin said, "I need to know where Garret and his older friend are."

"Garret?" Ailin echoed. "You've seen him?"

"Yes," Ferrin said. "I met him in Faillaigh; he and his companion."

Ailin's eyes closed, and she sighed with relief. "Good," she said. "I was afraid he didn't make it out."

Ferrin smiled. "He is alive and well," Ferrin assured her. "And is in the company of someone who may be able to help us."

"Helena will be happy to hear this," Ailin said.

Joran chuckled. "Probably not so happy when she finds out who this man is."

"What do you mean?" Ailin asked.

"He is an assassin," Joran said. "And he was interested in the boy the last we spoke."

Ailin nodded. "Well," she said. "I suppose there are worse things to get involved in."

"Don't worry," Ferrin said. "He is well taken care of. This stranger seemed like a man of honor."

186

"I agree," Joran said. "Though he snuck into my forge and scared the daylights out of me, I didn't see him as a threat. He was concerned about another assassin on the prowl."

Ferrin glanced at Joran, remembering the words he heard Darragh and the Queen speak. "Was this assassin a woman?" he asked.

Joran shook his head. "Don't know rightly," he said. "All we know is that the dagger Etanos brought me was one of Khem. He wanted to know if I could read the inscriptions upon it."

Ailin grabbed Ferrin's arm. "What do you know of an assassin of Khem?"

Ferrin sighed. "Nothing specific," he lied. "Only that Darragh knows of her existence."

"She seems to be after this Etanos fellow," Joran added.

"In that case," Ailin said. "Garret may be in danger."

Ferrin swallowed hard. He wondered if he should mention anything he heard. It probably wouldn't help the situation any. Though this assassin was being used in a plot against the king, he had faith that this Etanos could defeat her, making any mention of the plot pointless. Soon, he guessed, whoever this woman was she would no longer be a factor. He would hold his tongue for the moment. His primary focus was assisting this beautiful young woman and her sisters—and, of course, getting the children to safety.

Chapter Twenty-Two

eli's face was the first thing Garret saw when he opened his eyes. She sat next to him on the rickety cot, smiling down at him as his eyes fluttered. Though he had not seen her since they had first met, he had the strange feeling that she had been with him all night; watching over him and keeping him safe.

He was in much pain. Though a great part of it was the familiar cramp that always happened after strenuous activity, there was an underlying fatigue that he could not explain. Though in some ways, there was also a fulfillment that was unfamiliar to him; something new and unexplained.

Aeli's presence, however, warmed his heart, and he knew that she had healed him. From what, he was still unsure. All that he remembered was seeing the frightening woman land near him and pounce on him like a cat—a cat with fearsome, hellish eyes that burned into his very soul.

"How do you feel?" Aeli asked him softly, stroking his hair.

Garret looked up into her eyes, seeing the kindness there. "All right," he said. "What happened?"

"You were injured by a dark blade," she replied. "One that left its mark within you. It is gone now."

Garret struggled to remember what had happened while he was asleep. It felt like he had traveled somewhere else, as if he had left his body for a moment.

"I was…" he stuttered, "somewhere…"

Aeli smiled at him. "You were in the presence of the Great Mother," she said. "It was only through her power that you were saved."

Garret sighed. He had felt the warmth of someone's presence, he remembered. A mother's warmth, wrapped around him like a protective cloak. It was a feeling he had never felt before, but he guessed that was what it would be like.

"I feel different," he said.

Aeli nodded. "As you should," she said. "Not many people get to experience her presence and return to the land of the living. But it has happened to you, and she has taken notice of your soul. She has given you her blessing, and her strength. That is something even fewer people experience. It changes you; makes you stronger."

Garret was confused. He wasn't sure what she meant by her words. He did feel different, as he had said, but was unsure how he could possibly have changed, or *why* the Great Mother would have changed him. He was just a boy; and one who had killed many men that night.

"She has taken notice?" he echoed her earlier words.

"Yes," Aeli said. "And don't worry; she has not passed judgment on you for your deeds. You must remember that the Great Mother herself must kill to keep the balance of all things. Everything returns to her and is reborn in some other way. You needn't worry about her judging you. She is incapable of hatred toward her children."

Garret sighed. "I had strange feelings when she was near," he said. "They were feelings of guilt... or... I don't know."

Aeli leaned down to kiss his forehead. Her lips left a pleasant tingling on his skin and sent a jolt through his body. He stared up at her afterward, trying to comprehend her words, and why she cared so much about his well-being.

"You are a mortal man," Aeli said. "Such feelings are typical when in the presence of the divine. Even I am humbled by her presence. Though I act as her hand and am blessed in certain ways, I am still but a mortal woman. Someday, I will die and return to the Earth like everyone and everything else. Until then, her essence will always be with me, and it will always be with you."

"I do feel it," Garret said. "It's something I've never felt before."

"That is a mother's love," Aeli said. "It is with you now, and you deserve it. She knows that you never knew your mother, and has taken it upon herself to give you that which your soul needed."

Garret smiled. "It is a good feeling."

Aeli smiled again, standing. "It is," she said. "Let it be a driving force for you, and always do her bidding. You are now, and shall always be, one of her favored children. But now, it is time for you to rest. Etanos brought you here for me to heal you, but I must now attend to him."

"Is he all right?" Garret asked. "Was he hurt, too?"

"Only his soul," Aeli said. "And that will take even more time to heal."

* * *

"Her name is Ammarah," Etanos said.

He and Kuros sat outside in the rays of the rising sun, and the sounds of the forest awakening surrounded them like a comforting shield.

"Who is she?" Kuros asked.

"She was an assassin I had encountered on many occasions," Etanos explained. "Not a member of my order, but someone independent. I don't know where she learned the trade, but it was always obvious that she never learned the creed, or she simply chose to ignore it."

"I am not a seer," Kuros said, "or anything magical, for that matter, but even I could feel her innate darkness."

Etanos glanced at him, nodding. "It was always strong," he said. "But now it is overpowering."

"Why does she hate you so?" Kuros asked. "Why is she so intent on destroying you?"

Etanos was silent as he gathered his thoughts—and the courage to proceed. Despite knowing that his actions were noble, he couldn't shake the feeling that he might be judged for them. She was, after all, a woman; and a young one, at that. At least, she was at the time.

"We fought many years ago," he explained, "atop a temple of Imbra in Khem. I defeated her in combat, and I assumed she was dead."

"Why did you fight her?"

"She gave the guilds a bad name," Etanos said. "We worked to maintain the balance. She worked for the recognition and the notoriety. She took contracts without question, killing her marks without even the slightest of concerns for their legitimacy. Along the way, she killed the innocent, including women and children who stood in the way. She had to be stopped."

Kuros nodded. Etanos studied his face, which was turned upward at the morning sky. He saw no judgment there, which comforted him greatly.

"So," he continued, "I took it upon myself to go after her. I found her a year or so later, always finding death in her wake. She was at the temple to kill the high priest of Imbra, at the order of someone unknown, a necromancer, possibly. I confronted her on the rooftop, and we fought there. I was intent on destroying her and destroy her I did. But, not as thoroughly as I had thought."

Aeli came out then, gently closing her door behind her and taking a seat next to them.

"She tried to justify her actions," Etanos said. "She said that she was acting on behalf of the balance and that her cause was greater than the guild's. But I knew that was not the case. We fought furiously on that rooftop, and I could feel her hatred even then. But I was able to get the upper hand in the battle, and she fell into the beacon that burned high above the streets. It was then that I felt the guilt of what I had done. She was set aflame and thrashed and screamed in the most agonizing way one could imagine. I felt sorry for her, and despite her evil, I did not wish to see her suffer. So, I put an arrow in her heart. She fell from that rooftop to the street below."

He paused then, closing his eyes as he pictured her falling to her presumed death, crashing into the stones below.

"There is no way she could have survived," he said finally.

"She did not," Aeli said. "At least her body didn't. She was broken in that fall; killed as you would have expected. But something brought her back. Someone skilled in dark arts, perhaps. I could feel the darkness within her, and though some of it was hers, there was something else, too. A death magic of some sort. What we saw last night was not human, but something less than human. A construct of some kind; a simulacrum of steel and dead flesh driven by pure hatred. This is something the women of my family called a revenant; a spirit that has returned to its body to seek revenge."

"Created by whom?" Etanos asked.

Aeli shook her head. "I do not know," she said. "You mentioned a necromancer. Perhaps it was him or her. Either way, it was Ammarah's hatred that allowed her body to be resurrected and infused with unnatural materials. There is very little of her body left, and none of her soul. Her soul, though dark, has returned to the Great Mother, as all souls do. She is now nothing but pure physical form, driven by revenge. She is nothing but mind and body, driven by a spirit of pure evil."

Kuros shook his head. "So, she is a monster; a soulless one at that. And that is the most dangerous kind."

Aeli nodded slowly. "Etanos," she said. "She *must* be destroyed."

* * *

Kuros had gathered his gear and ate some small morsels that Aeli had given him. As he strapped his bow to his back, Etanos reached out to shake his hand in friendship. The two locked eyes for a moment, knowing that their combined efforts had been for the greater good and that they had done a most noble deed in freeing the slaves.

"It was good to meet you, Kuros," Etanos said, just as Garret appeared outside.

"Likewise," the ranger said.

Garret nodded in greeting, and Kuros took his hand as well. Aeli looked on, smiling sadly.

"You did a great thing, Garret," the ranger said. "Make no mistake about that. I hope our paths will cross again in the future."

"I'm sure they will," Garret replied.

Etanos looked at Garret with pride. The young man had performed well, and he had done so on a mission that was unmatched in its noble cause. Garret would be a great assassin; he knew and would embody the true cause of the Brotherhood of Perses.

"I must return to my brothers now," Kuros said. "I do not doubt that you will be investigating Daeglan's estate. Keep in mind that we are watching him as well, and we will be there when we are needed."

Garret nodded.

Etanos kept his eyes on Aeli, who continued her saddened stance. There was something in the way she looked at the two young men that was disturbing to the assassin. She seemed to feel something that he did not. Perhaps it was admiration, but there was no way of telling.

"Goodbye, my friends," Kuros said.

"Goodbye, Kuros," Aeli said to him. "And remember to keep this house in your thoughts. If you are ever in danger, I am always here to help."

Kuros smiled as he turned to leave; giving them one last wave before he departed into the forest.

Garret turned to Etanos. "The slaves are freed, then?" he asked.

"Yes," Etanos replied. "You did very well. They are safe, and presumably on their way back to their families."

Garret smiled.

"My friend," Etanos said. "We have much more work to do. Gather your things, and we too will depart."

Garret nodded, returning to Aeli's cottage. Etanos approached her carefully, keeping an eye on her expression. She kept her face turned down, still bearing that look of sadness.

"What is it, Aeli?" Etanos asked. "You look as if you see or feel something disturbing."

She shook her head. "It is nothing," she said. "Just the quiet musings of one who sees things others do not."

"You know something," Etanos said. "Something of the future, perhaps."

She looked up at him, and he stared into her eyes. "There are things in the future that have been set into motion," she said. "Things that cannot be changed."

"What do you mean?" Etanos asked.

"I cannot say," she replied. "Or go into too much detail, as you will try to change them. You must remember that everything happens for a reason and that changing the future can have a detrimental effect on the greater good."

"I do not understand," Etanos said. "Tell me. Please."

Aeli lowered her head again, clenching her jaw. "The fates of Garret and Kuros are intertwined," she explained. "Their bond is strong, as their friendship will be. But they share a fate that is more than just that. It is more than friendship and more than just their parallel paths."

Etanos clenched his jaw, feeling that Aeli's words were about to get much worse. And they did.

"In the future," she said. "Those two boys will die by the same hand."

* * *

"We will follow the river back to Gaellos," Etanos said. "Then, we will come up with a plan to get the sisters of Gaia out of Daeglan's grasp."

"Kuros mentioned his rangers keeping watch on his estate," Garret said.

"That's right," Etanos said. "And if my guess is correct, Joran the smith will be sympathetic to our cause."

"Should we stop in and see him?"

"Of course," Etanos replied, smiling.

Garret had noticed how troubled his mentor had seemed since they departed Aeli's cottage. He kept quiet, though, assuming his mood was simply due to the encounter with the horrifying assassin. Etanos had explained who she was, how she had died, and why she was after him. The young man found the story remarkable and strangely familiar at the same time. He had heard stories of dark wizards creating strange things in the past; golems and the like.

Why would this warrior be any different?

"You shouldn't feel guilt," Garret said, truly believing it. "Like you said before, she was evil, like the men we killed at the mines. Even more so, from what I gathered of your story."

Etanos nodded half-heartedly. "True," he said. "I cannot explain the guilt. Perhaps it is because I created her in a way. Her hatred of me is what made her who she is."

"Now you're blaming yourself as well as feeling guilty. If a warrior blames himself for every vengeful monster he creates, he would have a very miserable life."

Etanos chuckled, reaching out to pat Garret on the back. "You are wise beyond your years, my friend," he said. "And I suppose the guilt will go away once she's destroyed."

"Can you stop her, do you think?"

"I did once," Etanos replied. "I will do so again."

Garret accepted his answer, though the man's tone told him that there was some doubt. He had not witnessed the woman's prowess himself, but the aura of power that he felt when she was on top of him was overwhelming, even for those few seconds. Anyone who could stand against her would have to be very powerful. Garret did not doubt that his mentor was that skilled.

"So," Etanos said. "How do you feel?"

Garret rubbed his collarbone, feeling the slight tenderness that persisted. "It's not that painful," he said. "It just aches a little."

"The healing ritual was the strangest thing I have ever seen," Etanos said. "I can't explain it."

"It was strange for me as well."

"What did you see on the other side?"

Garret thought for a moment, remembering Aeli's words. "I think I was in the presence of the Great Mother," he said. "But she allowed me to return for some reason; like I was meant to."

Etanos was quiet again, but Garret did not press the matter.

"What did Aeli do?" Garret asked.

Etanos looked up, half-grinning. "She ate your soul, my friend," he joked. "Ate it right up."

Garret chuckled half-heartedly, not sure whether Etanos was serious or not.

And his mentor gave no indication either way.

Chapter Twenty-Three

ilin looked disheartened when they arrived at the ruins of the convent. Very little remained; only the blackened skeletons of the wooden buildings and the crumbled walls of those made of stone. Even the small statue of Gaia had been toppled and scorched during the chaos. Though the city guards and other volunteers had done their best to put out the flames, the damage had been extensive, and there was no hope of ever rebuilding.

Ferrin noticed the tears that were welling up in the young woman's eyes. It saddened him greatly to see her cry, but he hesitated to comfort her. In his heart, he wanted to embrace her and pour his soul out in support; reassuring her that everything would work out. But they had just met, and such an action might seem a bit... strange.

She, however, felt different. Without warning, she burst out in tears and heavy sobs, turning to bury her face in Ferrin's tunic. He wrapped his arms around her tightly, feeling a deep stirring in his heart. He felt his own eyes welling up and had a sinking feeling in his heart. He wanted to cry with her and make everything all right. The sound of her crying simply tore at his soul like nothing ever had before.

What the hell was going on?

"Where is this temple?" Joran asked.

"Give her a moment," Ferrin pleaded.

Ailin broke away, looking up into Ferrin's eyes. "No," she said softly. "He's right. The city guards would wonder why we are here."

"Well," Joran said. "Not likely. As much as it irks me to say it, Ferrin's presence is a good thing. It is well known that he works for Lord Darragh. They likely wouldn't bother us or ask questions if they saw him."

Ferrin grinned. "That must have been torture to say," he joked.

Joran grumbled, kicking through the rubble. Ailin turned away, leading them further into the complex. "The temple entrance is in the grove," she said. "It is disguised as a fountain, so no one ever knew it was there. Even the children were unaware — unless they were initiated, anyway."

Ferrin followed her close, glancing at Joran occasionally as the smith grunted and groaned his discontent. Ferrin knew the man respected the worship of the Firstborn and the Great Mother, and it was obvious that seeing such a complex burnt to the ground was quite disturbing to him.

"Thank goodness the trees were unharmed," Ailin said. "This used to be a wellspring, like the one further south. But things have changed since Daegoth's time."

Daegoth II, Ferrin echoed in his mind. He was the first Dragon King, anointed by the High Priest of Drakkar, Erenoth, many thousands of years ago. He had usurped the throne from Dag T'kar — so it was said — and defeated the great armies of Firbolga that served him. The legends said that he was the son of the Dragon himself, and the grandson of Daegoth I, and that he simply took the name Daegoth II to indicate that he was the rightful heir.

It was a fascinating story, but Ferrin had no time to ponder it now.

"Here it is," Ailin said.

They stood before a limestone fountain that was as white as the clouds above but weathered and cracked with age. It was at least fifteen feet in diameter, with a six-foot bowl in the center. Though decorated and carved with intricate swirling designs, it was dry and non-functional. The spout that sprayed water up into the air was broken and bent, forever empty and inactive.

"How do we get inside?" Joran asked. "And how do we get the weapons out?"

"If what Ferrin said is true," Ailin began, "then there should be a connecting tunnel to his guild house. These tunnels were built thousands of years ago by the Alvar, long before the Order of Baleron. They span the entire city underneath, and even outside in some areas. If we can find the connecting tunnels, then we can transport the weapons to Ferrin's guild and prepare them to be delivered from there."

"Then why didn't we just go through the guild side?" Joran asked.

"Because I am unfamiliar with its layout," Ailin said. "Plus, that would be too easy."

Ferrin shot Joran a questioning glance. The smith shrugged.

Ailin approached the fountain, stepping into the giant basin with cautious feet. Ferrin watched her with admiration. Though she had seemed like a meek and gentle woman, her stance was now confident and steady, as if she had done this a thousand times before. And likely she had.

"*Iak sakkat a beru na,*" she chanted, with raised arms.

There was a slight rumbling, and Ferrin glanced at Joran again. The smith was deadlocked on the fountain and didn't notice.

"*Forah den muti ka ahn,*" Ailin continued.

Suddenly, a loud grinding sound shook Ferrin from his trance, and he watched with wide eyes as the fountain's center bowl began sinking into the basin. It spun slowly, descending lower and lower into the darkness with audible clunks that sounded every so often. He realized the bowl was descending on gears and dropping stone slabs along the way that formed a spiral stairway leading downward.

"How did that work when the fountain..." Joran began but stopped when Ferrin waved his hand at him.

Ailin lowered her arms, turning back at them with a smile. "Come now," she said. "The temple is below."

Ferrin stepped forward, but Joran hesitated.

"I don't feel right going into such a sacred place," the man said.

"The Great Mother welcomes all good people into her house," Ailin assured him.

Joran grinned. "Then Ferrin best wait outside."

Ferrin half-smiled at her. "He jests," he said. "He likes me. He really does."

He shot Joran an annoyed glance as he followed Ailin down the stairs.

"I've always wondered how this entrance worked," she said. "There are no places in the walls where the steps would be stored when the entrance is closed."

"It's probably some kind of Alvar magic," Ferrin suggested. He ran his hands along the surface of the stone. It was smooth, almost ivory-like — with only the slightest of seams between the perfectly flat blocks.

"Those Alvar were crafty fellows," Joran said. "And this material is strange. I've never seen anything like it."

"It's limestone, Joran," Ferrin said. "Just limestone."

He heard the smith grumble behind him.

The staircase opened into a circular room below. The circular wall was carved with reliefs of the Great Mother in the various states she had appeared to her followers in the past. Among them, was one carving that appeared to be Alvar; complete with slim, angular features, and slightly pointed ears.

Opposite the landing was a steel door, beveled on all four sides with vine-like carvings surrounding its central panel. In the center of that panel was a raised relief of the swirl sigil; about the size of a large man's fist and made of pure gold that seemed to shimmer with a life of its own. Ferrin was mesmerized by its beauty, and the thief in him pondered the possibility of prying it off the door. But, he quickly shook his head in frustration when he realized the ridiculousness of the idea. He was there to help, not to steal.

Ailin raised her arms once more, turning her palms upward, and lowered her head. She chanted silently this time, and Ferrin and Joran waited patiently as she mouthed the words to her spell. When she was finished, the sigil began to glow and slowly slid out. It turned clockwise one full resolution, clicked into place, and then sank back into the steel door.

A loud click sounded, and then the steel door ground back several feet until it settled into a perpendicular wall behind it. On either side of it, nestled in the limestone blocks, were tiny green orbs of glowing magic that lit the hallway with their pleasant light. Above them, the fountain's bowl rose to its original spot, closing the stairway behind it.

"This is the inner sanctum," Ailin said. "Three priestesses go left, three go right, and they all meet on the other side, where the high priestess awaits."

"Helena?" Ferrin wondered.

"Yes," Ailin replied. "She is the headmistress, high priestess, and captain of the Sword Sisters."

Ferrin glanced at Joran again, who returned his curious expression.

"Women with swords," Joran mused, smiling. "Angus' mother carried a sword. I fell in love with her at first sight."

Ferrin grinned. "I can see that," he said.

"Come," Ailin said.

Ferrin followed her as she went to the left, noticing that the wall was not part of a hallway, but had been built as a standalone blockade. On either side of it, stairs led downward along limestone walls that were carved with smooth columns.

"The wall is a deterrent," Ailin said. "Much like the entrances to the temples in the east."

Ferrin understood. Temples of Yin-Kai, the Firstborn of the far eastern lands, had walls like this facing their entrances. They were meant to prevent foul spirits from entering hollowed grounds, as the spirits themselves could only move in straight lines for some reason. The Alvar must have had similar beliefs.

They descended the short stairway, which ended at a landing decorated with reddish-brown tiles of sandstone that formed the symbol of Gaia. They continued down to the right, along the beautifully decorated walls, and into the inner sanctum below. Ferrin gasped when he beheld the chamber.

It was a square chamber, with wide columns along each of the side walls, and a giant Gaia symbol on the floor. At each of the three spirals were two smaller circles, where Ferrin assumed a priestess would stand. At the center was a larger circle for the high priestess, where she would stand surrounded by her servants.

The ceiling was vaulted, carved like the canopy of a thick forest, and hung with lanterns that glowed with the green energy of the Earth. At the far end was a large ornate door, emblazoned with Alvar runes and a large relief of two crossed swords. It appeared to be made of bronze, with its carvings of shining silver.

"Ach," Joran exclaimed in disbelief. "I've never seen anything like this."

Ferrin nodded. "It's beautiful."

"This is where we hold our prayer," Ailin said. "Helena stood in the center circle, and the other sisters would stand in the smaller circles."

"And where did you stand?" Ferrin asked.

"Along the sides with the other initiates," she replied, pointing to the columns that lined the chamber. "I am new to the sisterhood. I only arrived a year ago, when my parents disowned me."

Ferrin turned to her, seeing the sadness in her eyes. His heart sank. "And why did they disown you?"

"They wanted me to marry a merchant in Bray," she said. "It would have been a loveless business arrangement."

"And who did you *want* to marry?"

"If I marry someday," she said, smiling, "it will be someone of my choosing. Someone valiant, handsome, and cares for others."

Ferrin smiled, staring into her eyes, daydreaming about standing next to her in front of an altar to the Great Mother.

"Can we get on with it?" Joran interrupted, gruffly.

Ailin shook her head, seemingly clearing away her daydreams. "Yes, of course."

She went across the chamber, leading them to the bronze door. It was twice as tall as she was, and almost the same width. Without a word, she placed her hands on the hilts of the crossed swords, silently chanting another spell. The swords came to life, uncrossing and spinning to a vertical position with a loud clunk. She then pushed the door open and turned to smile at them.

"This is the armory," she said. "And somewhere beyond is where these tunnels connect to your guild."

"Do you know where?" Ferrin asked.

"Not exactly," she said. "But there is a strange door that we were previously forbidden from entering. I believe it has a ward cast upon it, but I may be able to dispel it. That may be the entrance."

Ferrin nodded. He remembered seeing a door on his side of the tunnels that seemed out of place. It was buried behind rubble—broken columns and such—but was visible at the top. He had never paid much attention to it, thinking it led to a ruined area. The tunnels, after all, were thousands of years old. There was no reason to believe the entire lot of them was pristine and intact.

Ailin entered the chamber and raised her arms, bringing several globes of green energy to life. They shone brightly upon their poles, shining almost white, and illuminating the small room as if it were daylight. At the far end of the square chamber, in front of yet another barricade-like wall, was a single straw mannequin, dressed in shining steel-like Alvar armor. On either side were three other mannequins dressed in similar armor; all of them decorated with highly detailed designs of Alvar origin.

Each breastplate had a shield and longsword attached to the front, emblazoned with the symbol of Gaia. Ferrin looked at the gear in awe, but not quite as much as Joran, who approached the suits with the sparkling eyes of a child in a candy shop.

"My, my, my," he said. "This is the most beautiful work I've ever seen. I am truly humbled. These are Alvar, correct?"

"Yes," Ailin said. "Forged thousands of years ago, when the Alvar resided here on our world."

"If only I had the skill to forge armor and weapons such as these."

"The daggers you made for me were exquisite," Ferrin reminded him. "Don't sell yourself short."

Joran shot him a strange look, a half-smile with a skeptical slant of his brow. Ferrin wasn't sure what it meant, but he guessed it was a semi-gracious reaction to an unexpected—and uncharacteristic—compliment.

"The gear is extremely lightweight," Ailin said. "It was made for Alvar shield maidens."

Ferrin grunted, reaching out to touch the strange metal. "I had no idea there were Alvar women who carried weapons," he said. "But then, I had no idea there were priestesses of Gaia who bore weapons, either."

"This isn't even steel," Joran said. "I thought it was steel. What is it?"

"Helena says it is a metal of Alvheim," Ailin said. "Stronger and lighter than even Adamantium."

"Well, I'll be damned," Joran said. "It doesn't even dent when I press on it."

He flicked the breastplate with his finger, expecting to hear a metallic ding. What sounded was more of a hollow, wooden sound. He furrowed his brow, drawing a curious laugh from Ailin.

"If it's as light as you say," Ferrin said, "we should be able to get it into the Thieves' Guild with no problem. We just have to find the way in from here. Once we get there, I can find my guild mates. They will help us move everything. Then, it will be up to us to find a Red Hand caravan to hijack."

"As I said," Joran reminded him, "the rangers will know their routes."

Ailin clasped her hands before her, smiling and sighing with delight. "I am so glad I met you both," she said. "I was worried I wouldn't be able to fulfill my duties and get these weapons back to my sisters."

Ferrin smiled. "Fear not," he said. "We are *both* on your side. That is why I created the guild in the first place; to help those in need."

"And to steal from those who are not," Joran added.

Ferrin ignored him, continuing to stare at Ailin. She stared back for a moment, and then turned away with a blissful grin.

"I will show you where the door is," she said. "Then I will try to open it."

They followed her around the wall, where another bronze door stood facing it. Ailin performed the same spell she had before, and the door slid out and settled into the wall. Ferrin realized that there were no tracks on either the floor or ceiling. The door just seemed to know where to go.

Beyond was a long hallway, just wide enough for two people to walk side by side. It was separated into sections, each one formed by support columns that were flush with the walls. It was tall, with an arched ceiling, and large green globes hung from each section. At the far end there was yet another door, with one door on each wall beside it.

They hurried along, marveling at the craftsmanship of the stone supports. Again, the limestone was smooth and featureless, with only the slightest of seams. Even the floor was pristine, built of tightly packed blocks with golden veins running parallel to its length.

The door at the end was arched and made of carved white wood. Ferrin couldn't tell whether it was painted or naturally white. Its grain showed through, giving him the impression that this was its natural color. Either that or the paint was simply translucent.

"Beautiful work," he said, admiring the smoothness of the finish.

Ailin smiled, going to the door on the right and turning its golden handle. "The doorway is down this hall," she said. "This is the only area where there are doors I've never been through."

"What else is here?" Ferrin asked.

"Some of the old forges," she said. "But they are no longer used."

"Hmm," Joran grunted. "Likely because there is nowhere for the smoke to vent to."

Ailin shook her head. "These were Alvar forges," she said. "They used magical fire to forge their blades. There was no smoke."

Joran's eyes lit up, and he began to stare off into space as if daydreaming. Ferrin grinned, knowing the smith would likely love to use an Alvar forge. Perhaps when everything was done and over with, something could be arranged for him to do so.

Ailin entered the hallway, motioning for them to follow. Ferrin had to nudge Joran out of his daydreaming, but the smile on the man's face persisted. They followed Ailin inside, noting the gruff look of the hallway as compared to the rest of the complex. The walls were made of rough, gray stone, a material more befitting of a forge.

At the end, there was a dark-stained wood door, oak, perhaps. It was thick, and its slabs were held together with iron bands riveted directly into the wood. There was a single handle in the center in the shape of the spiral of Gaia. Ailin reached out and turned it, stepping aside as she pushed it open.

"Here you are," she said with a smile. "The largest Alvar forge."

Joran pushed past Ferrin, almost knocking him down. Ferrin shook his head at Ailin and followed him in, hearing him gasp as he beheld what was probably a treasure trove of smith's tools.

And it was.

The room was domed, with the forge in the center rising to meet the ceiling. Though as Ailin said, there would be no smoke, the heat from the magical fires would have vented upward and dissipated into the stone above.

The entire room was built of grey stone, with circular walls that were lined with countless empty racks. Piles upon piles of ingots were stacked everywhere and surrounding the forge itself were racks of tools and various stations where the Alvar smiths worked their magic.

"This is the most glorious thing I have ever seen," Joran whispered as if looking upon a veritable dragon's treasure. "I would never leave this place."

Ailin shot Ferrin a mirthful glance.

"Joran," Ferrin said. "I would be glad to help you figure out how to get it working when this is over." He glanced at Ailin again. "That is if the sisters deem it acceptable to do so."

"I'm sure they wouldn't mind," Ailin said. "Come now. The door is this way."

They followed her across the room, where another door stood ajar. The hallway beyond was dark and damp, lit only by the dim light of several fading orbs of magic. At the end of it, there stood a relief, carved directly into a limestone slab that seemed oddly out of place. It was a mural of strange design; a large four-armed swirl made of hundreds of thousands of tiny dots. It was oval-shaped, and stood vertically along the face of the stone, flanked on all four sides by rows of diamond-shaped depressions.

"What is that?" Ferrin asked, intrigued.

"I don't know," Ailin replied. "None of us do. But I suspect it has something to do with the wards that are placed upon it."

Ferrin approached the door, pressing his ear against the stone. There were faint humming sounds coming from the other side; sounds he could not identify. He stepped back, confused, staring at the swirling design.

"I know what that is," Joran said.

Ferrin and Ailin turned to look at him.

"It's the symbol of the Keeper," he told them.

"Who or what is the Keeper?" Ferrin asked.

"Ah," Ailin said in recognition. "It is he who holds the power of our universe. He is like the druid of the cosmos."

"I've never heard of him," Ferrin said. "Where did you learn of this, Joran?"

Joran grunted, scratching his chin in thought. "I don't remember," he said. "But I believe Jodocus spoke of him once."

"You've met the Great Druid?" Ailin asked.

"Hmm," Joran replied. "Many years ago, when I was a... *younger* man."

He stepped forward, examining the spiral. He placed his hands on the design, feeling along its spirals and staring off into space. His hands gradually reached the center, where the tiny dots were far more concentrated, and then leaned in to get a closer look.

"Well, I'll be," he said.

Ferrin leaned in closer. "What is it?"

Joran pointed at three small depressions in the center. They were spaced about three inches apart and connected by lines; forming a triangle.

"I know how to open this," he said. "And this is not a door. It is a portal."

"How do you know this?" Ailin asked.

"Because the Keeper travels through portals, and the key to opening them is through this triangle design."

He stepped back, thinking for a moment, mumbling the word *key* repeatedly. Finally, his eyes lit up, and he clenched his fist in the air.

"I'll be back!" he said, excitedly, turning and running back down the hallway.

Ferrin looked at Ailin, confused. She shrugged, leaning against the wall, shyly looking at the floor.

"He'll be back," Ferrin said. "But I have no idea where he is going."

Ailin glanced back at the portal, shaking her head. "He must know something the sisters don't," she said. "And that makes me curious."

"Well," Ferrin said. "He may seem to be just a smith, but he's a lot smarter than most would give him credit for."

She looked at him and smiled. He instantly felt the strangeness again; that stirring in his heart that stole his words — and his calm demeanor. There was something about the way her eyes sparkled that made him feel like a small child wanting to hide from a kind stranger. All he could do was grin stupidly and chuckle uncomfortably.

Thankfully, Joran returned quickly, running as fast as he could, cackling with knowing laughter. "Got it!" he said, holding up what looked to be an engineer's divider. "This is it!"

He fumbled with the golden instrument for a moment, pulling apart its arms to fit the distance between two of the holes in the portal. He then placed a point in the top hole and the other point in the lower right hole. A click sounded, and the portal thumped slightly. He grinned, and then swiveled the top point out and to the left, resting it in the bottom left hole. Another click sounded, and the portal thumped again. With one last grin, he swiveled the other point up to the top hole. The click sounded once more, and the portal began to rumble.

"It's opening," Ailin said. "It didn't need a spell at all. No wonder we couldn't open it."

Before their very eyes, the stone began to shimmer and roil like churning milk. The surface became chaotic and swirled slowly in the direction of the design that was upon it. They all stepped back in wonder — and slight fear — their mouths and eyes wide open.

Then, with a burst of light, the stone opened like an iris, pulling threads of reality with it in little swirls of green. When the light died down, the room beyond was visible.

As were the two thieves who stood there, shocked and bewildered.

"Ah," Ferrin exclaimed. "Tad, Bolan, I'm glad you're here!"

The two thieves nodded slowly, unsure as to what was going on. Ferrin stepped into the room, noticing that the portal had opened in a different place than he had expected. This was the proposed training room, and the two thieves had been setting up the training dummies when — apparently — the fancy plaque on the wall had suddenly opened.

"We are in business, friends," Ferrin continued, happy to see his colleagues. "You know Joran, the smith. This is Ailin of the Temple of Gaia."

The two thieves nodded wordlessly, their eyes still wide and their mouths gaping.

"Gather whoever else is here," Ferrin said. "We have work to do. Are you ready?"

Without a word, Tad and Bolan looked at each other, turned, and left to find the other thieves. Ferrin chuckled, putting his arm around Ailin.

"You see," he said. "My brothers and I will see to your weapons. Not a problem."

The smile on Ailin's face warmed his heart. But the kiss she planted on his lips did much, much more. Joran smirked, shooting him a crooked smile and one raised eyebrow as Ailin returned through the open portal.

"You devil," he said. "Why, she's young enough to be your... well, sister maybe."

Ferrin grinned proudly. "Someday," he said. "I will marry that girl."

"Ohhh," Joran laughed. "And a fine wife she'll make, too. That is if she likes sneaky little bastards."

Ferrin started to protest but realized Joran was right. He *was* a sneaky little bastard, and he would train all his children to be so, as well.

"Let's hope so," he said, grinning.

CHAPTER TWENTY-FOUR

mmarah's mind was clouded. Despite her strong sense of discipline, the mere sight of her nemesis had brought the past swirling back into her thoughts. His face was burned into her memory, and the hatred she felt for him was growing by the day. He had ruined her life all those years ago, destroying any hope she had for passing on her own legacy.

The legacy she carried in her belly when her body was broken and burned.

Her child had died that day. That dark seed of death and destruction the fates had given her. She had great plans for it; plans that would bring the underworld to its knees. With her spawn, she would rule the guilds, being the mother of death itself. Her child would be feared, respected, and would stand above all assassins; he would be their lord and master—the *new* Perses.

But all of that was taken away by Etanos.

His name brought a snarl to her lips. She gritted her ruined teeth in anger, stretching her cauterized lips over them until they cracked painfully and pleasantly. She loved the pain. She revered it. It was all she had left. With only a small portion of her true body remaining, any sensation at all brought her unfathomable ecstasy. Pain and pleasure, to her, were inseparable.

She closed her eyes to take it all in, feeling the throbbing waves of pleasure spread across her face. It reminded her of the past, when she lay there staring at the night sky; shattered on the stone street, and waiting for death. She remembered the dark face of the cloaked man who had found her. The strange shape of his brow; the way his dark skin reflected the moonlight. And those eyes—those dark, dark eyes that burned with the fires of hate.

A hate that matched even her own.

The necromancer had brought her back to life. He had given her a new body; one that was far better than what she had before. He had made her whole again—mostly. Her limbs, broken beyond repair, were now machines of iron; driven and fueled by the dark magic of this blessed mage. Her eyes were now reflections of her burning soul; orbs of hatred that showed through the iron mask that had been made to conceal what was left of her face.

She was flesh and blood melded with iron; a destructive machine remade to bring death.

"Rise, revenant," the necromancer had said. "Be that which you were meant to be."

"Who are you?" she had whispered.

"I am He," came the reply. "I am He who has been and shall always be."

What he had meant, she never knew. He had left her after that, giving her the will to seek her killer, but not the knowledge of his own identity—nor why he had given her this gift.

Was it a gift?

She hissed at the thought of it. What had seemed like a gift at first had grown into something of a curse. She had sought Etanos, feeling his presence so many times, and the anger and hatred that came with it. But she had not faced him until now. She had delayed the conflict, not knowing what would happen to her once she stood over his corpse.

Would that be the end?

She had only decided to seek him out to finally put an end to her pain. She didn't even care about the outcome, as long as the pain was gone. She wanted nothing more than the satisfaction of looking down at his lifeless body, but some part of her longed for her own end; an end to the inner pain that outweighed the sensations of her body.

A final rest for her soul would be… comforting.

In her dark pocket of reality, shielded from the light of the sun, she clenched her fists and shattered the silence with her cries.

* * *

"What was that?" Garret asked.

Etanos craned his neck to listen. Garret lowered the bow Etanos had lent him as he watched.

"I didn't hear anything," the man said.

Garret was confused. Surely Etanos' senses were sharper than his. Why could he hear something when his mentor could not? It didn't make any sense. Shrugging, he raised the bow again, loosing the magical arrow at his target. The missile streaked across the clearing, embedding itself in the trunk of a dead oak, shimmering and fading away.

"Good shot," Etanos said. "What did it sound like?"

Garret shook his head. "I'm not sure," he said. "Something like a hawk's screech combined with a bear's roar... or something."

Etanos raised his brow. "Interesting," he said, skeptically. "Are you sure?"

Garret shrugged again. "Not really."

"Try that shot again," Etanos said. "See if you can hit the exact same spot."

Garret pulled back the bow again, feeling the warmth of the magical arrow that appeared. He gazed down its length, focusing on the tiny black dot where the previous arrow had struck. When he was confident in his aim, he loosed again.

Bullseye!

He grinned, lowering the bow and glancing at his mentor. Etanos smiled proudly, coming over and scruffing his hair. "You learn quickly," he said. "You'll be an expert archer in no time."

Garret handed him the bow, turning to rest on a nearby log. The day's march had been long, and now after a few lessons with the bow, Garret was ready to rest. His mind, however, was plagued with questions. Etanos had told him the story of Ammarah, and how he had defeated her in Khem. After hearing of her fall, and the fact that had been set aflame, he was curious as to how she had survived.

In the back of his mind, though, he couldn't help feeling that he knew the answer somehow. His time with the Great Mother had given him the impression that there was more than survival involved. Someone—or something—else had revived her; resurrected her body with some dark magic.

There was something else that bothered him as well; why her soul seemed to be composed of two spirits. He had also gotten that impression while he was unconscious. Why, he could not guess.

"I saw and felt strange things when I was with the Great Mother," he said, finally.

"What kinds of things," Etanos asked, taking a seat next to him.

"I'm not sure," Garret said. "Just strange things that don't make any sense to me. There is a reason she survived. I don't think it was mere luck. Even before, when I saw her eyes as she crouched over me, there was something in there. It was something more than just hate and revenge. There was... pain and torment. Not just of her body, but her soul."

Etanos nodded in understanding, but Garret knew that he did not fully comprehend his meaning any more than Garret did himself.

"There was sadness," Garret said. "Loss."

Etanos looked at him blankly for a moment and then turned to stare at the forest around them.

"I cannot explain it," he said. "Perhaps you should have asked Aeli."

Garret shrugged. "I have the feeling she has no idea, either."

"She knows a lot of things, Garret," Etanos said. "But you may be right. This may be beyond her sight."

A sudden rustling brought them to their feet in an instant. Etanos' blades were out before Garret could even reach his. The two stood guarded, listening closely as the sound of snapping twigs approached them.

Garret's heart raced as he waited. Something was coming, and his thoughts could only go to Ammarah. He pictured her iron mask in his mind and the burning eyes that showed through it. It took his breath, and he felt only panic.

But when the tall, dark figure stepped through the tree line and Etanos lowered his blades, his heart slowed, and he sighed with relief.

"Baurus!" Etanos said, sheathing his blades.

The figure lowered his hood, revealing very dark skin, a bald head, and a shining white smile that told Garret this was a friend. Etanos raced toward the man, clasping his arm in greeting. Garret sheathed his blade, feeling embarrassed at his fear.

"What are you doing here?" Etanos asked.

Baurus glanced at Garret for a moment, his smile still wide across his face. "I bring word from the Grandmaster," he said.

"It was revealed that your contract has been fulfilled, and he requests your services again."

Etanos nodded. "The contract has been fulfilled," Etanos confirmed. "But it was not I who fulfilled it."

Baurus cocked his head curiously. "What do you mean?"

Etanos turned, and the two walked back to where Garret waited. He moved aside humbly, curious as to whom this new person was.

"A rival," Etanos said. "One of dark origin. She left this."

Etanos pulled the obsidian blade from his cloak, showing it to his friend. Baurus took it hesitantly, turning it over in his hand and pursing his lips.

"I will return after I tie up this loose end," Etanos said.

Baurus shook his head. "You chase ghosts, my friend," he said. "This belongs to a dead woman."

"That is what I have believed all of these years," Etanos said.

"She lives," Garret said, interrupting them.

Baurus looked at him. "Who is this?"

Etanos put his hand on Garret's back. "This is my apprentice, Garret," he said.

Baurus nodded, offering his hand in greeting.

"Garret," Etanos continued. "This is my friend and guild brother, Baurus."

"Pleased to meet you," Garret said, looking into Baurus' dark eyes.

He had not noticed before, but through Baurus' dark skin, he could see strange and intricate tattoos crossing the man's face. They accentuated his angular features, making him appear almost wraith-like. He was very intimidating, to say the least.

"Likewise," the man said. "I trust Etanos is teaching you well?"

Garret smiled. "Far better than I have taught myself all these years."

Baurus laughed out loud, turning his head to the sky and bellowing like a bear. "All of these years," he echoed. "You are no more than a boy of fifteen, I would say."

Garret shrugged. "That is correct," he said.

Etanos chuckled. "This boy has killed more scoundrels than you and I did at his age combined."

Baurus laughed but stuck out his bottom lip. "Very impressive," he said. "Then I bow to you, Garret, apprentice of Etanos."

Garret smiled as he bowed, unsure as to whether he was being genuine or sarcastic. He would accept it either way.

"How did you find us?" he asked.

Baurus put his hand on Etanos' shoulder, grinning at the man. "The same way I always do," he said. "I simply follow the chaos. That was quite a ruckus you two stirred up."

"It was for a good cause," Etanos said. "Now the slaves are free, and a major hub of a criminal organization is inactive."

Baurus nodded. "Where are you off to now?"

Etanos took the obsidian blade back from Baurus, stuffing it in his cloak. "I will find this ghost as you call her and put her to rest. She is a danger to not only the guild but to everyone in this kingdom. I have the feeling she is here for more than just revenge."

"Is there anything I can help you with?" Baurus asked.

"Not that I can think of," Etanos said. "Tell the Grandmaster I will return as soon as possible, and I will have a new brother in training."

"Very well," Baurus said. "May the eye of Perses watch over you."

Baurus bowed his head, and Etanos returned the gesture.

"Farewell, brothers," Baurus said, turning to disappear into the forest once more.

Garret watched after him until he was no longer in sight, longing to know more about him and the guild.

"That was an unexpected encounter," Garret said.

Etanos chuckled. "Not really," he said. "That's the way the Brotherhood operates; someone is always watching. Now, we should continue while the day is still young. We have work to do."

Etanos was right. Freeing Helena and the sisters would be a lot of work—and a lot of planning. They couldn't just walk in and free them. Daeglan would likely have many guards at his estate, and they would be much more skilled than the bandits of the Red Hand. And then, there was this Ammarah to deal with.

Whatever she was, it was clear that she would be the most difficult problem; one that posed a danger to *everyone* involved.

"To Gaellos, then," Garret said.

* * *

"What do you two have to say for yourselves?" Baelion demanded, glaring at Turgon and Kuros as they stood at attention.

Kuros had met the rest of the company near their camp outside of Faillaigh, and now having waited for him to return, Baelion had gathered him and Turgon together before him.

"I felt that getting involved with the strangers' quest would be best," Kuros said. "I know it is not our duty to engage in outright battle in the streets, but seeing the enslavement of our people demanded that we go outside our usual realm of action."

Baelion came and stood in front of him, folding his arms across his chest, glaring straight into his eyes. Kuros' heart pounded.

"I commanded you to watch these strangers," he said. "Not to join their raid on a known criminal compound."

Kuros nodded. "Yes, sir," he said. "I take full responsibility for our actions. The decision was mine alone."

"It was not," Turgon protested. "Once we realized what was going on, we *both* knew what we had to do."

Baelion pursed his lips, turning around to face away from them. Kuros peeked over at Turgon, who looked back with the same apprehensive expression.

"You disobeyed my orders," Baelion continued, "went outside the scope of your duties, and caused a great deal of chaos in the process."

He paused for a moment, looking up into the canopy above. Kuros shifted nervously. That was not a good sign. Baelion always looked up when he was about to deal disciplinary actions.

"Good work, men," Baelion said, surprisingly.

Kuros' heart fell back to a normal rhythm. Baelion turned and approached again, a crooked grin on his lips.

"You showed initiative," he said. "And drive. You saw a bad situation and you acted accordingly; altering your orders to best fit the situation. *That* is what being a leader is all about."

He reached out and put his hand on Kuros' shoulder, leaning in to stare directly into his eyes. "You will make an excellent captain someday," he said. "And I hope you will consider your friend here as your second."

Kuros grinned, looking over to Turgon. "Absolutely," he said.

Baelion turned again, putting his hands on his hips. Kuros and Turgon relaxed.

"Now," Baelion said. "Since we have gotten involved, what is next?"

"The younger man, Garret, will no doubt want to free the sisters and the children from Daeglan's estate. He and his companion are headed there now. But there is something else. There is another assassin involved, one of unknown origin."

Baelion turned. "Who is this assassin?"

Kuros shook his head. "I do not know, sir," he said. "But she is of the darkness. I could feel it. She was at the mines, and then at Aeli's cottage."

"What were you doing at Aeli's cottage?" Baelion asked.

"We took Garret there to heal," Kuros said. "This assassin had wounded him with a dark blade. Aeli was his only hope of survival."

Baelion nodded, furrowing his brow in worry. "Very well," he said. "But why is this assassin here?"

"She is after this older man, Etanos," Kuros said. "He is an assassin of Thyre, and he knows who the woman is. He had fought her in the past and defeated her. But now she is back for revenge."

"Let *him* deal with her, then," Baelion said. "That is none of our concern. Meanwhile, take ten men and travel north to Gaellos. My scouts tell me that Ferrin is up to something. Find him and give him our support if it is needed. Keep watch on Garret and Etanos, and do not let them fail. If they are rescuing the children, they will need our help. When that happens, keep them all safe in their escape, but do not allow Daeglan to be aware of your presence."

Kuros nodded. "Yes, sir."

Baelion stood silent for a moment, staring at them both.

"Well," he said, finally. "What are you waiting for?"

Chapter Twenty-Five

elena's prayers were frequent of late. Despite keeping her sisters safe from the advances of Daeglan's unscrupulous cohorts, she still maintained her duties as a priestess of Gaia behind the prying eyes of her captor. Her sisters were growing restless; torn between the desire to revolt, and the need to keep the children safe. Though not in any direct danger, the children were not as well off as they could be.

Daeglan cared nothing for them, or anyone else for that matter.

The noble had proven himself to be exactly what Helena had always suspected; nothing but a power and money-hungry rat who would likely sell his own mother if the price was right. His massive estate was nearly half the size of Gaellos itself and employed hundreds of soldiers of equally rotten stock.

How she longed to cut them all down with the swift blade of justice.

As Helena stared out the window of her bedroom, her thoughts went to Ailin. She had sent the young woman out early in the morning to find a sympathetic person to assist them in their escape. Helena had watched the front gates faithfully all day long, hoping to see the diminutive young girl walk through them victoriously. She had faith that Ailin could attract the right kind of man, as, despite her young and naïve demeanor, she was highly skilled at judging a person's true intentions.

She would find the right man to help them.

Once the sisters had hold of their weapons, they could take down Daeglan and his forces, get the children to safety, and escape to the tunnels. There, the Temple of Gaia would keep them safe, and they could worship in secret, working behind the scenes to keep the people of Gaellos safe from the likes of Daeglan.

Whom she now realized was standing at her doorway.

She turned, casting him a dark glance, but forging a half smile of indifference. He stood there in his silk robes; his hair neatly trimmed and styled, his boots shining like glass, and his body soaked in musky perfumes that threatened to gag her.

"How are you this evening, Helena?" he asked.

She turned back to the window, clasping her hands before her. Her heart pounded with hate, and the mere presence of the man made her stomach turn.

"It is getting late, my lord," she said. "I worry for those who are outside."

She heard him step into her room, and she gritted her teeth in preparation for the inevitable unwelcome touch on her shoulders; that false gesture of caring that disguised Daeglan's dark desires.

"The city of Gaellos is a safe place," he said, putting his disgusting hands on her. "Your servants will be fine. My guards keep the road safe, as well. There is no need to worry."

It's your guards I worry about, she thought but kept it to herself.

"Yes, my lord," she whispered.

"Now," he said. "Can we forget our hostilities? I *did* offer you shelter; you and the children. Surely you are grateful."

She felt his hands slide down her back, one of them resting on her waistline. She felt the bile rise in her throat, and the anger welling up in her heart. Without thinking, she grabbed his hand, pulling it off of her and squeezing it until she heard the knuckles crack. She turned as he pulled his hand away and glared into his eyes. Instead of expressing his anger, Daeglan smiled as he rubbed his hand.

It was the disgusting smile of a man who enjoyed such things.

"That wasn't very nice, Helena," he said, still grinning.

"I will return your kindness in my own way," she said, keeping her composure—she was slightly relieved that he had not reacted the way she expected to.

Daeglan politely bowed his head, backing away; his eyes moving up and down her body. She kept her glare, watching his face as he smiled coldly and turned to leave.

Oh, how she wanted to cut that smile from his face.

"Have a good night, Helena," he said.

She turned back to the window to resume her watch, her heart still beating wildly. Her breath came labored and rough for a moment before finally settling down. But it was the sight of Ailin coming down the center road that sent a wave of relief through her.

Helena went to her desk, turning the knob on her lamp to brighten its flame. She sat in silence, allowing her racing heart and reeling mind to settle down to a more normal state. Daeglan's touch had riled both her revulsion and her anger. His presence always did.

She knew deep down what he truly wanted. His desire was less than noble, as would be expected. He cared nothing for the convent, or the children, or the other sisters. He just wanted her. He wanted to ravish her and throw her away, sealing his fate as an enemy of the Great Mother forever.

She would put him in his place one day; one day soon, she hoped.

It was only a matter of minutes before Ailin wandered into her room. Helena stood as she closed the door behind her and went to embrace her tightly. She was pleasantly surprised that Ailin was smiling.

"I'm glad you're safe, Ailin," she said. "What happened? Did you find someone to help us?"

Ailin looked up at her and she released her embrace. Her face was beaming and bright.

"I did," the young woman said. "I met a young noble named Ferrin who has agreed to deliver the weapons to us."

She knew the name, and it brought a smile to her face.

"Ferrin?" she echoed happily.

"Yes, Helena," Ailin continued. "I met him in the square. He is sympathetic to our cause."

"Good," Helena said. "And did he tell you his story?"

Ailin pursed her lips, shaking her head. "No," she said. "Why?"

Helena motioned for her to sit beside her on the bed.

"Ferrin is not himself a noble," Helena explained. "He is the son of a spice merchant who had a shop in Faerbane. His father became indebted to Lord Darragh somehow, and the only way to escape his wrath was to send Ferrin to work off the debt. He was only ten years old, then. I'm glad to hear that he is still in good spirits."

"He is a slave, then?" Ailin asked, her eyes saddened.

"No. He is an indentured servant. But I would imagine after all these years, his debt would be paid."

"Then why does he stay?"

Helena knew the answer, and it brought another smile to her lips. "Because *that's* what you do when you plan to seek your revenge."

Ailin smiled slightly, but Helena knew she did not quite understand. But that was not important now.

"Tell me of your encounter with him."

"He took me to Joran's forge on the square," Ailin said. "And I told him of the temple, and our need to have the weapons returned. Joran overheard us and offered to help, as well. When I took them down into the sanctum, we were able to open the strange door with Joran's help. It leads to another area of the catacombs where Ferrin himself has been building a secret organization."

Helena cocked her head, intrigued. "What sort of organization?"

"A thieves' guild," Ailin said. "A guild made up of all of the young men and women in the area who hate the nobles and seek to restore freedom to the people."

What a wonderful development for their cause, Helena felt. With the help of highly skilled thieves, they could accomplish more than just a simple escape. The sisters could employ them as silent guards if need be; sort of like urban rangers, so to speak.

"We carried the weapons into the guild tunnels," Ailin said. "And even now, Ferrin and his friends are seeking a way to bring them to us. And the best part is Ferrin is close friends with many of the king's rangers. They work together somehow, but I did not quite understand what he meant."

Helena stood, clasping her hands together with excitement. She could almost feel the air of freedom rush through her. Something was rushing through her.

"Ailin," she said, turning, "I knew you would find someone. But this… this was just unexpected. We could very well topple the nobles and restore the rule of law; even without the king's help."

She held out her arms and Ailin rose to meet them. She clasped the young girl tightly, feeling a sense of pride in her that she had never felt for any of her initiates.

"You have done well," she said. "Very, very well. I am so proud to call you my sister."

Ailin looked up at her, smiling oddly.

"Was there something else?" Helena asked.

Ailin turned away, but Helena knew she was still grinning. After a moment, Ailin turned again, her hand clasped tightly below her chin.

"It's Ferrin," she said. "I cannot stop thinking about him."

Helena smiled, knowing full well what that meant. Though she had hoped Ailin would eventually become a Sword Sister, and devote her life to serving Gaia, she knew that nothing would make the girl happier than to follow her heart. And, if Ferrin was anything like his father, he was likely handsome and dashing. But she hoped he was a stronger man; strong enough to stand against those who would oppress him.

And strong enough to usurp Darragh's title... if that became necessary.

* * *

The shadows had begun to overtake the road to Gaellos. Garret and Etanos had passed the fork that led to Faillaigh, and the young man was trying to remember how to reach the road to Daeglan's estate. It was near a small trading post, he remembered, somewhere between the two cities, but the post seemed to be nowhere in sight.

Perhaps they had simply not reached it yet.

"What kind of post is it?" Etanos asked.

"A fur trader," Garret said. "One that buys and sells pelts and leather. I swear it was in this area."

"Are there no signs for it?"

Garret shook his head. "I don't imagine Daeglan would allow it," he said. "He owns the road since it only leads to his estate. We might just have to go to Gaellos and proceed from there."

"I don't think it would be a good idea to show our faces in Gaellos," Etanos warned. "I got you out of there for a reason."

Garret shrugged. "True," he said, sadly. "But I would like to see it again."

"You will," Etanos assured him. "Once this is all over."

Garret smiled as he thought of roaming the streets of Gaellos in the past. He could wander down any alley, pass any shop, or climb any tree, and there would always be someone there who knew his name. The town had gotten to know him well through his association with the convent, and he considered everyone there a part of his family — and his history.

The new path he was on, however, would eventually lead him away from that family. Things had already taken a turn in that direction. The convent was gone, the town would be besieged by Daeglan's forces, and he would forever be just another shadow working behind the scenes. His life as a social center point was over.

He could, effectively, no longer exist in the eyes of those who knew him.

"Things will never be the same, will they?" he mused out loud.

Etanos didn't speak; he merely pursed his lips, nodding slowly as they trudged along the road.

"There is one of the sisters that I would like to see again," Garret said.

"Oh?" Etanos said, grinning.

"Her name is Ailan. She was an orphan, I think, but when she came of age, the sisters initiated her as a nun."

"Well," Etanos said. "I suppose she would be off limits, then."

"True," Garret said. "But I have always known that. Had she not been initiated, I would have pursued some kind of..." He trailed off, not really knowing what he meant to say.

"I get it," Etanos said. "But sometimes a particular woman was meant for greater things. I have a feeling that your sisters are far more than they appear."

"What do you mean?"

"A true servant of Gaia, *or* her children, must always work for the greater good; the balance. That involves life *and* death. Understand?"

Garret nodded. He understood as well as he could understand the complex mathematical calculations that were scrawled inside the journals of a mad wizard.

"No," he said. "Not really."

"Is that it?" Etanos said suddenly, pointing ahead.

The trading post stood there at the corner of the main road and a smaller path that led into the forest. It was a small building made of weathered wood with a sandstone and mortar base and finely crafted glass windows... all of which were busted out.

"What the hell happened?" Garret wondered.

They approached the empty booths that were out front, scoping out the areas where the tanning racks were obviously located at one time. It was all but deserted, with only a few scraps of leather, some prepared but useless hides, and a few random copper coins lying about. Inside, where the operators would have lived, there was also nothing; only an empty building with barely a scrap of furniture left.

"Well," Garret shrugged. "I suppose it doesn't matter. It was just a landmark for us, after all. The road is what we were looking for."

"I hear something," Etanos said.

Garret craned his neck to listen. There was the distinctive rumble of wagon wheels and horse hooves approaching from the south. He looked at Etanos for a sign of what they should do.

"Shall we hide?" Etanos asked.

Garret ducked down, crawling around the empty booths to Etanos' position. They crouched there in wait as the wagon approached. From their vantage point, it appeared to be driven and escorted by Red Hand bandits. Four of them were on horseback, dressed in the same armor and cloaks as those who had been at the mines. The driver, a strange-looking man with a hawk-like face, also bore the Red Hand sigil on his tunic.

The procession turned at the fork, heading down the road to Daeglan's estate. Garret nodded to Etanos, grinning slightly.

"This is it," Garret said. "They're making some kind of delivery. It's too bad we can't follow them very closely. I would very much like to see what they are carrying."

"We'll be there tonight," Etanos said. "If all goes well, we will find out what they are smuggling."

Garret nodded. "It's still another half day's travel," he said. "But that just means we'll arrive late. Perfect for sneaking inside the walls."

"We'd better get on with it, then," Etanos said. "After you, my friend."

As the wagon disappeared down the tree-lined road, the two assassins fell in step behind it. Later that night, all would be revealed, and if things went as planned, the sisters and the children would be freed. But, in Garret's mind, one task remained. It was obvious that Lord Daeglan had to die.

And he wanted that honor for himself.

CHAPTER TWENTY-SIX

his is the worst idea anyone could have come up with," Joran said.

Ferrin leaned in to glare at him, his lips curling into a sneer. "Why do you say that?"

Joran shook his head, scowling. "We're dressed like bandits, hiding in the bushes, attempting to rob *actual* bandits, and we don't even know if they'll be coming this way."

Ferrin shrugged, lolling his head from side to side in partial agreement. "It's the best we could do on such short notice," he said. "Besides, this is the most logical route for them to take. It's the only road that leads directly to Daeglan's estate."

"It's still a bad idea."

Ferrin sighed. Joran was probably right. In his haste to impress Ailin, Ferrin had not thought the plan through. They were pressed for time, however, and the idea seemed as good as any. A delivery was bound to come this way, as Daeglan had constant visitors of the less desirable type. Surely, Red Hand operatives would pass by sooner or later. But there was a chance that the several hours it had taken to carry the weapons into the guild and load them onto their cart had caused them to miss the opportunity.

"We should have consulted the rangers first," Joran added. "They actually know things."

"My scouts watch these roads, too," Ferrin reminded him. "They can see just as well as the rangers can. We are affiliated, you know."

Joran exhaled sharply. "Whatever you say, *Grandmaster*."

A thief came up behind Ferrin, tapping him on the shoulder. He was a younger one, probably no more than fifteen, a new recruit.

"What?" Ferrin asked.

"What do we do if a wagon approaches?" the young man asked.

"Signal your nearest brother, and they'll pass it on."

The thief nodded but still seemed unsure. Ferrin clapped him on the head roughly, leaving his hand there to direct the boy's gaze toward him.

"Just watch the road," he said slowly, "and let us know when something approaches. Now, run along."

The boy turned away and disappeared into the brush. Ferrin looked at Joran, who was staring at him with a grin.

"Are you sure you picked the right people for your little guild?" he asked.

"Shut up," Ferrin said.

He stared down the road as well as he could, trying hard to forget the fact that he was probably wrong about everything. The road was silent, with only the slight rustling of leaves breaking the utter stillness. Dispersed among the brush, his thieves also waited patiently, probably thinking the same thing as Joran. Ferrin's confidence was beginning to wane.

But then, a hand on his shoulder startled him, and Joran's grunt broke him out of his trance. Kuros was there, grinning as he always did when he snuck up on his friends.

"Cripes, boy," Joran exclaimed. "You scared the daylights out of me."

"What are we looking at?" Kuros asked.

"We're waiting for a caravan or wagon to go by," Ferrin said. "One of the Red Hand's deliveries."

"Why?"

"We're going to rob it," Ferrin said.

"Oh," Kuros said, grinning skeptically. "To what end?"

"We have weapons that need to be delivered to the sisters in Daeglan's estate," Ferrin replied. "We need one of their wagons and their uniforms."

Kuros nodded knowingly. "The weapons from the temple?"

Ferrin furrowed his brow. "You know of them?" he asked.

"Of course," Kuros said. "We know all about the Sisterhood. Didn't you?"

Ferrin scowled. "No. At least, not until this morning when I met a young initiate. She showed us where they were. We have them ready to be delivered. All we need is a way into Daeglan's estate. That's why we're here."

"Well, at least you picked the right road."

Ferrin smiled at Joran, who stuck out his bottom lip. "See?" he said. "It wasn't a completely bad idea."

"What do you plan on doing once the weapons are inside?" Kuros asked. "Surely a group of thieves is too small and inexperienced to stand up against Daeglan's forces."

"The revolt is up to the sisters," Ferrin said. "We are simply delivering their weapons and helping them once they escape."

"All right," Kuros said. "We are here to help. Baelion gave us leave to do so."

"Where have you been, by the way?" Ferrin asked.

"Causing trouble at the mines," Kuros said.

"How so?"

"We followed the two strangers there at Baelion's orders," Kuros replied. "There was a situation. Slaves, bandits, sneaking around."

"Slaves?" Joran echoed.

"The mines were being worked by locals," Kuros explained. "And not of their free will. The Red Hand was operating the mines for some reason. We suspected it for quite a while, and now we know for sure."

"Why were they running the mines?" Joran asked. "Is there any of the special metal left?"

Kuros shook his head. "We don't know," he said. "But it's too late. Operations have been closed, the mine complex has been destroyed, and Garret and his companion are headed to Daeglan's estate to help free the sisters and the children. At least, that's what Etanos said would happen."

Ferrin's eyes popped open. "Really?" he asked. "Interesting. I would like to meet them again."

"You may get your chance," Kuros said.

"What do you mean the mine has been destroyed?" Joran asked.

"There was another person there," Kuros said. "A strange assassin with a magical nature. She had some kind of device that she used to collapse the entire complex."

Ferrin stared at him blankly. "Collapse?" he echoed.

"Buildings, tunnels, and all," Kuros said. "There is nothing left but the crater itself."

"Well," Joran exclaimed. "I'll be damned."

"There are too many assassins involved in this mess," Ferrin said. "How the hell did that happen?"

Joran chuckled. "I knew of this assassin before," he said. "From the blade that Etanos showed me. He... or she, rather, was of Khem."

Kuros nodded. "I will tell you the story he told me later on," he said. "Or perhaps *he* will. It is fascinating either way. I will tell you one thing, though; she is highly dangerous. It would be best to let Etanos handle her. She is focused on him anyway — and for good reason."

"I won't ask," Ferrin said.

The sound of an arrow striking a nearby tree startled them. Kuros turned to fetch it, grinning as he pulled it out.

"A wagon is approaching," he said. "Whatever you are planning, do it quickly. We will cover you from the trees."

Ferrin nodded, drawing his blade, and gestured to Joran. "Are you ready?" he asked.

"Of course," Joran replied. "I'll let you do the talking since you're so good at it."

Kuros disappeared into the gully behind them, and Ferrin stepped out onto the road. The wagon was not yet in sight, but he could hear the distant clopping of hooves and the squeaks and squeals of wagon wheels on rusted axles.

Ferrin motioned for other thieves to show themselves at the roadside. Several of them stepped out, seemingly as nervous as Ferrin himself. They were all dressed in dark clothing, large hoods, and face wraps that looked more like old women's scarves. Ferrin suddenly felt ridiculous and vowed to equip his men with some more formal attire for such jobs.

As he heard the wagon round the nearest curve in the road, he pulled his own wrap over the lower half of his face, standing defiantly in the center of the road. Joran stood beside him, sword out, one hand on his hip — briefly, until he realized what he was doing.

"Try to look more intimidating," Ferrin whispered.

Joran grumbled, gritting his teeth in a rictus grin.

"That's better."

"I hope you know what you're doing," Joran said.

The men on horseback appeared first, riding ahead of the wagon, apparently aware of the roadblock. They picked up their pace, riding toward the two men with swords in hand. Ferrin, though nervous and choking on the inside, held steady. He was confident that his fellow thieves along the roadside would give the riders cause to surrender.

"Clear the way!" the lead rider demanded. "This road is owned by Lord Daeglan."

"I think not," Ferrin said. "This road belongs to me. You will lay down your weapons, dismount your horses, and surrender your goods."

The riders laughed; the leader rode forward and leaned down to glare at Ferrin. "Or what?"

The rustling of leaves around them startled the riders. Rangers and thieves alike appeared; their bows drawn and ready to fire. The thieves on the road drew their blades, approaching the wagon. The riders looked around, confused, and held up their hands.

Ferrin nodded at Joran. "See," he said, smiling. "That was easy. Take the driver's weapons."

Joran did as he was asked, and Ferrin grabbed the reins of the lead riders. "Off now," he said politely. "We need your armor and your horses."

The leader grumbled, dismounting. He threw down his blade, glaring hatefully at Ferrin. "Lord Daeglan will have your hide," he said.

"Perhaps," Ferrin said, handing the reins to another thief. "But not today. Tell me, what are you delivering?"

The leader grinned. "Why don't you have a look for yourself?"

"*Ferrin!*" a thief called to him from the wagon.

He looked at the leader again, whose grin widened.

"Watch him!" Ferrin commanded his fellows.

Kuros stood by the wagon, his mouth gaping and his eyes as wide as plates. Ferrin sidled next to him and looked into the open flap of fabric the thieves had pulled to the side. Ferrin's jaw dropped when he saw the faces of several young children; bound and tied together wrist to wrist.

"Slaves…" Ferrin whispered, his heart pounding with rage. "Slaves in Eirenoch."

He turned to Kuros, whose face echoed his shock. "I told you," the ranger said. "The mines were only the hub. There's a slave trade right here under our noses."

Joran joined them, his brow furrowing in anger as he watched the thieves assist the children out of the wagon. "This is getting more and more infuriating," he said. "The king *has* to be told."

"Agreed," Kuros said. "I will rally more rangers, and we will make an official assault on Daeglan's compound. I'm sure Baelion will send a message to the king. It will be warranted."

Ferrin went back to the lead rider, who stood smirking as his hands were tied together. Ferrin's anger rose as he studied him. How could anyone condone the enslavement of children? How could anyone condone slavery *at all?* Ferrin found himself unable to speak. He could only grit his teeth with rage as the man's smile enflamed his heart. He felt his fist ball up tightly.

He decked the man's nose as hard as he could, feeling it splatter with the impact. The man was grounded immediately, falling onto his backside and rolling back on his bound hands, whining and crying as blood ran down his face.

Ferrin shook off the pain in his hand, satisfied for the moment. "That felt good," he said. "And as for you... the king will decide your fates."

"Now what?" Joran asked.

Ferrin studied him for a moment, looking at him and the wagon's driver. They were roughly the same size. "Would any of Daeglan's guards recognize you?" Ferrin asked.

"Not likely," Joran replied. "I've never met any of them."

"Good," Ferrin said, looking at the driver, who gulped, nervously. "You'll be driving the wagon, then. As for the children, I will find some of the younger thieves and disguise them. We will load the Sisterhood's weapons at the bottom of the wagon, and tie up the fake slaves. As for the real ones..."

He went to the children, who were gathered at the rear of the wagon, being tended to by the rangers. There were a dozen of them of various ages; from at least eight years old to a few in their early teens. Perfect.

"How many of you have homes and wish to return to them?" Ferrin asked.

Four of the children raised their hands.

"Good," he continued. "You will be returned as soon as possible. As for the rest of you, we will make sure you are taken care of."

"Who are you?" a young boy asked.

Ferrin smiled, going to the boy and putting his hand on his head. "My name is Ferrin," he said. "And you can be sure that my friends and I will put a stop to this nonsense once and for all."

"You're thieves, aren't you?" another said.

"Some of us are," Ferrin grinned, pointing to Kuros. "But my friend here is a ranger."

Another young boy sidled next to Kuros, looking up at him with a smile. "I want to be a ranger," he said.

Kuros put his arm around him. "It's not an easy job," he said. "Are you sure?"

"Yes," the boy said. "I will be Falgrin, King's Ranger."

Kuros chuckled. "Perhaps," he said. "Let's not get ahead of ourselves."

"All right," Ferrin said, motioning for his thieves to begin their work. "Bring up our cart. Let's get the weapons loaded up, four of you dressed in the riders' armor, and Joran drives. I want the smallest of us to dress up like these children and load up on top of the weapons. Make sure you're tied so you can easily escape, and look nice and oppressed for your captors."

"We will be outside the compound by midnight," Kuros said. "Tell the sisters to wait for our signal before they rise up. We will guard their escape."

"Right," Ferrin said, clapping his friend on the back. "This is getting exciting."

Joran cleared his throat, pulling the driver's tunic over his much larger belly. "I hope this works," he said. "Otherwise, I'll have paid Taen to watch Angus for nothing."

"Don't worry," Ferrin said. "Everything is working out well so far."

Ferrin watched as Kuros led the bandits away, minus their clothing, and rallied the children to follow. They would be taken someplace safe, and the criminals would be dealt with in whatever way the rangers usually dealt with criminals—Ferrin wasn't quite sure. The thieves had brought up the cart that held the Sisterhood's weapons and were now placing them carefully inside the wagon. Several smaller thieves were gathering rags and dressing each other up in waif-like fashion.

Ferrin watched the activity with pride. Everything was falling into place; not necessarily in the way he imagined, but well enough. His thieves had done well, the rangers had worked together with them perfectly, and the hijacking was a complete success. Smiling, he clasped his hands behind his back, looking up into the darkening canopy as he imagined himself as Lord of the House of Ferrin.

"Ferrin," Joran said with an approving nod. "Well done."

Ferrin smiled. Coming from Joran, that was quite the compliment. The smith had always acted skeptical of anything Ferrin did or suggested, and the confidence he had just conveyed gave Ferrin a well-needed boost.

Perhaps there was hope for his future as a nobleman yet.

CHAPTER TWENTY-SEVEN

here the hell is Ammarah?" Daeglan demanded.

The servant before him shrugged, lowering his head in fear of his master's wrath. "I do not know, master Daeglan," the young man said. "I have not seen nor heard from her since she left for the mines."

Daeglan glared at the boy, sickened at his uselessness. He saw no point in having servants if they did not "serve" his needs. The boy was worthless; just another orphan raised by an equally worthless convent. Did the sisters not even attempt to prepare their charges for anything in life?

Disgusting.

Daeglan briefly thought of skewering the boy for his own amusement. Surely it would show the others that they were to serve him to the best of their abilities, and not be such slothful and worthless show pieces. But, considering his attraction and desire for Helena, doing so would put any prospects of adding her to his house in jeopardy. He would let this boy live, against his better judgment.

"Out of my sight," he hissed.

The boy bowed low, quickly disappearing from Daeglan's chambers.

"Worthless piece of—"

"My lord," a voice said behind him. "We have been expecting a delivery for several hours now. The wagon has not yet arrived."

Daeglan grunted. Typical. Nothing was going right today.

"Patience," he said. "Slaves are not to be transported without care. I admire caution more than promptness. If the delivery is delayed, I'm sure there is a reason."

He turned, delighted to see the weasely face of his operations manager. Feyn was a reliable man who had served him since his ascent to houselord twenty years before. Never had Feyn let Daeglan down, and never had he given Daeglan any reason not to trust him. He was a favored servant and one with an equally dark personality.

"Have you heard anything from Captain Melin?" Daeglan asked.

"I have not, my lord," Feyn replied. "I have heard nothing from anyone at the mines."

Daeglan turned back to his window, running his fingers along the finely carved wooden sill. The sunlight was nearly gone outside, and its orange rays shone through his silk curtains in a pleasant, fiery burst that was pleasing to his senses. He found it relaxing; almost lustful in its glow. It calmed him, even more so than the presence of his most trusted servant. But the fact that no word had been heard from the mines was disturbing, and he found it hard to think of anything else.

"Ammarah went there to confront this assassin and his protégé," Daeglan said. "Surely she was not defeated."

"I would not think so, my lord," Feyn assured. "You must remember, however, that no matter what you have offered her, there is really nothing of yours that she wants. She has no reason to return here, nor to Darragh or his plot."

Daeglan glared at him for a moment before turning back to the duck outside. Feyn was right. The assassin was Ammarah's only reason for being in Eirenoch in the first place. She only entered into an agreement with him and Darragh for her own amusement; perhaps to even expose the plot to the king. After all, what reason would she have to honor any contract she was given? She was no longer a true assassin; only a dark creature with a vendetta.

Contracts meant nothing to her.

But, there was the question of logic. Darragh's plan to kill the king did not come without its downsides. If the king was killed, and Queen Igraina was to take the throne, things in the south would become much more chaotic. Only under the organized and stable rule of King Magnus were they able to operate the way they did. Igraina's rule would only expose them to the public. Perhaps Ammarah saw this and held her blade for that reason.

"When Ammarah returns, I may have a new contract for her that will be more to her liking."

"My lord?"

Daeglan smiled, grasping Feyn's shoulder like an old friend. "Darragh is of no use to us anymore, my friend," he said. "It's time for him to be removed, I think."

"That," Feyn said with a grin, "would definitely be to her liking."

"His interference only causes us trouble," Daeglan added. "With him out of the way, the Red Hand would be under my complete control. I think the slave trade is much more lucrative than anything he has suggested. Wouldn't you agree?"

"Completely," Feyn said. "There is a worldwide demand, and the people of Eirenoch are hardy and able. They would make excellent stock."

Daeglan grinned. "I like the way you think, Feyn," he said. "A worldwide market... such a bold statement, and a bold venture. I will make you a very wealthy man if you stick with me."

"You have always had my loyalty, Daeglan. No matter what. That will never change."

Loyalty. What a concept. In this world of backstabbing, betrayal, and debauchery, loyalty was hard to find. It was good to have one such as Feyn. He would stand beside Daeglan to the end, loyal to a fault.

On the downside, he would be much harder to cast to the side when he was no longer needed.

Another use for the deadly Ammarah, Daeglan thought.

* * *

The road was growing dark as Garret and Etanos heard the rustling of passing men in the forest. They crouched down by the side of the road, suspecting nothing more than rangers, but not taking any chances.

Garret peered into the shadows as the sounds neared. Etanos had his bow ready, and he too glared into the darkness. This stretch of road belonged to Daeglan, they knew, and there could be anyone in those trees. Garret's heart thumped in anticipation. He gripped his blades tightly, bouncing up and down slightly on his toes.

Two rangers appeared from the tree line.

"Kuros!" Etanos called out.

Garret's heart slowed and he sighed in relief. The two

rangers approached, and Garret and Etanos stood to meet them.

"Well met," Kuros said. "I was expecting you any time now."

"Is there any news?" Garret asked. "What is going on at Daeglan's estate?"

"A revolt will be happening tonight," Kuros said. "Weapons are being delivered to the sisters, and we will help them escape."

"Weapons?" Etanos asked. "Who is delivering them?"

"My friend, Ferrin," Kuros said. "You met him in Faillaigh."

Garret grumbled, shooting Etanos an annoyed look.

"He and his friends just hijacked a delivery wagon, and now they're preparing to take the weapons right through the front gates. We will be watching from outside the walls and will help the children escape once they are brought outside."

"Who exactly *is* this Ferrin?" Garret asked. "Why does he help?"

"I cannot go into much detail," Kuros said. "But let's just say that he is more than just a servant of Darragh."

"As I said," Etanos added, "he is a thief."

Kuros said nothing but nodded slightly.

"What is his interest in the sisters?" Etanos asked.

"He was asked to help," Kuros said. "He accepted. Joran the smith is with him, and they are now heading to the front gates. I must gather more rangers and return before midnight. Otherwise, we'll miss all the fun."

Garret was confused. Why was this thief so interested in helping anyone, much less a group of nuns whom he had never met? Perhaps he had misjudged Ferrin. Maybe Ferrin was more than just a simple thief. But why masquerade as a nobleman? What was the point?

"What should we do?" Garret asked.

"You do what you need to," Kuros said. "These sisters are more than just nuns. Focus on helping the children out. You needn't worry for Helena and the others. They can take care of themselves."

"I will have my hands full," Etanos said with a dark look. "She is coming. I can feel it."

Garret felt his concern but couldn't shake the thoughts that were now running through his head. He had known the sisters his whole life; they had raised him. He never knew them to take up arms before, much less *have* them in supply. But Helena *had* encouraged him to study fighting techniques with quite an unusual enthusiasm.

"Garret," Etanos said, shaking him out of his haze. "Whatever is bothering you, think about it later. We have work to do."

"I understand your trepidation, friend," Kuros added. "But remember, they are Priestesses of Gaia. Like the Priests of Drakkar, they must fight to maintain order. Make no mistake, they are warriors; all of them."

Garret shook his head. He just couldn't picture Helena shoving a sword into anyone's gut. Just the thought of such a kindhearted and soft-spoken woman doing so sent chills up his spine. If she were capable of fighting, then why hadn't the sisters taken up arms when the convent was raided? Was it to maintain secrecy? Was secrecy worth the danger they had put upon themselves and the children?

"It's hard to imagine," he said, finally. "But I suppose you're right. Some things make a lot more sense now."

Kuros grinned, clapping him on the shoulder. "We will see you at midnight," he said. "Do what you need to do, and we will be there as reinforcements."

The rangers rejoined their companions, leaving Garret and Etanos alone in the shadows. Garret remained confused but focused his thoughts on getting the children to safety. That was what was important. Still, the thought of the sisters in full battle armor perplexed him. It was a thought he couldn't shake.

"We probably have three hours before the rangers return," Etanos said. "Let's get to Daeglan's estate as soon as we can and stake it out. We can't just run in and start killing people."

Garret grinned half-heartedly. "No," he said. "That would be insane. But I wonder if Helena and the sisters will be enough to stand against Daeglan's troops. Kuros said they would support them from the outside and cover their escape. What about on the inside?"

Etanos shrugged. "I suppose once the sisters are armed, they will perform some kind of surprise attack and flee before his troops are even alerted. If things get too dangerous, I imagine the rangers will intervene, as we will."

That was good enough, Garret supposed.

"I wonder if Ferrin and Joran will get involved in the fight," he mused.

"Joran can handle himself," Etanos said. "He is experienced. I could see it in his eyes. I'm not sure about Ferrin though. He seemed confident enough, but I don't know how skilled he is in battle."

"Nor I," Garret agreed. "Nor where his true loyalties lie."

"We will see, my friend," Etanos said. "We will see."

* * *

Helena stood in the center of the circle of her six sisters. In the private chambers that had been provided for them, they often mimed this ritual, covering their conversations with the illusion of worship. Daeglan had thankfully not required that their rituals be supervised, and the sisters were left to use this time to their advantage.

"Ailin will ensure that we are informed when Ferrin and his friends arrive," Helena whispered, her head lowered in mock prayer. "Once she returns, we will make our way to the receiving building and take our weapons. Ferrin will have them ready."

"I worry for Ailin," another sister said. "She is young and may get caught up in the fight."

"She will be well protected," Helena assured her. "Ferrin will see to her safety while she rounds up the children."

"Once the insurrection is underway, where do we head?" another sister asked.

"We will lead the charge toward the western gate," Helena said. "The rangers will be there waiting for us, and will have already taken out the guards."

"And what of Daeglan?"

Helena raised her head, glaring up at the ceiling as she pictured Daeglan's hated face. "I will deal with him."

The sisters held hands in their circle, kneeling down as Helena took a knee.

"This will be our moment of truth, my sisters," she said. "This is what we have been training for all these years, and now the time has come to show the vile where we stand. It will be dangerous, to be sure, but fear not. Gaia is with us."

"Gaia is with us," the sisters repeated together.

"Tonight, we regain our freedom," Helena continued. "But we will sink into the shadows, never to be seen in the public again. It is the only way to keep our order safe and secret."

"But, Helena," another protested. "It is our duty to lead the worship of Gaia."

Helena sighed, not really sure how to explain the signs that

Gaia had given her. Things would change soon, she knew, and the Great Mother herself would be in danger. She had said so but had not explained why. She would need her own strength to protect herself from the impending threats that would soon come her way; threats from the divinities and powers of the Universe itself.

"The druids and the Firstborn will take precedence," Helena said. "Our time is nearing the end. We must now keep to ourselves and guard the spirit of the Great Mother, lest she fall to the darkness that she senses."

"What is this darkness?" the sister across from her asked.

"I do not know, sister," Helena replied. "But it has existed since the beginning, and it is not within our power to fight. These things will become prevalent to those who come after us, but *our* focus is getting the children to safety. What is left for us after that, I am uncertain."

"Who will care for the children?"

"The rangers and the thieves will care for them. They will protect them and give them a place to grow among their kind. They will live their lives as we do; as shadows who work to maintain order and balance."

The sisters were silent, and Helena took this as a sign that they accepted her explanation. She wasn't sure whether *she* even accepted it; nor if she even understood it. But it's all there was, and she felt that it was all there ever would be. In her soul, she felt that soon, their end would come. Never again would they draw swords in the name of Gaia, and never again would they lead the people in prayer. Tonight, if need be, they would give their lives in one last effort to lead the innocent to safety.

That was the oath they swore, and it was an oath they would follow to their last breaths.

Chapter Twenty-Eight

erves were coiled tightly as the wagon neared Daeglan's estate. Joran sat in the driver's seat, with Ferrin and three other thieves escorting him on horseback. Inside the wagon, several of his peers sat chained together, posing as the human livestock they had just rescued. Everyone—except for Joran—gritted their teeth in an apprehensive daze. They were about to perform an extremely dangerous deception, and it was one that could cost them their lives.

Ferrin's heart was about to burst from his chest.

"You need to settle down, lad," the smith called out to him, steering the wagon around the last curve before breaking through the tree line. "You'll mess yourself, and this whole charade will be for naught."

"I'm not going to *mess* myself," Ferrin replied with a sarcastic hand gesture. "Shut up and drive."

Joran grumbled, and Ferrin could see him shake his head with amusement. He stared at the road ahead, thinking that the smith was probably right—at least about settling down. If he faced the guards in his current state of mind, they would see through the farce for sure. He already looked suspicious, seeing as the Red Hand clothing was ill-fitting.

He felt out of place as well. He was cultured, clean-cut, and handsome—quite the contrast to the bandits of this criminal organization. There was also the possibility that all of the Red Hand operatives knew each other and would recognize the fact that he was not one of them. But, then again, Daeglan's guards were likely his own, and not associated, or familiar, with the gang members themselves.

So he hoped.

Ahead, the estate came into view. A high stone wall surrounded what looked like a dozen stone and wood buildings, all lit by a multitude of lamps placed everywhere around the compound. The rooftop of one large building dominated the view: probably Daeglan's house itself. The other visible buildings were arranged like a small town, several in line on either side of what was probably a wide street that led to the main house. But, even from the crest of the hill they now began to descend, it was all that was visible.

The massive wooden gate was closed, and four guards stood outside. They were armored in steel plate and bore long spears that were at least twice their height. They stood still as the wagon approached, obviously not alarmed.

"Here we go," Ferrin said under his breath, his heart still jumping around like a startled frog.

"Keep your wits, lad," Joran said. "I'll do the talkin'."

"Right," Ferrin replied, relieved.

He turned to look at the other thieves on horseback. They too were nervous, he noted, shifting uncomfortably on their horses and looking around with darting eyes. Their faces made him feel worse, and his heart began to thump even harder.

"Cripes," he muttered under his breath. "They're going to skewer us with those spears."

Perhaps this wasn't the greatest idea he had ever had. The only thing that made him feel any better was the fact that Joran was with them. Joran was confident, tough, and even-tempered. He would get them through this. He suddenly liked Joran.

A lot.

Two of the guards stepped forward as they neared, and Joran pulled back on the reigns to stop the horses. Ferrin and his men stopped as well.

"You're late," one of the guards said.

Without missing a beat, Joran replied, "So what? The road is full of holes. If Daeglan is such a wealthy man, he needs to fix his damn road."

The guard chuckled, poking the closest wheel with the butt of his spear. "Mayhap you need to fix your wagon wheels."

"After that ride, I might have to," Joran joked.

The guards laughed, and Ferrin chuckled nervously, drawing a narrow glance from Joran.

"He could pay us more, too," the guard said. "But that's another matter."

He motioned for the other two guards to open the gate, as he inspected the outside of the wagon. The thieves remained still and silent, keeping an indifferent posture as the guard looked them over.

"A bit young for such an important job, aren't they?" he said to Joran.

Joran shrugged. "I don't ask how old the escorts are," he said. "And I don't care."

The guard lifted the canvas flap and peered inside, grumbling as he looked over the costumed boys and girls inside.

"And these are a bit older than I was expecting," he said. "But, I don't care about that, either."

He closed the flap, returning to the front of the wagon. "Go inside the gate and turn left. The receiving building is there. You'll see the big door. Take the wagon inside."

"Right," Joran said.

He urged the horses on, and Ferrin followed behind, giving the guard a nod. The guard sneered, spitting on the ground in front of him. He was, apparently, not too thrilled about having to deal with Red Hand brigands.

Ferrin swore he heard the guard mutter, *rotten bastards*.

They rode through the gates cautiously, eyeing their surroundings. The compound was just as Ferrin expected; a wide street, with at least six buildings on either side. Some smaller buildings were interspersed among them, not tall enough to have been seen over the wall.

Joran turned the wagon left toward the receiving building. The door was wide enough for the wagon to fit through, and the smith guided it in. Several guards motioned for the men on horseback to dismount. Ferrin and his men did so and tied their horses off to the posts that were mounted in the ground to the right of the large door. Once the wagon was inside, the guards closed the door.

Joran got out of the driver's seat and joined Ferrin and his men near the rear of the wagon. The guards lifted the flap and ordered the occupants to exit. They played their parts well, moaning and crying with perfect mock fear. They stood together, wide-eyed and sulking. Ferrin found it hard to stifle his grin.

"Nice," one of the four guards said.

He seemed to be the leader and was dressed the part. His armor was gleaming and etched with strange triangular designs.

The tunic he wore was of blue silk, with an embroidered golden edge, and his demeanor was much like one would expect of a captain.

He inspected the slaves with scrutiny, patting their shoulders and checking their teeth. He even patted one of the girls on the rear, checking its firmness. The girl glared at him, clenching her fists.

"Problem?" the captain asked.

The girl was silent.

"Well, then," the captain said, turning to Joran. "Do you have the invoice?"

Joran pursed his lips, patting his tunic. "Invoice?" he said. "I..."

The captain gripped the hilt of his sword, narrowing his gaze. "Invoice," he repeated roughly. "We need to sign the invoice or the Red Hand will ask questions when you return."

"Hmm," Joran mumbled. "I'm afraid I must have lost it. I..."

"Who are you?" the captain demanded. His guards gripped their blades, moving closer to the group. Ferrin's heart pounded again, and he instinctively reached for his blade.

"I..." Joran stuttered.

The cracking sound of his fist smashing against the captain's face startled Ferrin. The man went down, falling straight back like a toppled tree. The other guards drew their blades but were quickly subdued by the chained-up thieves. They pounced upon them, using their chains to drag them to the ground.

Ferrin shot Joran a look of disbelief. "Why did you do that?" he asked.

Joran shrugged. "Sorry," he said. "I panicked."

Ferrin reached into his pocket for the key to unlock the chains. He undid the shackles one by one, and each guard was chained up and gagged. The captain was shackled last as he probably wasn't going anywhere any time soon.

"That was not part of the plan," Ferrin said. "What are we going to do now?"

A door opened at the rear of the room, and the pretty face of Ailin appeared. Ferrin grinned stupidly, urging her inside.

"You made it!" she said, excitedly.

"Yes, we're here," Ferrin said. "But now we're at a loss. How do we get the weapons to your sisters?"

Ailin clapped her hands together. "Don't worry," she said. "They will come to you. I will return with them and then I will start gathering the children for our escape."

Ferrin nodded. "All right then," he said. "But what do *we* do? We can't just stay in here and hope the other guards don't come in for a look."

"Don't worry about them," Ailin said. "I will create a distraction. It will be needed anyway so the sisters can get here. Just stay put, and don't let those guards get away."

"I don't think they're going anywhere," Joran said.

Ailin smiled again, rushing to Ferrin and shyly kissing him on the lips. Ferrin's heart pounded again, but for a good reason this time. As Ailin rushed back out the door, Joran shook his head, grunting.

Ferrin continued grinning.

✻ ✻ ✻

The rangers sped their way through the forest just west of Daeglan's estate. A thick fog was beginning to roll in, obscuring their view even more than the darkness that surrounded them. Kuros guessed that it was getting close to midnight, and their arrival would be just in time. With a total of thirty rangers, their force was sufficient to stand against any surprises, and the men were eager to engage the hated nobleman's army at long last.

Though Daeglan had been targeted for many reasons by the rangers, the new revelation about his involvement in the slave trade was the last straw. Despite their hesitation in confronting him in the past, now was the time to put an end to his criminal ways. His entire house would be dismantled, and Daeglan himself would be put down, if need be.

As the walls of the compound came into view, Kuros gestured for his men to take positions in the tree line. There were eight guards at the western gate and several on top of the wall. Taking them out was a priority, as the small force of thieves and nuns would have no hope of escaping otherwise.

Kuros drew his bow, and Turgon crouched next to him, drawing his own. "It would be best to take out the guards above first," Kuros said. "Then we will get rid of the guards at the gate and get inside."

"I thought we were supposed to wait outside," Turgon said, reminding him of Baelion's orders.

242

"Our goal was to assist in the escape," Kuros said. "And we will do that in whatever way we can."

Turgon nodded, signaling to the men behind him to ready their bows.

"Let's go," Kuros said, creeping forward.

The company snuck to the edge of the forest, keeping to either side of the road to Gaellos. They were about fifty yards from the gate; close enough for every archer among them to a get dead-on shot. At Kuros' signal, the men drew back their bows and released. The arrows took off with a swish, taking down every guard on top of the wall with barely a sound.

Kuros and the others immediately followed up with a ground-level volley, dropping all eight gate guards at the same time. Without hesitation, the company charged forth, keeping to the shadows of the roadside as they went to hide the bodies.

"Good work," Kuros whispered to his men. "Now, let's scale these walls and see what's inside."

Darragh's carriage arrived at Daeglan's estate shortly before midnight. He was let through the gate without question and led straight to the drop-off point directly in front of Daeglan's own house. Though he appreciated the welcome, it still didn't change the fact that he hated Daeglan with a passion.

Despite their allegiance, the two men had a strong disdain for each other for various reasons. In Darragh's case, Daeglan tended to try to overshadow him and take control. Darragh was the elder and more experienced of the two, and Daeglan was harsh, quick to react, and very indiscreet in every way imaginable. He was very public about his affiliations, much to the disdain of the other noblemen who shared their passion for money.

But the one thing that bothered Darragh the most was his doubt about how to profit. Darragh knew that smuggling stolen goods and hiring out thieves was the most lucrative—and least immoral—of ways to make money. But Daeglan scoffed at these ideas, saying they were beneath him, and beneath anyone who had any business sense. Daeglan's ideas were based around human suffering; something that even Darragh had no stomach for.

Slavery, Daeglan has said, was the most profitable business

there was, and what a better stock of people to buy and sell than the people of Eirenoch.

His *own* people.

What a devil, Darragh had thought. Who enslaves another human being to begin with, much less one of your own countrymen? Where would these slaves be sold? Even when Daeglan had sent them to the mines to work for the Red Hand, there was already doubt that they could be of any use to farmers or merchants. Who in Eirenoch would buy slaves?

No one, Darragh thought, that's who.

Now, with this upcoming meeting, Darragh was loath to look upon Daeglan's face again—or ever, for that matter.

He stepped out of his carriage, where two guards met him. One was Feyn, Daeglan's right-hand man. Another one Darragh hated.

"Welcome, Darragh," Feyn greeted him with a sneer that Darragh wanted to smack right off his face.

"Feyn," Darragh said with a nod. "I am here. Let's get this over with."

"This way," Feyn said, turning. "Daeglan has been expecting you."

Expecting me to bend down and kiss his ass, Darragh thought.

He followed Feyn up the front stairs, looking at the lavish estate with contempt. Darragh himself lived inside Faillaigh, placing himself among the people. Daeglan, however, built an elaborate estate outside of Gaellos, nearly half as large as the town itself. And the materials used were brought in from the outside; bought from the kings of foreign lands and shipped here at the cost of the people, no doubt. Likely, they labored unpaid to build the damnable place.

Feyn opened the large, oaken double doors, allowing Lord Darragh to step inside. His eyes widened as he saw the foyer, which was richly decorated with enough paintings and statues to fill Darragh's entire mansion. He cursed under his breath, following Feyn deeper into the main hall.

It was dominated by a large staircase that went up to a loft overlooking the hall. On either side of it were small sitting areas—probably unused. Feyn led him up the stairs, to an elaborately carved door.

"Daeglan awaits you, my lord," Feyn said, knocking once and then opening the door.

Darragh stepped in, noting the shadowy, candle-lit atmosphere. There was incense burning, and its smoke hung still in the air, broken only by the occasional wafting of a light breeze through the open balcony doors. Daeglan sat at his desk, wordlessly smiling as Darragh entered. He stood, offering Darragh the chair opposite him.

"Welcome, my friend," he said. "Please, sit."

Darragh clasped his hands behind his back and looked at the floor. "Why have you called me here at this hour?" he asked.

"To discuss business, of course," Daeglan replied. "Please, sit."

Darragh shook his head, hesitantly taking the chair and glaring at Daeglan from across the desk. He hated Daeglan's face; that smug smile that betrayed his mock politeness, and the cold blue of his eyes. They were a wolf's eyes, he thought.

"What business do you wish to discuss?" he asked. "Smuggling? Thievery? Slaves?"

Daeglan chuckled, reaching out to pour Darragh a mug of wine from a steel pitcher. "You always hated the prospect of slavery, have you not?"

Darragh sat forward. "Any man who has scruples would hate it," he said.

Daeglan's smile disturbed him. "Scruples," he echoed. "Who needs those? Besides, I'm not the one who is working with the queen to have her husband killed."

Darragh shook his head. He had constantly tried to explain to Daeglan his reluctant involvement in the plot but couldn't bring himself to tell him how much he feared disagreeing with Igraina.

"You know as well as I do that one does not stand against the wishes of the queen," he said. "Her power is great, and there is nothing she wouldn't do to ruin a man who does not play along with her little games."

Daeglan pursed his lips, a slight smile tugging at the corners of his lips. "She is just a woman, Darragh," he said. "The king is divine; the son of the Dragon. She is nothing but a sorceress to be ignored."

"Let us not forget that you are the one who provided the assassin," Darragh reminded him. He looked around then, holding his hands up in the air. "And where is that assassin now?"

"Ammarah is minding her business," Daeglan said. "She does not appear to be interested in the contract, and I don't blame her. She is focused on this Thyrean assassin for some odd reason."

"I know nothing of this assassin," Darragh said. "Assassins are your forte. My only concern now is my own house."

Daeglan leaned forward, staring Darragh in the eyes. "And where is this servant of yours?" he asked. "This boy... Ferrin?"

"I do not know, Daeglan," he replied. "His life is his own. As long as he serves me when I need him, I do not concern myself with what he does on his own time."

Daeglan chuckled. "How polite of you," he said. "Especially for the one who enslaved him."

Darragh picked up his mug, sipping the sweet wine. He only did so because Daeglan had drunk from the same pitcher. "He is not my slave," he said. "Ferrin was an indentured servant. He paid off his father's debt within two years and has chosen to stay out of his interest in politics."

"Ah, yes," Daeglan said. "He hopes to usurp your title, then?"

"There is no need for him to usurp anything. As I do not have children, he is the most natural successor to my title and heir to my house."

Daeglan nodded skeptically. "Aspirations," he said. "You have to love them, don't you?"

"He is a good man," Darragh replied. "His aspirations are noble. I respect him."

He meant to continue but was suddenly overcome with a strange feeling of dread. Daeglan seemed to notice, as he stood and turned toward the balcony doors. Darragh stood as well, feeling his heart race, and his skin tingling with strange magic, it seemed. The sound of metal tapping gently on ceramic tiles suddenly echoed in through the doors, and Daeglan turned to him, smiling.

"She has come," he said.

Darragh gritted his teeth. The foreboding feeling in his bones increased greatly; the anticipation within burning painfully. That clanking sound ground at his ears, filling his soul with a fear he had never felt before. Then, the shadowy figure of a woman appeared from behind the curtains.

She was not tall by any means, or physically imposing in any way. But the darkness that she exuded tore at Darragh's very soul. He felt himself unable to breathe as he beheld her dark form. She was armored in leather, with steel plates placed in strategic areas along her limbs. Her cloak was black, and its hood was raised, covering the dented and pitted iron mask that she wore over her face. From behind it, hellish eyes glowed red; eyes that seemed to lock at Darragh from the Abyss.

Though he desperately wanted to look away from her, he could not. His eyes were glued to hers, and his skin crawled as if it were trying to get away. He was mesmerized and terrified at the same time.

"Darragh," Daeglan said. "Meet Ammarah, our assassin."

Darragh swallowed, nodding his head slightly and averting his eyes, finally. He heard the woman step forward slowly, the sound of her metal boots causing his skin to jump every time they hit the floor. She stopped within three feet of him, pausing. He looked up at her again and could only imagine what was behind that mask.

"Do you fear me?" she asked him, her ghostly voice sending chills up his spine.

Darragh took a deep breath. He was terrified of her, but he could not answer. He was frozen.

Daeglan chuckled, taking a sip of his wine and grinning smugly. "Of course, he fears you, Ammarah," he said. "Who doesn't? Well… besides myself, of course."

Ammarah said nothing but turned her metallic face toward him. Darragh glanced at him as well, expecting him to continue his ill-conceived confident stance. Instead, he looked away and sat his mug back on the desk, turning to stand in front of his balcony doors.

"So, tell me, Ammarah," he said. "How are things at the mine?"

"The mine is no more," she replied. "I destroyed it. I find your practice of slavery repulsive."

Darragh was surprised to hear her say that. Surely such a vile and obviously evil creature cared nothing for slaves. Daeglan, however, was furious. He turned to her, his face as red as blood, a vein popping out on his forehead.

"You did *what?*" he demanded. "I gave you no leave to do so."

Though he could not see her face, Darragh knew that she was grinning underneath her mask. She, like Daeglan, enjoyed conflict.

"I do not need your permission to do anything," she whispered. "I do not work for you, nor shall I ever."

Daeglan narrowed his gaze, turning to rest his hands on his desk. "Those mines were our livelihood. Destroying them was not part of the plan."

Ammarah turned to Darragh, cocking her head strangely. "Plans change, now, don't they Darragh?"

Darragh swallowed hard. "I am not sure what you mean?" he said.

"You do not like to see people enslaved, either," she said. "Do you, Darragh?"

Darragh paused, then, "Not particularly, no."

She chuckled, turning back to Daeglan. "You see? You're the only one who approves of enslavement. Now you call this man here to insult him and tell him he is weak? He is weak because he chooses to smuggle goods and gold, not people?"

"I did not call him weak," Daeglan said. "Just foolish. Do not put words in my mouth."

"I will put my sword in your mouth if I so choose."

Darragh stifled a laugh. Though he feared this woman, he liked her attitude. She seemed to hate Daeglan as much as she did. And he would love to see her run him through — especially through the mouth. What a gruesome and hilarious sight that would be.

Daeglan sighed, shaking his head as he stared downward. "Why do you care so much about the people?"

"I care *nothing* for anyone or anything," she said. "What I *do* care about is the reason why I came to this island in the first place."

"Yes, yes," Daeglan said, nodding rapidly. "The assassin. So then, did you kill him? Did you kill the boy?"

Ammarah chuckled. "I took the boy from him," she said. "And with it, his heart."

"Good," Daeglan said. "I needed the boy removed. He would seek vengeance and try to take Helena away from me."

"Helena does not concern me," Ammarah said. "What concerns me is hurting Etanos before I finally put him to rest."

"Who is this Etanos?" Darragh interrupted. "And this boy?"

Daeglan stood. "The Thyrean assassin I spoke of before," he said. "And the boy is Garret. He was a servant at the convent I had burned to the ground. He would have been a danger to our... *my* plans."

Why did the name sound familiar to Darragh? He couldn't remember where he had heard the name, but he *had* heard it. Perhaps Ferrin had mentioned it before during one of his over-explained stories concerning his whereabouts.

Ammarah suddenly froze, drawing stares from the two men. She pulled her sword partway from its scabbard, letting it slide back in with a clank. She did this several times, her breathing becoming deeper and more urgent.

"What is it?" Daeglan asked.

"The time has come," she hissed. "Etanos is near."

"You can feel him?" Darragh asked.

"He has my dagger," she said. "And the wrath that it bears."

Darragh glanced at Daeglan in question. The man shrugged, folding his arms across his chest, and glancing back. "I suppose things are about to get ugly," he said. "Darragh, you should remain here. We may need to continue our business in the morning."

Darragh nodded. He didn't feel like riding back home anyway.

"Daeglan," Ammarah said. "Tonight is the night I end Etanos. And if it pleases me, I will end you as well."

CHAPTER TWENTY-NINE

The rangers were here," Etanos said as he and Garret paused just as the stone wall came into view ahead.

Garret studied the ground for a moment, trying hard to see what Etanos had noticed, but to no avail. He saw nothing, and that fact struck down any confidence he had in his ability to track.

"How do you know?" he asked his mentor.

Etanos grasped the stem of a nearby weed, showing him where the stalk had been bent slightly. Just below the bend was a clean-cut mark.

"This was made by a passing blade," he said. "One that is carried at the hip without a full scabbard. Kuros' friend carried an exposed blade like that, and he carried it with the edge facing to the front."

Garret nodded. That made sense. Etanos then reached down to pick up a small tuft of brown fluff from the ground.

"These are bits of an arrow's flight," he said. "The same feathers that Kuros himself used on his arrows."

"I see," Garret said, trying hard to take it all in.

"Plus," Etanos continued, grinning slyly, "Kuros said this is where they would be."

Garret grinned with him, shaking his head. "You're supposed to be my teacher," he joked, "not my personal jester."

"Come on," Etanos replied, emerging from the tree line.

They crept across the gap to the wall, just north of the gate. Etanos stopped and looked around, furrowing his brow. "There should be guards here," he said. "The rangers must have taken them out and went inside."

Though the area was shadowy, Garret could make out several dark lumps lying among the weeds. He approached one, seeing that it was a man.

"Here they are," he said. "Not very carefully hidden."

Etanos grunted. "Not much traffic on this side, I would imagine."

Garret counted the bodies. There were eight of them. Way too many for a low-traffic gate.

"There were quite a few of them," he said. "I wonder why."

"Let's not dwell on it. Let's just get over this wall."

Garret grabbed onto the highest block, easily pulling himself up to the next one. They climbed quickly, barely exerting any effort at all. When they reached the top, they paused for a moment to scan the walkway. It was empty.

"This wall is pointless," Garret said, remarking at how easily they had scaled it. "A cow could climb it."

"Bodies," Etanos said, nodding.

Several dead guards were lying about on the walkway; all of them pierced with arrows. They went to each of them in turn, lifting them and tossing them over the side to keep them from being discovered.

"First rule of guarding your fortress," Etanos said. "Make sure your guards don't stay in one place. These guards have been dead for at least an hour and no one found them."

"Well," Garret replied. "If his bodyguard was any indication, then I assume his other guards aren't too bright, either."

Etanos grinned, leading him to a darker section of the wall. They crouched in the shadows while Etanos scanned the area. He pointed to the north, directing Garret's gaze to that section of the wall.

"One guard is coming this way," he said. "So, there's at least a few of them that know what they're doing."

He pulled out his bow, handing it to Garret. "You take him," he said.

"I don't know if I'm good enough yet," Garret replied, doubtful.

"You'll be fine. Just remember everything I told you about your breathing."

Garret swallowed hard, taking the bow and drawing it back. He aimed for the lone guard, waiting for him to turn the corner onto their section. He held his breath, waited for his heart to beat, then loosed. The guard jerked violently, dropping straight down to the stone walkway.

"Good shot," Etanos said.

Garret handed him the bow, grinning in confidence. Etanos shook his head.

"Keep it for now," he said.

Garret shrugged, flicking his wrist to activate the bow's magic. It collapsed back into its compact size and Garret stuffed it in his tunic. They crept forward toward the largest of the buildings, knowing full well it would be Daeglan's private house. Garret watched Etanos closely, seeing the man's apprehensive demeanor. He knew that the assassin could feel the presence of his enemy.

Garret felt it, too.

"I wonder if Ferrin made it in," he wondered out loud.

"Likely," Etanos replied. "If Joran is with him, I'm sure they were successful. I have faith that the smith is an experienced trickster."

Below, a group of guards were patrolling the grounds. Their voices carried upward, warning the two of their presence. They crouched, looking through the crenellation. There were six men in light armor marching in formation along the wall. They were armed with spears and short swords and seemed to be preoccupied.

...which was always a good thing.

Without a word, Garret and Etanos draped their legs over the side of the wall and lowered themselves down to an acceptable level. They hung in silence until the troop passed them, and then dropped, drawing their blades on the way down. Each of them slashed downward at the back of a guard as he landed, taking them down instantly, and then rolled into a standing position. Before the other guards could react, the two assassins took them down with lightning-quick strikes.

"Leave them," Etanos said. "We'll head for the largest building."

"We should find Helena first," Garret protested.

Etanos shook his head. "As Kuros said, the sisters can take care of themselves. You needn't worry about them."

Garret had forgotten about the weapons and armor. He still could not picture Helena dressed as a warrior, so it had slipped his mind. He shoved away all doubt, however, and shook his head, grinning slightly as he thought of how beautiful Helena would look in shining armor.

She would be like a golden-haired Valkyrie of northern legend.

"Stick to the shadows," Etanos said. "We'll take out any troops we see along the way."

They tore through the darkness, keeping behind the row of buildings where the lamps could not reach. There wasn't much activity, although several patrols of guards marched down the center of the street and were visible from their route. It was only when they reached the last few buildings near Daeglan's house that the compound went on alert.

Alarm bells suddenly rang out for an unknown reason, and the visible guards began rushing toward the center of the complex. Garret and Etanos stopped, looking at each other in question.

"What's going on?" Garret asked.

Etanos shook his head. "I'm not sure," he said. "Ferrin must have been caught."

Garret raced toward the nearest building, mounting the stone wall and climbing up quickly. Etanos followed right behind. In the distance, no more than a few hundred yards away, a bell tower was plainly visible, its base and supports engulfed in flames.

Garret chuckled. "How ironic," he said. "The alarm bell is on fire."

Etanos nodded in amusement. "A good distraction," he said. "And you're right; irony at its best."

Garret scanned the grounds, watching the various troops of guards as they raced toward the tower. Other men were among them, probably workers or slaves. But there was another group that caught his attention, and he nudged Etanos to direct his gaze toward them. A small group of eight cloaked figures was heading toward the main gate, keeping to the row of buildings to stay hidden. Garret immediately knew who they were.

"The sisters," he said. "They're heading toward the gate."

"Ferrin must have taken the weapons there," Etanos said.

"We should make sure they get there safely," Garret said, pulling out the bow.

Etanos shook his head, pointing at the rooftops on the opposite side of the street. "No need," he said. "Our friends are here."

Garret saw the shadowy figures of several cloaked men on the rooftops. They followed the sisters from above; taking down any guards that were in their path. Garret smiled. He knew the rangers would keep their word — and then some.

Just as they were about to set off again, a squad of guards rounded the corner of a nearby building. The two melted into the shadows, waiting for the four men to pass in front of them, and then dropped to the ground behind them. Garret took the two guards in the rear, dropping them with one slash each. Etanos dropped the front two with a slash and a spinning thrust.

"To the mansion," Etanos said.

* * *

Ferrin opened the back door of the receiving building when he heard the sisters arrive. Seven tall, fierce-looking women entered, followed by Ailin, who smiled at him as she came through.

"Come with me," she said. "We will find the children and lead them toward the western gate. Joran, we will need your help to fend off the guards."

The smith nodded, drawing his blade and grinning with excitement.

"Ailin," Helena said, turning. "Be careful. We will join you at the barracks when we are dressed for battle. Do not approach the gate until we arrive."

"Yes, mistress," Ailin said.

She grabbed Ferrin's hand, pulling him outside. Joran followed, urging the other thieves to trail him.

"The children are in one of the old barracks," Ailin said. "It is guarded by four men. They are not likely to leave their posts despite the distraction."

"What did you do?" Ferrin asked. "I heard the alarm bell."

Ailin pointed off toward the center of the compound. Ferrin's eyes widened and a grin stretched its way across his face. The bell tower was burning, and the flames were climbing their way up its height. From what he could see, men surrounded it, desperately tossing buckets of water onto it to extinguish the flames. They weren't having much luck.

Joran chuckled. "Nice work," he said. "I feel sorry for the poor devil who's currently ringing the bell."

"Oh no!" Ailin cried. "I didn't think of that."

Ferrin pulled her away, urging her to lead them on. "Don't worry," he said. "He'll get out. Let's get to the children."

Ailin nodded hesitantly. "Follow me," she said.

Ferrin could tell she was worried about her actions. Though he too had some concern for the man at the top of the tower, his focus was on her. He hated to see her so worried, especially over something like the accidental death of a man whose only crime was his association with Daeglan. However, there was no time to be concerned. There were children to rescue.

Ailin led them through the complex toward the old barracks. The housing buildings were behind the main row on the west side, shorter and squatter than the rest, and hidden in the shadows of a sparse grove. While most of the buildings were currently empty, the children's barracks were well-lit on the inside, and there were four guards outside. Their swords were drawn, and they were focused on the fire in the distance.

"Stop," Joran said. "I can't take all of them at once. Are you allowed to go inside, Ailin?"

"Of course," she replied.

Ferrin looked at his fellow thieves, choosing the smallest girl and pulling her to him. "She can go with you," Ferrin said. "Tell them she's a new one, just arrived from Faillaigh."

Joran grunted in agreement. "Good idea," he said. He turned to the girl. "Are you armed?"

"Yes," she said, pulling a dagger from her tunic.

"Get one of them to follow you in and take him out."

"Wait," Ailin protested. "Not in front of the children."

"Ailin," Ferrin said softly, placing his hands on her shoulders. "These children are going to grow up around violence. Though my thieves are primarily in the business of stealing, they will no doubt have to resort to killing if it becomes necessary. The rangers… well, you know what they do."

Ailin sighed, glancing at the young thief with sad eyes. "All right," she said. "Just do it quickly and try not to draw too much attention to it."

"Don't worry," the thief replied. "I've done this before."

Joran's eyes widened for a moment. He seemed impressed. "Ferrin and I will take care of the rest."

Ferrin shot him a look. Joran nodded encouragingly. "Remember your own words," the smith said. "It's necessary."

"All right," Ferrin said. "Go on."

Ailin took the young thief by the hand and led her toward the barracks as Ferrin, Joran, and the rest hid around the corner. Ferrin felt his nerves tingle again, and his heart began to race. He was not looking forward to the prospect of killing. But, as Joran — and he — had said, sometimes it was necessary.

They watched the two as they approached the guards. The four men seemed indifferent, but stopped them anyway, looking over the young thief as Ailin introduced her. After a brief exchange, the guards motioned for her to enter, and one of them followed the two inside. Joran gave Ferrin a nod, and the two men snuck through the shadows toward the corner of the barracks. Ferrin watched through the window as Ailin led the young girl into the main bunk room. The guard began walking down the center aisle, inspecting the children as they lay sleeping in their bunks.

The young girl snuck behind him, drawing her dagger as the guard neared the end of the aisle. As he turned, the thief plunged her dagger into his heart, silently dragging him to the floor. Ferrin's heart skipped a beat. He had never seen this girl kill before. She seemed to be good at it.

When she and Ailin had dragged the guard's body into the corner, Ferrin nodded to Joran. "Done," he said.

He looked in one more time, seeing Ailin waking the children and instructing them to stay quiet.

"Let's do it," Joran replied, rounding the corner and drawing his blade again.

Ferrin motioned for his thieves to follow him as he trailed behind the smith. The three remaining guards were oblivious to their approach, keeping their eyes trained on the raging fire. Joran wasted no time with the first kill, striking down the nearest guard with a thrust, and then back slashing the next. Ferrin raced to the third guard, jabbing his blade into the man's ribs just as he turned.

The guard grabbed his blade arm, wrenching it tightly and twisting as Ferrin struggled to withdraw and thrust again. Ferrin kicked the man in the groin, pulling his arm free and jabbing him again. This time, the man went down with a groan, and Joran finished him off with his sword.

Ferrin stood breathless, his heart racing like that of a spooked horse. Joran glared at him with a grin.

"Not bad," the smith said. "But your technique could use a little work."

"That was frightening," Ferrin replied.

"You'll get over it," Joran said.

Ferrin smiled halfheartedly. He was sure Joran was right, but the thought of killing a man disturbed him. He couldn't imagine doing it as frequently as an assassin—or even a soldier. He wondered how many men Joran had killed, or Etanos, even Garret.

Was it even important?

"Inside," Joran said. "Grab a body and pull it in."

Ferrin grabbed the shoulders of the man he had killed and dragged him through the door. Ailin was inside waiting; the young thief, and several children standing near her. The children were wide-eyed and frightened, half-dressed and dazed. Ferrin dropped the body just inside the door, helping Joran carry in the other two.

"We will wait for the sisters here," Ailin said as Ferrin stopped to catch his breath. "They should be here soon."

Ferrin nodded. "I hope so," he said. "I am ready to leave this place."

CHAPTER THIRTY

Immarah charged through the alleys, intent on finally disposing of Etanos, her rage burning like the fires of Hell itself. She growled as she ran, drawing frightened stares from Daeglan's men as she passed them. Occasionally she struck one down, passing by and delivering a killing blow before the guards even knew she was there.

She could feel the assassin's presence growing ever closer, and her gaze narrowed as she blindly sought him out. He was near, she knew, he and his cursed protégé. The boy still lived.

But not for long.

She rounded a corner, seeing the main street alive with the crowds of rushing guards and workers. The bell tower blazed brightly in the moonlight, obscuring her sensitive vision, but she went forward on instinct alone. In the street, she lost the sense of her enemy's presence due to the massive amount of people rushing about. She growled in frustration, charging forth with her blades slashing in every direction.

Blood splattered in the air as she cut down all of those in her path. She could feel the satisfying friction of flesh beneath her blades, and that sensation drove her on. Underneath her mask, she licked what was left of her lips, sopping up the drool that ran from between her exposed and cracked teeth. Her breathing became rough and rattled as her excitement grew.

The time of her vengeance was near.

With a scream into the night, she leaped against the wall of a nearby building, vaulting herself up onto its roof. There, she perched, eyeing the darkness for her target. He was out there somewhere, she knew; she could feel him.

She could taste him.

"*Etanos!*" she howled his name out loud, drawing frightened stares from the soldiers around her.

They cowered from her presence, desperate to escape her wrath. To them, she was a demon of destruction, bent on slaying all who stood in her way. She was death itself; here in human form to bring terror to all of those who beheld her.

And she would gladly give it to them.

* * *

"What the hell is going on out there?" Darragh shouted as he looked out the window of his assigned quarters.

There was no one there to answer, but the question forced its way out. Everywhere outside, men were frantically rushing around. The bell tower was in flames for some reason, and he had seen the dark assassin dash across his field of view like a mad woman.

Something was going on, and it had something to do with this Etanos that Daeglan had mentioned.

He squinted through the glass as another small group dashed around in the shadows. One of them seemed familiar to him, but he couldn't place him. All he could focus on was the assassin. She had made a mad dash out the windows in pursuit of her target, leaving him and Daeglan behind.

Granted, she had frightened Daeglan with her threats, but why had she just left? Why was she so bent on killing this Etanos? She had said she would kill Daeglan. Why had she not done it right there and then? Why toy with him like that?

He wanted Daeglan dead!

Frustrated, Darragh turned and stomped his way to the door. He grabbed the handle, finding it locked. He pounded on the door in anger, banging his fist against the thick wood as hard as he could. Then, the handle turned, and the ugly face of Feyn was there, sneering as usual. Darragh felt his hatred of the man grow as he beheld his face.

"What is it?" Feyn asked.

"Let me out!" Darragh demanded angrily.

Feyn shook his head. "Lord Daeglan has declared that you are to remain here," he said.

Darragh leaned in closer, his teeth gritted with rage. "He has—*what!?*" Darragh hissed. "I am the Governor of Faillaigh, damn it! He has no authority over me."

"His orders were strict, milord," Feyn said, grinning. "No one is to leave."

Darragh narrowed his gaze. "You will step aside, young man, or I will have your head on a pole."

Feyn opened the door fully, stepping inside. There was another guard with him, gripping his sword tightly.

"You do not give orders, Darragh," Feyn said. "Daeglan's orders are for your own prot—"

Darragh's eyes widened as Feyn's expression changed to one of horror. Darragh didn't realize that he had drawn his dagger until he looked down and saw it sticking in Feyn's gut. The young guard that accompanied him stood frozen, his eyes also widening as Feyn slumped into Darragh's body.

Darragh met the guard's eyes as the lifeless bastard slid down and crumpled to the floor. They stood that way for a moment, both of them waiting for the other to make a move. Darragh briefly caught a glimpse of the young man skewering him with his sword.

But it never happened.

The guard dropped his blade and shield and fled down the hallway. Darragh stared after him wide-eyed and confused.

"All right..." he whispered, "now what?"

He looked down at Feyn's body, then at his dagger, then back to Feyn's body. What the hell just happened?

"Sorry, Feyn," he said, mindlessly. A grin spread across his face.

He knelt next to Feyn's body, retrieving the man's sword. In his youth, Darragh had not been so bad with a blade. Perhaps he could find Daeglan and kill the man himself—if he could remember his moves. Or maybe...

Feyn had a bow, as well.

Cackling, Darragh grabbed the bow, stuffed a few arrows in his belt, and gave Feyn a swift kick before escaping.

* * *

Helena led her sisters westward, avoiding the large crowds of men. Though they passed close by quite a few of them, the guards were preoccupied with the fire that was working its way up the bell tower.

Fully armored and ready for battle, the seven sisters slipped through the alleys on their way to the barracks. It seemed as if they would gather the children and escape without any resistance, as the number of men dwindled as they got nearer to the western gate. Helena was thankful for that. She had no desire to engage in open battle in front of the children.

She was aware of the presence of the rangers, who silently escorted them from the rooftops and the shadowy alleyways. She admired their skill, and their cause, and was thankful that they were there in case things went south.

Which they were about to do.

Ahead, she could see several rangers drop to the ground and rush forward. She halted her troops, keeping them at bay with an outstretched hand. She heard the ring of steel, and the twangs of several bows as the rangers engaged an unseen enemy.

"Hold fast, sisters," she said. "Our time is not yet here."

When the sounds ahead died down, a ranger appeared from the shadows, crouched down, and running toward them. She recognized the man as Kuros, the fledgling captain. He approached cautiously, one hand on his sword handle and the other gripping his bow.

"Something is happening at the western gate," he said, acknowledging her with a nod. "Outside forces have arrived. They must have spotted the guards we eliminated."

Helena sighed, crouching down on one knee. "Is there another way out?" she asked.

"There is another gate to the north," Kuros replied. "It's a secret entrance, located inside the main guard house. You would have to cross the main street to get there."

"We will do what we must," Helena said, her fear for the children growing. "But first we must meet Ailin and the children."

Kuros nodded. "The way is clear," he advised. "Just get there before the arriving forces breach the gate. We will hold them off."

Helena nodded, motioning for her sisters to follow her. Kuros disappeared again, and she looked after him as her troops sped away. She led her sisters through the last alley, scoping out the narrow street before crossing to the barracks. Ailin, Ferrin, and Joran awaited them just outside the door.

"The children are safe and ready to go," Ailin said.

Helena embraced her tightly, looking at her proudly. "You've done well," she said. "But the plan has changed. There are soldiers at the western gate, and we must detour to the north."

Ferrin sighed. "I wasn't aware there was a gate to the north."

Helena nodded. "Kuros says there is one inside the guard house along the north wall."

"I know where it is," Joran said. "I've been there. The way should be clear since everyone is running around like circus folk."

Just then, the frantic shouts of men were heard in the distance. They turned to the center of the compound where the bell tower was beginning to lean, its supports fully engulfed in flames and weakened to the point of collapsing. They watched, wide-eyed, as the tower slowly toppled, the sounds of its materials cracking and splintering filling the air as it crashed down.

The ground shook as it impacted a building on the east side of the road, crushing the structure under its weight and spreading the flames even further. Helena grinned, turning to Ailin as the young woman stood transfixed on her handiwork.

"Well done, Ailin," Helena said. "You chose the perfect distraction. Let's get the children out of here."

Ailin backed away to re-enter the barracks. The rest of them watched the chaos, keeping to the shadows as they waited for the children to be gathered. Helena turned to Joran, whom she had always admired. She placed her hand on his shoulder, gripping it affectionately.

"Thank you, Joran," she said. "You have proven time and time again that you are a man of great character."

Joran smiled, his eyes still trained on the fire in the distance. "It's all for a good cause," he said. "I have always been a friend of Gaia."

"We're ready," Ailin said from behind. "Lead on."

Helena drew her blade, rising to stand before her sisters. "Now is our time," she said. "The children will be freed at all costs. Leave no man standing who hinders our path."

"For Gaia," they said in unison.

With their hearts ablaze, the Sisters of Gaia charged forth, trailed by their newly found allies. Their exodus had begun.

* * *

The deafening crash of the bell tower collapsing startled Garret. The building near them exploded with the impact, sending bits of wood and stone flying everywhere. Etanos pulled him forward as he ran, and Garret could only watch in awe as the flames spread even further.

"It's going to burn down the whole compound," Garret said. "I hope Helena and the children are safe."

"Don't worry," Etanos said. "Kuros will make sure they're safe. Keep your eyes on the task at hand, Daeglan's house is ahead."

Garret tore his eyes away from the flames, peering into the street. There were men everywhere, running this way and that, carrying buckets of water and directing workers to help put out the flames. There were not, as of yet, any signs of battle, though Garret knew that sooner or later, they would be discovered. He only hoped that he could get to Daeglan before then.

They were a mere fifty yards from Daeglan's house now, and the crowds of men were dwindling rapidly. Everyone was rushing to put out the fire, leaving the main house mostly unguarded. Only the men posted at the front door remained, and they too were transfixed by the chaos.

As soon as the last rushing man passed, Garret and Etanos left the shadows and charged toward the southeast corner of the mansion. They were still out of the guards' line of sight, but Garret felt the strange sensation of being watched. Etanos felt it too, as his face became grim, and his grip tightened on his blades.

Then, from the alley behind them, the shouts of several guards got their attention. Six men rushed out from the shadows, swords drawn and prepared for battle. Garret spun in their direction, taking a defensive stance next to his mentor.

Etanos began the offensive, spinning away with his blades rushing about in a windmill attack. Garret did the same, avoiding the charge of the three guards who split off and rushed in his direction. He came around the nearest man's flank, back-slashing with his saber, and following with a thrust of his dirk. He felt his attacks blocked and heard the whoosh of a guard's blade just above his head as he ducked.

He turned to face his attackers, hearing the clang of steel as his mentor engaged the other three. He took his scorpion stance, waving his dirk out in front of him in challenge. The nearest guard grinned and then stepped forward with a double slash. Garret switched feet, stepping left and swiping at the attacker's blade. The man stumbled forward off balance, but the second guard took his place, attacking with a quick thrust.

Garret shot to the right, swiping inward with his dirk. The guard dodged just in time, and Garret leaped back to avoid his counterstrike. The third guard charged from behind him, and Garret fell to one knee and spun low, slashing at the man's legs. His blade sliced open the man's shin and continued in an upward swipe at the second guard, catching him in the chin.

As the first attacker stumbled forward in pain, Garret leaped toward him, placing his feet on the small of his exposed back, and vaulted toward the remaining guard. He spun in the air, switching the grip on his saber and jabbing downward as he landed. The guard batted his blade away and backed off, dropping his sword and drawing a bow.

Garret stepped forward, but the guard was quick. His arrow was knocked before Garret could react. He took his scorpion stance again, feeling his heart pound as the guard aimed. Without thinking, he released his saber, stepping to the side and reaching to the small of his back. He felt the grip of the strange dagger the old man had given him at the market and pulled it free from its scabbard. The world seemed to slow to a crawl as he drew it, reared it back, and flung it toward the bowman.

The arrow was released, and it soared straight toward him in slow motion. The dagger spun end over end as it left Garret's grasp. He instinctively reached for his saber as it fell, grabbing it right out of the air and spinning it into a backhanded swipe just as the arrow passed him. His blade cut the arrow in two, and the dagger buried itself in the man's forehead.

Then, the world sped up again. The transfixed guard fell to his knees, dropping his bow, and tumbled forward into the dirt. Garret stood staring in disbelief. How had he acted so quickly? Behind him, he heard the moans of the man he had crippled. He turned, seeing the wounded man crawling away.

He decided to let him go.

"Garret," Etanos said as he rushed over. "Good work. The guards at the front door didn't see a thing. Let's go."

Garret nodded wordlessly, still in shock. He followed Etanos, reaching down to pluck his dagger from the guard's forehead. They rounded the corner to the side of the mansion, stopping to scan the wall for a place to climb up. Just as they stepped forward to mount the wall, Etanos stopped, backing away and glaring to their right.

Garret turned, releasing the stone wall and stepping back as he followed Etanos' gaze. There, silhouetted against the flames, was the cloaked figure of the mysterious assassin. Garret swallowed hard as he saw her eyes burning through the darkness. He could feel her hatred, and it was overwhelming. He drew his blades again, stepping to the side to make room for his mentor.

Etanos gripped his shoulder. "Garret," he said. "This battle is not for you. She has a score to settle. Settle yours. I will take care of this."

Garret looked at his mentor's face. The man's expression was grim but determined, and his gaze was firm. There would be no protesting his decision, Garret knew. He would fight Ammarah alone.

He glanced at her once more, his fear becoming overwhelming. Whether it was the memory of her face glaring down at him, or the pain and suffering her blade had caused him, he could not tell. Either way, she was beyond his skill. He was no match for such a foe.

"Go," Etanos said. "Daeglan awaits you."

Garret's heart sank. Though he knew Etanos was skilled enough to face the assassin, some part of him felt a loss already. He had no desire to abandon his teacher — and friend. But Etanos would not take no for an answer. Garret had his own battle to fight; his own score to settle.

Reluctantly, he sheathed his blade and mounted the wall again. He looked at his mentor once more, proudly watching him as the man spun his blades into position. Ammarah cocked her head, seeming to smile behind her iron mask, her blades drawn in an instant and prepared for the battle.

Without a word, Garret began his climb, focused only on his target.

Soon, Lord Daeglan would pay the price for his deeds.

Chapter Thirty-One

he rangers scaled the western wall, gathering along its crenellations as the troop of outsiders lined up at the gate. Kuros could see the faint red hand symbol on their breastplates, telling him that these were not Daeglan's personal guards, but bandits from the outside. Either way, they were the enemy and must be eliminated.

He nodded to his men, knocking an arrow, and took aim. At his signal, his men loosed, releasing a barrage of arrows that caught the bandits by surprise. They fell by the dozens, shouting and scattering as the rangers continued to rain arrows down on them. Several archers in the rear fired back, missing their invisible targets: their arrows flying wildly over the rangers' heads.

"Keep at it, men!" Kuros shouted, knocking another arrow as he sought out the bandits' leader.

An arrow struck the stone next to his head, and he ducked down, surprised. Turgon was next to him, smiling.

"That was a close one," Kuros said, grinning.

He rose up, took aim at an archer in the distance, and fired. His target fell back, dropped his bow, and crashed into the men behind him. The bandits began to retreat, taking cover behind the rocks and shrubs outside the gate. The rangers continued to fire, and soon the ground was littered with arrows.

"The leader and his cronies are cowering by the gate," a ranger said nearby.

Kuros threw a leg over the outside of the wall, motioning for Turgon. "Follow me down," he said. "We'll take them out from here. Cover us, men."

At once, he and Turgon dropped to the ground just outside the gate. They drew their blades, pouncing on the leader before he even knew what was happening. Kuros took out one crony with a double slash, kicking the man's lifeless body at the gate. The captain, a large man of Anwar, drew his giant mace, swinging it from side to side with a deafening *woosh!*

Kuros dodged left and right as the great man charged. He crouched low, waiting for the right moment to strike. The captain then twirled the mace in a wide arc and raised it over his dark head. Kuros bounced on his feet in preparation, and the captain growled in rage as he swung the giant mace down. Kuros rolled to the side, and then forward, striking the captain's leg with his blade. The giant man howled in pain, and Kuros jumped up toward him with his heel poised to strike. He kicked the man hard in the face, knocking himself back as well. He impacted the ground hard, rolling onto his feet just as Turgon finished off the giant man with a slash to the back of the neck.

The captain toppled like a tree, crashing into the ground in a cloud of dust and dirt. The remaining men fled, running toward their hidden comrades. The rangers above cut them down with arrows, and Kuros and Turgon stood directly in front of the gate, challenging the gathered bandits to charge.

"*Come on, you cowards!*" Turgon shouted.

Kuros grinned. "That's not very ranger-like, Turgon," he said. The men above chuckled.

In the distance, a single figure appeared, standing in the center of the path. His hands were out in a gesture of peace, and he walked forward cautiously. Kuros eyed him suspiciously.

"What's this fellow up to?" he asked out loud, stepping forward.

"Be careful," Turgon said.

Kuros turned to look upward, nodding to his men to keep him covered. He and Turgon walked forward slowly, keeping their eyes on the bandit. Kuros assumed he wanted to surrender, or at least talk for some reason, but there was also the possibility that he was setting them up. The latter was more likely.

Then, out of nowhere, a company of riders crashed through the tree line in the distance and ran the man down. Dozens of horsemen rode out of the shadows, purging the bandits from their hiding places and cutting them all down as they charged back toward the gate. Kuros and Turgon rushed to the side of the road just as the riders passed.

Their leader stopped his horse, turning toward them. He was armored in shining steel and bore the banner of Gaellos.

"Ho there!" he shouted down at them. "What's all this chaos, ranger?"

Kuros stepped forward as the man dismounted. "You've been waiting for a reason to take Daeglan down," he said. "Now's your chance."

"What's going on?"

"Those men you ran down were of the Red Hand," Kuros said. "They've been working with Lord Daeglan, smuggling slaves and weapons. You'll find dozens of them inside."

"Where is Lord Daeglan?" the man asked.

"No doubt he is hiding somewhere in his mansion. You'll not likely find him alive."

The man nodded, mounting his horse again. "Care to join us?" he asked.

Kuros chuckled and whistled to his men above. Within less than a minute, the gates opened, and the horsemen charged in. With thirty rangers and a company of cavalry, Daeglan's forces were doomed.

Soon, Gaellos would be free of his scourge.

* * *

Guards seemed to be appearing from nowhere as Helena and her company crept through the shadows. Though the children were mostly silent, their mumbling and frightened cries worried her greatly. If they were spotted, the children's lives would be in great danger.

She noted how Ferrin kept close to Ailin, seemingly guarding her in a most noble effort. She knew that the young woman needed no protection, but admired Ferrin's heart. His ability to keep the children in order was also worthy of admiration. They seemed to like him, and that fact earned him her trust.

From what she could see, they were a mere two hundred or so yards from the north wall, and thus the northern guard house. With Joran at her side, there was no doubt they could find their way out without much of a hassle. Though getting the children out safely was her primary concern, she intended to return and dispose of Daeglan once everyone else was safe and away. She only hoped the rangers would figure out their detour.

Near the corner of an empty barracks, she paused, putting her hand out to halt her sisters. Something did not feel right to her. There was a strange, familiar darkness in the air; one that she and Ailin had felt before. Joran seemed to feel it, too, and the smith knelt next to her as she contemplated their next move.

"Do you feel it?" Joran asked her.

"I do," she replied. "I have felt it before, though I do not know what it is."

"I wouldn't worry about it," he said. "It is not our concern. This darkness does not seek to harm the children. It has a specific goal in mind."

Her eyes went to the smith's face. He was not telling her the whole truth, she knew, though she trusted his words. Joran had no reason to lie, but he seemed to be holding something back.

"I trust you, Joran," she said. "But if the children could be in danger, I need to know."

"As I said, the children are safe from this darkness. We only need to worry about Daeglan's forces."

Helena nodded, accepting his words. If he was keeping something from her, he probably had good reason. There was no need to press the matter, she supposed. He was merely keeping her sights focused on the goal.

She turned back to their path, creeping forward to find a way through the chaotic scene ahead. Men were rushing around, desperate to put out the fires that had been spread by the collapsing tower, and there was suddenly the thundering sound of horses coming from the west.

"Follow me," she said, turning to Ferrin and Ailin. "Keep against the front of the next building, and make sure the children follow in single file."

Ferrin nodded.

Helena rushed forward, heading straight toward a low, single-story house tucked away from the streetlamps. She kept as close to the building as possible, looking back to ensure the children were also in the shadows. All she could see was the occasional glimpse of Ferrin moving along their line to keep them in order.

Ahead, there was an empty field, dotted only by shrubs and rocks, and lit only by the light of the moon. Though dim, the area was too open to offer full concealment. They would have to risk being spotted. She hoped that the soldiers were too busy to notice them.

With a wave of her hand, she bolted toward the wall. The others followed right behind, and the sound of their footfalls, especially those of the children, was not quite as stealthy as she had hoped. But before she could turn and urge them to walk softly, she heard ringing steel. A small group of soldiers appeared from the west, heading straight toward them.

"Stop!" one of them shouted.

Helena froze, drawing her blade and stepping forward. Joran was at her side in an instant, his sword poised and his face stern and determined.

"Ferrin, protect the children," he shouted.

Joran and the sisters charged. Helena cried out in rage as she crashed into the soldiers, immediately breaking into a furious windmill attack that felled two soldiers. She bashed into another enemy with her armored shoulder, knocking him into Joran, who slammed him into the ground and stomped him into oblivion.

The enemy leader charged with a thrusting attack. Helena dodged to the left, spinning into a backhand swing that caught the man's breastplate. He stumbled back, breathless, and was taken down by another sister.

Helena growled with battle lust. She could feel the power of the Great Mother surge through her veins. She released it upon another soldier, driving him back with lightning-fast strikes. The soldier blocked every swing, and Helena felt the impact of their colliding blades. But she pressed on; delivering a blow that knocked his blade from his hands. She kicked him square in the gut, knocking him down, and pounced on him, driving her blade through his chest.

All around her, the sisters fought against their foes, taking them down with all the Great Mother's fury. The soldiers fought hard, but they were no match for the Sisters of Gaia and the mighty Joran. Soon, the guards were eliminated, and Helena caught sight of Ferrin and Ailin as they kept the children calm.

"Come!" she called to them. "The guard house is just ahead."

The thieves rallied the children together, leading them right behind the sisters as they continued forward. They reached the wall, and Joran led them east toward the guard house. Helena kept alert for any other guards and glanced back occasionally to ensure the children were still in line.

"Stay here," Joran said to her, holding his hand out before her. "I will check the guard house before we go through."

Helena nodded, allowing the smith to scout ahead. She urged the others to stay against the wall, where the shadows were plentiful and kept her eyes on the raging fires in the center of the compound. Through the thundering flames, she could hear the sounds of battle, and she knew other forces had arrived.

Then, as she glanced over at Daeglan's mansion, she saw a lone figure climbing the wall. Though she could not make out any details, she knew in her heart that it was Garret. The boy had come to seek revenge for the burning of the convent. She smiled as she watched him, proud to see that he had fulfilled his promise to always look after the children.

The Great Mother had chosen him well.

* * *

Etanos whirled his blades as he charged, crossing them in a diagonal pattern. Ammarah's blades sliced against his, throwing sparks out in bright bursts that illuminated the dark assassin's iron mask. Etanos focused on her burning eyes and the blind rage that dwelled there. Though he was not intimidated by her skills, he feared the darkness that she exuded.

She was pure, vengeful evil.

She swiped across with one blade, striking downward with the other when Etanos ducked. He blocked with his right blade, countering with a thrust that she easily dodged. He spun away, feinting left, and leaped into the air with a double thrust that caught her off guard. His left blade hit her gauntlet, cutting a leather strap that held it in place.

She cackled as he ducked away, letting the piece of armor fall from her forearm. Underneath was nothing but dark iron, segmented and jointed like some bizarre machine. He glared at it, wondering whether she was entirely iron, or just partially. Was there even any living flesh left on her body?

"You are an enigma, Ammarah," he said.

He heard her cackle behind her mask, and her eyes flashed orange for just a moment. It was almost as if she felt flattered.

"Who was this mad wizard who brought you back?" he asked.

Again, she cackled, swiping her blades quickly through the air in anticipation.

"No more words," she hissed. "Fight now."

She charged, leaping into the air and spinning as she descended. Etanos rolled out of the way, striking behind him and then spinning to slice across with his other blade. She dodged both attacks with a backflip, landing squarely in a strange, crouching stance.

"What is it that motivates you?" he taunted. "Is it your lack of skill? Or is it simply your anger at being defeated?"

She hissed again, ending it with a growl that gurgled with an unearthly timbre. Etanos felt his skin crawl but kept his composure as he glared at her shining mask.

"Answer me," he said. "Do you seek to prove yourself?"

"I seek to end you," she replied with a venomous tone. "Nothing more."

She charged again, this time twirling low. Etanos drove a blade into the ground and vaulted over her as she passed, delivering a pommel bash to the back of her head. Her blade impacted his, throwing her off balance. She rolled onto the ground, smoothly returning to her feet just as Etanos charged. He swiped his blades in a crisscross pattern, driving her stumbling back as she struggled to keep her balance. He pressed on, relentlessly pummeling her defenses with furious blows.

But a handful of dirt and rocks broke his attack, sending him reeling back with an eyeful of grit. He spat as he retreated, wiping his face with his gauntlet. Ammarah cackled as she rose, twirling her blades menacingly.

"I will stand over your body as you did mine," she said. "And my soul will rejoice in your death."

Etanos scowled, laughing on the inside at her words. "You have no soul," he said. "You never did. Only a monster murders women and children."

Ammarah cocked her head, chuckling strangely. "Then you are a monster as well," she said. "You are a murderer of children."

Etanos froze, keeping his stance, but glaring at her in shock.

"That's right, Etanos," she continued, tapping her belly with the tip of her blade. "You murdered my child."

His heart skipped a beat. Was she speaking the truth? Did it matter? What kind of child would it have been? If she had born any offspring, would it be like her; soulless and evil? Or had he truly taken the life of an innocent child?

Inside, he felt the pain of guilt growing. He was torn. Ammarah was a truly unscrupulous woman in her life. She had killed hundreds of innocent people; and had fulfilled contracts without question. She was a bringer of darkness without the soul of a human. He *had* to kill her. He *had* to end her career, lest she bring a scourge to the brotherhood — and the profession.

Pregnant or not, her existence was a bane to all that was honorable and good.

"Your child is with the Great Mother now," he said, determined not to allow the guilt to overcome him. "And soon, you will be, too."

He charged then, his heart burning to put an end to Ammarah's reign of terror. As the world slowed down to a crawl, his eyes locked with hers. Only by defeating her could he justify the death of her child; otherwise, it would have been for nothing.

As he reached the peak of his leap, he mouthed a silent prayer to Perses, asking the divine assassin to guide his hand one last time.

Chapter Thirty-Two

arret pulled himself up to a large, open window. The room inside was dark, with only the faintest hint of moonlight illuminating its far wall. The smell of spiced tobacco wafted out from inside, interspersed with the occasional hint of stale beer.

He settled on the sill, looking down behind him one last time before dropping onto the floor inside. The room seemed deathly quiet, unused, and layered in at least a month's worth of dust. Whatever purpose this room served, it had not been used as such for some time. He guessed that it was some kind of smoking room, where house servants could gather to engage in their vices.

Outside, the sounds of battle were escalating, which piqued Garret's interest. But with time running short, he had no time to watch or wonder. He had one purpose and one purpose only. Daeglan was his focus, and despite his concern for Etanos, he had to eliminate the lord of the manor before outside forces arrived—if at all.

Picturing Lord Daeglan's face in his mind, he crept toward the door, pressing his ear against the hardwood to listen. It was quiet beyond, and he reached up to turn the handle as quietly as possible. The door creaked slightly as he opened it. The hallway was well lit, with sconces every six feet or so, and sported at least two doors on the opposite wall in either direction.

He heard voices coming from the right. There were at least two men speaking in the distance; one of them formal and stern. Deciding it could be Daeglan himself, he went in that direction. As he approached a corner, the voices faded, as if moving in the opposite direction.

He crept down the hallway, stopping at a door that was ajar. Inside, a rough-looking man lay dead; stripped of his weapons. He appeared to have been stabbed in the gut, and carelessly left for dead. Though he had been dragged a short distance, his killer seemed to be unconcerned that he would be found.

Shaking his head, Garret continued. He followed the voices as well as he could, always keeping them within the same distance while keeping watch on the hallways ahead. The house was mostly empty, it seemed, and anyone posted inside was likely out participating in the battle.

…or had fled.

But, as a typical nobleman, Daeglan would be cowering in his house, away from the battle. That or he was already in the process of escaping. Either one was likely. From the brief encounter he had with Daeglan in Gaellos, Garret could tell he was nothing without his cronies. He was just another spineless bureaucrat, confident and commanding when in the presence of his bodyguards, but cowardly when alone.

"Where are you, you bastard," Garret muttered under his breath.

The voices were getting louder as he continued down the hall. Either the speakers had stopped, or they had changed direction. Either way, they were about to die. Garret peered around the corner, seeing the hallway lined with the same sconces. The men were just around the next corner; their voices were loud and clear now. He crept down the hallway, keeping his back to the wall, and approached. Their words were audible, and he stopped to listen.

"Why do I always get stuck inside?" one asked. "I would rather be out there in the thick of battle."

"I would rather not be here," the other said. "It would probably be a good idea to flee while we have the chance. To Hell with Daeglan."

The first guard chuckled. "Right. The bastard's up in his tower hiding out like a rat while all of us are risking our lives protecting him."

"Well," the second said. "I hear Darragh pays well. Maybe we should go work for him. He doesn't cavort with those nasty brigands."

"Ahh, the Red Hand," the first exclaimed. "I hate those monsters. Thieves, murderers, slave traders."

"That's not all they are, Hern. Rumor has it there's much more to them than meets the eye. But one would have to delve deep into their group to find out everything."

"I'm not sure what you mean."

"They have dealings with the cults on the mainland," the second said. "And some of the cults here in Eirenoch. I hear they relate to the queen somehow."

Garret furrowed his brow. What did the queen have to do with all of this?

The first guard grunted curiously. Garret got the impression that he too was unaware of the queen's involvement, or at least was skeptical of her apparent dark nature. This was the first Garret had heard of it. He wanted to know more.

"Maybe Darragh is the better choice," the first said finally. "We should go talk to him, at least."

"Should we?" the other said. "His room is right down the hall."

So, Garret realized, Darragh had been there and had killed the man back in the open room. He wondered where the man was now. How unfortunate for Ferrin if he were here. It would be embarrassing for both, Garret imagined, if they were to find each other outside.

"All right," the first guard said. "Let's go talk to him. Maybe he'll pay us if we help him escape."

Garret pressed closer to the wall, slowly drawing his blades. He was about to be discovered. But he had no desire to kill these two men. They didn't seem to like Daeglan any more than he did. Maybe they could be persuaded to flee without any trouble.

As soon as they turned the corner, they spotted Garret, and their hands went to their blades. But Garret stood quickly, jabbing his saber into one man's face, just inches from his eye.

"Stop right there," he said.

Both men were startled but did not seem aggressive.

"Who are you?" one of them asked.

"I am here to find Daeglan," Garret said. "If you choose to turn and walk away, I will let you. I am not your enemy."

"Why are you looking for Daeglan?" the other asked.

"I am here to kill him," Garret said. "In return for burning down my home and putting the children there in danger."

The man on the left gave an odd expression of surprise; his eyes widening and his brows rising almost to the top of his head. "Ah!" he said. "You're the one."

The other guard grinned, lowering his hands. "Daeglan is in his tower," he said. "You'll find it if you go down this hall and go through the double doors at the end."

Garret eyed him curiously. "You would give up your employer so easily?"

"Daeglan is a rat," the man answered. "I care nothing for him or his operations. I want to work for Darragh."

Garret chuckled. "From what I hear, he is a rat, too. And he's no longer here."

"What do you mean?" the first man said.

"He killed a man in his room and escaped."

The two men looked at each other, smiling. "Feyn," they said in unison.

Garret cocked his head. "I don't know who that is," he said. "But I don't care."

He lowered his blades and moved to the side of the hall. "Get out of here and find another person to work for. I'm sure you could catch Darragh if you hurry."

The two men nodded and wordlessly ran down the hallway, not even looking back. Garret turned the corner and peered towards the end of the hall. He could see the double doors the guard spoke of. There, probably up a ridiculously long flight of stairs, Daeglan waited... and hid like the coward he was.

Abandoning stealth, he raced down the corridor, intent on ridding the world of Daeglan's treachery. He could only think of the look on Daeglan's face when he confronted him, and it drove him on. He couldn't wait to see the shock, the fear, and the pleading eyes that he would no doubt get to see.

He would enjoy it.

The double doors were unlocked — surprisingly — but extremely heavy. Garret had to strain to pull them open, and it was likely he was making an excessive amount of noise in doing so. When he finally slipped through, he was faced with a fancy spiral staircase with sconces along the outer walls, and murals of the Great Mother along the inside.

Fake sentiments, perhaps?

Garret hugged the inner wall as he ascended, keeping his ears open for any sounds above. All he heard was the crackling of a large fire. The smell of burning wood was slight and was interlaced with the aroma of tobacco, not quite the same aroma as earlier, but similar. Daeglan was up there, smoking and probably watching the battle from the comfort of his tower.

Garret had his blades drawn when he reached the top, and as he had guessed, Daeglan was there. He stood at his window, smoking a pipe, and holding a tankard of ale in his other hand. The circular room was a mess; clothing, bottles, and other items were scattered everywhere. The smell of decayed food and dirty clothing lingered, barely masked by the other smells.

Daeglan cleared his throat. "I knew you would come," he said, turning.

He was calm, collected, and seemingly unsurprised by Garret's presence. He took a pull from his pipe, and sipped his ale, waiting for Garret to respond.

"Then you know why I'm here," Garret said.

Daeglan smiled. "Of course," he said. "But let me offer you an alternative."

"I am not interested in an alternative," Garret said. "You must pay for your crimes."

"Of course, I must," Daeglan said, taking another sip of his ale. "That was my alternative plan—to *pay* for my supposed crimes."

Garret held his saber out in front of him, pointing it directly at the nobleman—who still seemed unshaken.

"Do you really think I am interested in gold?" Garret said. "You put the lives of those children in danger, you destroyed a convent dedicated to the Great Mother, and now you offer me gold?"

"I can offer you more than gold, my friend," Daeglan insisted. "How about title, an estate of your own?"

"In case you hadn't noticed," Garret said, "your estate has fallen. The rangers have overrun your guards, city troops are here to arrest you, and my mentor is here to destroy your assassin. What can you possibly offer me?"

"Allow me to show you my plan," Daeglan said. "If only for your own amusement."

"Daeglan, it is time for you to pay for your crimes."

Garret took a step forward, swishing his saber from side to side. Daeglan glared fearfully as it cut through the air.

"Listen to me," Daeglan said, holding up his hand in a pathetic gesture. "I have all the money and influence you could ever want or need. Whatever you want, just name it, and it's yours."

He backed away then, nearly stumbling over a pile of clothing. Garret followed him, his eyes locked with the nobleman's.

"It doesn't have to be this way," Daeglan pleaded. "Just let me show you what I have planned. I can escape from here. No one will ever know where I am. You will never see me again."

He turned, shuffling toward a nearby bunk where a pile of rags and other clutter lay atop the blanket. Garret narrowed his gaze, feeling a strange sense of danger. The dagger at the small of his back—the one given to him at the market—began to vibrate. It was an odd feeling, one that seemed to heighten his awareness.

Suddenly, Daeglan turned back, a crossbow poised in his right hand. The weapon clicked as its bolt was released. Garret spun away just as the missile passed by his chest, and he instinctively reached behind him to retrieve and throw the dagger. Before Daeglan could react, the blade buried itself in his chest. He dropped the crossbow, staring at Garret with a look of horror.

Garret regained his balance, watching as Daeglan's eyes glazed over. The nobleman began to sway as he reached up to grasp the dagger's hilt. He inhaled with a rasping breath, his face trembling and pale. Garret sheathed his blades, folding his arms in front of him as he waited.

Without a word, Daeglan fell to his knees, glaring at Garret with hatred before pitching face-first onto the floor. Garret felt a sense of relief inside; satisfied that he had done his duty to the convent. Daeglan had paid the price for his treachery, and the entire city of Gaellos was free from his tyranny.

As for his men, and their association with the Red Hand, things seemed to be falling apart. Outside, the sounds of battle were raging, and soon, the entire operation would fall. The rangers would overrun the compound, Daeglan's men would flee, or face the local magistrate, and the sisters would find a new place of worship.

Everything would be alright, he thought.

He retrieved his dagger from Daeglan's body, holding it out in front of him as he stared at it in wonder. The blade had warned him of impending danger, as if it were magic. But there had never been any indication that it had any such properties before; it had simply been a mundane dagger. Had it just been his imagination? Was it his own intuition that had saved him?

Shaking his head, he wiped the blade clean and sheathed it once more. He looked down at Daeglan's body as he did, feeling a small amount of pity for the man. It was pity that was quickly replaced by worry as he suddenly remembered his mentor's current situation.

"Goodbye, Daeglan," he said, racing toward the window.

He could see the fire spreading to other buildings, and the frantic mob of soldiers and guards running about and fighting randomly amidst the flames. Etanos was down there somewhere, facing the dark assassin in a battle to the death. Helena and the sisters were fighting a battle of their own, and he knew that the fate of the children was in their hands.

He raced out the door, eager to join the battle below. For the first time in his life, Garret felt that he mattered and that there were those who relied on him.

He would not let them down.

CHAPTER THIRTY-THREE

tanos struck hard, his blade crashing into Ammarah's own as he landed. The sparks flew, and he heard the dark assassin groan with anger. He let loose with everything he had, driving her back with every blow. Still, she blocked and countered, her blades whirring with blinding speed and becoming an almost impenetrable wall.

She flipped and spun, striking out at unexpected moments. Etanos skillfully blocked her attacks, ducking and weaving as he tried to gain the upper hand. He was growing tired, and yet Ammarah seemed to be growing stronger as her anger built.

She leaped against the wall, flipping off it and striking before hitting the ground. Etanos blocked and countered with a low spin, striking out at her legs. She flipped into the air, landing behind him, and slashed out with both swords. Etanos jabbed his own blades over his shoulder, blocking the attacks, and struck out with a spinning counter. Ammarah rolled to the side, spinning into an odd stance; both blades held up and out to her sides.

Beneath her mask, Etanos heard her cackle.

"It seems we *are* equally matched," she hissed.

Etanos said nothing, charging at her with a blinding twirl of both blades. She parried each strike, stepping back as she taunted him. With the last blow, she countered, swinging both blades together in a horizontal slash. Etanos ducked and rolled forward, crashing into her legs with a force that knocked her back. He instinctively twirled his blades into a dagger-like grip and jabbed downward, but felt his swords impact the rocky ground.

He flipped over his blades, drawing them out of the dirt, and took a guarded stance. Ammarah's eyes glowed with fury, and she glared at him, her heavy breathing giving her a threatening aura. Etanos studied her carefully, noting her tiny movements, and her gentle swaying. She seemed to tense up before she attacked, and the tensing was coupled with the strange whirring that drove her movements.

He glanced at her exposed arm, still in awe at its metallic structure. Though quick and accurate, the limb seemed stiff and predictable. Unlike a true limb, it was not flexible and fluid and this would be his advantage.

He charged again, this time feinting to his right. As she swung to block, he shifted left and spun both blades, striking her shoulder with a debilitating slash. She pitched forward, stumbling, but spun around to face him, ready for the next attack.

He had felt his blade impact on her body and knew that there was metal underneath. Surely somewhere in there was human flesh, and he would find it. He would find it and strike her down once more.

Ammarah slowly circled him, her eyes glowing brighter as her wrath grew. He grinned to taunt her, and the red brightened to an almost blinding orange. She hissed her contempt and charged once more, slashing left and right. Etanos dodged from side to side, countering with thrusts and backhand strikes.

He leaped back when she attacked with an aggressive horizontal slash. Her momentum carried her around and she struck with her other blade. The attack met with empty air as Etanos flipped over it with a sideways leap and jabbed straight at her neck. He felt the tip of his blade strike soft flesh and knew he had injured her.

Ammarah hissed with rage as Etanos landed behind her. She spun quickly, staggering back and clutching her wound, her growls growing in volume as Etanos laughed. She backed away, mumbling unintelligible words behind her mask.

Etanos approached; confident the battle had been won. One more strike and she would go down. As her knees became weak, he crossed his blades, intent on decapitating her when she fell. His heart raced with anticipation as he contemplated her demise.

Soon, it would be over.

* * *

Darragh exited Daeglan's residence through a window on the east side of the house. He knew there was a guardhouse along the north wall, but there were too many guards on that side of the building. He would have to sneak around the front and hope that no one would see him.

He had contemplated going up to Daeglan's tower and disposing of him for good, but escaping seemed the more urgent matter. Besides, it had been decades since he had held a blade and fought against another man. He did not know how well Daeglan fought, and it was likely that he could best Darragh if it came down to it.

But, Ammarah had threatened to do the deed herself. Perhaps if he could find her, and offer her a deal...

He went around the southeast corner of the house, staring at the many fires that burned throughout the compound. He was amazed at how the flames had spread so quickly. Men fought here and there, some of them Red Hand, some of them Daeglan's men, and some of them city guards. He also caught glimpses of green-cloaked men among them, fighting alongside the city guards. Rangers, he guessed. They were always in the middle of something.

But, despite the chaotic scene, a nearby fight caught his attention. He focused on the rings of steel that echoed off the front of the house, seeing two figures battling fiercely in the light of the surrounding fires. As he crept closer, he saw that it was Ammarah and some unknown foe.

From his vantage point, he could see that this man in the dark cloak was winning. He had scored a devastating blow and looked as if he were about to finish her off.

Darragh could not let that happen.

Ammarah was needed. She was needed to dispose of Daeglan, and possibly other members of the Red Hand. Perhaps he could even hire her to kill the queen herself. Surely the assassin was much more likely to kill the queen than the son of the Dragon.

He had to help her.

Darragh drew the bow, knocking one of the three arrows he had taken from Feyn. It had been quite a long time since he had fired one, but he had once been an excellent shot. He hoped he still had the skill.

His livelihood depended on it.

He held his breath and aimed, steadying himself as he focused on the bastard warrior who was about to destroy his plans. He gritted his teeth as he loosed, watching the arrow fly through the fiery sky as it sailed home.

＊ ＊ ＊

Ammarah's heart thumped wildly as Etanos bore down on her. Inside, her machinery was struggling to repair her flesh, but she knew there would not be enough time. She felt a lump rise in her throat as she closed her eyes. This was the end, she knew. Etanos had won, and she would go into the darkness with only hatred in her soul.

Her child would not be avenged.

She felt the urge to weep, but her tears would not come. It was not possible. She could only moan with anguish as she watched those blades cross before her. It would be quick. It would be painless. That was Etanos' way.

She was glad for it.

She would welcome death; it would be an end to her pain and suffering. Her years of torment would be over, and she could finally rest in peace. Her heart slowed as she gave in to her fate. It was comforting.

"Well fought, Etanos," she whispered.

"Rest now, vengeful spirit," she heard him reply.

Then, there was a sudden groan of pain. She opened her eyes to see Etanos' face twisted into a mask of shock and horror. An arrow protruded from his neck, still quivering from the impact. He dropped his blades, stepping back and grasping the arrow in terror. Ammarah's heart began thumping again. She could feel the blood returning to her system, repairing the damage that had been done.

She was healing.

She chuckled as she watched Etanos fall to his knees. The joy she felt was greater than anything she had experienced in many years. Just the look on his face alone was enough to drive her spirit again. She reached out to retrieve her blades, feeling their comforting steel in her hands again. She stood, towering over the prone assassin as he choked on his own blood.

She would end him the way he was going to end her.

She didn't know who had fired the arrow. She didn't care. All she cared about was crossing her blades around Etanos' neck and laughing with pleasure as he stared up helplessly. His eyes did not plead. He said not a word. He merely waited for his fate, accepting it with commendable stoicism.

"Goodbye, Etanos," she said.

She ended him quickly.

* * *

Garret had just landed on the second-floor balcony when he saw his mentor fall. His heart nearly stopped as Ammarah crossed her blades across Etanos' neck and struck off his head. He stared in disbelief, shocked at what he saw.

As the headless body of his mentor fell forward, the dark assassin reeled back in victory, her blades up and out above her head, and her howls of triumph filling his ears like the keening of a banshee. Garret screamed in pain; having just lost the only father he had known since his own had died so many years ago.

The pain was too much to bear. His heart ached, and his mind reeled. He had never felt such anguish in his life, and there was nothing that could hold back his cries. He let his rage loose, spewing out his hatred like a dragon's flame.

Ammarah lowered her blades, turning her head up toward him. Through his tears, he could see those red eyes glaring at him. He could almost hear her laughter, her taunting cackles. She enjoyed his pain. He could feel it. He only hoped that she could feel his hatred burn in her heart. He glared at her with that hatred, and it consumed him from within. He would destroy her, as she had destroyed his teacher, his father, his friend.

Etanos' teaching came to him then. He had said that hatred would lead to defeat.

Never ignore it, but do not let it consume you, lest it weaken your defenses and cloud your mind.

Too late.

Garret drew his blades, never taking his eyes off Ammarah as she turned toward him. He held out his saber in challenge, showing his teeth like a rabid dog. She accepted. Her dark form streaked at the stone wall of Daeglan's house and mounted it like a spider. She shot upward, climbing faster than anything that Garret had ever seen.

He turned, going back into the house. He would face her there, somewhere in the main hall or the grand gallery. Anywhere but here. As he raced out of the room, he heard her land on the balcony behind him. Her metallic movements echoed in his ears as he sought out a place to make his stand.

Win or lose, Garret would prove his courage and his skill. He was terrified, to be sure, but in his heart, he made a vow to Etanos. He would kill Ammarah, or he would die trying.

Either way, he knew that his mentor would watch him with pride.

* * *

Joran moved quickly through the guard house, carefully checking each room for soldiers and making as little noise as he possibly could. Though he heard voices from all directions, he could not see anyone or anything. The guard house seemed empty, and the main hall where the gate lay was open and abandoned.

The gate itself was locked from the inside with a large beam. It looked heavy, but Joran was a large man. He leaned his sword against the wall and poised himself to lift the beam. He groaned with the weight, but the beam gave and came off its hooks. Joran let it fall to the floor and retrieved his sword. He could now lead the others back and outside to safety — assuming the outside was clear as well.

Just as he was about to open the gate, several men ran into the room. He turned, startled, but ready to face any foe.

"Stop!" one of the guards commanded.

"Come get me!" Joran said, hefting his sword out in front of him.

The guards charged, splitting up and attempting to flank him. Joran went to work immediately, swinging his sword in a wide arc. It sliced just inches from the guards' faces, and they backed away in caution.

"I said come get me," he repeated, stamping his foot on the floor and winding up for another attack.

One of the guards charged, jabbing with his blade. Joran dodged and swung upward, catching the man in the ribs and flinging him against the wall, broken and bloodied. The other guard came at him from behind, but Joran ducked, kicking back with his booted foot. The guard was knocked senseless, and Joran finished him off with a thrust of his blade.

"Worthless guards," he muttered, turning to open the gate.

It opened with a creak, and Joran was surprised to see Baelion and his company standing outside, waiting. The ranger greeted him with a smile.

"It's about time, Joran," he said.

Joran grinned. "The children are safe," he said. "I'll lead them out."

"I'll come with you," Baelion said. "The rest of you wait here and get the children to our compound." He clapped Joran on the back. "Come, my friend. Let's send some devils back to Hell."

* * *

The children huddled together against the north wall. Ferrin and his thieves gathered around them to protect them as Helena and her sisters readied themselves for any surprise attacks. The compound was bustling with pockets of fighting, men trying to put out the fires, and small bands of fleeing guards.

Ferrin kept close to Ailin, hoping to make her feel more secure. Though she probably didn't need his protection, it made him feel better, at least. Her skills with the children were impressive. He watched her with admiration as she comforted them, talked to them, and kept them in line. His attention was focused on her, and he almost didn't notice the man with the bow approaching from the west.

He heard the sisters' blades ring in the night as they were drawn. He drew his sword in response, running to the front of the line to join the sisters. He was, however, not needed. It would have been better if he had stayed hidden.

"Ferrin!" Darragh exclaimed.

Ferrin's heart skipped a beat as his master glared at him strangely. Helena and her sisters relaxed their posture, keeping their weapons drawn but lowering them as the nobleman approached.

"Lord Darragh," Ferrin said bowing his head.

"What are you doing here, boy?" Darragh asked, looking at the group of thieves. "And why are these others here?"

"Lord Darragh," Helena interrupted. "Ferrin is assisting us in freeing the children from Daeglan's clutches. You know as well as I do that he is not the man his title indicates."

Darragh pursed his lips. "Of course not," he said, looking back at the burning buildings. "But it looks like his career is over."

"May I ask what *you* are doing here?" Helena asked him.

Darragh cleared his throat, looking at Ferrin. Ferrin knew he was about to lie, but something inside him didn't care.

"I was here to investigate Daeglan's part in the destruction of the mines when I realized his connection to this band of brigands," Darragh said. "And then all of this happened. He had me imprisoned in his mansion under guard."

"Sir," Ferrin said. "Your efforts are most noble, but it is time to flee. If any of us are spotted by the guards, we may be implicated in Daeglan's plots."

Darragh stared at him for a moment, and Ferrin knew fully that he would receive a tongue-lashing when they returned home. Darragh looked at Ailin, then, who was standing close to Ferrin.

"Who is this young lady?" he asked.

"This is Ailin," Ferrin said. "She is a priestess of Gaia."

Darragh nodded but reached in and pulled Ferrin close. "Listen boy," he said. "I know what you're up to. I know about this little group of thieves you got in your pocket. I must say, I don't approve."

Ferrin swallowed. "It seems we both have our secrets, my lord," Ferrin said, boldly. "I know you are here to do business, not to investigate. You and Daeglan are connected in this conspiracy."

"How do you know all of this?"

"I listen," Ferrin said. "I know everything; even the plot against the king."

Darragh furrowed his brow. "My dealings with the queen are not of my doing," Darragh said. "Do you think a man of my station can just refuse the queen's wishes? No. What choice did I have?"

Ferrin nodded. He knew Darragh was right. The queen herself was corrupt to the core, and she had every nobleman in the South on a leash—most of them anyway. Refusing her wishes could mean death.

"All right, my lord," Ferrin said. "But we keep this all between us, and Ailin will stay with us. I want her to be a member of your house."

Darragh looked over to her, his face scrunching up into an irritated expression. "Fine," he said. "But you will marry her—if she will have you, that is. I don't want any bastard children in my house."

Ferrin grinned. "Of course, my lord." He bowed low, returning to the group just as Joran and Baelion emerged from the guard house.

With a wave of Joran's hand, the sisters stepped aside and led the children inside. Ferrin waited for all of them to pass, smiling at each one of them. Joran came over to him, nodding strangely at Darragh.

"What's he doing here?" Joran asked.

"It's a long story, my friend."

Joran shook his head. "The rangers are outside waiting. They will take the children to the ranger compound. It's up to your two groups to decide which ones will go where. Your part is done here."

"All right," Ferrin said. "Thank you, Joran. Take care of the sisters."

Joran chuckled, patting him on the back and urging him through the door.

He watched as Joran, Baelion, and the sisters charged back into the battle. Darragh seemed to have little interest and was likely eager to get out before anyone important noticed that he was there. Ferrin grasped Ailin's hand as they left, happy to have her at his side. Soon, if she accepted, they would be together, living as Master and Mistress of House Darragh.

And someday, Lord and Lady...

CHAPTER THIRTY-FOUR

arret's pulse quickened. His pursuer was hot on his trail and getting closer with every second. Though he twisted his way through the maze-like hallways of Daeglan's estate, Ammarah seemed to sense him somehow and stay right behind him. Perhaps she could smell his fear.

He made his way upward toward a massive staircase that led to the open balcony. It overlooked the great hall below — far below — and was surrounded by an iron railing that was no more than three feet high. As he traversed it, he looked down at the floor below, ignoring the dizzying height.

At the back of the balcony there was another staircase leading upward. Though there were no more floors, the structure of the house allowed for a massive attic, and that is exactly where the staircase led. He mounted them and made his way up, drawing his blades halfway up. Behind him he could hear Ammarah's metallic footfalls, and her mechanical breath.

…and the heavy thumping of his terrified heart.

The attic was massive, with a high, vaulted ceiling. Beams crossed overhead, providing support for the heavy roof, and three dormers with open windows lined each side of the long structure. There were very few items stored here, almost as if Daeglan had planned on using the space but never got around to it.

It was a dark and open area, lit only by the eerie light of the moon. It was perfect. It was where he would make his stand, and if needed, the open windows would provide a means of escape.

He crossed the entire length of it, stopped at the opposite side, and waited. He knew Ammarah would come stalking up that staircase, her dark form emanating evil itself, and her red, glowing eyes cutting through the shadows.

It was all he could do to keep his heart from beating out of his chest.

On top of his terror, there was the heartbreak he felt for Etanos. Even in such a short time, he had grown to love the man. He was truly like a father to him, one that he looked up to, and now he was nothing more than a memory.

Etanos would be missed.

Fighting back his tears, he glared ahead. He could feel the assassin approaching. He could feel her anger, her hatred, and the very evil that fueled her strange and alien body. Whatever drove those mechanical limbs was pure darkness. Darkness amplified by the evil in her own heart; the heart that still beat in there somewhere inside that bulk of metal and ruined flesh.

The dagger at the small of Garret's back began to vibrate again, telling him that the battle was near. He was thankful the old man had given it to him as it had saved his life once before. It would likely save his life again.

He heard the clanking of Ammarah's boots at the foot of the staircase and tensed up as he waited. His heart had never beaten so fast in his life. He felt the sudden urge to flee, but knew he wouldn't get very far if he did; she was too fast and much too frightening.

Even her voice was bone-chilling.

"Garret," she called up to him, her voice echoing like demonic whispers. "I have something for you."

Garret gritted his teeth, remaining silent, his eyes locked ahead.

"It is a gift," she continued, taunting him. "From me to you."

A large object sailed up the stairwell, bounced off the floor of the attic, and rolled in his direction. Blood splashed out of it in a ring as it rolled, covering the floor, and spattering on the beams above.

It was Etanos' head.

Garret's heart stopped in terror. He held his breath, clenching his eyes shut, desperately trying to avoid locking eyes with the severed head of his mentor. It rolled past him, settling in the shadows behind him.

"Do you like it? I picked it just for you."

Garret's emotions stirred. He lost any semblance of logic, unsure as to what emotion he was feeling. Was it horror? Hatred? Hopelessness? Anger?

"I bet Helena's head would make an even better gift," Ammarah said, chuckling.

"*No!*" Garret blurted out.

He clenched his jaw, knowing that his outburst would draw her up to attack. He was right.

Ammarah's dark form shot up the stairwell like a shadow. She drew her blades in the air and came down hard on the wooden floor, rolling and sliding toward him with all the speed of a streaking arrow. Garret rolled to the side to avoid her blades, and she slid past him, rolling over onto her feet, and pouncing in his direction.

Her blades twirled like a windmill as she spun in the air. He countered blow after blow, backing away to avoid her charge. Sparks flew as their blades connected, lighting the attic like the flickering flame of a forge. Ammarah's growls and groans were those of a ghost; horrifying and soul-sapping.

This was her weapon, Garret knew, fear and intimidation.

Garret cart-wheeled to the left, landing in the scorpion stance. Ammarah charged once again, coming in low and kicking out to sweep Garret's supporting leg. He leaped forward, slashing downward with his saber as he went over her sliding form. He felt his blade connect with something metallic and landed facing her as she rose.

She stood menacingly, her blades out to her sides. Her eyes glowed fiercely in the darkness as she glanced over at her shoulder. Her leather pauldrons were cut, exposing the metal underneath. But she cackled at the sight, knowing that Garret stared at it in wonder.

"Your skills are impressive, young one," Ammarah hissed.

Garret swished his saber from side to side, taunting her, but kept silent. He stared into her glowing eyes, feeling the hatred even out within him. He repeated Etanos' words in his head, remembering to keep his focus and allow his mind to stay alert. If he let his guard down due to his hatred, he was doomed. Focus was the key during the battle. There would be plenty of time to grieve later.

She charged then, coming at him with a windmill attack. He alternated his blades to block each swing, waiting for an opening as they clashed. Once her attack shifted and she attempted a horizontal strike, he blocked with his right blade and swung across with his left, barely missing her face mask as she leaped back. At the end of her leap, her balance shifted incorrectly, and she stumbled slightly.

Garret saw it, and a plan entered his mind. He charged forth, delivering a furious array of random swings to throw her off guard, then turned and sped toward one of the open windows. If he could make it to the roof, where there was only a small strip of flat fighting ground at the peak, he could throw her off balance and win the fight.

He crawled through the window quickly, planting his feet firmly on the roof, and climbed upward. The slope was steep and fairly slick, but he managed to get a grip with his boots and rise to the top. He heard Ammarah climb up after him, effortlessly scaling the slope to meet him at the peak.

She stood against the bright fires in the background, a sentinel of death in front of a hellish wall of flame. He watched her movements as she stood there. She did not sway slightly as a normal person would. Her stillness told him that her sense of balance was not like that of her former self but was worked by something else—something not quite as accurate and effective.

And thus, a weakness.

Without a word, Garret rushed forward. He slashed left and right, adding a thrust here and there with his dirk. Ammarah was all too quick with her parries, slapping his blade away effortlessly and countering with equally effortless attacks. Garret held his dirk with the blade back, using it to block, attempting to score a strike with his saber.

Ammarah surprised him with a spinning attack. She slashed multiple times, each pass at a different level. Garret backed away as he blocked, and then countered with a punch from his right hand. His fist, gripping the handle of his dirk, impacted her mask. The hit jarred his knuckles, but it was solid and knocked her off balance. He continued with a slash of his saber, but she blocked it and backed away. Garret returned to his scorpion stance.

"If only you knew the pain I have suffered," Ammarah whispered as she crossed her blades, "you would understand my need for vengeance."

Garret scoffed, smirking as he gazed, hatefully, into her burning eyes. "I have no interest in your pain," he said. "I only want to see your lifeless body on the ground."

Ammarah cackled, bringing the tip of her blade to the edge of her mask. She pried it up and over, revealing the horror that lie beneath. Garret felt a wave of revulsion as he beheld her face — or what was left of it. Her skin was deeply scarred and missing in some places. Her blackened and rotting teeth were exposed, her nose burned away, and her eyelids were shriveled back to reveal her blank, fleshy eyes.

What was left of her lips curled into a rictus grin that sent chills up Garret's spine. He narrowed his gaze, ignoring the horror that was before him, and gritted his teeth in response.

"As I said, your pain is of no importance to me," he said, slashing his saber from side to side.

Ammarah let her mask fall back into place, and the glowing of her eyes returned. She then held up her right arm, showing Garret where the armor had been cut away. Underneath was a false limb, comprised of banded metal.

"You cannot kill me," Ammarah said. "I am no longer flesh and blood."

"What flesh is left," Garret taunted, "I will destroy."

Ammarah growled and charged again. Garret jumped back, swatting her blades away as she let loose. They alternated attacks, and the sounds of their steel echoed loudly in Garret's ears. He struggled to keep up with her, focusing on both of her blades as Etanos had instructed.

She drove him back to the edge of the roof, just inches from where the peak dropped off to the ground below. Garret could hear the chaotic battle all around, and the roars of the fires as they raged on. Ammarah seemed to draw back for a finishing blow, seeing that he was distracted, but at the last minute, he pushed back at her, charging forward aggressively. He drove her back, switching to a right-handed stance and releasing a barrage of strikes that threw her off guard. As she spun to once again attempt her cyclonic blows, Garret switched back to left-handed, dodging her initial spin, and countering with a jab of his saber.

He caught her on the shoulder, just above the collarbone, and felt the tip dig into her soft flesh. She howled in pain, and he slipped around her, swiping with his dirk. But she was quicker; she countered with a back-handed strike that caught the cross guard of his dirk, knocking it from his hand. It clanked onto the roof, sliding down the slope and resting against an upturned shingle.

Garret jumped back just in time to avoid her follow-up, and he felt the wind of her blade as it passed just inches from his neck. He swung his saber wildly, guarding his retreat.

Ammarah, enraged and bleeding, came like a madman, slashing repeatedly with diagonal attacks that seemed to cut through the air itself.

Desperate, Garret crouched and stood his ground, slashing at her legs with a double attack. She leaped into the air, flipping over him, landing behind him. He turned and blocked her last strike just as she landed, countering with a sweep of his foot. She leaped up just in time, landing with a spin kick that caught Garret right in the face. He was knocked back, and his saber impacted the peak of the roof, bouncing out of his hand and joining his dirk in the shadows.

Garret kicked himself back with his feet, digging his heels into the surface of the ledge. Again, the dagger at the small of his back trembled, and as he rose, he reached back to pull it from its hidden scabbard. Ammarah leaped into the air and flipped her blades around to stab downward as she sailed toward him. Garret's world slowed to a crawl. With the last ounce of his strength, he rolled forward, passing beneath her just as she reached the peak of her jump.

He could feel the points of her swords rushing at him, and the painful grinding of the roof as his body rolled over it. As he finished his roll, he rose, spinning around just as Ammarah landed with her blades jabbing into the roof. She pulled them hard, turning to attempt another attack. But her left blade would not come loose. She faced him, unarmed, as he charged right at her. Garret reared back the dagger, screaming his fury into the night.

Ammarah's eyes burned with the brightest red, nearly blinding him as he thrust the blade into her heart. He felt the hilt of it smack against her breastplate as he drove it through. Ammarah wailed when the blade penetrated her heart. Garret could feel the rapid thumping as he gazed into her eyes. They stood still for a moment; Ammarah's wails settling into a whimper as the fires in her eyes faded.

Garret withdrew the dagger and stepped back. Ammarah's remaining blade fell from her grasp, tumbling down the slope with a series of clanks. The assassin staggered, her breathing becoming ragged. Garret's own heart thumped wildly, and his breath quickened as he realized he had won. He had defeated the dark assassin, and now she glared at him with what could only be hatred.

It had to be.

But as the glow of her eyes faded even further, becoming a calmer purplish color, her whispers, barely audible, uttered one final phrase.

"Thank you," she said.

Then, her body went limp. She fell straight down, wobbling on her knees for a moment before collapsing to the right and sliding down the slope like a rag doll. Garret let himself slide down with her, following her to the edge and watched her body fall to the ground below. There, amidst the flames, was the body of his mentor, and the familiar form of a young ranger staring up at him.

He looked at Ammarah's body for a moment, fully expecting her to rise again and kill Kuros where he stood. But she lay still, strangely positioned with her arms lowered but out at her sides and her face staring up. He saw Kuros wander over and nudge her with his bow. Nothing changed.

Garret looked again at the dagger, wondering why it was so connected to him. Why had it warned him, and how had it done so? It was nothing special from what he could tell. It was just a dagger like any other. If he lost it, he would not miss it. He would likely not even look for it, until now.

Shaking his head, he put the dagger back in its sheath and retrieved his blades. He climbed down, knowing that Kuros was there waiting for him. The ranger stood over Ammarah's body, still transfixed on her strange form.

"What was she, do you think?" Kuros asked.

Garret looked down at her, gazing at the empty eye holes in her mask. There was nothing but blackness there now. "She was human once," he said. "*Who* she was is still a mystery to me. All I know is what Etanos told me, and I'm not sure even *he* knew why she was the way she was."

"She's certainly dead," Kuros said, sticking out his bottom lip and nodding sarcastically. "That was one hell of a good stab."

Garret nodded wordlessly. Though he did find some humor in Kuros' words, he knew he would eventually have to see Etanos' body. He did not look forward to it.

Kuros knelt, moving her cloak to the side. Underneath, where her collarbones were, was flesh—albeit scarred and ruined. The edges of it seemed to be melded with the steel plates that made up the covering of her limbs. He could only imagine what kind of strange machinery lay beneath it all.

"This is truly fascinating," Kuros said. "Maedoc would love to see this. Maybe even Traegus if he were here."

"Do what you want with her body," Garret said. "Maybe this madness could be put to good use someday."

He turned to look at Etanos, whose body lay prone several yards away. Slowly, hesitantly, he walked toward it, his heart aching with every step. His mentor's swords were nearby; one of them thrust into the ground, the other lying flat several feet from his right side.

He stopped, kneeling to place his hand on the man's back. He closed his eyes as the tears came, choking back the pain that grew in his heart. He would miss Etanos greatly; this man that had saved him and given him a purpose in life. In the short time he had known him, Etanos had taught Garret more than anyone had in his whole lifetime. But, most importantly, he taught him how to learn for himself.

Out of all the lessons Etanos had shown him, he would remember how to observe and deduce things on his own. Learning by experience seemed to be the best way, he realized. Etanos had shown Garret very few of his own techniques; he had allowed Garret to figure things out on his own—by using ways that worked best for *him.*

That was the sign of a good teacher.

On top of everything, however, were the moral lessons the man had taught him. Never would Garret have ever considered an assassin to be honorable, but Etanos had shown him that he, and others like him, showed true honor.

Garret could only hope to live the same kind of life.

"We never forget our mentors," Kuros said behind him.

Garret stood, nodding in agreement. "I will never forget him," he said. "No matter who I meet in the future, he taught me the most important things of all."

"Remember what you see here, my friend," Kuros added. "One other important lesson; there is always someone better—or luckier."

Garret looked closer at Etanos' neck. Just below the point where it was severed, there was the stump of an arrow. Someone had shot him.

"Ammarah was lucky," Garret said. "She had help."

"I saw that," Kuros said. "But I cannot say who could have done it."

Garret gritted his teeth in anger. Someone had turned the tide of the battle. Ammarah was not the better warrior. If Etanos had not been shot, he would have killed her. His victory was stolen and handed to his enemy by the pull of a bow.

"I will find who did this," Garret vowed. "And I will kill them."

Chapter Thirty-Five

oran and Baelion led the charge against the last remaining group of defiant guards. The enemies had been backed against the east wall, desperate and unorganized, but still intent on escaping. The rangers and the newly arrived city guards had rounded them up, forcing them to retreat to make their final stand. Nearly one hundred of them were left, and they weren't about to give up.

Joran felt the exhilarating rush of battle lust as the group clashed with the soldiers. His sword went to work, plowing through the men and scattering them like roaches. As he fought, he looked with admiration at the nuns, who fought with equal ferocity. They had a score to settle, and their dedication to destroying Daeglan's forces was obvious.

They fought together, crushing everyone who stood against them. Even the enemy archers who climbed the wall were no match for the rangers and their bows. They were picked off before they even had a chance to fire.

The captain of the city guards brought his horsemen into the battle from the side, cutting a wide swath of destruction through the enemy ranks. Those that were left over after the pass gave up, turning to flee. But they too were cut down by the rangers that had followed the city guards in.

Soon, the enemy forces gave up, surrendering to the superior numbers that stood against them. The allies cheered together, not only for this small victory but for the complete destruction of a known criminal's compound.

However, Joran realized that this was only a minor victory against what he knew was a larger problem. The Red Hand was not broken by any means; they would persist, and eventually, they would have another nobleman in their collective pockets.

It was the way of the world.

Now, as the smith put away his sword, he clapped Baelion on the back, giving his respect to the old ranger.

"That was fun," he said. "It's been a long while since I've felt the thrill of battle."

Baelion laughed, putting away his blade as his men gathered nearby. "Things may pick up yet," he said. "My scouts tell me this Red Hand operates in more than just the south. There are still groups in the north and on the mainland. We are dealing with something larger than just a band of brigands."

Joran nodded, knowing Baelion spoke the truth. "There's always more than what meets the eye, my friend," he said. "Always."

Helena joined them, her armor dented, bloodied, and worn with the rigors of battle. "Thank you both for all of your help," she said. "We couldn't have done it without you. Daeglan's forces were larger than we thought."

"And there's still the problem of putting out the fire," Joran said.

"Let it burn," Helena said, drawing agreeable nods from her sisters. "The rains will come when the Great Mother deems it."

"Where will you and the sisters go?" Baelion asked her.

"We will remain in our temple," she replied. "Hidden away from the world. But we will be there when we are needed. Please take care of the children, Baelion—you and the thieves' guild."

"You have my word, Helena," Baelion said, clasping her hand. "And you have our protection. We will ensure that your temple is kept safe from intrusion, and Ferrin's boys will be right there alongside you."

"So I've heard," she laughed, rolling her eyes. "And I hope he takes care of Ailin."

"He will," Joran said. "I have the feeling he is rather enamored of her."

Helena smiled, resigned to believing him. "Goodbye Joran," she said. "Take care of yourself, and your city."

He embraced her, patting her on the back. "I will, Helena," he said. "And I will always keep my shop open for you if you ever need anything."

As Helena led her sisters away, the captain of the Gaellos city guard rode up, dismounting and giving them both a salute. "Joran, Baelion," he said. "Thank you for your help. We can take it from here. You've earned a night's rest."

"What will happen to the men here?" Joran asked.

The captain removed his helmet, watching as the collective allies rounded up the remaining criminals. "They will spend some time in jail," he said. "But we will take the higher-ranking ones to the king for judgment. And this place... well, I suppose it's going to burn to the ground."

"Good," Baelion said. "Whatever remains will be of some use, I suppose."

"I'm sure we will rebuild it as a guard outpost, or perhaps a barracks for the king's armies."

"Good idea," Joran said. "My shop is right where it's always been. Don't hesitate to draw up some contracts."

The captain grinned. "Always looking for business aren't you?"

Joran bellowed in laughter. "A man has to eat, sir."

* * *

Garret and Kuros were surprised to see Helena and the sisters as they approached in full armor. Garret had never seen the headmistress in such attire, and he had to admit, he was impressed. But what was most important to him was seeing that Helena was still alive. He ran to her, embracing her tightly, relieved to be in her presence once again.

"Garret," Helena said, fondly. "I'm so glad to see that you got out alive."

"Likewise," he said. "I've been hoping that you were all safe. I had no idea that you were all..." he paused, gesturing at their armor and weapons.

Helena smiled. "Some things are better kept secret," she said. "But our work is not yet done. We still must find Daeglan."

"Don't worry about him," Garret replied. "I took care of him in his tower."

Helena nodded in relief. "So, you have fulfilled your first mission as a Brother of Perses," she remarked.

"How did you know?" Garret asked, confused as to how she knew of the guild.

"We are all aware of the guilds," Helena said. "Anyone who serves the divine is connected to his or her peers. To serve one Firstborn is to serve them all. Perses, as a lesser divinity, is well known to us, as are his followers."

Garret nodded. "I suppose I should seek them out now that Etanos is gone."

Helena put her hand on his shoulder, and he could feel her sympathy. "Has he been lost?"

"Ammarah struck the final blow," he said. "But he would have won had it not been for an outsider. He was shot with an arrow."

"And what of this dark assassin?"

"Garret killed her, too," Kuros said, clapping him on the back.

Helena smiled proudly. "Good," she said. "She did not belong in this world. I could feel it when she was near. I must say, Garret, I am very proud of you. You have done well; not only for the sisters, your land, but for yourself as well. I know Etanos will look down on you proudly. Never lose your spirit, no matter what. I can feel the Great Mother's blessing within you, and I know that you will serve her faithfully."

Garret's heart began to ache once more. He was glad for Helena's words, her praise. Though she had always been encouraging, hearing her express her pride was a gift like no other.

"Thank you, Helena," he said.

They embraced again, and Garret said goodbye to the other sisters. He was sad to see them go, but he knew that they had work to do. Garret, however, was unsure what to do next. The children were safe, the sisters were safe, and he was now without a mentor. He was not bound by anything anymore, only the desire to seek revenge for the death of Etanos.

But that could take a lifetime.

"Where will you go now?" Kuros asked him.

"I don't know yet."

"Well," Kuros said, taking his hand. "If you ever need guidance or a place to call home, there is always the King's Rangers. We could use a warrior of your caliber."

Garret smiled. "Someday, perhaps," he said. "But I think I need to find a way to tell the Brotherhood of Perses that Etanos is dead."

Kuros nodded sadly. "Very well," he said. "Good luck in finding them, my new friend. I hope we will cross paths again someday."

"As do I," Garret said. "It was good to meet you, Kuros. Thank you for everything."

As Kuros left, Garret looked at the chaos around him. Daeglan's mansion was now in flames, and the rest of the compound was nearly in ruin. The battle had died down around him, and it looked like the remaining groups of Daeglan's men were being rounded up. Men on horseback led them away in irons, and those who had been enslaved walked freely among them, celebrating their release.

Garret sighed. It was all over now. At least this part of it. Though Daeglan was dead, his operations put to rest, and his estate burned to the ground, there was still the matter of the Red Hand. He supposed he could hunt them down, leader by leader, and bring the entire organization to its knees. But could he do that alone? Was such a thing even possible?

Either way, the prospect of seeing men in chains disturbed him. If what he had heard was true, the group engaged in a slave trade worldwide — and probably worse. He could make that his life's mission; to free slaves wherever he found them, eventually finding the true leader of the Red Hand and bringing him to justice.

And then there was the matter of finding Etanos' killer. He would seek his revenge but was unsure as to how to begin. Where would he look? Who would he seek for information?

There were too many questions.

All that remained now was to honor his mentor and find a place to rest for the night.

* * *

"What is it that troubles you, Darragh?" Ferrin asked his lord as they rode back to Faillaigh.

"It is nothing, Ferrin," Darragh replied.

Though his servant didn't press the matter, Darragh knew that the young man saw through him. His guilt was overwhelming. The thought of firing an arrow at the warrior — all to serve his own selfish purposes — was eating at him like nothing ever had before. He had contributed to the death of a man he didn't know, just so the assassin he was fighting could dispose of his enemy.

And it was all for nothing.

He had heard that Daeglan was killed during the battle by some unknown hand. He had gotten what he wanted without the need for murdering another man. He was free of Daeglan but was now burdened with the guilt of killing someone who would probably have killed Daeglan himself.

The turmoil was too much to bear. He knew that if Ferrin found out, the young man would lose any respect he had left for him. Ferrin was already at odds having heard his conversation with the queen. Though the young man had seemed to agree that speaking out against the queen was dangerous, some part of Darragh felt that Ferrin would always think he was truly plotting against the king.

He couldn't have that.

"Ferrin," he said. "I want you to know how much I respect you."

Ferrin said nothing but lowered his head.

"I have no sons of my own," Darragh continued, "but I have always thought of you that way."

Ferrin looked at him curiously. Even Ailin and the other young thieves shot him a glance.

"When we return to Faillaigh I want to make you my official heir. To Hell with custom."

"I thank you, my lord," Ferrin said. "That is very generous of you."

Darragh sighed. "I hope you understand that I respected your father greatly. The only reason I requested your service was to avoid making him feel like a beggar."

"I don't understand," Ferrin said.

"He was unable to pay the debts he owed," Darragh explained. "I was going to relieve him of them, but I knew that his pride would not allow it. He *needed* to pay his debts. That was just the kind of man he was, and I respected that. That is why I asked for your service in return."

Ferrin nodded. "He respected you, too," he said. "And I know your gesture gave him some relief."

"I only hope that he didn't resent me for doing what I did," Darragh said, meaning every word.

"He did not," Ferrin assured him. "Believe me. I think deep down he knew what you were up to. He was a smart man, not a conniving scoundrel like most merchants."

Darragh laughed; glad to hear Ferrin's words. "You are a lot like him," he said.

"Was he handsome and dashing, too?" Ailin added, drawing chuckles from the other thieves.

"No," Darragh said. "And I'm sure Ferrin will grow old and warty as he did."

The thieves chuckled again, and Ferrin shook his head. "You boys can go now," he joked. "We can take it from here."

"Well, Lord Ferrin," Darragh said. "We should pick up our pace. We have a wedding to plan."

Ferrin smiled and looked over at Ailin, whose face was turned down and beaming with a huge smile.

Darragh turned his eyes back to the road. Outside, he was the model of composure as he rode. But, inside, he was still in turmoil. He would probably never live down the guilt he felt, but he hoped that he could at least hide it long enough for Ferrin to forget about the events of tonight.

Only then could he be at peace.

EPILOGUE

arret sat before the small grave he had dug for his mentor's heart. He had taken it before leaving the compound, along with the man's blades, and the strange black dagger that had once belonged to Ammarah. Now, as he stared up at the stars, he asked the Great Mother to look after Etanos and bring him the peace he deserved.

Garret's own heart was heavy with grief. Even the sight of the two blades jutting out of the ground on either side of the grave gave him pause and brought tears to his eyes. He felt lost now; alone, as he was once before. But at least at the convent, he always had someone to talk to, or to rely on for comfort.

Now, out here in the wilderness, he was solitary. Though he had made friends, and could still seek them out when needed, he knew that a sedentary life was not for him. At least not yet. He had work to do, he knew; slaves to free, scoundrels to bring to justice, and people to protect. That would be his life.

And his fate.

As he turned to his fire to warm his hands, he noticed that a lone figure stood a short way away. Though startled, he felt no danger. It was a familiar person; dark and cloaked in equally dark clothing. When the figure stepped forward into the firelight, he realized who it was.

"Baurus," Garret said. "Well met."

Baurus sat across from him, hanging his head in grief. Garret realized that he knew.

"Etanos is gone," Garret said. "I was going to find the Brotherhood and tell them, but I see you are here now."

"We lose brothers, Garret," Baurus said. "We lose mentors. All of us do. What is important is that he died protecting the innocent and bringing justice to those who deserved it."

"He did," Garret said.

"And what of this Ammarah?"

"I killed her," Garret said. "She is no more."

"As the apprentice of our brother," Baurus continued. "You are now welcome to seek out the guild and join us. I will vouch for you. I trust Etanos' judgment."

"Thank you," Garret said. "I will do that. But I think there are some things I must take care of first."

"I understand," Baurus said. "But when you are ready, you will find us in Thyre. Seek out the symbol you saw on Etanos' wrist and follow it. There you will find our sanctuary. You will be asked a question. No matter what that question is, the answer will always be *By the Hand of Perses*."

Garret nodded, holding up the obsidian blade. "I think the guild should have this," Garret said, "as a reminder of Etanos' life."

Baurus smiled, taking the blade and holding it out before him. "The Grandmaster will want this," he said. "I thank you. You may keep Etanos' blades. As his student, they are yours to claim."

Garret shook his head. "They will always belong to him in spirit," he said. "Besides, they are not conducive to my fighting style."

"Then let some lucky young warrior find them and put them to good use."

Garret nodded, silent.

"Etanos had asked me to seek out information," Baurus said. "What I found out was more profound than what was previously thought. The Red Hand not only operates as a criminal organization, but they are also involved in sorcery and other dark things."

Garret listened intently, surprised at the revelation.

"Though they engage in criminal activity, it is merely a front for their true purpose."

"What purpose is that?" Garret asked.

"I do not know for sure," Baurus said. "But some have reason to believe that several kings and queens around the world are involved. Queen Igraina, your queen, may be involved as well."

"That doesn't surprise me," Garret said.

"Whatever they are up to, it involves more than just a slave trade. If you seek them out, be wary. They are in league with dark things. Never underestimate what they can conjure."

"I will remember that."

Baurus stood and Garret rose with him. The two clasped hands as brothers.

"Remember," Baurus said. "Wherever you go, follow the Path, and you will never go wrong. I look forward to seeing you in Thyre, no matter how long it takes. Goodbye, brother."

"Goodbye, Baurus," Garret replied. "And thank you."

"Never forget what your mentor has taught you," Baurus reminded him. "These are the things that will shape your life and your reputation."

Garret nodded as Baurus turned and disappeared into the shadows. He sat down again, leaning back against the log that lay behind him. He would sleep here tonight, and in the morning, he would begin his journey. To where, he was unsure.

The only thing of which he was certain was that Etanos would always be with him.

ABOUT THE AUTHOR

Shawn is a web developer and graphic artist living in the hills of Brown County, Indiana. In his spare time, he plays and builds guitars, and hunts rocks and artifacts with his best friend, Lisa, and their three cats.

THE DRAGON CHRONICLES

TALE OF THE SCORPION

THE DAEGOTH TRILOGY